POOR TOM
IS
COLD

POOR TOM
IS
COLD

— ✦ —

MAUREEN
JENNINGS

THOMAS DUNNE BOOKS / ST. MARTIN'S MINOTAUR
NEW YORK

THOMAS DUNNE BOOKS.
An imprint of St. Martin's Press.

POOR TOM IS COLD. Copyright © 2001 by Maureen Jennings. All rights reserved.
Printed in the United States of America. No part of this book may be used or
reproduced in any manner whatsoever without written permission except in the
case of brief quotations embodied in critical articles or reviews. For information,
address St. Martin's Press, 175 Fifth Avenue, New York, NY 10010.

www.minotaurbooks.com

Library of Congress Cataloging-in-Publication Data

Jennings, Maureen.
    Poor Tom is cold / Maureen Jennings.—1st ed.
        p. cm.
    ISBN 0-312-26892-0
    1. Police—Ontario—Toronto—Fiction. 2. Inheritance and succession—
Fiction. 3. Toronto (Ont.)—Fiction. 4. Stepfamilies—Fiction. I. Title.

PR9199.3.J397 P6 2001
813'.54—dc21

                                                                00-045766

First Edition: February 2001

10 9 8 7 6 5 4 3 2 1

To Iden with love and gratitude as always

ACKNOWLEDGMENTS

There are always so many people who help along the way in the process of writing a novel. I would like to thank Cindy Boht, who helped me with the horse material; Dr Jerome Chen, who was my generous resource person; my brilliant dentist, Dr Stephen Forgacs, who checked my facts and also sent me over to the archives of the Toronto School of Dentistry, where Dr Dale and I literally climbed over old dentist chairs so she could show me the wonderful collection of dentures; and Larry and Eileen Richard, who kindly instructed me in the finer points of Catholicism. I am grateful that Dr Geoffery Rheaume made his doctoral thesis on the history of the Queen Street Mental Health Facility available. It gave me invaluable material. I am particularly indebted to Cheryl Freedman, who read the book in manuscript form and gave me extremely helpful feedback. As always, I am grateful to my agent, Teresa Chris, and my editor, Ruth Cavin, for their patience and perspicacity.

POOR TOM
IS
COLD

PROLOGUE

Since the boy had died, she didn't sleep and many nights she prowled around the house, searching. She was quiet so as not to wake any of the others, but they knew and talked about it when she wasn't there. This night was particularly bad. It was long past midnight and she had heard the grandfather clock in the hall chime. She counted out the number of gongs, not wanting the sound to die away as it was comforting, like a voice. After a while the snuffles and groans of her sleeping husband were insufferable and she got out of bed. She didn't put on her dressing gown or slippers, even though the room was chill. She went out to the landing. A slit of light was showing beneath the door opposite and she knew he was not yet in bed. She walked over and went in without knocking. He was seated at his desk, writing, and turned quickly when he heard her enter. She was glad she had startled him. She smiled, a false smile, hiding her fear. He regarded her coldly. He didn't get up, didn't exclaim in concern or bewilderment; he merely sat and waited for her to say something.

She moved closer. "You are up late," she said.

"And you."

"You must be cold."

"Not at all."

He indicated the fire, which was still burning in the hearth, and the woollen shawl that was around his shoulders.

1

She wanted to flee, to run from that icy stare but she knew this might be her only chance.

"I have seen the looks you give me. They burn my skin like the hot sun."

"I must disillusion you. I have no such desire."

Some of her earliest memories were of witnessing the power her mother could exercise over the many men who visited her, and Peg knew she had no other recourse. She slipped her arms out of her nightgown, letting it fall to her ankles. She tried to take a bold stance, feet apart, the way she had long ago seen her mother do. But her legs were quivering and she couldn't force herself to stand other than with her knees pressed together. Cupping her small breasts in her hands, she pushed them up.

"I ache for your suck," she said. She tried to make her voice coy and sweet, but even to her own ears, she sounded unconvincing.

He scanned her thin body, studying her dispassionately, critically, making it clear how much the choice was his. Then he took the candleholder from his desk and came over to her. She tried not to flinch but she couldn't help herself. He bent down and pulled up the nightgown.

"Allow me to take you back to your room," he said.

CHAPTER ONE

———•———

IT WAS STILL dark out, not yet dawn and the flickering street lamps made little dint in the sodden November darkness. Acting detective William Murdoch pulled his astrakhan hat tighter over his ears, thrust his bare hands deep into his pockets, and shoulders hunched against the cold driving rain, plodded up Ontario Street toward the police station. Pain from an infected tooth had sent him from his bed, and in an attempt to distract himself, he had dressed and set out for work well ahead of his duty time.

He turned onto Wilton just as a cab was going by and stepped back to avoid being splashed. The cabbie slowed his horse in case Murdoch was a potential fare, realised he wasn't, and tipped his whip in acknowledgment as he passed by. He was wrapped in a voluminous black oiled slicker, the high collar masking his lower face and the hood pulled down so low over his forehead that only his eyes were visible. The horse had no such protection and its coat was dark from the rain. Like a lot of cab horses, the beast looked underfed, as if it had barely a trot left in it, but the driver snapped the reins and they heaved into a faster clip. Murdoch watched the rear lamp swaying, warm and bright in the gloom, until the carriage turned south on Parliament, leaving him alone on the dark street.

What if I am the last man on the earth? he thought. *What if I'm really dead and in purgatory? Is this what it is?* Physical pain and loneliness melding together until he couldn't separate one from the other. Suddenly, somebody, probably a servant, lit a lamp in the upstairs room of one of the houses he was passing and the light winked out through a crack in the curtain. Murdoch was somewhat embarrassed at the relief he felt and he grinned at his own nonsense. He shook his head to clear out the morbid thoughts and was rewarded by a current of white-hot pain along his jaw, so severe he yelped. Trying to move cautiously to avoid aggravating matters, he continued on his way. He was heartily glad to reach the steps of the station. The outside lamp was burning and the windows were bright.

He pushed open the door, greeted by the familiar smell of wood-stove, sawdust, and a lingering sourness from the old clothes and unwashed bodies of the local constituents. The fourth division served Toronto from the working-class streets of River and Sackville in the east, to the nobs who lived in grand houses on Jarvis and Church Streets in the west. The east-siders were the ones whose backsides polished the wooden benches in the station hall.

The night-duty sergeant, Gardiner, was seated on a high stool behind the counter, entering his report in the register. He glanced up in surprise to see Murdoch.

"Gawdelpus, you're the early bird."

The detective grunted, not feeling up to a long-winded explanation. His tooth had started hurting about a week ago, but he'd managed to ignore it until yesterday, when the pain had worsened. His landlady, Mrs Kitchen, sent him to bed with a brown paper and vinegar poultice to hold to his face and had padded his gum with some cotton wool soaked in carbolic. That had helped for a while, but at five o'clock he had been dragged to consciousness with the sensation that every nerve in his body had gathered at a point on his lower jaw and was pulsing there.

He took off his fur hat and shook the rain out of it.

"What's up?" asked the sergeant.

Gardiner was regarding him curiously and Murdoch knew he must look like a pauper's pal.

4

"Got a toothache," he mumbled. He tried to talk without moving his mouth very much.

"Awful things them toothaches. Keep you up don't they?"

Murdoch blinked in agreement.

"Better get yourself into the dentist. There's a fellow right at the corner. You could drop in on him."

Murdoch grunted. Not if he could help it. George Crabtree had been forced to visit Dr Brodie last year and, big and tough as a moose though he might be, the constable had almost fainted when he staggered out of the chair. His face was swollen for weeks.

"My landlady's good," said Murdoch. "Knows a lot . . . carbolic . . ."

"Wondered what it was I could smell. Helped did it?"

"Hm."

The sergeant sniffed. "Or is it fish? Did the cat bring something in?"

Murdoch shrugged. The smell was from his sealskin coat, which developed a distinctive odour when it was wet. He'd got it from an old lag a couple of years ago, in exchange for some tobacco, and he considered it a good bargain in spite of the pong.

He started to head for the sanctuary of his office, which was a tiny cubicle across from the cells.

"While you're over there, put some more coal in, will you?" called out Gardiner.

Murdoch opened the stove door, picked up a pair of tongs, seized a large piece of coal and dropped it into the red maw. The action hurt.

There was a waft of chill air as the hall door opened and Ed Hales, the patrol sergeant, came in. He hung his dark lantern on a hook.

"Perishing cold out there."

"It's nothing to what it will be," said Gardiner. "Wait till we get winter."

"You're early this morning, Will."

"He's got toothache," Gardiner answered for him. "Kept him up. He's going to have to have it pulled."

"Hey, I don't know that yet," protested Murdoch.

The sergeant grinned at him. "That kind of pain means abcess. If

5

you don't look after it you could be in bad trouble. Second cousin of the wife's nearly died from an abcess. Poison got into her blood. She was bad for months after, still not right. It affected her mentally. She cries all the time."

"Glad to know that, Gardiner. Lifted my spirits no end did that little tale."

The duty sergeant shrugged, undaunted. "It's the truth, I tell you."

"How about I brew up a pot of tea, Will?" interjected Hales. "Cheer us both up. Come on."

Murdoch was about to refuse but Hales, out of sight of the duty sergeant, nodded warningly. He had something to say.

"I wouldn't mind a mug myself," Gardiner called after them. "I'm parched."

Murdoch followed Hales through to the small back room where the officers ate their meals. The morning shift hadn't arrived yet and the fire was low in the grate, the room chilly.

"Why don't I look after the pot and you see to the fire; you're better at it than me," he said.

"All right," said Hales but he didn't move. He pulled at the ends of his moustache. He was a tall man, ruddy-faced. He was invariably pleasant and even-tempered, qualities that made him popular in the station, but this morning he was visibly distressed.

"Need your ear a minute, Will . . . I didn't want to say anything in front of Gardiner, he's got a sniffer for trouble like a rat on offal but," he hesitated, reluctant to admit the bad news. "Fact is, young Wicken seems to have gone missing."

"Missing?"

"Well, he don't seem to be on his beat." He rubbed at his moustache. "I did my first check on him at twenty-five minutes past eight. All correct. Did the second at a quarter past ten like normal. Again all correct. But when I went to check in on him at a quarter past two, he was nowhere to be seen. Supposed to be up at River and Gerrard. I thought maybe he'd stepped into a laneway to have a piss, even though he shouldn't, and I waited a bit. No sign of him. I walked back along Gerrard. Not a whisker. I put pebbles on the doorknobs. You know that little trick."

Murdoch nodded. The constable on the beat was supposed to check the doors of the vacant houses to make sure they were secure, no vagrants camping out. The patrol sergeant sometimes tested the officers with a small stone or piece of dirt. If it was still there at the next round, heaven help the constable on duty.

"When he wasn't at the four o'clock checkpoint, I walked his entire beat in reverse but he was nowhere to be seen. All of the pebbles were still there."

Murdoch frowned. "That's bloody strange. Is he playing up d'you think? Hiding?"

The younger constables sometimes teased the good-natured patrol sergeant by hiding out until he went by, then innocently meeting him on the return route. It was childish but it relieved the boredom. Murdoch had done it himself when he was on the beat.

Hales shook his head. "He's never done it before and it's past a joke by now. If he isn't here at changeover he could be put on a charge."

"Ill then? Could he have been taken ill? Gone home?"

Even as he said it, Murdoch knew how unlikely that was. Wicken would have gone to the closest alarm box and telephoned in to headquarters.

"He looked healthy as a doctor when I saw him last. He wasn't drunk neither."

The two men looked at each other, mirroring each other's uneasiness.

Murdoch reached for his hat. "I'll go and have another gander? You've got your report to do."

"Thanks, Will. If he is just acting batchy, I'll overlook it as long as he's back on the beat when the next shift comes in. But if he's not there without a damn good reason, it'll be dire."

"Where should he be right now?"

"Coming down River Street from Gerrard. Maybe you could try going the reverse way."

Murdoch stood up. "Save me some tea."

"The whole pot if you find him safe." said Hales. "And you'd better take my lamp. But don't let Gardiner see you if you can help it."

Murdoch went back to the hall. He managed to whip the lantern off the hook while the duty sergeant was turned away, getting a file from the cabinet. However, Gardiner saw him at the door.

"Where's my tea? What are you doing, growing it?"

"Hales's doing it," muttered Murdoch. "Got‑tuh go."

The sergeant called after him. "Have them all pulled out. You'll be better off in the long run."

Murdoch waved his hand.

Outside, dawn was coming in begrudgingly and the rain had slowed to a drizzle. He set off at as fast a pace as he could manage, heading east along Wilton to River Street. Even though moving quickly caused the pain to pulse through to his eye socket, he felt the need to hurry. He couldn't imagine why the young constable wasn't on his beat. No one with a brain in his head would take a joke this far and risk losing his job. That left the possibility that something had happened to him and that wasn't good either.

River Street wasn't as heavily populated as the other streets in the division and there were several vacant lots. They reminded him of missing teeth, a gap between molars. Quickly, he checked the doors of the houses that were boarded up. On each knob was balanced a small pebble. Wicken's beat started at the corner of Parliament Street and Gerrard and would have taken him in an easterly direction toward River Street, where he turned south to Queen, back west, then north again up Parliament. During the long night, he walked this square many times, making sure all the God-fearing were safe in their beds. If he had the bad luck to miss any criminal occurrence, such as a break-in, he was held accountable. As far as the chief constable, Lieutenant-Colonel Henry Grasett, was concerned, a crime meant the constable on the beat was remiss in his duty and he was always reprimanded.

Murdoch turned left onto Gerrard and paused, looking down the deserted street. More lamps were showing in the houses now, welcome smudges of light. If the constable had run into any kind of trouble, it had been silent. No one had raised an alarm.

He continued to Parliament Street, past Toronto General and the Burnside lying-in hospital on the north side of Gerrard. *Even as I'm going by, an infant might be squawling its first cry.* His mind skittered away from the thought because that lead straight to Liza, and what they had hoped for. *Four children, Will, and then we'll see. I'm not going to be one of those women whose job in life is to be a breeding mare.* Murdoch sighed. *Fat lot of good all that nattering did us. There won't be any at all now.* The memory of her sudden death from typhoid fever, two years ago, was still a cause for anguish.

He forced himself to focus on what he was doing. Across from the hospital grounds was the medical school. Quite a lot of lights burning there. It took him about fifteen minutes to reach Parliament Street but there was absolutely no sign of Wicken. He stopped for a moment until the throbbing in his jaw subsided. On the southeast corner there was another vacant house. It had once been quite grand, but now the windows were boarded up and the front fence was protecting only weeds, colourless and drooping. He squeezed by the stiff iron gate and walked down the path to the front door. Shrubs, heavy with raindrops, brushed against him as he went up a short flight of steps into a deeply recessed porch. Hales's pebble was where he'd put it. Murdoch knocked it off, turned the doorknob and shoved. The door had lost much of its paint but was solid wood and it didn't yield. He stepped back, fished out a box of matches from his pocket, and lit the dark lantern. The bull's eye beam was bright and strong and he directed it at the windows. They too looked intact, no sign of breakage.

There was a flagged path that branched off to the rear of the house and, pushing his way through the long grass that had overgrown it, Murdoch tramped around to a high gate that opened into a walled garden. This was neglected and overgrown, but like the house, suggested a former grandeur. To his right was a patio with a fancy design of yellow and red brick. He walked over to the back door. Around the lintel there was a climbing rosebush, two or three frostbitten buds still on their stems. An image of the church window, Christ's blood on the thorns, jumped into his mind, taking him by surprise with its intensity.

He turned the handle and the door opened easily. He stepped inside.

The light shone on Wicken's body.

He was lying on his left side, facing the door; his head was uncovered and surrounded by a halo of blood, which had soaked much of his blond hair. His legs were crossed at the ankles and between his thighs was wedged his revolver, barrel uppermost, stiff and protruding like a grotesque symbol of manhood.

CHAPTER TWO

———•———

PEG HAD ALREADY wedged one of the armchairs underneath the doorknob, but in a sudden rush of fear, thinking she heard Nathaniel's voice, she dragged over the chiffonier and pushed it so that it toppled against the chair. There were two doors she had to worry about. This one, which connected with the master bedroom, the other, which opened onto the landing. The latter had been fitted with a bolt some time ago. Nathaniel said this was so he and Harmony could have some privacy from the children. Everything he said had an implied reproach. His previous wife had liked nothing better than to spend time with him alone; she had been loving and compliant.

Not like you. Never like you.

She went back to reassure herself that the bolt was in place. They would have to break the door down to get in. She stood still as she could, listening. Whatever she'd heard had gone. The house was silent.

She shivered. There was no longer any heat in the room as she had used up the last piece of coal the night before. The tips of her fingers were cold. Suddenly she caught a glimpse of herself in the chiffonier mirror and she stared, hardly recognising herself. There was a crust of dried blood at the corner of her mouth where his ring

11

had cut her lip. She touched it gingerly with her tongue and shuddered. The salty taste of her own blood frightened her. He was an old man but still strong and made more so by his rage.

She looked again at her reflection. Her eyelids were reddened from lack of sleep, her hair unpinned and lank. The sight repelled her—a doxie's face if ever there was one. She could have been looking at her own mother. She snatched the crocheted antimacassar from the Morris chair and draped it over the mirror.

You and the boy will be well looked after, my sweet. I promise. That's what he'd said when he first came courting, and foolishly, desperate, she had given in. She moaned. That promise would not be kept now. His feeling for her had withered away, corroded by his own humiliation.

She's a whore, father. You've married a whore.

Jarius was calm, his voice as dispassionate as if he were reciting the order of hymns for the day. And they had stared at her from the table, all of them there, even the child.

Did you do this? Did you go to Jarius's room and offer yourself like some Jezebel?

And all she could answer was, *He is trying to murder me. He put poison in my food. He killed Charley.*

But he repeated. *Did you go to his room?*

When she said yes, Nathaniel hit her hard across the face.

One of the candles in the wall sconces sputtered and Peg's heart thudded.

I must save them for nighttime. They're burning down too fast. She reached for the candlesnuffer but stopped herself.

It's all right. He'll be back long before then . . . he believed you.

She returned to the couch, suddenly so tired she thought she would fall down. She would rest for a moment, just a moment, then she had to think. She had to make plans. She lay back and closed her eyes.

Off the dining room of the Village Home was a tiny pantry that the matron referred to as "the calming room." Naughty children were put in there, in the dark, until they thought better of their behaviour and were willing to act like grateful Christian children

12

and not heathens. Not too long after she had been admitted, Peg was locked in there for using bad language and for scratching and biting another child.

She stole my cup. The bint took it. It's mine. The matron, Mrs Southgate, was firm.

Nobody owns the furnishings here. The cups and plates, the knives and forks belong to everybody. You have behaved most wickedly and you must pray for forgiveness.

Although Peg had kicked and fought, the matron and two of the bigger girls easily subdued her. She was closed inside the pantry to think about her wrongdoing. Perhaps Mrs Southgate did indeed forget; she was a busy woman with many cares. Perhaps the time in the darkness was not as long as Peg experienced it. However, when she was finally let out, she had messed in her drawers and was hoarse with crying. Overnight, she became a model child and was frequently paraded before visitors as an example of the miracle of love and Christian teaching. When she was sent to Canada as one of the quotient of child emigrants, Mrs Southgate handed her a splendid testimonial and kissed her.

Peg sat up. The memory burned like acid in her gut.

She got off the couch, went over to the window, and raised the blind. The sky was lighter and relief ran through her body. The night was over. She gave a quick hard tug on the window sash but she knew it was futile. Frank had nailed it shut earlier in the week. She leaned forward, pressing her forehead against the glass. Even if she smashed it, there was nobody to call to, nobody who would help her. She hadn't been friendly with the neighbours, sensing their disapproval. If word of Jarius's accusation ever got out, they would turn away completely. And she knew he would make sure it did get out.

He was young, fair-haired. His eyes were kind and she could tell he was listening so she tried to speak calmly. She told him everything. About Charley, about the poison she'd tasted the two nights she'd become ill. How they all hated her. She also told him about Jarius and lastly about Frank. "Show me," he'd said to the others and they took him off. "I'll come back," he had said. And he would, she trusted he would.

13

She felt short of breath, as if the air was being sucked away, and she returned to the couch and lay down again. She'd brought this piece of furniture with her when she'd married Nathaniel and its familiarity was a comfort. She stroked the plush surface as if it were a creature and pulled the velour cover over her face. Under the tent of it, she could smell her own stale flesh.

All she had to do was wait.

Suddenly, there was a sharp rapping on the door and she jumped.

"Stepmother? Stepmother?" the voice outside called to her and the doorknob rattled. "Please let me in, stepmother. I've made you some porridge for your breakfast . . . you must eat something."

Augusta was speaking softly, falsely, as if she were trying to trick a child to take foul medicine. But Peg knew it wasn't medicine that she wanted her to swallow.

She didn't answer and the doorknob shook again. Augusta's voice was less patient this time.

"Stepmother, open the door." Another rap.

A rush of white-hot rage surged through Peg's body and she jumped off the couch and ran over to the door.

"Sod off," she screamed. "You can all sod off. All the frigging lot of you."

She banged with her fists on the unyielding wood.

CHAPTER THREE

MURDOCH BROUGHT THE lantern close to the ravaged face. The source of the injury seemed to be a small circular wound near the right temple, and the blood which was covering the right eye was from that wound. The left eye was open.

What in God's name happened?

Slowly, he swung the beam along the length of the body. The metal of the gun barrel gleamed in the light and abruptly Murdoch tugged the gun loose from between the thighs. Placing the lantern beside him on the floor, he crouched down and snapped open the cylinder. All police pistols had six chambers but for safety reasons, officers were allowed only five cartridges. The hammer was always to rest on the empty chamber. Wicken's gun held four undischarged cartridges; the fifth had been fired. Near his right shoulder was the empty shell case. Murdoch left it where it was. Hurriedly, he tugged off his own glove and held the back of his hand beneath Wicken's nose to check for any indication of breath although he knew there could be none. He touched the chin, the skin was grey and cold, and when he tried to move the jaw from side to side, it was stiff. The rigor of death had already started. The constable must have died four or five hours earlier. More carefully, his hands steadying, Murdoch began to scrutinize the body.

15

Wicken was lying with his left arm underneath him and the right arm was flung across his chest, the gloved hand touching the floor. Just beyond the reach of his fingers was his notebook and underneath that was tucked a piece of paper.

Gingerly, Murdoch extricated it. Printed neatly in pencil were the following words:

LIFE IS UNBEARABLE WITHOUT YOUR LOVE. FORGIVE ME.

He felt a rush of anger. *You stupid boy. May God forgive your sin. I won't.*

He stared at the note again as if there was some answer in the terse words.

LIFE IS UNBEARABLE WITHOUT YOUR LOVE.

Whose love? Why had it been withdrawn?

Murdoch didn't know much about Wicken's personal life. As an acting detective, his rank was above the constable's, and off-duty they were not expected to have much to do with each other. On the occasions when they had met, however, he'd liked the young man. And in fact, he'd talked to him only last evening when Wicken had come on duty. What was it they'd chatted about? He couldn't remember because his toothache had obliterated everything else. No, of course, that's what it was. Wicken expressed sympathy. Said he'd had a tooth pulled when he was young. Murdoch was too proud to ask if it had hurt but Wicken had told him cheerily, "Hurt like the deuce at first but the pain doesn't last that long." The constable had seemed in perfectly good spirits. Quite normal.

And now look at him.

He took out his own notebook and placed the piece of paper inside. He was tempted to inspect the body further but Wicken's rubber cape was wrapped tightly around him, which meant he'd have to be lifted. Murdoch decided to wait until the coroner arrived.

16

He picked up the lantern and started to walk around the kitchen. The room was totally bare of furnishings although the original rush matting remained. He examined the door and the window next to it. Dust was thick on the sill and there was no sign of forcing around the frame. How had Wicken got into the house? And why choose this particular place to take his own life? Murdoch looked out of the window at the neglected garden, forlorn and grey in the predawn light. The fence was high all around and the house abutted a laneway on the east side. Parliament Street was on the west. There was no other house overlooking this one. Wicken had made sure his sin was a private one.

He turned back to the body. *Who was the note addressed to?* It didn't sound as if the beloved person had died—more likely rejected him. *You get over it, my lad. Nothing is worth committing such a mortal sin.You might want to die to escape your pain but God says that is according to His will not yours.* But Murdoch knew he himself had thought such things not so long ago when his fiancée had died. And he wasn't completely sure he was over it.

A few feet away was Wicken's helmet, standing upright as if he'd put it tidily on a shelf. Murdoch picked it up and held it in the light of the lantern. It seemed clean, free of blood. He replaced it in the same spot then he paced around a second time, saw nothing more, and returned to the body.

He was about to say a brief prayer but he stopped. He could as yet find no forgiveness for Wicken. His pity was with those left behind. He'd heard that the boy's mother was a widow and that there was a younger sister. And he wondered also how the unnamed woman would feel when she learned she had precipitated this self-murder.

He left the house, closing the door tightly behind him. The sky had turned from black to dull grey but the drizzle was unalleviated. He started to jog-run back to the front gate and along the street to the neighbouring house. There was a plaque on the wrought-iron gate proclaiming this was a livery stable and he could see into a long yard. At the far end was a low building, which he supposed housed the horses. He tried the gate but it was bolted on the inside and he shook it impatiently, prepared to knock the shicey thing off its hinges if need be. However, at that moment a man emerged from the stable, leading a saddled horse.

"Hey you, come over here," Murdoch shouted.

The man hesitated then approached slowly, the horse swaying behind him, its hooves clacking on the cobblestones.

"Who the sod are you? What'd you want?"

He was quite young, perhaps in his mid-twenties, short and wiry, dressed in corduroy trousers and jacket. His cap was low on his forehead.

"I'm sodding William Murdoch, acting detective, that's who. Now open up."

The fellow's expression changed.

"Sorry, officer. What's up? Here—"

He threw back the bolt on the gate and started to swing it open.

"What's your name?" Murdoch asked.

"Eakin, Frank Eakin."

"Well Mr Eakin, I'm commandeering you. I need somebody to run over to the police station. At once. Ask for Sergeant Hales. Got that? Hales."

"Yes, sir."

"Tell him I've found Wicken. Tell him we need the ambulance and the coroner."

"Somebody dead then?" he shifted nervously.

"That's what it usually means when you get the coroner. Now hurry." He pointed. "I'm in the empty house on the corner. Tell them to come to the back door."

Eakin indicated the horse standing listlessly behind him.

"I was just going to exercise Sailor. Shall I take him?"

"Of course take him, unless you can run faster. Get going. Scorch!"

The man swung himself into the saddle, kicked his heels hard into the horse's sides, and lunged into a gallop out of the gate.

Murdoch turned around and half ran, half skittered back to the scene of death.

CHAPTER FOUR

JARIUS GIBB PULLED the candlestick closer, selected a fresh pen and dipped it into the inkwell. He did these actions deliberately, watching his own hand to determine if it would betray him with a sign of human weakness. It didn't and, as he entered the date in the ledger, his writing was steady, even and precise as always.

TUESDAY, NOVEMBER 12, 1895
I write this entry in good health. My tongue is furred but my pulse is quite steady. I have pissed copiously in the chamber and my water is of good colour. I have slept for at least four hours but fitfully. I had expected to experience a natural fatigue but so far that is not the case. In fact, I would say I am quite invigorated.

He paused. Even in his own diary, he had difficulty writing down the absolute truth. He blotted what he had written so far, and continued.

I doubt Father will be with us much longer. He looks more aged every day, although I regret to say, his temper is unabated. This failing is made worse of course by the present situation. I must admit, even I

19

quailed when we spoke on Saturday night. But he has brought it all on himself so I have no pity. So utterly, utterly unsuitable.

His hand had betrayed him and the writing was suddenly untidy. She was a young woman it was true but plain as a mouse, skin like lard, no diddies or arse to rouse a man, no wit or liveliness to explain Nathaniel's infatuation with her.

Frank said in his delicate way that father was "cuntstruck." To me it was less of the human. Father lusted after her like a dog after a bitch in heat. I thought he would take her on the dining room table that first night he brought her here. "This is your new mother," he said. None of us had an inkling. He was barely out of mourning. She is younger than Frank. A widow she said and she brought her own by-blow with her. A vile boy who immediately made it apparent he carried criminal blood. Within a week, I was missing several coins from my trousers. Frank said he stole from him also. All this denied of course; Father was determined to side with the boy at all costs.

He had written an account of these events several times before but he found himself returning over and over again to that day and the weeks that followed.

I thought at first my "stepmother" must practice whore tricks to keep him panting the way he did but I stood shamelessly outside their bedroom and I heard her refusing him, crying "no" while he grunted and rutted like the goat he had become. I might have felt pity except I thought her coyness must be a way to keep him hot. Augusta says she has not yet conceived but I thought she would when it suited her.

The thought was still so unbearable, Jarius had to lay down his pen and stand up. He went to the table beside the bed where he'd left his pipe and, not bothering to fill it, stuck the stem in his mouth and clenched down hard. He returned to his desk.

I am glad to say the possibility is now remote. I am almost able to rest.

Once again he noticed a tremor in his hand and he forced himself into steadiness.

I cannot pretend I was sorry when the boy died but I must admit it was quite convenient. She plays so easily, I almost feel compunction for her state. Of course nobody believes her. She has given up any pretext of affection for dear Papa and this has been bringing about a rapid cure of his obsession. I have seen his distaste although he attempts to hide it whenever I am present, cooing and caressing with her as he did before.

The memory filled him with contempt. She was as unresponsive as stone. An unpaid whore would have more life.

Like a preening peacock he seems intent on proving his feathers are the brightest. How sweet then that she revealed what she really is. How beautifully she has played into my hands. I could hardly wait to tell him. I had expected he would throw her out immediately but he didn't go that far. And what a pity that has proved to be!

Another pause, another struggle to contain the surge of excite-ment through his body.

There was quite a scene I must say. Worthy of the stage. She scream-ing that I was a liar, which ironically is true but not in this case. Poor Augusta had to hurry Lewis from the room with her hands over his ears. I was not surprised. Only a whore knows language like that and it is my conviction that is what she is.

He had checked the marriage registry and discovered she had been, in fact, legally married and her son was legitimate.

That does not eliminate the fact that she was and still is a tart.

Unfortunately, it didn't mean Nathaniel wouldn't continue even now to dip his sugar stick in her honey pot. And she could catch. She had shown she was fertile.

"Fertile—capable of producing issue."

Jarius had insisted on having connections with his wife, Caroline, almost daily, but even his most vigorous pushing and shoving could not create the heir he yearned for. Her monthly courses had arrived with the regularity of the moon. Then she became ill and there was no possibility.

I will now write down the events of last night.

He was distracted by the sound of somebody talking outside in the hall. Augusta's voice, although he couldn't quite make out what she was saying. Then there was an enraged scream that he knew came from his stepmother, followed by the sound of bangs and thumps. He closed the ledger quickly and waited, listening. Almost at once, there was a sharp rap at the door.

"Jarius! Are you awake?"

"Yes."

"Can I come in?"

"Yes."

Augusta entered, a tray in her hands. Her eyes were bright with anger.

"Did you hear her?"

"How could I not?"

"She was shouting at me in the foulest language. Listen, she's still banging on the door."

"What did you do to provoke her?"

"How can you ask that? I did nothing. I thought she might want something to eat and I brought her up some porridge. She's had nothing since Saturday night. She spewed filth at me for thanks."

"How odd. I was under the impression she liked her porridge."

"Jarius, please! I will not tolerate her behaviour any longer. We have to do something."

"What do you suggest?"

"I don't know. Perhaps you can speak to Papa. He will listen to you. He always does."

"Is he up yet?"

"Not so far."

"And the others?"

"Frank has not shown his face . . . nor has my husband."

He lifted his hands in a placating gesture. "I understand how difficult it is for you, my dear, I do truly understand."

In contrast to his soothing voice, his thoughts were full of irritation and contempt for his half-sister. Regrettably, Augusta did not live up to the grandeur of her name; she was short with an unprepossessing figure. Even at this hour, she was already fully dressed and her hair was pinned in a tight coil on top of her head. She insisted on remaining in mourning for her mother and was wearing a black bombazine gown— even though the woman had died more than a year ago. The dull colour didn't suit her fair complexion and she looked washed out.

Augusta gave the tray she was holding a shake, as if it were a live creature and responsible for the situation.

"I have Lewis to consider. He is being exposed to the worst kind of language and behaviour in his very own home."

"That won't do." Jarius clutched the woollen shawl tight around his neck as if he were a woman going to market. "But the poor soul needs our love and sympathy, Aggie. She needs special care. More than we can possibly provide."

She gaped at him. "What do you mean?"

"I have been thinking and praying most of the night. I think we should send for Dr Ferrier. I fear for her mental stability."

"Oh, dear, Jarius, I don't know if we should go that far."

He came over to her, removed the tray from her hands, and drew her to his chest. "Try not to fret, little Cissie. It will be for the best. Think of your son."

She stood leaning against him. "Jarius, why did he do this to us?

My mother was as good a Christian woman as you could wish for. She was devoted to him. Your mother was the same. How could he marry such a one as this?"

He stroked her cheek tenderly. "Hush little one. He is an old man in his dotage, that's why. But I promise the situation won't continue. Now, why don't you go and stir up Cullie to make me some breakfast."

Augusta stepped back and picked up her tray.

"I had better do that. She's a clumsy girl. She'd set us all on fire if I didn't watch her."

"I'll come down shortly."

She left closing the door softly behind her.

Jarius went back to the ledger and opened to his last entry.

So far all is proceeding beyond my greatest imaginings. I am sure we will have no difficulty in persuading Ferrier that she belongs in an asylum. In my deepest heart I know it has all been worth it.

In spite of what he wrote, for a brief moment, quickly controlled, he quailed.

The Eakin's servant girl, Janet Cullie, was grating sugar from the loaf into a bowl. Because she was near-sighted, she was bent over close to what she was doing. The low kitchen windows didn't let in much light at the best of times and this morning the rain was virtually obliterating the dull early morning light. There was one oil lamp, which hung from the ceiling, but the wick was turned low. Augusta watched every expenditure, making Janet's life miserable by her constant carping about wastage.

There was the sound of a footstep on the uncarpeted stairs and, involuntarily, the girl flinched.

Sure enough the door was thrust open and her mistress entered. She was carrying a tray, which she put on the kitchen table.

"Clear this away, Janet."

Her voice was cool but the girl knew her well enough by now not

24

to be fooled. Something had riled her bad. Worse even than she'd been for the last two days and Janet thought that was very bad. Very high up riling.

"Must I finish this first, ma'am?"

"Of course, finish. You should have been done by now."

"Yes, Mrs Curran. Sorry, ma'am."

She gave a quick curtsey as she had been taught to do in the school. Janet Cullie was only fourteen and this was her first placement. Augusta had taken her from the Industrial Refuge for Girls, a school where orphan girls who might be in danger from bad influences were set to rights by being trained in working skills, mostly domestic service. Janet knew she should be grateful to Augusta, but many nights she cried herself to sleep, her head pushed into the pillow so as not to wake anybody. The school had been strict but there were other girls to chatter with and the work was not anywhere near as hard as what she was expected to do here. Besides, no matter how much she tried not to, she seemed to irritate her mistress and Augusta's voice became sharp and impatient. This only made the girl more nervous and ingratiating.

Augusta picked up the porridge dish from the tray.

"No sense in throwing this out; it wasn't touched." She scraped the porridge back into the pot that was cooking on the stove. "You can start the bacon for Mr Jarius."

"Shall I do up some for you, ma'am?"

"No, just toast and coffee will suffice. Why isn't the pot on?"

The girl grimaced. "We've run out of coffee, ma'am. There isn't any."

It wasn't Janet's job to order supplies but she was supposed to tell Augusta when they were getting low.

"Make me tea then."

Augusta dropped the porridge dish into the pail of water which stood beside the sink.

"I have a task for you after you have served breakfast."

Janet glanced over at her nervously. Her tone of voice suggested something disagreeable.

"Yes, ma'am."

"I want you to go for Dr Ferrier. Mrs Eakin has been taken poorly."

"Yes ma'am. I'm sorry to hear that ma'am."

She meant it. Ever since Peg had come to the house, she had felt an affinity for her. The new Mrs Eakin was a watcher the same as Janet. She knew the poor woman had shut herself up in her sitting room for the past two days, but so far nobody had said a word about it.

"Come from losing her little one, doesn't it?" she continued.

"What?" Augusta turned to stare at her.

"Our under-matron had a little girl that died. Only two she was. Missus never came back to work after. We heard she'd lost her mind. She had—"

She halted. Even though Augusta was standing a few feet away, Janet felt the sudden rage that came from her body.

"Whatever gave you the notion that this was any of your business?"

"I, er . . . I'm sorry, ma'am, I didn't mean anything—"

"Don't ever, ever, overstep your position like this again, or you will be dismissed instantly without reference. Do you understand me?"

Janet curtsied. "Yes, ma'am."

"You are a very ignorant girl. There are many women who have the misfortune to lose their children and they do not become lunatics. They continue on with their lives." There was a fleck of spittle at the corner of Augusta's mouth. "Is that clear?"

The girl ducked her head. "Yes, mistress."

Augusta looked as if she could have said much more, but with an ostentatious gesture of self-control, she turned and swept out of the kitchen. Janet sniffed hard trying not to cry in case Augusta came back in and saw her. But she couldn't help herself and the tears welled up in her eyes. She used her sleeve to wipe away the dribble from her nose. Then she dipped her forefinger in the soft, shiny sugar and stuck it in her mouth. The sweetness on her tongue was comforting and she sucked on her lips to make it last. She wished desperately that she had somewhere else to go but she didn't.

CHAPTER FIVE

———— ◆ ————

WHILE THE CORONER did a preliminary investigation, Murdoch went to inform Oliver Wicken's mother that her son was dead. They lived on Wilton Street, not far from the police station. He found himself inwardly rehearsing the words he would use.

The house was narrow-fronted with brown gables that even in the dulling rain looked freshly painted. The small yard behind the iron fence was neat and the shrubs trim. At the door, Murdoch took a deep breath, then knocked on the door. There was no response and he was forced to knock again, harder. This time the door opened. A tall woman of middle age stood looking at him enquiringly. The resemblance between her and the dead constable was striking and he assumed this was Mrs Wicken. He raised his hat.

"Ma'am. My name is Murdoch. I'm a detective at number four station, I, er . . ."

His words stuck in his mouth. The truth was too dreadful to say while he was on the doorstep. "May I have a word with you?"

Fear flashed across her face but perhaps with some instinct of self-preservation, she suppressed it immediately and nodded graciously. "Of course. Please come in. We're in the back."

She lead the way down the narrow hall toward the rear of the house. There was an elegance to her that Murdoch hadn't anticipated. Her abundant fair hair was stylishly dressed, her silk wrapper a smart sky blue stripe with cherry red yoke and flounces.

"We can talk in here," she said and she drew back the portieres that covered the door to the kitchen. They were velvet and a rich garnet colour. Like the outside of the house, the interior gave the impression of care and pride. Green durrie strips had been placed on the linoleum of the hall and there were several framed paintings on the walls, mostly equestrian portraits as far as he could tell.

"You must excuse us, we were just finishing breakfast."

By the window was an invalid chair, tilted back to a reclining position. Murdoch blinked, fighting the reflexive impulse to look away. There was a child lying in the chair although it was impossible to tell whether it was male or female. The head was enormous and virtually bald, except for a few sparse strands of white hair that straggled across the forehead. The neck seemed thin as a stalk although it was probably normal size, and he saw that there was a leather brace under the chin to hold the weight of the head. The pale blue eyes beneath the bulging forehead were vacant.

"This is my daughter, Dora."

She bent over and held a sipping cup to the girl's mouth. Murdoch waited. The kitchen seemed to serve a double function as a sitting room; it was crammed with furniture.

Mrs Wicken concentrated on her task, wiping away the dribbles from the child's chin. Then she turned around and regarded him.

"I beg your pardon, Mr Murdoch, please have a seat." She indicated a comfortable armchair but he was reluctant to take it.

"Is there somewhere we could speak in private?"

She shook her head. "It makes no matter where we talk; Dora can neither hear nor see."

She met his eyes and what she saw there frightened her dreadfully.

"What is it? Is Oliver hurt?"

He plunged in and his mouth was dry. "I'm afraid I have very bad news, Mrs Wicken. Oliver has met with"—he was going to say, "met with an accident," but that wasn't true. He tried again. "I deeply regret to tell you that your son is dead."

The words were out unsoftened and he would have given anything in the world to call them back, to make them palatable. As if that were possible.

She didn't cry out, or show any immediate sign of grief. She simply stared at him.

"I'm not sure I heard you correctly, sir. Are you referring to my son, Oliver Wicken? He is a police constable."

"Yes, ma'am, I know him well."

Her face had gone the colour of chalk. "I don't understand. What has happened?"

"I myself discovered his body in a vacant house a little while ago . . . he had been shot."

"Shot? By whom?"

"I, er . . ." Murdoch didn't want to tell her. "He was shot through the head. The bullet was from his own revolver."

He could see her absorbing the implications of what he said but she shook her head.

"I still cannot comprehend what you are saying. Was this an accident?"

"I'm afraid that doesn't seem likely."

"Then I don't understand."

"There was a note beside his body."

He removed it from his notebook and handed it to her. She took it reluctantly and read the message.

"This is preposterous. It makes no sense to me. Who is this addressed to?"

"Did he have a sweetheart?"

"He did not."

"Are you certain, ma'am? That is what the letter implies."

"Of course I am certain. Do you think I don't know my own son? He was devoted to me and his sister. Her care was a vital part of his life." Her chin and lower lip were shaking uncontrollably and she turned abruptly to the crippled girl and began to fuss with her covers. The child gurgled some sounds of distress, sensing what she couldn't hear or see. Her mother picked up the sipping cup again but held it suspended in the air. Her hand was trembling so badly, however, she couldn't hold the cup steady and she put it down on the table. Murdoch wanted to reach out and comfort her but he couldn't. Finally, she turned back to face him.

"I know what you are implying, Mr Murdoch. You think he took his own life."

"We won't know for certain until after the inquest but I'm afraid it does seem that way."

"That is utterly impossible. He isn't that kind of boy. My son would never commit suicide. He loved both of us too much."

Murdoch did not reply.

"Let me see that letter again." She examined it. "I am not even sure if that is his hand."

He knew printed letters were hard to distinguish but he didn't contradict her. Abruptly, she returned the letter to him.

"Where is he?"

"At the moment he is still where I found him in the empty house on Gerrard Street. After the jurors have viewed the body he will probably be taken to Humphrey's Funeral Home for the inquest."

Suddenly, she sat back in her chair, "I beg your pardon . . ." She put her hand to her mouth, turned to the side and retched violently, two or three times.

Murdoch crossed over to her and put his hand on her shoulder.

"I am so terribly sorry, Mrs Wicken."

CHAPTER SIX

————◆————

WITH A GRUNT, the coroner, Arthur Johnson, got to his feet. He was getting on in years and his knees were plaguing him. The wet weather made the ache worse and his temper fractious. He had been examining the wound in Wicken's temple. Murdoch was standing to his right and jammed around the room were the thirteen members of the jury. Constable George Crabtree was at the door. He had been appointed constable of the court and commissioned to find and swear in at least twelve men to serve as jurors. Because of the early hour, he'd managed to net thirteen, catching them before they went to work. For most of the men, this meant missing a day's wages and they had griped and complained. Only two of them were genuinely willing. Albert Chamberlin, retired and lonely, was more than happy to do his duty, and Jabez Clarke, a traveller, was eager because he knew the situation would make for a good tale to recount at a dinner party. However, the sight of the corpse had silenced all of them, even the vociferous labourer, Sam Stevenson, who would sorely miss the money he would have earned that morning.

Johnson beckoned to them irritably. "All of you men, come in closer. What you expect to see from over there is beyond me."

Reluctantly, the men shifted and shuffled forward.

"Come on, come on. Unlike the constable here I haven't got all day."

Murdoch thought for a moment Johnson was referring to Crabtree, then the flippant remark hit him. He would've loved to have made some sharp retort but he daren't show his disapproval too openly. He already had a dickey relationship with his inspector and if he antagonised Johnson, he ran the risk that the coroner would report him. The fine for insubordination was hefty.

"Have you chosen a foreman?" asked the coroner.

"Yes, sir. I am he." The speaker was a tall, lean-faced man, middle-aged, who was dressed in the sombre clothes of a clerk.

"Your name, sir?"

"Jarius Gibb."

"Mr Gibb, are you prepared to be sworn in?"

"I am."

"Constable, please address the jury."

Crabtree clasped his official papers and in a voice that would have been easily heard in the rear seats of the new Massey Hall, he read:

"'Gentlemen hearken to your foreman's oath; for the oath he is to take on his part is the oath you are severally to observe and keep on your part.' Mr Gibb, take this Bible in your right hand."

Gibb did so. He had a rather prissy face with tightly pursed lips as if he was used to disapproving of the transgressions of humanity. Murdoch wondered where he was employed. Crabtree continued:

"'You shall diligently inquire and true presentment make of all such matters and things as shall be here given you in charge, on behalf of our Sovereign Lady the Queen, touching on the death of Oliver Wicken now lying dead, of whose body you shall have the view; you shall present no man for hatred, malice, or ill will nor spare any through fear, favour, or affection; but a true verdict give according to the evidence, and the best of your skill and knowledge. So help you God.'"

"Amen."

Crabtree addressed the remaining jurors:

"'The same oath which Jarius Gibb, your foreman upon this

32

inquest, hath now taken before you on his part, you and each of you are severally well and truly to observe and keep on your parts. So help you God.'"

There was a varied chorus of "Amens" and then the jury was sworn and ready. Johnson had been waiting impatiently for it all to be concluded.

"All right then. Pay attention all of you." He indicated the wound at the right temple. "The bullet entered here, exited here." He raised Wicken's head releasing trapped blood, which dripped onto the floor.

"Blasted butcher's shop," the labourer muttered to his neighbour.

"Watch your language, Stevenson," Crabtree warned. "This is Her Majesty's court now present."

Johnson pushed at the dead man's shoulder. "See, he's getting stiff as a statue. That's what we call 'rigor mortis.' Happens to all of us when we die—man, woman, or babe." He started to warm to his role as demonstrator. "Anybody know what we can tell from the development of rigor?"

The men avoided his eye.

Murdoch said. "When I found him, at about six o'clock this morning, rigor had started in the chin and neck. I figured he'd been dead for approximately five to six hours."

He didn't want to show off, just let Johnson know there was somebody else in the room he couldn't lord it over.

The coroner nodded. "That's right. So let's see. Rigor is now more advanced. I would agree with the detective. He probably died some time between midnight and two o'clock last night. It's quite cold in here so that slows down the stiffening. Now what else can you tell me about the body? Hm? One of you men speak up. What do you see?"

The jurors stared at him, trying to figure out what he wanted. Johnson shook his head impatiently.

"Well, it's obvious, isn't it? He's in uniform. He was on duty. Isn't that right, Murdoch?"

"Yes, sir. The patrol sergeant last spoke to him at a quarter past eleven."

Sergeant Hales had seen Wicken's body before the coroner

arrived and he had been very upset. Saying he didn't want to watch them poking and prodding, he'd put himself in charge of keeping back the curious onlookers who had gathered outside.

"His helmet is about six feet away from him. You didn't move it did you, Murdoch?"

"I did examine it, sir, but I replaced it in the same spot."

"You said the constable's pistol was wedged between his thighs. Show us exactly where it was, will you."

Murdoch had no desire to do so but he couldn't refuse. He walked over to the body, picked up the gun, and holding it by the handle, tried to push it between the rigid thighs. It was obscenely difficult.

"All right," said Johnson. He scanned the jurors, then pointed to one of them, a short, squat man who looked as if he were trying to make himself invisible. "You at the back. Yes, you. You with the scars."

The man's nose was wide and flattened across his face and the lower lid of his right eye was pulled down by the pucker of a scar, exposing the red. The pupil was dull and unseeing.

Murdoch hoped the fellow wasn't sensitive about his appearance.

"What's your name?" asked the coroner.

"Peter Curran, sir."

"Occupation?"

"I work in the livery stable next door, sir."

"What happened to you? A horse kick you?"

"It was a cow actually, sir. I was just a nipper at the time."

"Unfortunate," said the coroner, his tone brisk as if Curran might be one of those malingerers who are always pleading for sympathy. "Now, then." He held up the note that Murdoch had given him. "The detective found this close to the right hand, under the constable's notebook. What did it say again, Murdoch?"

"Life is unbearable without your love. Forgive me."

"Rather poetic wouldn't you say? You can all have a look at it."

Murdoch handed the note to the closest juror who took it gingerly, studied it, and then passed it on. One of the men raised his hand as if he were in the classroom. He had a chubby, weather-roughed face and bright, dark eyes.

34

"Excuse me, sir. But do we have the pencil that this note was wrote with?"

Johnson frowned. "Do you, Murdoch?"

"No, sir. Perhaps he returned it to his pocket."

"We'll look in a minute."

"I do have another question, sir."

"Yes? State your name so I know who I'm dealing with."

"Stevenson, labourer."

"Speak out."

"Why was the gun between Wicken's legs? It seems an odd place for it to be."

"It must have fallen there as he collapsed, then it was fixed in the grip of death. Don't you agree, Mr Murdoch?"

"Actually, I was wondering about that myself, sir. It would seem more likely to fall beside him."

There was a palpable ripple of uneasiness among the jurors, who sensed the coroner would not take kindly to contradiction. Most of them had learned to be intimidated by authority.

Johnson shook his head. "Typically, in the case of sudden death, the body can go into seizures. The gun must have been trapped at that moment. Let's move on. The spent casing was here, as you see. What now, Stevenson?"

"Where is the bullet?"

"I don't know, still lodged in his head probably. The post mortem examination will tell us."

"Beg pardon, sir."

It was constable Crabtree who had spoken. "There is a hole in the wall right here beside the door. Can I examine it?"

"Do, please do."

The constable felt into the small hole and, breaking off some of the plaster, he fished out a bullet and brought it over to Johnson.

"Probably the one that killed him. Take care of it will you, Mr Murdoch?"

Murdoch took out one of the envelopes he had at the ready in his pocket and put the bullet into it.

35

"The entrance of the bullet into the wall seems rather low, sir. Certainly not six feet."

Johnson stared at the spot he indicated. "What religious denomination was the young man?"

"I don't know, sir."

"Hm, an important facet of a man's life I would say. Strange not to know. Constable?"

"He was Episcopalian, I believe, sir."

"So there. He was no doubt kneeling and saying his prayers. At least he stands a chance of divine forgiveness. Lucky for him he wasn't a Papist. He would head straight to hell for a sin like this."

Murdoch didn't think the coroner could possibly know that he was Roman Catholic but he was stung by the contempt in the man's voice.

"Excuse me, Mr Johnson." He tried to keep his voice devoid of expression. "At this juncture, we are not absolutely sure he did shoot himself, are we? Won't that be determined at the inquest?"

As soon as the words were out of his mouth, he regretted saying them. They were more likely to close up Johnson's mind than open it.

"No, we are not *absolutely* sure but as close to as makes no difference. We have a farewell note and the position of the wound is consistent with suicide. I fail to see how we can come to any other conclusion."

The jurors were quiet, aware of the rebuke, sympathetic. Then one of them, an elderly man with an old-fashioned full beard, indicated he had a question. Johnson nodded at him.

"Chamberlin, sir. Retired. I was wondering why his helmet was beside him?"

"You are most perspicacious. If he were wearing it, the strap would prevent it from being blown off. Conclusion, Wicken must have placed it where he did prior to shooting himself. As to why he did, I have no idea. Some kind of mental preparation I suppose. People who drown themselves often take off their clothes and fold them up neatly. Like going to bed."

"Can we see his notebook, sir?" This was again from Stevenson.

"As you wish." Johnson handed him the book. A couple of the other men looked over his shoulder.

"There are two entries with yesterday's date. *Monday, November 11.9.07 Gerrard and River. All secure.* The second entry says *Monday, November 11.11.12 Queen and Parliament All secure and accounted for.* He sounds quite normal here, sir."

"Come man, what do you expect? He'd not going to use his official notebook to write down his inner turmoil. Typically self-murderers vacillate, sometimes for days, until the actual moment."

Stevenson handed back the notebook.

"Let's move on. We'll examine his clothes, then we'll call it a morning."

Murdoch signalled to Crabtree to help him. He undid the neck button of the rubber cape and tugged it away so they could reach into Wicken's pockets. He started with the trousers and pulled out a clean handkerchief from the right-hand pocket and, from the left, a small, brown paper package that contained a half slice of cheese. The pencil was here and an iron key.

"Constable, see if it fits the back door," said the coroner.

Crabtree, who seemed even bigger than usual in the cramped room, walked to the door and tried the key. It fit the lock perfectly.

Johnson glanced around at the jurors. "I don't know if there's any more to be done here. We will request a post mortem examination and you will hear that report at the inquest. Murdoch, will you take charge of the effects?"

"Yes, sir."

"Excuse me, Mr Johnson, could I ask something?" Once again it was the labourer Stevenson who spoke.

"What now? I've got to be getting on. I don't have all day to speculate."

"I've just been thinking, you see."

Johnson made a surprised face that caused some of the other jurors to titter sycophantically.

"What I mean, is, I'm wondering why Wicken didn't do himself in the first time?"

"What on earth are you talking about?"

His tone was so withering, the man was abashed. Murdoch interjected.

"If I may speak for Mr Stevenson, sir, I was about to ask the same question. If we are to assume that Wicken was so despondent, why did he wait so long to kill himself? He could have come into the house immediately."

Mr Johnson smiled. "You weren't listening, Detective. As I said, people can shilly-shally for a long time. To me it is very clear. He is ambivalent about what he is thinking of doing. He knows it is a blasphemy against the Divine Will. He walks his beat, round and round through the empty streets, trying desperately to decide. His sweetheart has abandoned him. His heart is broken. He does not want to live. He has the means at hand to commit the act but he cannot make up his mind. Finally in the darkest hours of the night, he can bear it no longer. He enters the house and . . . well you can see the rest."

"Where did he get the key?" asked Murdoch.

Johnson frowned, annoyed that Murdoch had spoiled the effect of his little speech. "I don't know. Don't the police keep the keys to vacant houses?"

"Occasionally we do, but I don't recall ever seeing this one at the station."

The coroner waved his hand dismissively. "We might not be able to tie up all the loose ends. This is something you, yourself, can investigate. Now, I'm setting the inquest for tomorrow morning at eleven o'clock, Humphrey's Funeral Home." He pulled on his fur-lined kid gloves. "Constable, please read the jurors their duties and obligations. And Mr Murdoch, as you seem so anxious to have this case *absolutely* certain, you have my permission to investigate further. You can tell your inspector I have requested it."

He made his way to the door then he paused and turned around, a bemused look on his face.

"You're not Roman Catholic by any chance, are you, Detective?"

If Murdoch could have controlled his own flush by sheer willpower, he would have done so, but he couldn't. All the other men were gazing at him curiously. The coroner had a fine sense of an exit line.

"As a matter of fact I am, sir. But I don't understand why you ask?"

"It's just that you people are so jumpy about suicide. Mortal sin or something in your religion, isn't it? Go to everlasting damnation, don't you?"

"That is the teaching, yes sir."

"Well don't let it blind you to the truth, that's all I ask. Remember the oath. We want a true verdict."

Johnson was busy wrapping himself in his muffler or he would have seen the expression on Murdoch's face. Crabtree saw and said loudly, "Off you go then, you men. And don't forget to report in tomorrow. No feeble excuses. You don't show up, you'll be fined."

The jurors shuffled out and Murdoch was left alone with the constable.

"Don't let him get to you, sir. He's a first-class fart if I can put it that way."

"You certainly can, George."

"Do you think it's a suicide, Mr Murdoch?"

"Let's say I'm keeping an open mind."

"Shall I have him off to the morgue now?"

"Yes. Ask Hales to go for the ambulance. I'll wait here."

The constable left and when the door had closed behind him, Murdoch crouched down beside the dead man.

"May our Lord have mercy on your immortal soul."

He made the sign of the cross with his thumb on Wicken's cold forehead.

CHAPTER SEVEN

Frank Eakin sliced a piece off the apple he was holding and held it underneath the mare's nose. She smelled at the fruit and went to take a nibble but Frank stepped back quickly and put the slice between his own teeth.

"Kiss me," he said and he poked his head forward. The horse tossed her head but didn't move. Frank said again, "Come on, Duchess, kiss me."

Peter Curran was leaning against the stable partition watching. "Doesn't want to, does she? Can't say I blame her."

Suddenly, Frank kicked out and his heel caught Curran right on the shin. He yelped and grasped his leg.

"For God's sake, Frank. What are you doing?"

Eakin didn't deign to answer but he made more seductive noises at the mare and this time she stretched her neck and gently nibbled the piece of apple away from his mouth. He grinned.

"See, she's learning."

"That's wonderful," said Curran sullenly. "You can both join the frigging circus."

However, he made sure he had stepped out of reach as he spoke.

"And you could join the freak show," said Frank, "but I doubt they'd take you. Your face would scare the nippers off."

Peter Curran was used to his brother-in-law's jibes but he didn't ever like them. Only fear of the younger man's temper kept him from retaliating.

"So are we going to twitch her or not? Fellow said he'd come by tomorrow."

Frank gave Duchess the remainder of the apple and stroked the horse's soft nose.

"She's a lovely little tart, isn't she?"

Then he grasped her upper lip and twisted it, holding it tightly pinched between his fingers. Far from shying off, the mare stood motionless as if she had gone into a trance. Curran picked up an iron file from the shelf and started to rub at the exposed front teeth, which were splayed out with age.

"There you go my pretty. You're going to look like a filly all over again," said Eakin.

"Only in the dark. They'll notice for sure."

"You're a cheerful charley, aren't you? Is something the matter? Is there something darkening your view of life?"

"Leave off, Frank."

He worked on in a sullen silence, while Frank spoke soothingly to the horse.

"Almost done. You just keep your mind on one of those enormous stallion dongs."

"Do you need to be so crude?"

"You only say that because you aren't stopping your beak in my sister. The mares like knee tremblers. And speaking of that, is Aggie still giving you the go-by?"

Curran shrugged but didn't respond.

"I'll give you some advice, even though she's my own flesh and blood. You've got to show her the whip. Give her a goffer about the head. She'll start talking to you."

Curran scooped out the filings from the mare's mouth. "I didn't notice I'd asked for any advice."

"Suit yourself. But she's a mule when she wants to be. Look, you did me a favour by marrying her. I've never seen a woman more anx-

41

ious to snare a husband. Before you came along, she'd take things out on me. Wouldn't speak to me once for almost two months. I gave a piss about her stupid conversation but it got to be aggravating that she wouldn't answer anything. One day, I just got fed up and I picked up the slop pail in the kitchen and dumped it all over her. That brought her voice back fast."

Curran rubbed away in silence, the mare still transfixed by Eakin's grip on her lip.

"I'm done," he said and Eakin let go. Duchess ducked her head a few times and snuffled. "Do you think we should puff her glims?"

Frank regarded the mare's sunken eyes. The upper skin had collapsed with age.

"No. She'll have to do. Keep the lamp down low. This fellow is nothing but a country sot. He won't notice." He stroked the horse's neck. "She'll look beautiful."

"Why'd the old gasser pick on me at the viewing?" Curran asked suddenly.

Frank shrugged. "Must have been your open and honest face."

"He made a comment about my eye. I told him the cow kicked me."

"You should have said the truth—it was some poor heifer you were trying to stick it to."

Curran scowled. "Leave off, Frank, I mean it."

"I was joking, for Jesus' sake. Just trying to lighten the mood."

"You needn't bother. You'd be low too if you'd been there when they were examining him. It'll haunt me for the rest of my days."

"Like I said, you should have made yourself scarce when the frog came around recruiting."

"You know I didn't have a chance. The fella came right into the stable and nabbed me."

"Well, put it this way, one good thing is you'll be up on all what's going on, won't you? You and Jarius both."

"He don't show much, does he? Didn't even blink an eye when one of the fellas nominated him as foreman. 'I'll be honoured,' was his very words."

"Don't surprise me. He don't have blood in his veins like normal people. I should know."

"Know what?"

Jarius had entered the stable unheard. Frank jumped as if there was a loud noise.

"Nothing," he said.

"We need some help," said Jarius.

"What with?"

"Dr Ferrier's come but she won't open the door. She's screaming like a street slut." He nodded at Frank. "Where's the axe?"

"In the back."

"Bring it."

"What does Pa say?"

"Nothing. He's leaving everything up to me. Hurry up, I don't have all day. I want to get to my office before the day's wasted completely." He was dressed in outdoor clothes—a smart plaid cape and a black crusher.

Frank tapped his forehead in a mock salute and went to do what he was told. As he went past the last stall, the big, grey gelding poked his head over the gate and gave him a quick, hard bite on the shoulder. Frank yelled, spun around, and fetched the horse a savage punch on the side of the head.

CHAPTER EIGHT

⎯⎯⎯•⎯⎯⎯

AFTER THE AMBULANCE had taken away Wicken's body, Murdoch and Crabtree started the tedious process of knocking on doors. The constable took the west side of the street and Murdoch the east. There was a string of stores from Gerrard down to Wilton Street and he was able to speak to the shopkeepers, who for the most part were huddled by their stoves with the lamps fully burning. None of them could give him any information. Two or three were familiar with the constable and one confirmed he had seen Wicken walking the beat at ten o'clock last night and said he had seemed quite normal. They had heard nothing. Mrs Bail, the widow lady who ran a confectionery at number 327 was particularly upset.

"Oh dear, oh my word," she kept repeating. "He came in here once a week on Friday night without fail. He'd catch me just before I closed when he was on his way to work. Very partial to my buttercups with the nut centre. Oh dear, oh my."

She had seen Wicken as usual on Friday last. "He bought a box of chocolate creams. Raspberry flavoured. For his sister he said, but I suspect it was a sweetheart. They are my best candies."

She was so distressed, Murdoch felt sorry that he had to press her. "In your opinion, Mrs Bail, did the constable seem in any way despondent or out of sorts?"

44

She eyed him, puzzled. "Not at all. He was cheery as always. 'Good evening to you, Mrs Bail,' he'd say. 'What have you got for me to try today?' I experiment with new candies you see and I'd let him taste them. I'd made some maple toffee and he really liked it. Oh my, Mr Murdoch why are you asking such a thing?"

Murdoch had said little about the way Wicken had died but she picked up the implications of his question immediately. He hesitated.

"I'm afraid there are indications that he may have taken his own life."

"Oh, no. I cannot believe that. He was too happy. No, Mr Murdoch, that cannot be."

"Did he ever mention to you that he had a sweetheart?"

"No, he never did. But as I said, I wondered sometimes when he would buy a special box of chocolates. I knew he lived with his mother and a sister who is poorly." She indicated one of the large jars on the shelf behind the counter that was filled with small, brightly coloured candies. "His sister was partial to the Tom Thumb mix and his mother liked the marshmallow drops."

She was close to tears and Murdoch wished he could offer her some solace but he couldn't.

"The coroner's inquest is tomorrow and we hope we'll learn what exactly happened. For now, I'm just trying to find out if anybody heard or saw anything that might have to do with him."

She shook her head. "I did not. I closed up the shop as usual at seven o'clock and retired for the night at a half past nine. Saves the lamp oil."

She gave him a wan smile that nevertheless had the ghost of the coquette in it. She was a small woman, grey-haired and neat in her green silk waist and crisp white apron. She reminded him of his landlady, Mrs Kitchen, and he responded warmly.

"Indeed it does, ma'am."

She went on to express concern for Wicken's widowed mother. She was as adamant as Mrs Wicken had been that Oliver was not the kind of man to take his own life.

Finally, as Murdoch was leaving, she took some barley sugar sticks from a jar, put them in a brown paper bag and thrust it into his hand.

"Freshly made this morning."

The shop had a wonderful sweet smell of boiled candy.

Because of his painful jaw, Murdoch didn't want to risk eating anything now but he thanked her and stowed the bag in his pocket.

The next half hour was unforthcoming. From across the road, Crabtree indicated he had no success either. They continued making their way south and Murdoch was glad the constable had the dentist Brodie on his side of the street. He wondered if revisiting the scene of his pain would distress him but Crabtree emerged looking much the same.

About half a block below Wilton Street, there was a Chinese laundry and when Murdoch stepped through the front door he was immediately enfolded by the hot moist air. A Chinaman was working on an abacus behind the counter. He was wearing a traditional blue smock and round black hat and his hair was braided into a long queue.

"Can help you?"

Murdoch tapped his own chest. "Me police officer. Need to ask questions."

The man looked at him uncomprehendingly. Murdoch paused trying to think how to communicate. "Me police officer," he repeated in a louder voice. "Ask questions."

"Washing very cheap. Very clean."

Behind him in the long narrow shop were two large steaming washtubs. Another man was forking out piles of boiled linen with a long stick and dumping them into a basket, ready for mangling. To his right was a large iron range where a variety of irons were heating.

Murdoch pointed. "He speak English?" He made motions at his mouth but realised he looked as if he was wanting to eat. He called out instead. "Hey, you back there. Do you speak English?"

The Chinaman stopped what he was doing and approached Murdoch. He was young and seemed as wary as a dog with a stranger.

When he was close enough, Murdoch asked, "Speak English?"

"Ay. What ken I do for ye?"

For a moment, Murdoch was confused by his accent, expecting Chinese. Then he realised the man had spoken with a strong Scottish burr.

"Early this morning, a police constable was found dead up at the corner of Gerrard Street. He was on duty last night and I was wondering if you saw him at all or had anything to do with him. He would probably have been walking past here on his beat at various times during the night. Any information you can give me would be much appreciated."

The older man apparently asked a question and there was a spirited exchange between the two of them. Murdoch couldn't tell if they were excited or if it was the rhythm of the language. The younger man turned back to Murdoch.

"I perhaps should present my father, Mr Sam Lee. I myself am called Foon Lee."

He bowed in such a formal way that Murdoch almost reciprocated. He nodded an acknowledgment.

"I'm acting detective William Murdoch from number four station."

"My father would like to know a description of the officer in the case."

"He was young, about the same height as me, but he had a blond moustache, not dark."

"And this unfortunate officer has been the victim of an accident?"

"Something to that effect."

Sam Lee spoke to his son and Murdoch wondered if he understood English better than he was letting on. Foon bowed.

"I must tell you that I myself had got myself off to my bed but my father did encounter the constable last night. The officer opened the door. Apparently it was not locked and he was concerned that all was well. When he was secured that all was as it was intended to be, he left."

He stopped and they both watched Murdoch, waiting for the next move.

"What time was that?"

Foon translated the question to his father.

"It would have been at approximately twenty minutes past eleven o'clock. Mr Lee is quite assured of the correctness of this time." He indicated a large clock that was hung on the wall, its glass face obscured by steam.

"Will you ask him if there was anything strange about the constable. Was he calm? Distracted in any way? Do you understand what I mean?"

"Ay, I do."

Again the exchange in Chinese.

"My father says the officer has come here on two prior occasions to check on his well-being and they have had pleasant words. Last night was not an exception. The constable seemed quite equal in his temper."

Mr Lee senior interceded, saying directly to Murdoch, "Lady. Had lady."

"I don't understand."

"Lady, was a lady with him."

Exasperated, Murdoch turned to Foon. "What is he saying?"

"The officer was accompanied by a young woman. She was standing back but he saw her clearly then they walked up the street together."

Murdoch sighed. It was strictly against regulations for anyone to accompany constables on their beat. However, in spite of what Mrs Wicken believed, the evidence was pointing to her son having a lover. Someone he was willing to risk his job over.

"Please inform Mr Lee that he will have to be a witness at the inquest. A constable will come back today with a subpoena."

There was a flurry of talk, both of them obviously alarmed.

"Mr Lee wishes to ask what is the charge he is under? He has paid his licence most recently."

"No, no. He isn't being charged with anything. At an inquest anybody with information has to tell it. There will be others doing the same. Then the jury can decide what has happened."

"My father is now wondering if he was not in truth mistaken. That it was not this night that he saw the officer."

Murdoch faced the older man, gave him a little bow, and spoke slowly and distinctly.

"Mr Lee. You need not be afraid. You are not in any trouble. All I want you to do is to tell the coroner, the judge, what you have just said to me. That's all."

He turned his hands palms up in a universal gesture of openness. As far as he could tell, the Chinaman calmed down.

"You will have to come as his translator," Murdoch said to the son.

"Very well."

Both the Lees bowed deeply and Murdoch gave a quick bob himself. It was infectious.

He left. Outside on the grey street, the air was even more chill after the warmth of the laundry and he shivered. He wondered when the mysterious woman was going to turn up and he hoped he wouldn't be the one to give her the news.

CHAPTER NINE

———◆———

BY THE TIME he got to the end of the beat, Murdoch was getting tired. His jaw was still pulsing and when he touched his cheek, it felt swollen. He would have to find a dentist soon and stop being such a lily liver. His moustache was dripping and his hands were freezing because he'd left his lodgings without his gloves, and to make matters worse, he was overly conscious of the fishy miasma all around him from his wet coat. He took out one of the barley sugar sticks and stuck it in his mouth. As long as he kept it away from the bad side of his jaw it seemed fine, and the sweetness filled his mouth.

He had almost reached the corner of Gerrard and Parliament Streets, when two men emerged from the house that was next to the livery stable. They were carrying a chair between them on which was sitting a young woman. She was squirming and it took a moment for Murdoch to realise she was strapped to the chair. Her actions were peculiarly lethargic as if she were a mechanical piece that was winding down. A frightened-looking girl, dressed in servant's grey, was endeavouring to hold an umbrella over all of them while an older man, a doctor by the look of him, followed behind. He was speaking in a quick, anxious voice to the woman in the chair.

"Calm yourself, madam. Please calm yourself."

One of the men carrying her was Frank Eakin, the other, the scarred juror whom Murdoch had seen earlier.

The bizarre entourage was heading for a carriage drawn up at the gate but even as he watched, Murdoch saw the woman's struggles begin to subside completely. They came through the gate and he waited to let them pass. The woman's head was lolling back against the chair, but she turned in his direction and her eyes, wide with terror, met his.

"Help me," she whispered. "Please mister, help me."

He had no chance to respond because the doctor stepped in front of him. The coachman opened the door of the carriage and she was lifted in, chair and all. The doctor climbed in himself, immediately pulled down the window blind, and they drove off. The two men, both of them panting from their exertion, watched.

"What's going on?" Murdoch asked.

Curran realised who Murdoch was and he gave him a quick salute.

"Morning, officer. That's Mrs Eakin. I'm afraid she's lost her slates. We're getting her to the loony bin."

Murdoch was about to make some polite murmur of condolence but he didn't get the chance.

Eakin snapped at the servant girl. "For God's sake, Cullie. We're getting soaked. You're as useless as a stuck pig. Bring the frigging thing over here."

She jumped to obey and Eakin took the umbrella. "Anything we can do for you, sir?"

"I was coming to speak to the members of the household concerning the death of constable Wicken. I'm sorry if this is not an appropriate time. I can come back later."

"What is it you're after?"

"Any information. Whether anybody heard the gunshot. That sort of thing."

"Nobody's said anything about it."

"I'd still like to talk to them. We're asking questions of everybody in the vicinity."

Eakin managed to produce a friendlier expression. "Of course. Terrible tragedy, that."

He was studying Murdoch from the shelter of the umbrella and the detective began to get irritated. He was sorry for the man's circumstances but he didn't feel like spending more time in the rain than he had to.

"It shouldn't take too long," he said.

Eakin looked toward the house. The front door was open and a woman was standing on the threshold watching them. She was dressed in mourning clothes and her hands were clasped in front of her as if in prayer. Whatever Eakin saw there made up his mind.

"You might as well come in now. Get it out of the way."

He extended the umbrella to cover Murdoch and they walked toward the door in awkward intimacy.

"Augusta, this is detective Murdoch. He wants to ask us all some questions about the fellow they found in the empty house." He was closing up the umbrella as he spoke. "This is my sister, Mrs Curran." He gestured with his thumb. "Hitched to him."

She stepped back so they could enter, then over his shoulder, she noticed the servant girl who was trailing behind them.

"Janet, you can get back to work. Go in the side entrance."

She bobbed. "Yes, ma'am." She scurried off.

"Come this way, Mr Murdoch," said Mrs Curran. "We can talk in the drawing room."

She turned and lead the way down the narrow hall but not without a quick glance at Murdoch's boots to determine just how wet they were. He wiped them hurriedly on the doormat and set off after her. Peter Curran was at his heels, and at the door, he tapped Murdoch on the shoulder.

"You don't want me, do you, sir?" asked Curran. "Me being on the jury and all."

"Yes, as a matter of fact I do. It won't affect anything. It can all be repeated for the inquest."

He'd found that asking questions of an entire family at the same

52

time tended to yield a lot of information, if not about the case, certainly about them.

The drawing room fire was laid but unlit and the air was chill. Frank went straight to the fireplace and reached for the box of matches standing by the fender.

"That won't be necessary," said his sister, "I'm sure Mr Murdoch won't keep us."

Eakin turned to her, glaring in a little spurt of anger.

"Aggie, it's frigging freezing in here. I'm going to light the bloody fire."

His sister didn't retaliate for his rudeness except by a visible tightening of her lips.

"Mr Murdoch, will you take that chair." she indicated an armchair next to the fireplace. He sat down, took off his damp hat and placed it beside the chair. The mantle was draped with black crepe and the mirror above was covered with a grey gauze. He wondered who had died.

Eakin had got a blaze going right away and stretched out his hands to the flames. Then predictably, he turned to warm his backside. Mrs Curran took a seat on the Turkish couch opposite him, while her husband remained by the door.

"Shall I light the lamps, Augusta?" In the gloom, Peter Curran would have been a sinister-looking fellow except that his whole bearing was so hangdog, Murdoch felt sorry for him.

She didn't look in his direction at all but addressed the air in front of her. "I would have thought it was obvious we need some light."

Murdoch took a quick glance around the room. There were other crepe trimmings on the sideboard and around the pictures on the walls. The furniture was dark hued and although the plush green coverings were thick and patterned with gilt flowers, the effect was gloomy. The house wasn't that grand and he had the impression the drawing room wasn't much used. Probably a family aspiring to a lifestyle beyond their class. Fine furniture but not fine manners. On

53

the other hand, to be fair, it had been his experience that ungraciousness could be found at any level of society.

Curran lit a lamp from the sideboard and brought it closer to where they were sitting. Augusta pointed wordlessly at a small japanned table and he placed it there.

Murdoch took out his notebook to indicate he was ready to start. Frank Eakin, smelling slightly of singed corduroy, came and sat beside his sister. The family resemblance was strong. Short nose and round chin, fair complexion. Augusta had light brown hair that she wore pinned tightly in a knot on top of her head. Eakin was trying without much success to sport side whiskers and a moustache.

"Is this everybody in the house?" asked Murdoch.

"No, there's Mr Eakin, our father, but I'm afraid he is indisposed. Besides, I'm sure he could not help you. He always takes a sedative at night. Nothing would wake him."

"Anyone else?"

"There's Mr Jarius Gibb. You must have met him. He's the foreman of the coroner's jury. He is our older brother."

"Stepbrother," interrupted Eakin. "His mother was a widow when she married our father. Unfortunately, she did not live too much longer afterward. Father married for the second time. This Mrs Eakin, Harmony by name and nature, was our mother."

He was offering this information in a chatty way that Murdoch found odd. As did his sister, obviously, because she frowned at him.

"Frank, really! I doubt that is relevant to the officer's enquiry."

Murdoch had a vivid image of the two of them as small children ready to squabble at any moment. But that early animosity seemed to have hardened into mutual disdain.

He addressed Eakin, trying to be as delicate as he could. "And your wife, sir? She was in the house last night, I assume."

"Who?"

"Mrs Eakin, the lady who . . ." he waved vaguely in the direction of the door.

"That's not my wife. She's married to my father. As I said, Mother

54

died last year. My father married again this April. Quick you might say. Properly speaking the woman you saw is my stepmother, young as she is."

There was a strange sound from Curran, and Murdoch could have sworn he had guffawed and stifled it immediately. He looked over at Curran but he was sitting in the shadows behind the light and he couldn't see his expression.

"Mrs *Nathaniel* Eakin was indeed in the house," answered Augusta. "But as you saw, she is dreadfully ill. Her doctor has been forced to commit her to the Provincial lunatic asylum. I doubt she would be aware if Beelzebub himself visited us."

Her tone was sharp. No love lost there, Murdoch thought.

"Do you have other servants?" he asked.

"Only Janet, the girl you saw. We hire extra help as we need."

Murdoch felt a twinge of pity for the young servant. He could imagine the amount of work that was foisted on her.

"I assume your husband has spoken to you about the tragedy I am investigating, Mrs Curran?"

"My brother told me. But I thought the coroner declared him a suicide."

"We won't know anything for certain until after the inquest. That is why I am conducting this investigation."

"'Scuse me." Frank got up and went to the fire. He grabbed the poker and gave a recalcitrant piece of coal a couple of good thwacks. Flames leaped out. He stayed where he was, watching the fire.

"I am interested in any information you can give me," said Murdoch. "We think the constable died some time between midnight and one o'clock. Did any of you hear anything?"

"I for one am a very sound sleeper," said Augusta. "I heard nothing at all."

"Where is your bedroom, ma'am?"

"On the third floor. My husband and I have a suite there."

Murdoch nodded at Curran. "What about you, sir?"

"Not a peep. I sleep like the dead."

"You were on the third floor as well?"

Augusta looked at Murdoch as if he had said something quite rude but his guess was right.

Curran chuckled in embarrassment. "Not last night I wasn't. I snore. Keeps my wife aggravated. I was in the stable loft. Better."

"So was I," added Frank. "I have a room there so I can keep an eye on the horses. I didn't hear anything except them farting."

This remark was obviously intended to offend his sister, who took the bait.

"Frank, how many times must I ask you not to be so coarse?"

"That's not coarse, Aggie. It's a fact of nature. Horses fart all the time. Noisy buggers."

Any further argument was halted by the mantel clock which began to announce the hour in such a deep-toned gong, it was impossible to speak. Involuntarily they all looked in its direction. It was a massive bronzed piece, more than two feet high, and the clock face nestled in the middle of the bust of a smiling woman, rather Roman in appearance. Her hair and collar were lavishly hung with imitation coins and the word "Fortune" was embossed on the base. As the sound died away, Murdoch closed his notebook, picked up his hat, and stood up.

"I won't keep you any longer. What time might I catch Mr Gibb?"

"He works at the city offices. He issues marriage licenses. He is usually home by six o'clock."

"Either me or a constable will come back then. For now, I'll just have a word with your servant before I go."

Frank Eakin grinned. "Janet's a fanciful girl, Mr Murdoch. Don't take everything she says as gospel. She believes in ghosts. She's always going on about hearing them wandering round the house."

"I'll take that under advisement. Where would I find her, ma'am?"

Augusta stood up. "I'll take you. She should be in the kitchen."

"We'll get back to the stable," said Eakin. "You won't want us any more will you, officer?"

"Not for now."

At the door, Mrs Curran paused and apparently speaking to nobody in particular, she said.

"It won't be necessary to leave the lamp lit."

Her husband hurried to obey and blew out the light. The sour, smoky smell of the extinguished wick wafted on the air.

Murdoch left with a feeling of relief. Being with this family was like sticking your hand in a wasp's nest.

CHAPTER TEN

———◆———

PEG THOUGHT SHE must have been in the bathtub for a very long time but it was hard to be sure. There was no clock in the room and her memory of coming here, of being put into the tub was not quite real, as if she had been dreaming violent, vivid dreams. However, her eyes were focusing properly now and even though her head felt as if she were inside a blanket, she was no longer under the influence of the sedative. She knew she was in an institution.

She shivered. The water had cooled to the point of discomfort. She turned her head. There were three large bathtubs in the room and she was in the middle one. On her left was a woman whose face, with its well-defined nose and chin and good wide brow, showed some refinement of features. She wasn't young but her hair was still brown and abundant, braided and pinned into a crown on top of her head.

"Hello," said Peg softly.

The woman's eyes were closed and she didn't respond.

"Good girl." The woman in the other tub had spoken loudly. "You'll go to heaven, my dear." Her hair was white and stringy and Peg could see there were large bare patches on her scalp, the skin showing pink.

"Hello," she said.

The woman looked over at her but her eyes were blank and

58

unseeing. Suddenly she burst into harsh crying. Peg could offer no comfort but the tears stopped as abruptly as they'd begun and the woman started to sing a cheerful hymn.

All three women were in the same position. A canvas cover was stretched across the iron tub. There was a hole for the patient's head; the rest of the body was completely immersed. There was a canvas harness which sloped backward and Peg was fastened to it by a strap at the waist. Her arms were tied at the wrists and her legs were similarly restrained at the ankles. The bonds weren't tight but she couldn't slip out of them. Even if she had been able to get loose, she knew she wouldn't be able to lift the canvas cover because it was tied to rings at the side of the tub.

Somebody will come soon. Keep calm, keep calm.

But the panic swept over her and she couldn't stop it bursting out of her mouth.

A woman in attendant's uniform came hurrying in. She was large and her features were strong to the point of being masculine but her expression was kind. She clucked sympathetically.

"What's this now?"

"Let me out, please let me out."

"Are you cold?" the attendant asked.

"Yes, yes, I am. Can I get out?"

"I'll just warm up the water a bit and that'll feel better. All our ladies show great improvement after a time in the tub. Wish I could do it myself; my beaters get real sore at the end of the day."

"I don't care a frigging toss about your feet. I want to get out of this goddam tub."

The woman wagged her forefinger. "Nasty words like that won't get you anywhere except into trouble."

Peg felt a wave of terror pinch her stomach. This attendant seemed quite kind really but she was like all of them. If you offended, retribution was inevitable. Sometimes it was angry and overt, more often subtle. Small withholdings. Leave her there longer, just fifteen minutes longer in the solitary room. Fifteen minutes that would make the difference between sanity and madness.

She tried to gain back some control. "I'm sorry, truly I am. Please forgive me. I didn't mean it. I was . . ."

She was interrupted by her neighbour bursting into sobs again. The attendant nodded over at her.

"Don't worry about Miss Anderson. She's quite harmless."

"Why is she crying like that?"

"She is afraid she won't go to heaven. She was a missionary most of her life."

She went over to the white-haired woman and leaned over close to her face.

"Why don't you sing us another hymn now, Miss Anderson? I do dearly love to hear 'Waiting by the River.'"

Almost without pause, the woman changed from crying to singing. Her voice was hoarse but the rendition was tuneful, years of habit still strong. The attendant came back to Peg and turned on the taps at the end of the tub.

"Is that better? Do you want it hotter?"

"No, thank you. I'm sorry I was so rude. What is your name please?"

"Trayling."

"How long have I been in here?"

"In the bath or in the asylum?"

"The bath."

Trayling consulted the steel watch pinned to her grey apron. Peg noticed the swell of her large breasts which seemed soft even beneath the starched bib. Her sleeve was rolled up past the plump forearm and her skin was freckled and reddened from the water. Peg had to fight hard to keep back a rush of tears. The attendant reminded her of somebody but she couldn't quite recover the memory. It was somebody who had appeared in her dreams many times. Familiar yet unidentifiable, like a place you know you must have visited some time in the past, but cannot name. She'd been told a neighbour had delivered her to Dr Barnardo's orphanage when her mother disappeared and she thought it might be her she dreamt of.

"You were admitted this afternoon. Dr Clark thought a bath

would calm you and you've been in here for two hours. He wants you to stay for at least three."

She must have seen the fear because she picked up a sponge from a basket beside the tub, and dipping it in a bowl of cool water, she wiped Peg's brow.

"Best thing is not to fight so. You'll feel better before you know it."

"What is going to happen to me?"

"That's for the doctors to decide. If you act like a good Christian woman, no cussing like you did just now, do what you're told, and you'll soon be allowed to go home."

"And if I'm not good?"

"Then you'll have to stay in here with all the other lunatics."

As if in answer, the woman who hadn't said a word up to now burst into loud laughter. They could hear her splashing her feet in the water. Trayling clucked her tongue disapprovingly.

"Mrs Stratton, stop that noise. You sound like a heathen if ever I heard one."

She got up stiffly from her stool, rolled down her sleeve, and started to dry her hands on the piece of holland toweling on the chair. She smiled down at Peg. "I'll leave you for now. See if you can get some rest."

She left, her clogs splashing against the water-splattered brick floor.

Peg was so afraid again, she felt nauseated. Her mouth was dry and she wished she had asked for a drink of water. She didn't want to call again, though. She couldn't risk using up the goodwill that the attendant was showing toward her. She lay back, her eyes open wide, looking at the ceiling, which was stained with watermarks from the steam. She forced herself to be calm, to think.

Her memories were returning and at first she wanted to shy away from them, to get lost in the fog of the drug.

No! Think. Get it back.

They'd broken down the door. It had splintered when somebody, Frank probably, wielded an axe. They had all come in, Dr Ferrier behind them with his black bag. He had talked to her, she remembered that, but she didn't know how long that had taken. He had turned away to his bag, and when he faced her again, he was holding a syringe. She had screamed and kicked it out of his hand. Then Frank and Peter had held her in the chair and Dr Ferrier got another syringe.

At that moment, she had stepped out of her body and stood to one side, watching. The two men holding her were exerting painful pressure and Frank was cursing because she was fighting so. "I must ask you to temper your language," said the doctor, and she thought what an old-fashioned expression that was. The woman who was struggling to get free was very strong and could easily throw them off if she wanted to but somehow she was being slowed down. She was falling asleep; she was so tired she couldn't help herself.

If you go to sleep now you will die, said the separate self. She moved further away from her body as if she were actually floating near the ceiling. She saw the other Peg tied to the chair with some binding the doctor had brought with him. Then they were carrying her downstairs.

Don't give in. Stay awake.

But sleep was inviting—safe and irresistible. They were outside. She saw Cullie and was sorry the young servant was afraid. Then she was looking at a tall man in a fur hat and a long coat. He had a dark moustache and his eyes were noticing. The Peg in the chair spoke to him.

Help me. Please help me.

He was worried. "I'll help you," he said, although his lips didn't move.

"Psst, you, new woman."

She turned her head to the left. Mrs Stratton was watching her.

"Yes?" She tried to make her voice friendly.

"Allow me to introduce myself. I'm Mrs Harold Stratton of Chatham, Ontario. What is your name?"

"Margaret Eakin."

"Are you married?"

"Yes."

"Children?"

62

"Ye-no. That is, I did have a son but he died."

Mrs Stratton gazed over at her; her eyes were fierce. "Murdered was he?"

Peg turned her head away as abruptly as if she had been struck. "Yes," she said. "Yes, he was."

CHAPTER ELEVEN

WEARILY, MURDOCH HEADED for Ontario Street and the comfort of Mrs Kitchen's parlour. He was cold and hungry, his back ached from walking so long and the pain in his jaw was all-consuming. Between them, he and Crabtree had questioned virtually every household member on Wicken's beat but nothing significant had come of it. Many of the people were familiar with the young constable; some of them were sincerely distressed. One or two of the women wept openly. "Such a nice, polite young man," cried Mrs Jackson, who was the cook at a grand house on Gerrard Street. But she hadn't seen him since the end of the summer when she'd been sitting on the front veranda, it was so scorching that day. "Madam allowed all us servants, even young Eddie, to come outside after evening chores. Very kind it was. The constable went by and we joked at him. He looked so hot he did in his uniform."

Most people tried to be helpful, would have manufactured information if they could, but essentially nobody told him anything new. Nobody other than Mr Lee had actually seen Wicken or his companion. It was a night when everybody was as snug as they could be in their own houses.

Lamps were lit along the street; the macadam black and slick in the rain. Not for the first time Murdoch wished he were coming home to Liza. Closely following on that thought, however, like a herding dog on the heels of a sheep, was an image of Enid Jones, the young widow who was also a boarder at the Kitchens. Under different circumstances, Murdoch had to admit he would have been paying court to her but she was a devout Baptist, he, a Roman Catholic, although not so devout. Those differences of faith seemed irreconcilable.

He was passing one of the big houses on Wilton Street. The curtains were not drawn and he could see into the front sitting room. Two men, one about his own age, were lounging in their armchairs in front of the fire. They were wearing claret-coloured smoking jackets and he saw them both, in unconscious unison, take a protracted luxurious pull on their respective cigars. The furnishings were opulent and the room was golden from the bright firelight. Murdoch knew the two men slightly, knew they were both lawyers and that the son had joined his father's firm. He felt a sharp stab of envy. He walked on by, realising it wasn't the affluence of the men that he was jealous of, so much as the feeling of security surrounding them and how comfortable they seemed to be in each other's company. He hadn't thought about his own father in a while, deliberately keeping his memories as buried as possible, but he wondered if he was even still alive. The life of a fisherman was a dangerous one, after all. However, he assumed somebody would have informed him of any catastrophe.

Murdoch didn't particularly like his own envy. He'd seen too much of it in his father and had experienced over and over again the man's rancour, his unrelenting jealousy of his own son. Once again his thoughts flew to Liza. If she had lived they would be married by now, probably with a babe, and he himself would have been struggling with the complexity of fatherhood.

Oh, but I would have wanted it. The words were so strong in his mind, he thought for a moment he'd said them out loud. At times, his grief at her death seemed as fresh as ever. He looked for her in the women he passed on the street, dreamed of holding her in his arms, dreamed that she wasn't dead but merely gone away. After those dreams he awoke angry; after the loving dreams he awoke aching.

However, over the past few months he had found himself actively seeking for a sweetheart. He had started dancing lessons, taken to it quite well really, even though his only dancing partner at first was the instructor himself, Professor Otranto, who took the lady's part. Then in the summer he'd attended his first mixed class and met a young woman who worked at the music store on King Street. She had seemed most receptive towards him until she discovered he was Roman Catholic. She was Methodist. "My father would disown me. And I'm all he's got now," she had said sadly. As a result, Murdoch had given up his dancing classes, reluctant to see her there and be tantalised by what he couldn't have.

And now, stronger all the time, were his feelings for Enid. Would he change his faith in order to fit with a woman's? He tried to be honest with himself, sighed and had to admit, fair or not, he couldn't see himself doing that. He'd never even set foot in a church other than a Catholic one. In that respect he'd been thoroughly indoctrinated by the priests of his childhood. About time I gave this some thought, he said to himself, again not for the first time. But later, not when his head was pounding, not when the rain had washed all colour from the world, and certainly not on the same day a fine young man had been ripped from life before he'd even lived much of it.

As he approached the house, he experienced a rush of pleasure. The lamps were lit in the front parlour and he knew Mrs Kitchen would have his supper waiting for him. She prided herself on being a "plain cook," which meant that the meat was often overdone and the potatoes boiled into tastelessness but he didn't mind. Since he had moved in with the Kitchens three years ago, they had become dear friends. The closest thing to a family he had ever known. He opened the door and entered the narrow hall, also well-lit tonight. He had hardly taken off his hat and coat when his landlady came hurrying out of the kitchen.

"Oh my, what dreadful weather. Come and get yourself warm this minute. The fire's going in the parlour and your tea is all ready. I'll bring it right in."

Murdoch blew on his cold hands.

"I forgot my gloves this morning."

Then he noticed that the chenille curtains across the rear door were lowered.

He nodded in that direction. "How's Arthur?"

"A bit poorly. This damp weather is hard for him."

She took his astrakhan hat from the coat tree where he'd hung it and shook off the rain drops. "I've minced up some lamb for you and mashed potatoes. And I've boiled up the rutabaga. I thought you'd be glad of soft food. I'm sure that tooth is bothersome. I don't suppose you've had it tended to have you?"

"I confess I have not. Cowardice won out."

"I'll bring you some more clove oil."

"Thank you, Mrs K. Can I go and see him?"

"Of course. He's been brooding too much. See if you can take his mind off things."

As he lifted the curtain aside, Mrs Kitchen said, "He asked me to close them, said the draft was bothering him. Fact is he's wrapped up tight so I don't know what it could be."

The ever-present worry about her husband was close to the surface tonight. Usually, she acted as if he were suffering from a bad head cold that would clear up before long.

She returned to the kitchen and Murdoch went into the room.

Arthur Kitchen was wrapped in a tartan blanket, sitting in his wicker Bath chair. He seemed to be asleep, but at Murdoch's entrance, he opened his eyes and grinned with pleasure.

"Hello, Will. You're late tonight. Something happen?"

"I'm afraid so. I'll tell you about it after my tea."

They both knew Mrs Kitchen wouldn't let them talk until Murdoch had been properly fed. But he valued their chats and both the Kitchens loved to hear about his experiences with what Arthur termed, "the fascinating diversity of the criminal strand in the fabric of society." Arthur almost never went out and certainly hadn't stirred from home during the entire last six weeks of wet, chilly weather.

"How's your tooth?"

"Making itself known. You've been a bit poorly today, Mrs K. said."

Arthur nodded and suddenly coughed. He had a cloth which he held close to his mouth but Murdoch could see how much blood he expectorated. There was a fetid odour in the room that not even the bucket of carbolic Mrs Kitchen had placed in the corner of the room could disguise. The window was closed tonight. Another deviation from the usual routine. Even in the bitterly cold winter months, Mrs Kitchen had kept the window open in the hope that fresh air would arrest the progress of the disease. She tried out every treatment she heard of and Murdoch couldn't tell whether it was, in fact, the efficacy of these cures or her desire that had kept Arthur alive this long.

A fire was burning in the hearth but there was only one lamp lit on the mantelpiece and the room was gloomy. He was about to offer to light a lamp when Mrs Kitchen came in. She was carrying a jug and a glass.

"Good heavens what are you doing sitting in the dark like this?"

Arthur shrugged listlessly.

"I'll light the sconces, shall I?" asked Murdoch.

"Yes please, and those two lamps on the sideboard. Poor light is unhealthy."

Murdoch set to and Beatrice poured water from the jug into the glass.

"Here you are, Arthur. Drink it right down." She saw the bloodied rag and whisked it away into the bucket that stood beside the chair. She handed her husband a fresh piece of cloth.

"Mrs O'Brien's niece has a friend who was completely cured of the consumption by drinking several glasses of hot water every day. We're going to try it," she said to Murdoch.

"Mother, it's a good thing my kidneys aren't in the same condition as my lungs. I have to make water on the hour every hour."

"Arthur! Mind what you're saying."

Mrs K. treated Murdoch the same way she treated the priest—as if their ears must be kept pure from any reference to body parts or functions and, God forbid, any obscenity.

Arthur sipped the hot water, then immediately went into a fit of coughing. This time the fresh cloth was filled. The water had spilled all over him and Mrs Kitchen wiped at the blanket. There was blood there too.

"I'll get another glass. Won't be a minute."

Arthur shook his head. "No, Mother, please. I can't."

"Of course you can. It was too hot was the problem."

"I thought it was supposed to be hot," he whispered.

She ignored his remark, shaking her head in disapproval as if he were being a finicky child.

"Mr Murdoch, your tea will be ready in just a minute."

"Has Mrs Jones eaten yet?" Murdoch kept his voice as casual as he could knowing his landlady's avid interest.

"Yes, she was down at six. She has a big piece of work to do."

"Another legal brief?"

"I believe so. Such a hardworking young woman. She hasn't stopped all day."

She held out her hand for the empty glass. "I'm going to bring you some of Arthur's medicine. It'll help you sleep until you get that tooth looked after. If I may say so, you look quite exhausted."

She left for the kitchen. As soon as the door closed, Arthur turned to Murdoch and gave him a wry grin.

"There's something makes you sleep better than any laudanum and it's natural."

"What is this, a riddle?" asked Murdoch, pleased by the revival in his landlord's spirits.

"No riddle. I'm referring to conjugal relations. The best cure for insomnia is to have connections with the woman you love."

Murdoch could feel himself blushing like a green youth. Arthur had never spoken so personally to him before.

"I am assuming from your expression this is not a joy you have yet experienced, Will?"

"Well . . . I . . ."

Murdoch thought his passionate but unconsummated caresses with Liza didn't count, and before her there had only been awkward fumblings with a neighbour's daughter when he was seventeen.

69

"I must say I don't have the interest right now," continued Arthur. "But I miss it. So I am being so bold as to give you some advice, Will. Don't let the differences get in the way."

Murdoch was confused as to what he meant by that.

"She's a good woman, no matter that she's Baptist. Still young. Her face lights up whenever she sees you"

"You're referring to Mrs Jones?"

"Who else? I saw the way she was at the police games when we were all watching the tug-of-war." He spoke in a good imitation of Enid's lilting Welsh accent. "What does the blue marker indicate, Mr Murdoch?" Ha. She didn't care a jot. She just didn't want you paying attention to that other young woman."

Mrs Kitchen came in and overheard these last words. "He's better off without that one. Flighty I thought. Here you go Arthur."

While she stood over him, Arthur drank all the hot water. This time he didn't cough it back. "There, you see!" said his wife.

"I'll go and change into my slippers," said Murdoch, glad to escape any further talk about his love life.

Mrs Jones's room was at the top of the stairs, across the landing from his. Her door was closed but he could hear the rapid clack of the typewriting machine. Her face lit up, did it? His too probably. But what on earth was he going to do about it?

THE CLOVE OIL and the vinegar compress had relieved the toothache somewhat, and although he could hardly stop himself from yawning, Murdoch felt better. He and the Kitchens were in their sitting room. All three of them were tucked under covers, as Mrs K. had opened the window. Arthur's mood had swung in the opposite direction, typical of a consumptive. Murdoch had just finished telling them about Wicken's death and the subsequent round of questioning he and Crabtree had gone through.

"How's the latest arrival?" asked Mrs Kitchen, referring to the constable's newborn son.

"Healthy as a horse and growing like a weed according to George."

"That's good."

Her husband glanced over at her and Murdoch knew they were both thinking about the son they had lost so many years ago. He had lived for only three weeks.

"When's the inquest going to happen?" asked Arthur.

"Tomorrow."

"Your Inspector Brackenreid isn't going to be too happy if the inquest comes in with a suicide verdict. Not on his force."

Arthur carefully removed a dried pansy from the waxed paper where it had been pressed and started to glue it onto a strip of stiff cardboard. He was helping his wife make bookmarks. She earned a little money by selling handmade articles to the fancy goods shop on Queen Street.

"I feel sorry for his sweetheart. Poor thing, having that on her conscience. Suicides are always hardest for the survivors," said Mrs Kitchen.

"Not as far as the Lord is concerned," said Arthur.

Beatrice selected an ivy leaf for the bottom of the bookmark. "Of course. But I do wonder why she would reject such a nice young man."

Mrs Kitchen had never met Wicken but it was enough for her that Murdoch had liked him and that he had had a widowed mother.

"I'll light a candle tomorrow for the sake of his mother. How ever she will cope I don't know. She won't get any insurance compensation will she?"

"Not if the verdict is suicide."

Murdoch yawned again.

"Off to bed with you, this instance," said Mrs Kitchen.

"Yes, ma'am." He pushed away his blanket.

"I put the portable oil heater at the end of the landing. Why don't you leave your door open and you'll be warmer. And don't forget to take two spoonsful of the syrup. It'll make you sleep like a baby," said Beatrice.

"That or the other thing I mentioned," added Arthur.

Mrs Kitchen looked at him with curiosity. "What other thing?"

"Nothing," said Murdoch. "He means counting the rosary beads."

71

"Really? That shouldn't be so boring as to put us to sleep though, should it?"

Mrs Kitchen was very devout, especially when it suited her.

"You're quite right, Mrs K. But toothache or not, I think I'll be out the minute I put my head on the pillow."

He shook hands good night. Arthur's skin was hot with the fever but at least he wasn't moping.

Murdoch left them and went to his room. Enid's door was slightly ajar and he could hear the sounds of sleep from her and the boy. He undressed quickly and got into bed but he closed his door. He thought that even drugged with laudanum he might be kept awake with what the priest would call impure thoughts.

CHAPTER TWELVE

———•———

CULLIE KNOCKED ON the door softly. On damp days such as this one, Jarius liked to take a foot-bath before bed in the conviction that it kept away colds and influenza. She had brought up the pitcher of water.

"Come in."

She could hear the impatience in his voice and she shrank. Jarius never shouted at her or slapped her the way Frank did, but she was more afraid of him than anybody else in the household. Whenever she had a task to do, like build up the fire or, as now, bring him hot water, he never allowed her to get on with it but sat watching. She sensed something in that scrutiny not exactly malevolent, but not kind either, and her nervousness always made her clumsy.

She entered the room. He was sitting by the fire, wrapped in his shawl, already undressed for bed. His nightshirt was pulled up to his knees exposing his spindly calves.

"Ah Janet, good. I've been waiting."

"Sorry Mr Gibb, I had the water bottles to fill for Missus."

He waved his hand, indicating she should pour the water into the enamel bowl that he'd placed by his feet. She came closer but as she poured the water, it splashed over his legs.

He yelped. "Damn it girl, what are you doing?"

"Oh I'm sorry, sir, I . . ."

"Get a cloth."

She put the pitcher on the floor and scurried to the washstand by the bed to fetch a towel. He didn't take it from her but pointed at his legs.

"Wipe them off."

"Yes, sir."

She dabbed at the pale, hairy shanks, all too aware of the parted knees protruding from the flannel nightshirt. Jarius made no attempt to assist her or to do it himself.

"That's enough. Finish pouring the water and be more careful."

She tried again but he didn't move back which forced her to bend closer to the bowl on the floor. This time she managed not to splash. He eased his feet into the water. Gibb was of middle age but his feet were old man's feet, his toes bent, reddish corns on the joints.

Janet hovered beside him waiting for her release.

"Where's the mustard?"

She gasped. "I, er, I-I'm sorry, Mr Jarius, I'll go get it."

"No! It's too late now. Remember next time."

"Yes, sir."

The girl squirmed in her misery.

Jarius hitched his nightshirt up his thighs. He was looking into the fire, not at her, and when he spoke his voice was quite gentle.

"I hope you weren't too frightened by the police officer today."

"No sir. He was very kind. Not frightening at all."

"I see. That explains it."

She waited but he didn't seem as if he were going to continue. The silence was unbearable. Like a fly caught in a web, Janet could only hold out for so long.

"Beg pardon, sir. What does it explain?"

Now he looked up at her. "My sister tells me you had a lot to say to the kind detective. You seem to have told him all sorts of things about the family. Unnecessary things."

"I'm sorry, Mr Jarius. It sort of burst out. He asked me to tell him anything I could."

74

Gibb reached over and caught her hand. He started to stroke it with his thumb.

"Janet you are a silly girl to imagine gossip is of any importance to the police. But tell me truthfully, what exactly did you say?"

"Nothing really, sir. Just that there'd been a big row on Saturday night and that Mrs Eakin had shut herself up in her room. Wouldn't eat nor drink."

He continued to stroke the back of her hand and his touch burned.

"Did you by any chance also load the poor man's ear with why there was a quarrel?"

"No, I didn't. If you remember, Missus sent me out of the room when it all started."

"Quite so. Was the detective at all curious?"

"I can't say especially. He listened to everything and wrote down things in his book."

Jarius released her hand.

"I'm sure that is the last we will see of him but if by chance he does come back, you will be more discreet won't you my dear? You will keep family matters to yourself from now on."

"Yes, sir. I'm sorry, sir. I didn't mean no harm."

"Of course you didn't. Now get off to bed with you. It's eleven o'clock."

Janet curtsied and headed gratefully for the door. Her legs were trembling. In fact she did know what the quarrel was about because she had listened at the dining room door. But she hadn't told Murdoch that. Her mistress had insisted on being present during the interview and she knew if she had told everything, she would have been dismissed sure as houses.

She was just about to close the door behind her when Jarius called out.

"Janet, you forgot to bring me my writing box."

He indicated the scribe's desk that was on the dresser. She hurried back and he waited for her to place it in his lap.

"Thank you, my dear. Good night."

"Good night, sir."

She hurried off.

Jarius waited a moment, then fished under the chair cushion and pulled out a flat leather pouch. He untied the thongs, removed a key and unlocked the lid of the desk. He took out his ledger and the fountain pen. Then momentarily distracted, he watched the fire. As a child he'd sat like this many an evening, making up stories about the castles and cliffs he saw in the glowing coals. He had created that imaginary world to escape from the misery of his life. A mother who was never well, hardly ever laughed that he could recall, and who demanded from her young son an emotional sustenance he could not provide. His eyes were starting to itch and he looked away. Then, taking up his pen, he began.

So draws to a close this most difficult of days. I had little patience with any of my customers today, which I suppose is not surprising. There were five all together wanting to marry before the year is out. One of the women showed clearly that she was already with child, but she and the prospective groom dabbled in each other's palms as if the prize was still to be had. The men smack their lips when they name the wedding date. You can practically see their members quivering in their breeches. Most of the girls, for that is what they are, act coy but I can always tell the ones that are pretending. Who are as eager for a screw as their men. There are more of that kind than we think.

Jarius paused. He'd understood at once when Peg came into his room that it was not from desire for him. He hated her even more that she thought he would be brought down by such a pitiful display. He was not the least like the eager men he saw in his office everyday.

They said she fought like a trapped vixen when Ferrier came. She had to be sedated. "A needle right into her arse," was how Frank put it, in his usual delicate way. They intend to keep her in the asylum for several days to assess her state.

He stopped writing and wiped his pen with a piece of felt. The clock on his dressing table chimed the hour. He heard the sound of footsteps coming up the stairs. Augusta was going to bed. She paused and he knew she was considering coming in to talk to him, but she thought better of it.

Father has stayed in his room all day. I went to see him before supper but he had little to say. "A peck of trouble," was all he would offer. I am sure he is sick of her but who knows if that will stop him rutting. It is strange to write this but I am quite exhilarated. Tired yes, but excited. It seems as if I am able to resolve these same troubles.

He had been out of mourning for one month for my wretched stepmother when he claims to have met up with the tart. However, I strongly suspect he was dallying with her long before. And she of course would have no respect for his state. The sooner married, the better for her. A chance for his money.

The memory of that first meeting was bitter to him. Peg, small and plain, but dressed in a cream silk and lace gown for her wedding day. His father doting over her, kissing her on the mouth without heed to anyone else. Her child, silent and watchful, ugly.

He blotted his page and closed the ledger. There was a carafe of water and a glass on his desk and he poured out some water, swilled it around in his mouth, and spat into his handkerchief as if he had a foul taste in his mouth.

For a moment he wavered, wanting to go to bed but his need was too great, overriding the desire for sleep. He took up his lamp and left his room quietly, hurrying down the backstairs as if he were a harried servant.

CHAPTER THIRTEEN

━━━◆━━━

SHE WAS TRYING to wake up but her eyelids were stuck together and she couldn't open them. She'd been crying, she knew that; the salty taste of tears was caught in her nostrils. She could hear her mother talking to somebody, a man. "Shut her up," he said. "Give her something to shut her up else she'll get what for." Her mother was clad only in her drawers, her breasts swinging as she bent over the bed. The man was naked. "I did. She'll be out in a minute," said her mother. But Peg fought against the weight of sleep until she could do so no longer.

She opened her eyes and lay still, listening. Where was she? She could hear the sounds of other people, a soft snore, a bed creaking as somebody turned over. She was in a narrow bed that felt hard, the sheets rough. She wasn't at Dr Barnardo's—she was too old—nor at home with Harry. The bed wasn't the soft luxuriant feather mattress that he loved.

Think. What has happened?

Then, as suddenly as if the stereoscope had come into focus, she found the details.

I'm not married to Harry anymore. He died. I married Mr Nathaniel Eakin.

As fast as she registered that knowledge, she felt everything she was trying to keep at bay rush toward her, bringing such desolation the pain was almost physical.

I have been committed to the lunatic asylum. I have been here since yesterday.

The occupant in the adjoining bed, Mrs Mallory, turned, muttering some unintelligible words. Peg waited to see if she had woken up, but she hadn't. She was a farmer's wife who had been in the asylum for several months suffering from mental anxiety. She wouldn't talk above a whisper and sat in a chair, rocking ceaselessly.

Over by the window were Miss Anderson, whom she'd met last night in the baths, and Mrs Foster, an elderly woman who confessed she'd been in the asylum for six years. She knew everyone's history and was curious to know about Peg. She had insisted on taking her by the arm and leading her down the corridor where the patients were taking a walk before lights out.

"It's the change of life that's affected her," she said, referring to the farmer's wife. "You've got that to look forward to, dear. It comes to us early in here."

Peg knew from her experience in the orphanage that there was always somebody who wanted to befriend the newcomer, somebody who knew the ropes. So she'd been glad to stroll along the corridor with Mrs Foster listening to her talk about the other inmates and the attendants.

"Reid is a good sort but she's strict. Furness is cold as a frozen cod. Try not to cross her. Oh, there's poor Miss Green. She thinks she's related to Her Majesty, a distant cousin or some such. Do give her a nod; she gets very upset if you snub her."

Peg wanted to ask Mrs Foster why she herself was in the asylum but she knew it was best to wait. She'd find out sooner or later.

She put her hands between her knees to warm them. There was a steam radiator in the room, but there was a strong draft blowing from the window and the cotton quilt on the bed was thin. What time was it? The blinds were lowered, shutting out all light, but she sensed that it was close to morning. There was a night candle on the window sill and it had burned low.

She felt wide awake now. Ever since she could remember, at times of great distress, she couldn't sleep. Paradoxically, she felt worse if she was sharing the room or bed with somebody else. The sound of the regular breathing of the sleeper created more and more anxiety. She was awake in a world that slept; she was abnormal in a normal world. When she was in the cottage home, she never dared to wake one of the other girls, afraid of possible anger, and she had slept so badly for weeks that finally the matron had prescribed a daily tonic, convinced that the dark circles underneath Peg's eyes were from anaemia. Later, when she was married to Harry, desperate, ready to risk wrath if it meant somebody would talk to her, she had awakened him. He was always impatient, didn't understand, and soon turned away, putting his pillow over his head to shut her out.

There was a sound from the other bed. She raised her head. Mrs Foster had gotten out of bed. She trotted over to Mrs Mallory and opened the door of her bedside cupboard. Then she realised Peg was watching her and she stopped, glancing over her shoulder with a mischievous grin.

"She had some bonbons," she whispered. "She won't eat them and she's always offering them to me. I was feeling a bit peckish." She reached in and helped herself to one of the candies, popped it into her mouth and took another handful.

"Do you want one?"

"No thank you," said Peg.

Mrs Foster scampered back to her own bed and stashed the stolen candy in her own cupboard.

"Good night dear."

She was so childlike in her pleasure and lack of guilt that Peg smiled. She wanted to go on talking, to engage her, but the older woman immediately pulled up her quilt and turned over.

Peg curled up tighter, trying to will herself into sleep. She must have been lying like that for a while when she heard the soft creaking of footsteps outside the door. There was a gleam of light through the small window and she heard the key turn in the lock. Somebody came into the room with a lamp, sweeping back and forth over the beds. The person came nearer to her and she could hear wheezing in the chest. It was the night attendant, Reid. Her skirt rustled as the hem dragged on the rush matting. The light became brighter and Peg knew she was standing next to her bed, watching. She rolled over onto her back.

"Oh dear, Mrs Eakin, not asleep?"

"I was, the light woke me."

"Try to go back to sleep, it's not time to get up yet."

"Yes, Mrs Reid." She closed her eyes obediently, listening as the other woman checked on the remaining occupants. She heard her blow out the night candle then she left, locking the door behind her.

Peg sat up and waited until her eyes grew accustomed to the darkness, then she swung her legs over the side of the bed. She hitched up her nightgown. When she arrived she had been issued a flannel gown and a grey dressing robe, both too large for her.

"When you're feeling better, you can wear your own clothes," said the matron. "Your gown did need to be laundered," she added, and Peg knew that she must have been filthy when she'd been admitted.

Keeping her in nightclothes ensured she was conspicuous and vulnerable. The better you behaved, the better you were treated and the more privileges you got. Peg had soon realised the asylum was run on very similar principles to the orphanage where she'd grown up.

She went quietly over to the window. The sash was stiff but she managed to push it open. There were bars that smelled metallic and they were cold and wet with rain. She knew she was on the third floor and as she sniffed the damp night air, she caught the smell of livestock. She must be facing the south side of the building, which overlooked the vegetable gardens and stables. Mrs Foster had told her proudly that the asylum tried to be as self-sufficient as possible and that they raised pigs and a few milch cows.

"The bacon's really quite excellent," said the old lady with glee.

Suddenly, Miss Anderson sat bolt upright.

"Good morning," she said to Peg in a loud voice. "How are you Annabel?"

Miss Anderson called everybody Annabel, which was apparently the name of the family household maid, long since dead.

"I'm very well, thank you."

Miss Anderson burst into song.

"Onward Christian soldiers, marching as to war . . ."

She was well launched into the first verse when the two other women in the room both woke up. Mrs Foster called out, "Please be quiet over there. I'm trying to sleep."

Miss Anderson was oblivious and began to sing louder. "With the cross of Jesus going on before."

Mrs Foster glared, then flung back her covers and jumped out of bed. Before Peg realised what she intended, she ran over to Miss Anderson and attempted to put a hand over her mouth.

"I'll make you be quiet, then, you silly canary."

The older woman grabbed at the hand across her mouth, trying to pry the fingers loose. Mrs Foster wasn't big but she was much more vigourous than her victim. She started to push her back into the pillows.

"I'll shut you up once and for all."

Her ferocity was so alarming, Peg had to do something. She rushed over and tried to pull her away.

"Stop it! Come on now, stop it."

The woman let go and turned her fury on Peg. Her fingernails hadn't been cut for some time and the claws aimed straight for Peg's cheeks. She would have inflicted a serious injury but Peg managed to grab her by the wrists and keep her at bay.

Next to them, Miss Anderson was trilling at full voice. "Forward into battle, see His banners go."

Mrs Foster was trying to get at Peg's face, spitting at her and kicking. Her toenails were likewise untrimmed and she scratched Peg's shins badly. Suddenly, the door opened and Reid swept in.

"What's going on in here? Stop that at once. Mrs Foster! Let go of her, Mrs Eakin."

Peg grunted too intent on protecting herself to answer. The attendant caught hold of Mrs Foster's arms from behind and, quickly and expertly, spun her around and two paces back.

"Mrs Eakin, please get into bed," she managed to call over her shoulder. Panting, Peg retreated and at that moment another attendant who had heard the noise came hurrying into the room. Reid was holding Mrs Foster tightly but she was bucking and struggling like a wild creature. Miss Anderson sang on. The second attendant went straight over to her, took out a strip of linen from her pocket and in one swift movement, bound it around Miss Anderson's mouth. She made no attempt to remove the gag, but continued to sing in a much muffled way, staring at the ongoing struggle between Reid and Mrs Foster. Abruptly, the fight stopped; Mrs Foster went limp and sagged in the attendant's arms. Reid spoke to her soothingly.

"That's my good girl. Shush now."

The fourth occupant of the room, Mrs Mallory, had covered her head with her quilt but she was moaning to herself. Reid led Mrs Foster back to her bed.

"Are you going to be good, now? I don't have to tie you down, do I?"

"No, dear, not me." She pointed at Peg. "It's her who's the troublemaker. Tie her down."

Peg shrank back, shaking her head. "Please, I was just trying to help Miss Anderson. Mrs Foster was hurting her." She spoke in her best English manner. "She began to sing and Mrs Foster got angry."

"And why shouldn't I?" interjected the other woman. "That's the third time this week she's started bellowing and woken us all up. Listen to poor Mrs Mallory over there."

The two attendants exchanged glances and Mrs Reid went over to Miss Anderson, who immediately became silent.

"It's too early to be singing. You're just being naughty. You can sing after dinner. Now do you promise to be a good girl and go back to sleep?"

Miss Anderson nodded, her blue eyes wide and bright above the gag. The attendant removed the linen strip from her mouth. She waited until the elderly woman lay down, patted her lightly on the head, and went back to Mrs Foster's bed. She brought her face so close their noses were almost touching.

"You will not move a muscle until morning bell or you will have only bread for breakfast. And tomorrow is Wednesday and it's ham. You know how much you like ham, don't you?"

Mrs Foster nodded. "I have to use the commode."

"Are you sure?"

"Yes, it's coming fast."

Reid sighed. "Very well." She turned to the other attendant. "Thank you, Mrs Furness, I think we'll be all right. I'll keep her with me until morning."

"What about that one?" Furness indicated Peg, talking as if she were invisible.

"I just want to get back to sleep, if you don't mind." She suited her actions to her words and quickly got into bed and under the covers. Her legs were stinging from the scratches but she wasn't about to add to the trouble by mentioning it.

Reid, who was the senior of the two, was satisfied, and holding Mrs Foster by the arm, she led her away to the water closet. Furness wagged her finger in a warning at Peg and followed.

The room seemed to rock as unsteadily as a dinghy in the wake of a steamer. Peg lay staring at the ceiling.

Be calm. Think! You've got to think!

CHAPTER FOURTEEN

THE CHAPEL AT Humphrey's Funeral Home was used regularly for coroner's inquests because the post mortem examination could be easily conducted on the premises. The room was panelled in dark oak with a sober brown carpet and pews. A large portrait of Her Majesty and the prince consort, surrounded by their young children, was hung at the front of the room. Murdoch assumed Mr Humphrey had chosen this particular reproduction because of the family aspect. Queen Victoria and Prince Albert as a source of parental comfort to the bereaved.

The chapel could comfortably hold about forty people but there were at least sixty jammed into the room, extra benches having been provided. Word had spread about Wicken's death and Murdoch also recognised many of the people he had been questioning the previous day. There were four or five constables from the station and Inspector Brackenreid himself was present. He was looking quite disgruntled and Murdoch knew he considered Wicken to have brought disgrace to the force and particularly his station. He gave a curt nod as the detective went to take his seat near the front with the other witnesses.

In the first pew were the thirteen jurors. Murdoch slipped into the aisle seat in the second row and was almost knocked over by the various odours of camphor, violet pomade, and shaving soap. Several of the men had cleaned themselves up and taken out their Sunday best suits, as befitted their important role in the proceedings.

Across from him was Oliver's mother. She was in deep mourning and a heavy crepe veil fell to her shoulders. Her head was bowed and she was very still. She didn't acknowledge anyone and she seemed alone and friendless, even though there was a woman next to her who Murdoch assumed was a neighbour. She too was in black and he saw her wiping her eyes with a black-edged handkerchief. Mrs Wicken was not weeping.

Beside the neighbour was the patrol sergeant Hales, who had to testify, and next to him was a young woman that Murdoch didn't recognise. She was soberly dressed in a dark grey walking suit and plain black felt hat with a short veil to the chin. He wondered if this was the woman that Wicken had apparently died for. She seemed to be alone and her head was bowed in prayer. He could imagine what an ordeal the inquest was going to be for her.

The spectators were behaving with respect and there was only a subdued murmur as they waited for the proceedings to start. A table had been placed at the front of the chapel for the coroner and the constable of the court. The side door opened and Crabtree strode in followed by Mr Johnson.

"Oyez! Oyez! Everybody please rise."

There was a rustling of garments and creaking of seats as the spectators obeyed.

"An inquisition is now in session, taken for Our Sovereign Lady, the Queen, at the house of Benjamin Humphrey, situate in the city of Toronto in the county of York on the thirteenth day of November in the ninety-fifth year of the reign of Our Sovereign Lady, Victoria, before Arthur Edward Johnson, Esquire, one of the coroners of our said lady to inquire when, how, and by what means Oliver Wicken came to his death. All of the jurors here present being duly sworn and having viewed the body."

Johnson took his seat behind the table.

"Everyone may now sit."

Crabtree's booming voice filled the chapel. There was an expectant silence; nevertheless, the constable picked up the rubber mallet on the desk and banged it. He addressed the jurors.

"Oyez! Oyez! Oyez! You good men of this county, answer to your names as you shall be called, every man at the first call, upon pain and peril that shall fall thereon."

He checked off their names as they answered.

Johnson waited impassively for Crabtree to finish, staring at a spot three feet in front of him. The roll call finished, he blinked and spoke out in his raspy nasal voice.

"I shall proceed to hear and take down the evidence respecting the fact, to which I crave your particular attention."

He nodded at Crabtree who turned slightly to face the row where the witnesses sat. Murdoch felt a slight quiver of stage fright in his stomach. Crabtree declaimed, "If anyone can give evidence on behalf of our Sovereign Lady the Queen, when, how, and by what means Oliver Wicken came to his death, let him come forth and he shall be heard."

He beckoned to Patrol Sergeant Hales who stood up and approached the table.

"State your name, place of abode, and occupation."

"Edward Hales, Number fifty, Sydenham Street. I am night patrol sergeant at number four police station, which is located on Wilton Street."

"That your full name?"

"No, sir. My full name is Edward George Wilbur Hales."

"Say so then. This is Her Majesty's court now convened."

Johnson frowned at the rest of the witnesses as if they too had transgressed. Crabtree waited until the coroner had finished entering the information in his ledger, then picked up the Bible that was on the desk and held it out. Hales took it in his right hand.

"The evidence which you shall give to this inquest on behalf of our Sovereign Lady the Queen touching the death of Oliver Wicken shall be the truth, the whole truth, and nothing but the truth. So help you God. Do you so swear?"

"I do."

"Stand over there and address the coroner and make sure the jurors can hear you."

Hales moved so that he was an at angle to the court.

"Constable, second class, Oliver Wicken went on duty at a quarter to seven on the night of Monday last, the eleventh of November . . ."

"Don't gabble," interrupted Johnson. "I have to write this down you know."

Hales continued, trying to speak more slowly. "I did my first check at twenty-five minutes past eight at the corner of Queen and River Streets. The second was at twenty past ten when I met up with him at Parliament Street. Constable Wicken was present and correct. He was not under the influence of liquor. He showed me his report book and to that point his beat had been without incident."

"Did he seem in any way morose or dispirited?"

"No, sir, he did not."

"Other than giving his report, did he say anything to you?"

"Just about the weather."

"His exact words if you please, Sergeant."

"I can't say as I remember them exactly, sir. Something like, 'Good weather if you're a duck. I'll be glad to be done.'"

"In your opinion was there anything at all in Mr Wicken, either that night or on any other previous occasion, that would have indicated a man with suicidal tendencies?"

"Absolutely not. He was always a good-natured fellow, never whinged like some of them do. I would say he was of a cheerful disposition. And if I might add, Mr Johnson, in all my experience as a police officer, I have never known a pistol to end up stuck between a man's legs in the way it was found . . ."

Johnson stopped him. "Members of the jury, I should remind you that we demonstrated this point to our mutual satisfaction. The gun could in fact fall into that position. I am not suggesting this would happen every time. Of course not. We are not talking about an arcade. But there is quite sufficient probability. However, Patrol

Sergeant Hales is entitled to his opinion. Nobody wants to accept the fact that a fellow officer was a weakling."

Murdoch could see Mrs Wicken had bent her head and he cursed Johnson for his lack of tact.

The sergeant had turned even redder than usual. "I returned to the station to make my report and went out again at about two o'clock. At this time I did not encounter the constable, who should have been in the vicinity of Gerrard Street east between Parliament and River Streets. I went around his beat the reverse way expecting to meet him but he was nowhere visible. I returned to the station."

"Hold on," said Johnson. "Why didn't you sound the alarm?"

Hales hesitated. "Sometimes the younger constables liven up the dullness of the watch by playing tricks—harmless, sir, quite harmless and don't affect their duty at all. Monday was a drear, wet night."

"What sort of harmless little tricks, pray tell?"

The sergeant shifted uncomfortably. "Sort of hide-and-seek. They might duck into the laneway when they hear me coming, then jump out as I go past."

"I see. So you thought Constable Wicken was simply playing games with you?"

"Yes, sir."

"Had he done that on other occasions?"

"No, sir. No he hadn't."

"But this night, as it was as you say, so drear, you thought he had got it into his head to act like some child with his tutor?"

Hales was stung by Johnson's tone.

"It crossed my mind as an explanation. Wicken was a responsible young fellow. I didn't think there was any harm if he did want a bit of a laugh. I did the rest of my rounds, made my report, and then I went out again at four o'clock. There was no sign of him. At this point I was getting worried. I started at bit of a search, thought he might have been taken ill and be in one of the laneways. I didn't find him."

"Didn't you think to inspect the empty house?"

"No, sir. For one, there were several vacant properties along the beat, and second, my pebble was still on the doorknob . . ."

"Explain if you please, Sergeant."

"Sometimes just to test that the constables are doing what they're supposed to do, I place a pebble on the doorknob of the vacant houses on the beat. It's small so as they can't really see it in the dark but if it's still there when I come round next, I know they haven't bothered to check."

"And you put a pebble on the doorknob of the Gerrard Street house?"

"Yes, sir. When I went by at two o'clock."

"Did you do the same to the back door?"

"No, sir."

"So when did you finally decide something might be seriously the matter?"

"When Wicken hadn't shown up at the end of his shift or called in. That's when Detective Murdoch offered to go in search of him."

Johnson frowned. "Long after the horse had left the barn, wouldn't you say?"

Murdoch felt like throttling the coroner. He knew that the patrol sergeant had been chastising himself severely. All the "if onlys" tearing at him. Not that it would have made any difference if he had raised the alarm, unless he'd happened on Wicken in the act of aiming his revolver at his own head.

"You can step down, Sergeant. Constable of the court, call the next witness."

"Acting detective William Murdoch, please come forward to be sworn."

Hales went back to his seat and Murdoch stood up and went to the table. He tried to give Hales a sympathetic glance as they passed but the sergeant averted his eyes.

He made sure to give his full name of William Henry Murdoch then Crabtree handed him the Bible and swore him in.

Johnson laced his fingers together and cracked his knuckles.

"Address the jury and give your statement. Please be clear and precise."

Murdoch faced the jurors, who were still highly attentive, and related his discovery of Wicken's body. Most of this ground had already been covered at the viewing so there were no questions. He assumed he had been clear enough.

"Do you yourself have an opinion as to the manner of death?"

"I do not, sir. I have known Constable Wicken for some time and like Sergeant Hales, I have always found him to be uncommonly even-tempered. It is hard to conceive of him committing such a violent act as self-murder. However, the situation in which I found him does seem to indicate that is the case. I am frankly puzzled by it."

"Are you indeed? Well, as I remarked to the sergeant, we are not visiting an arcade. Men do not function like mechanical pieces. Perhaps any one of us is capable of irrational acts at times in our lives when we are unbalanced by our passions."

There was no answer to that.

"You can step down, Mr Murdoch."

Johnson addressed the jurors. "There was a post mortem examination of the body conducted by Dr Grieg, a licenced physician. Unfortunately, he is not able to be here in person today but I do have his written report. Members of the jury, you will be able to study this said report when you are deciding on your verdict, but I will ask the constable of the court to read it out for the benefit of the rest of the people here present."

Crabtree did so, handling the medical terminology remarkably well. ". . . the anterior fossa of the base of the skull was much shredded. The base of the brain was torn and lacerated almost to a pulp . . . in the interior of the brain was a pepiculer of bone about the size of three quarters of an inch long and one half an inch broad . . ." Again, Murdoch felt bad for Oliver's mother. No matter how Latinate the language, what she was listening to was a description of her son's head being shattered.

Crabtree concluded with ". . . abdominal organs healthy. Heart healthy."

The only new piece of information for Murdoch was that Wicken had eaten shortly before he died. There was partially digested meat and bread in his stomach.

"Thank you, Constable. Mr Samuel Lee is our next witness I believe. Please swear him. His son will act as interpreter."

Crabtree called out their names and the two Chinamen approached the desk. There was a murmur from the spectators, many of whom had probably never seen such a sight.

Both of the men were wearing padded silk jackets of red silk embroidered with green and gold thread. On their heads were black, tri-cornered hats. They were like exotic birds among the sparrows and crows. And the rustle of whispers expressed a rather hostile curiosity.

Johnson said to the young man. "State your name and address first, then his, and the constable will swear him in."

The son's name was Foon. "This is my father, Samuel Lee. We live at number two hundred plus twenty-four on Parliament Street. We run the laundry."

There was a giggle from somebody in the crowd and Murdoch guessed it was because of Foon's accent.

Crabtree took a flat box from the desk and lifted out a china saucer. "Tell Mr Lee he must kneel down."

Foon translated and rather stiffly his father obeyed. Crabtree handed him the saucer. Bewildered, the Chinaman took it in his hand.

"Instruct him he must break the saucer in two," said Crabtree. "He can smash it on the floor if he likes."

A short fast exchange happened between Foon and his father, and with a slight shrug, Mr Lee slammed the saucer hard, breaking it in two.

"Now repeat to him the following," said the constable. "You shall tell the truth and the whole truth. The saucer is cracked and if you do not tell the truth, your soul will be cracked like the saucer."

Foon translated.

"Does he understand?"

Lee nodded.

"You can stand up now," said Johnson.

Crabtree picked up the broken pieces and returned them to the box.

The audience had watched this ritual as avidly as if they were at a magic show. The coroner looked at Lee. "As a witness in this investigation you are required to tell the jury exactly what you told the detective when he came to question you yesterday."

Foon repeated what he'd said and his father answered animatedly. Foon translated it all back into English. When he mentioned seeing a young woman with Wicken, a ripple of excitement ran through the crowd. When he had finished, Stevenson put up his hand.

"What now?" asked the coroner in exasperation.

"Just want to make sure the gentleman knows what he is saying. That there's no mistake. How did he know for certain it was twenty minutes past eleven o'clock when Constable Wicken came to the door?"

Lee spoke at once to his son.

"My father says he looked at the clock, wondering who was coming so late."

"He tells the time then, does he?"

Johnson saved Foon the embarrassment of a reply.

"Mr Stevenson, you are revealing an appalling ignorance. The Chinese invented clocks, isn't that so Mr Foon?"

"Ay, sir."

There was a titter at Stevenson's expense but Murdoch had the impression most of the listeners were surprised to hear this.

"Any other questions for the witness?"

Jarius Gibb, the foreman, indicated he had one.

"In the opinion of the Chinaman, was the constable in low spirits or good spirits?"

Foon translated and his father paused for a moment before he answered.

"My father regrets to say he could not distinguish what sort of demeanour the constable was in. Nor the lady. But he must emphasize, he only glimpsed them as they walked up the street together."

"Talking or not talking?"

"He believes talking."

The coroner consulted a sheet of paper in front of him. "He can step down but he is still sworn. Remind him, Mr Foon. Call the next witness."

"Miss Mary Ann Trowbridge, please come forward."

The young woman edged her way along the row. As she crossed in front of Mrs Wicken, she hesitated, made as if to reach out her hand, thought better of it, and went on.

Crabtree swore her in and she answered in a soft, light voice.

"Give your statement, Miss Trowbridge," said Johnson. "And please speak up; I won't bite."

She nodded but more volume seemed beyond her and Murdoch had to strain to hear.

"I am, that is to say, I was betrothed to Oliver Wicken." She glanced over at Mrs Wicken. "It was a secret betrothal. Nobody knew, not even his mother. We became engaged two months ago but . . ." she stopped, swallowing back tears. "On Monday evening I broke off our engagement. Oh, if only I hadn't." Her voice trailed off.

"You really must speak louder, my dear young lady. The jurors need to hear you." Johnson was being most solicitous.

Miss Trowbridge lifted her veil to wipe her eyes and Murdoch had a good view of her face. She was a pretty girl with fair skin and light-coloured brows. Her eyes were well shaped, blue or grey, and her chin was rounded. He judged her to be less than twenty.

"Oliver was most upset. He begged me not to abandon him . . . he said his life was nothing without me. I was dreadfully worried but I could not go back on my decision. I felt we were not suited to each other and that eventually he would be happier with another. He did not think so . . . We quarrelled dreadfully."

"Did he make threats at that time to take his own life?" Johnson asked.

Mary Ann nodded. She reached into her reticule and took out a folded piece of paper.

"I live with my aunt Mrs Avison. She would have come here today but she is in poor health. However, she wrote out a letter to you, Your Honour. I spoke to her the moment I returned home so she can vouch for what I said."

Johnson took the missive, scanned it quickly, and put it into the folder that was on his desk.

"So, the last time you saw Oliver Wicken was this Monday past?"

"Yes, that is correct."

"And where did you see him?"

"I must confess, Your Honour, I met him on his beat. I know I should not have done this as he was on duty but . . . I felt safer. I did not think he would dare to pursue me. So I arranged to meet him in the empty house. I knew he had the key because he'd begged me to meet him there before which I had not done . . . When we were inside, in the former kitchen, I told him my intention . . . He became very angry. He began to shout at me, dreadful cruel things . . . I was afraid he would actually strike me. I ran off . . ." She was having a hard time speaking. "I wish now I had stayed, tried to talk to him until he was in a more reasonable frame of mind, but I was afraid . . ."

Suddenly, Mrs Wicken burst out. "That girl is not telling the truth. Oliver was not like that. He would never have become engaged without informing me."

Her voice was harsh and she was panting as if she had been running. Unnecessarily, Johnson thumped the table with the mallet.

"Order please. Mrs Wicken, I do appreciate your distress but you cannot call out like that. This is a law court. If you wish to make a statement you have to be properly sworn. Is that what you want?"

Her neighbour touched her arm and whispered at her but Mrs Wicken shrugged her off.

"Yes. I would like to testify."

"Very well. When Miss Trowbridge has finished you can come up. But I must ask you to control yourself. I will not allow any hysterics."

He turned back to the young woman. "Do continue."

95

She wiped at her eyes again. "I'm sorry, sir. I cannot bear to upset Oliver's mother in this way but I can't lie because of that, can I?"

"Absolutely not. Is there anything else you want to add?"

"No, sir. That's all that happened. He must have remained in the house until . . . until he . . ."

"That's all right, Miss Trowbridge. We understand. Now, does any member of the jury have a question? Oh no, Mr Stevenson, not again?"

"Yes, sir. I just wanted to know how long this encounter lasted?"

The girl answered. "Not long. Ten or twelve minutes at the most. As I said, I was afraid and I left as soon as I could."

"And what time of night was this?"

"I'm afraid I can't say exactly. I don't carry a watch. It was after midnight, I believe."

"One more question, miss. Isn't that very late for a young woman to be out unescorted?"

She turned to Johnson. "Would it be too much to ask for a glass of water?"

"Of course not." There was a glass and a carafe of water on the table, and Johnson poured some out and handed the glass to the young woman. She sipped some of the water.

"I'm sorry, sir, what was your question?"

Stevenson repeated it.

"You are quite right, sir, and believe me I would not have done such a thing if I were not desperate. As I mentioned, my aunt is in ill-health and I am the sole watcher. I could not leave her any earlier. But where I live isn't too far away and I hurried as fast as I could."

Miss Trowbridge was looking more and more frightened. Murdoch wished for her sake that the ordeal was over.

Chamberlin waved his hand. "One question, sir . . . Ma'am, how did you find out what had happened to the constable?"

"I read about it in the newspaper this morning. I came directly to the coroner as I thought it was my duty to say what had occurred, even though there were those who might blame me."

"Nobody of a reasonable mind would blame you, Miss Trow-bridge," said Johnson.

Murdoch thought he was acting like a besotted old fool and it added to the list of grievances he held against the man.

Gibb indicated he had a question. "Miss Trowbridge, had Wicken shown any previous signs of mental instability?"

"I regret to say that he did. If I even had a cross word for him, which was not often, he would become distraught. He said he could not rest until I had forgiven him. He was horribly jealous and made mountains out of molehills over everything . . . That is why I broke off our engagement. I know he didn't show that part of his nature to the world but please believe me, I saw it all too often."

"I think we've heard what we need," said Johnson. "You may return to your seat, Miss Trowbridge."

She did so, this time ignoring Oliver's mother.

Johnson pulled out a large gold watch from his waistcoat pocket and consulted it.

"We will hear from Mrs Wicken."

She stood up, swayed for a moment on her feet. Murdoch was afraid she was going to fall. But she held tightly onto the back of the pew in front of her until she was composed and then she approached the table. When Crabtree swore her in her voice was audible, in spite of the encumbering veil.

Johnson nodded at her and ostentatiously dipped his pen at the ready for her statement.

"I know of no such engagement entered into by my son and I am entirely unacquainted with Miss Trowbridge. However, even if Oliver were betrothed to her, I cannot believe for a moment he would kill himself because she rejected him. From an early age, Oliver was a sensible boy."

In spite of the sympathy that was her due as bereaved mother, Mrs Wicken was not endearing herself to the spectators. Her composure, which had momentarily deserted her, was now firmly in place and Murdoch knew that most of those listening would see her as unnat-ural and unfeeling. They far preferred a story of love and passion and the evidence of heartbreak that Miss Trowbridge had given them. However, he knew how Mrs Wicken had reacted when she'd heard of her son's death and his heart went out to her.

The indomitable Stevenson raised his hand again and Johnson nodded permission for him to speak. "Excuse me, ma'am, for asking, but was your son's life insured?"

"Yes, it was. After my husband died, Oliver became the sole support of me and his sister. We took out modest policies for both of us."

"Thank you, that is all."

He didn't have to press the point. Everybody knew that if it was determined that Wicken had killed himself, there would be no payout from the insurance company.

"I myself wish to ask one thing, Mrs Wicken," said Johnson. "I commiserate with you most sincerely but this is a court of law and you are sworn under oath to tell the truth . . . you do understand that don't you?"

"Of course."

"Did your son show any signs of a melancholy disposition at any time prior to his death?"

"No, he did not. Never."

"Thank you, madam. That is all."

Tall and erect she returned to her seat.

Stevenson's hand was in the air immediately.

"I'd like to ask the previous witness, Mr Lee, a question, Your Honour."

Johnson sighed. "Is this the last?"

"Yes, sir."

"Very well. Mr Foon, please tell your father to stand up. Remind him he is under oath."

Foon spoke to his father and he obeyed the instruction.

"I do want to make it clear, Your Honour, that I mean no disrespect to Miss Trowbridge in any way at all," said Stevenson. "This is strictly for confirmation, you understand . . ."

"Spit it out, man. We don't have all day."

"Mr Lee, is the young woman who has here testified the same person that you saw when Oliver Wicken came to your laundry? Miss, would you be so good as to stand and raise your veil again. Thank you."

Mr Lee regarded her for a few moments then spoke quickly to his son. Foon nodded.

"My father says that is of certainty the young woman he saw on the street with the constable."

A sigh of gratification went through the room. Mrs Wicken only sat straighter.

Johnson banged the mallet on the table. "We will adjourn for fifteen minutes."

Crabtree stepped forward. "Court, please rise."

With much shuffling and scuffling of boots, the spectators stood up while Johnson left.

CHAPTER FIFTEEN

THE JURORS WERE seated around a table in the viewing room of the funeral parlour. On two shelves at the back were displayed empty coffins; the quality ranging from expensive polished oak lined with white satin to plain pine with no brass and thin cotton lining. At first these eternity boxes had served as silent *momento mori*, but now they had assumed the same invisibility as a sideboard.

The men had taken out their pipes and the air was thick.

"Has everybody now read over the witness statements?" asked Gibb. There were murmurs of agreement.

Gain, a porter, called out. "Wonder if they could bring us a bite, Mr Gibb? It's past my dinner time and my belly is starting to eat itself." There were some grins at this. Thomas Gain was a stout man with heavy jowls and an abundant stomach. "And as for Peter Curran here," he continued, "his is growling so loud I can't hear the half of what's being said."

The man beside him answered before Gibb could respond.

"If you want to eat, you'd better hurry up and settle the verdict. They're not going to give us anything until you come to a decision. It's the rule." His name was James Slade and he owned a grocery store on Jarvis Street. He wasn't at all happy at being subpoenaed to serve on the jury, but at the least, he thought he should have been foreman, given the social standing of his clientele. He spoke in a condescending tone that had already set the rest of them on edge.

"That used to be the practice, Mr Slade," said Gibb, "but I don't believe it's the case nowadays. If you men want some refreshment, I'll order it right away."

"They won't, you'll see."

Stevenson, who was next to him, groaned, glanced around for somewhere to spit, caught Gibb's eye and refrained.

"Can we at least have a jug or two of Dominion?" asked John Shaw, who was a coal merchant. His jacket and flannel shirt were clean enough, but around his neck and wrists the skin was dark with coal dust. He considered it weakened you to bathe more than once a month. A tarry odour of coal emanated from him but it wasn't totally unpleasant. Better than the smell of hides coming from Emery Nixon, the tanner.

"Why don't we just get on with it? Cast our vote now," said Chamberlin, who was an avid temperance man.

"You're the one who's been insisting on going over everything like you're combing your head for lice," interjected Jabez Clarke. "In my view the constable was a silly arse lad who thought it mattered what woman you get a bit of dock with. As for me, I'm as confused as a priest in a brothel. In other words, gentlemen, soon as the lassie with the lovely tiddies stood up, I knew at once where to put my vote—and my member." Clarke was a corset salesman for Mr Simpson's store. Perhaps in reaction to the need to be constantly deferential and discreet, when in male company he was unremittingly vulgar. Some of the men considered him a wag, some did not.

"Show some respect, Mr Clarke," said Gibb.

"No offence meant." He flicked his heavy moustache, which was an unnaturally black tint, as was his thick, glossy hair.

Gibb laid down his pipe and picked up the ledger where he'd been taking notes.

"Is everybody ready then?"

A chorus of "ays" but one man shook his head.

"I hate to see the lad's mother destitute. And she will be if she don't get that insurance money," said Mr Bright, an elflike man with large ears. He was a druggist who had his shop on Parliament Street.

"I feel the same way," said Gibb, "but our job is to find the truth and we must present that unflinchingly. I'm afraid we cannot worry about the consequences."

"Why not?" interjected James Slade. "We are decent Christian men after all."

Gibb took a long pull on his pipe but before he could answer, Chamberlin spoke up.

"Jarius is right. Unpleasant as that may prove to be, our duty is to present the truth as we see it. What happens after that is out of our hands. I say we should vote."

"Hear, hear," agreed Stevenson. "I might even be able to get to work and not be totally out of pocket."

Gain, who was at the far end of the table, waved his pipe to get Gibb's attention.

"There's something niggling at me, Mr Foreman. It's about the food."

"I promise I'll send for dinner as soon as we're done . . ."

"No, I don't mean that. I mean the food the doctor said was in Mr Wicken's stomach. When did he eat it?"

"I don't quite follow . . ."

"According to what I'm looking at here, the constable ate his meat and cheese shortly before he died. If he shot himself at one o'clock, after his sweetheart had given him the push, when did he eat?"

The rest of the jurors were regarding him with some exasperation.

"You would be the one to focus on that," said Slade.

"I'm quite serious. Think about it for a minute. Here's your lady-love breaking it off; you're not going to be munching on your sandwich while she's telling you that. So she leaves; would you eat then? Doesn't seem likely to me. You'd be more likely to go off your feed than not."

"Well, it's obvious you've never been lovelorn, Mr Gain," said Stevenson, and the others chuckled.

"Thomas has got a point," said Chamberlin. "People have been known to fade away to nothing when they're pining. But usually they're women."

"I've known the exact opposite," said Slade. "One of my customers had a cousin who lost his fiancée in a boating accident. He couldn't stop eating. Built up over fifty pounds in less than a month. It can go either way."

The jurors looked as if they were about to plunge into a lively argument but Gibb called them to order.

"I thank Mr Gain for bringing up this matter but we're missing the point. The time of death is approximate. It's impossible to pinpoint exactly. It could be earlier. And Miss Trowbridge was not clear as to when she left Wicken. He probably had plenty of time to polish off his sandwich before he met her." He smiled at them. "And speaking of polishing off, let's do it."

"One thing I can't get off my mind is his mother saying she wasn't aware of a fiancée," said Bright.

"Of course she's going to say that," said Slade. "She don't want a suicide verdict. She needs the money bad." He fished in his waistcoat pocket, pulled out an enamel snuffbox, took a pinch of snuff, and sneezed satisfactorily. "Don't forget, there's an invalid sister to take care of."

"Are you for a verdict of death by his own hand then?" asked Gibb.

"Absolutely. It's crystal clear that's what the fool did."

"The patrol sergeant and the detective seemed to think differently," said Bright.

"They're going to stick with their own, aren't they? Nobody wants to admit a police officer shot himself." Slade shook out another pinch of snuff onto the back of his hand and inhaled it. He didn't offer any around.

"Gentlemen? Other comments?" Gibb asked.

"You haven't said much yourself, Jarius," said Curran. "We'd like to know your views."

Gibb leaned back in his chair, tapping the stem of his pipe on the table. "If it wasn't by his own hand, whose was it by? There's no sign of a fight, or a disturbance. He didn't seem to have any more enemies than normally go to a police officer. He's in that vacant house for no other reason. Think of it, if you were going to do yourself in, where would you go? Not home where your mother is going to find you. You'd want to spare her that. Not at the station where there's people about all the time. You'd want a bit of privacy. Time to compose yourself to meet your Maker. I have to say that it all adds up the same way, no matter what direction I put the sums. He was plunged into a state of extreme melancholy by the rejection of his fiancée. She told us he was of a jealous and highly strung disposition. When she left, he must have stood there mulling things over, getting more and more het up. His mind goes completely, he takes out his revolver and shoots himself. My verdict is for suicide. I'm truly sorry for his mother and wish I could say otherwise but I can't. None of us here present is so old we don't know what it feels like to have a woman turn you down. Am I right in this?"

"Right," said George Griffin, the butcher. He spoke with such vigour, the others stared at him and he squirmed. "I had more backbone than that constable but love sure does put you in a miserable state."

"Shall we take the vote then so Mr Shaw can have his beer before he faints away? Here's some paper; pens are in that box. Write down 'ay' and the word 'suicide,' or 'nay' and 'cause of death unknown.' Add your name."

He handed around the slips of paper. Inkwells had been placed in front of each place and for a few moments there was only the sound of pens scratching.

Jarius wrote down his own vote and began to collect the slips as the men finished. All were done but one.

"Mr Griffin, your paper if you please."

"Coming."

The butcher was not much used to writing and he formed his letters as slowly and carefully as if he were in the classroom. Finally he passed the folded paper to Gibb who looked at it.

"That's it then." Gibb recorded the votes on his sheet and placed them all in an envelope. He got to his feet and addressed the men in front of him, reading from a card. "By a unanimous vote, we the jury here present do upon our oath all say that at the city of Toronto on the eleventh day of November, 1895, from injuries received by a pistol fired by his own hand, the deceased, Oliver Wicken, came to his death."

"So be it," added Chamberlin and there was a corresponding murmur of "amens" from the remaining jurors.

CHAPTER SIXTEEN

MISS ANDERSON WAS at the piano and she was singing and accompanying herself to "Onward Christian Soldiers." She seemed to have a small repertoire, three hymns at the most, which she had been rotating for the last hour. Immediately after luncheon, all the inmates of the ward had been shepherded into the sitting room. Peg hated it at once. It smelled like an institution—carbolic cleaner and not enough fresh air. The chairs and couches were old and shabby, the plush worn threadbare at the arms. The lamps were lit but to her it seemed as if the entire place, including the inhabitants, existed in a grey wash that leached out colours from clothes and faces.

"... with the cross of Jesus going on before." Miss Anderson's voice was cracked but still strong enough to reach the unconverted.

If she plays that tune once more I will surely go stark staring mad.

Realising what she'd just said to herself, Peg had to smile. She got up and walked over to the fireplace where she stood and gazed at the bright, dancing flames, hoping they would burn away the grey film from her eyes. Suddenly she was aware that Shelby, one of the attendants, was watching her. There was something implacable in her attention that made Peg uneasy. So far the attendants had been quite kind but she had the feeling that in this woman's eyes, once committed as a lunatic, always a lunatic. She was alert for any evidence of what she would see as madness. In spite of the fire, Peg shivered. The knowledge of her own helplessness was cold in her stomach.

There was a tap on her shoulder and she turned around. Mrs Foster was smiling at her.

"Would you like to take a walk around the room, Mrs Eakin?"

The older woman seemed to have forgotten totally about their altercation of the previous night and was beaming at her happily. Glad to escape her thoughts, Peg nodded and Mrs Foster linked arms. They strolled over to the window for all the world as if they were two well-to-do ladies promenading along King Street.

"I'm so glad I have you for a friend," said Mrs Foster, giving Peg's arm a hard squeeze.

In spite of herself, Peg felt a thrill of pleasure. She had always had trouble making friends. She was too stiff and awkward and gave the impression of being standoffish. For as long as she could remember, she had been trying to understand the subtle signals that seemed to go back and forth between people, making some acceptable and others not.

Miss Green was sitting on the couch next to another attendant, and as they went past she called out in an affronted tone.

"I beg your pardon, I do beg your pardon."

Peg hesitated, not sure what transgression had occurred.

"Bow to her," said Mrs Foster and bobbed in the other woman's direction.

Peg had already curtsied to Miss Green twice as they passed her in the corridor but she did so again. However, the other woman was not satisfied.

"I beg your pardon," she said in an even more indignant voice. The attendant stood up quickly and interposed herself between them.

"I think it's time for you to write your letters, madam. Her Majesty relies on you."

She led her away to a desk at the far side of the room. Miss Green was well into middle age but she had styled her hair into side ringlets more suitable for a young woman. She was wearing an out-of-fashion dress of green and blue check taffeta. The bodice was tight and the full skirt was pulled back into a bustle with a drape of blue ruffles that cascaded into a long train.

"Poor woman," said Mrs Foster. "She gets most upset if she thinks she's been slighted."

"What did I do wrong?"

"I don't know, dear. She's quite changeable on the matter."

Mrs Stratton, the woman Peg had talked to in the bath, was sitting alone on the window bench. She was oddly dressed in a one-piece loose garment of brown holland. It had legs like a man's trousers and was fastened at the ankles and wrists.

"Good afternoon," said Mrs Foster. "May I introduce Mrs Eakin?"

The woman turned her head but gave no sign of recognition.

"I believe we've met," said Peg.

Mrs Stratton nodded. "Yes, of course. Do you have children?"

Peg recoiled. "I told you yesterday that I did."

"They're all dead, I assume. Murdered no doubt."

She was saved from answering by Mrs Foster, who pulled at her arm.

"Come on, my dear. Good afternoon to you, Mrs Stratton." She patted Peg's hand. "Don't mind her. She has ten fine healthy children, seven of them boys, but she fancies they're all dead and that her husband murdered them." She lowered her voice. "It's been brought on by the change. Poor thing, her flushings are very bad."

"Why is she wearing that peculiar outfit?"

"That's what they call an untidy suit. She must be in one of her bad spells. She's worse than any baby during those times. Wipes her food all over herself. Not to mention her you know what."

"How long has she been in the—in here?" Peg couldn't bring herself to say the word "asylum."

"Not that long. She came in last March." Mrs Foster continued. "She probably should be on the second floor with the really bad patients. It's not nearly as nice as our floor. They don't have any singing or dancing and nobody is allowed sweets." Suddenly, she stroked Peg's cheek. "You don't want to go down there, my dear."

Peg involuntarily moved away from her touch. "I have no intention of doing so."

As they turned back toward the fireplace, the door opened and Miss Bastedo, the matron, and two nurses came in. All the attendants stood up in deference and one or two of the patients followed suit. Miss Bastedo was a tall woman, mature and strong featured. Like the rest of the staff, she wore a plain dress of blue wool but she omitted the apron and the cap. Her dark hair was pulled into a tight knot at the nape of her neck. She began her tour of the room, chatting to the patients as she went. Her assistants walked quietly behind her.

Peg could feel her heart beating faster as she approached. She felt as if she had gone backward to her own girlhood and this was one of the mistresses of the orphanage. Unexpectedly, Mrs Foster dropped her arm and wandered off in the direction of the hearth, leaving her stranded.

Miss Bastedo halted in front of Peg. "How are you feeling today, Mrs Eakin? The nurse tells me you are settling down quite nicely."

"Indeed I am, thank you."

"I heard you ate a hearty breakfast this morning."

"Yes, ma'am, I did."

Peg had been ravenous and she'd devoured two servings of ham and toast.

"You wouldn't take your tonic though."

"No, ma'am. I did not feel the need."

"You really must take it. You will feel so much better. All of the other ladies do."

"Yes, ma'am."

The matron's expression was kind. "I understand how new everything must seem. I know you have been very frightened. Tonight, I will come by myself and give you the tonic. And just so you will know it is perfectly safe, I will even have some myself. I could do with it these days. Will that be more acceptable to you?"

"Thank you, ma'am."

Peg had been afraid the tonic contained sedatives and she couldn't bear the drowsy, helpless state they induced.

One of the assistants came forward and said something to the matron.

"Ah, yes. Before your marriage you had the occupation of dressmaker I understand?"

"Yes, ma'am."

"We encourage our ladies to do some simple occupation while they're with us. It calms the nerves. We have a wonderful sewing room here. Would you like to do something? Embroidery if you wish. Or we are always in need of garments."

"I would like that, ma'am."

"Excellent. Perhaps on Friday then, you can go to the sewing room."

"Yes, ma'am."

"And I think you can have day clothes tomorrow. You will have to make do with what the asylum provides for now, but I will send a message to your family to bring in your own clothes."

She was about to move on but Peg reached out and caught her sleeve. Both assistants tensed but Miss Bastedo stayed, looking at her calmly. Peg let her go.

"I was wondering if anybody has been to see me."

"Not yet. On the whole we prefer to see our patients settled in before they have visitors. Are you anxious to see your husband?"

Peg was quite aware that in spite of the pleasantness of Miss Bastedo's manner, like Shelby, she was watching for any signs of delusions or unnatural behaviour. But she wanted to scream out, *No! Don't let him near me. Don't let any of them near me.* Instead, she bowed her head.

"Yes, ma'am."

Mrs Foster had wandered back and the matron greeted her warmly.

"I see you've been taking good care of our new arrival."

The old lady beamed. "I most certainly have. She's my dear friend. We were just about to go for a walk down the corridor."

110

"Very good. And I must continue with my rounds. Good afternoon to you both."

She moved away and Mrs Foster took Peg's arm.

"My dear, you are trembling. Are you cold?"

"Yes. Yes, I am rather."

There was another attendant sitting by the door. She was round featured and rather jolly looking.

"Good afternoon, Mrs Foster, Mrs Eakin. Where are you going?"

"Just for a turn down the corridor and back," answered Mrs Foster. "Matron approves."

"Very well. But don't be gone too long, will you?"

"That's Wylie," said Mrs Foster as they went outside. "She's a good lassie; never has a cross word for anyone."

They began to walk down the corridor. There were no other patients out there except for one of the charity inmates who was sweeping the floor. She was quite elderly and bent and, as they passed, Peg heard her cough so hard, she had to stop what she was doing and lean on her broom.

"She sounds consumptive," she whispered to Mrs Foster.

"Oh, she is, my dear. That's Effie Callahan. She was quite all right when she came in here but she caught the consumption last year from another patient. She'll probably be gone by spring, you mark my words."

They walked by her but she didn't look up.

"Who was it you wanted to see, my dear? Oh, don't be surprised. Nothing escapes me, especially where my friends are concerned. I myself only want my daughter. She is such a love. She is married now with her own family and she cannot visit as often as she would like. My husband, Mr Foster, doesn't approve and hardly ever comes."

She reached up and pinched Peg's cheek. "You can tell me."

But she couldn't. Her protestations only got her into trouble. A dog that barked and bit was tied up and rendered helpless. It was the silent cat who moved in the darkness that remained free.

111

"How many grandchildren do you have?" she asked, and Mrs Foster was diverted and chatted to her merrily until they reached the end of the corridor. Here, there was a pair of double doors. Mrs Foster made to turn back.

"We can't go through there."

"Why not?"

"It leads onto the verandah and we're only supposed to be there in warm weather."

Peg tried the door and it wasn't locked. Mrs Foster dithered. "We'll get into trouble."

"Don't worry. If anybody scolds, I'll tell them it was entirely my idea."

"I'll wait here then. I'm not allowed."

Peg pushed open the door and stepped through. The semicircular verandah was quite large and roofed but otherwise open. She drew in her breath sharply. Her flannel wrapper and nightgown were little protection against the chill air. She walked over to the far side and peered through the bars. In the distance, the pewter-colored lake was hardly distinguishable from the sky. Below her stretched the sodden garden, denuded now of all vegetables. There was a thin plume of smoke coming from the chimney of the gardener's house and the hominess of it made her want to weep. She pushed up her sleeve and thrust her bare arm through the bars and held it there while the rain wet her skin.

"I don't know what will happen to me if you don't come. Please don't leave me here," she whispered.

"Mrs Eakin? We should be getting back."

Mrs Foster had the door partly open and was peering in anxiously. Peg turned.

"I'm coming." She returned to her companion. "There, you see, a little air has done me wonders."

In fact, she was shaking uncontrollably. Mrs Foster took one of her hands in hers and chafed it briskly.

"My dear, you're so cold. And look at your slippers. They're quite wet. Let's go back to the fire."

She looked into Peg's face, her eyes knowing.

"I heard you say something. Were you praying?"

Peg gave a wry smile. "Yes, I suppose I was."

"That's good, dear. I myself pray all the time."

CHAPTER SEVENTEEN

———•———

THE MOOD AT the station was subdued. Everybody felt bad about Wicken, who had been well liked. The discussions were ongoing, but most of the constables were resigned to the verdict and the inexplicable nature of the human mind. Murdoch retired to the cubicle behind the tea room that served as his office. He wasn't in the mood for talking. Mrs Wicken's devastation haunted him. She had left immediately after the verdict had been delivered and he hadn't had a chance to speak to her again. Mary Ann Trowbridge had departed quickly as well and he hoped she had somebody to comfort her.

With a sigh, he turned to his battered metal filing cabinet. He should look over his old reports at least, see if he could follow up on anything. He took out the folder labelled Piersol, which was a charge of embezzlement against a young clerk who worked for an insurance company. It was a complicated case and Murdoch had to admit he didn't much care about it. Piersol was underpaid and overworked and if he syphoned off some of the considerable profits of the company, good for him. Before Murdoch could go any further with these thoughts, there was a tap outside. His cubicle was too small for a proper door so visitors had to signal their presence by knocking on the wall. Through the reed curtain, he could see the outline of Sergeant Seymour.

"Come in."

Seymour pushed through into the tiny space.

"Thought you could use a spot of tea." He was carrying a mug, which he held out to Murdoch.

"Thank you, Sergeant."

Murdoch took the mug and sipped at the hot brew.

"Ow."

"Will, you'd better get that tooth looked at. Your jaw is all swollen."

"Yrr, tea'sot."

The sergeant smiled at him. "Listen, it's quiet here this afternoon. I'll book you out early. Go over and see Brodie."

"He's a butcher."

"Maybe, but he does his job."

The hot drink had set up such a clamour in Murdoch's mouth that he could hardly sit still.

"Come on, Will. You can't keep putting it off."

"Yes, I can," said Murdoch, trying to grin.

But the sergeant prevailed and he soon found himself setting off along Wilton Street in search of a dentist, any dentist other than Brodie.

A chill wind was blowing in from the lake and the sky was grey, sunless, threatening more rain to come. He wrapped his scarf around his face. *Are you a miserable coward or not?* He said to himself, and the answer was a loud *Yes*.

He remembered passing a dentist's office not too far from the station on Wilton Street and he decided to try there first. His feet had kept moving and he was now standing in front of a dry goods shop. Just to the right of the window was a green door that looked newly painted. A shiny brass plaque announced Dr F. Stevens, Dentist. 2nd Floor. He hesitated. Well, at the least he could look at the place, determine if it looked decent. No blood and discarded teeth on the floor. He opened the door and stepped into a narrow hall which lead to a steep flight of stairs. The walls were a cheery yellow tint and the oilcloth floor covering was a flowered pattern. Everything appeared

115

to be well swept and clean. So far so good. Slowly, he mounted the stairs. At the top was a small landing with another green door and another plaque that said Please Enter. Murdoch paused and touched his sore tooth with the tip of his tongue. The resulting jolt moved him to open the door. He poked his head around. In front of him was a tiny room with just enough space for a desk and three straight-backed chairs lined up against the wall. A pretty young woman was seated at the desk and at his entrance she rewarded his courage with a welcoming smile.

"Good afternoon, do come in."

She was wearing a sober blue dress with a starched white apron over it and her auburn hair was pinned up beneath a stiff white cap.

"You're here to see the doctor, I presume?"

Murdoch mumbled. "Yes, bad toothache."

She looked at him sympathetically. "I can see your jaw is swollen. But never mind, Dr Stevens will have you right as rain before you know it."

She stood up and came over to him. "Let me take your things. It's another nasty day, isn't it?"

She hung his hat and his coat on a brass coat stand. Murdoch added the muffler and stood awkwardly waiting. There was some kind of telephone board on the desk and she sat down, plugged in a wire and leaned closer to the mouthpiece.

"A patient here to see you, doctor. A Mr? . . ." She looked up.

"Murdoch, William Murdoch."

She repeated that into the telephone, then held the receiver to her ear. Murdoch heard crackling as the invisible doctor replied. She gave a smile, so quickly suppressed, he wondered what the man had said. He perched on one of the chairs while she took out a large ledger.

"I just need your name, address, and occupation."

He gave her the information.

"Oh, my, a detective. We haven't had one in here before. It must be exciting work."

"Sometimes." He wasn't up to explaining all the different shades of liveliness that his job entailed.

Suddenly, he noticed a shelf behind the desk. Sitting on it was a glass box, inside of which was what looked like a set of teeth. He got up and went closer to investigate. The young woman smiled.

"Those are an old set of dentures. Dr Stevens collects them. They are what we call 'Waterloo' teeth. The back molars are made from ivory but the front teeth were taken from the corpses at the Battle of Waterloo. They were very popular as they are so natural looking. They're glued to a copper plate."

"Must have been hard to eat with those things. How did they stay in?"

"There is a little spring at the back. But you're right, they would be quite uncomfortable and we believe they were only worn for show. Special occasions. I suppose you had to eat as best you could with your gums. Nowadays we have vulcanised rubber that we use for the plate. Much better. People can have all those troublesome teeth removed and hardly know the difference."

Murdoch thought her glance fell to his lips as if sizing him as a prospect but just then the door opposite opened and Dr Stevens came into the waiting room. He too seemed very young and Murdoch's stomach quailed. He had hoped for an elderly man with much experience who knew what to do, who wouldn't hurt any more than necessary. Stevens looked to be barely into his mid-twenties. He was tall, clean shaven, with dark-brown hair trimmed close to his head. Seeing Murdoch he stretched out his hand and smiled, revealing perfectly white and even teeth. Murdoch supposed that was a good advertisement and he wondered if they were real. Weakly, he shook hands.

"What can I do for you, sir?"

"I've got a bad toothache," he jabbed his finger in the air, indicating the side of his jaw.

"Ah. Come this way, we'll have a look."

The nurse gave a reassuring nod and Murdoch followed the dentist through to the adjoining room. This was larger, with deep windows on two sides. Even with this much light, the afternoon was so gloomy that all the wall sconces had to be lit. In the far corner was a Chinese screen of black laquer, hiding who knows what instruments of torture. There were two tall oaken cabinets flanking the door. However, what dominated the room was The Chair. It was on a pedestal and stood dead centre.

Stevens walked over to it and patted the backrest invitingly. "Sit here, if you please," as if Murdoch were going to get a haircut.

The chair was covered with plush, burgundy in colour. The better to hide blood stains, he thought. There was a wooden footrest with a Grecian scene painted on it. Probably nymphs chasing Zeus. He climbed in. There was a metal spittoon attached to the arm of the chair. For blood he assumed.

"Open your mouth wide."

He did and Stevens peered into it. He'd picked up some sharp instrument from another tray without Murdoch noticing and he tapped the gum where all the pain was emanating.

"Ow." Murdoch tried not to make that a bellow.

"Hm. Did that hurt?"

His face was very close to Murdoch's, and at this intimate distance, he saw that the dentist had a small cut on his chin where he'd nicked himself shaving.

"Um," he replied.

"How long have you had the ache?"

" 'Bout two weeks."

"Oh, dear, that is a long time. You really should have come in sooner. I'm afraid it looks infected. It will have to come out."

Murdoch's thoughts must have been obvious because the dentist patted his arm.

"Don't worry. I have all the latest equipment. The extraction will be quite painless."

"How long have you been practicing?" Murdoch asked.

Stevens looked disconcerted. "To tell the truth, I graduated from dental college this spring. But I was in the top five of the class."

"How many altogether, six?"

Stevens smiled uneasily and Murdoch himself grinned. "Just a joke, sir. My apologies."

He was afraid to ask him how many patients he'd had. His tooth was throbbing again. Besides there was something jolly about the man and sympathetic. That must count for a lot surely.

"If that's the only thing to be done, then we'd better do it."

"You'll be glad. Better this than weeks of pain. And an abcess can cause the devil of a lot of problems. Look."

He pointed at his neck just below the jaw and Murdoch saw a rather deep, round scar.

"The result of an abcessed tooth. The infection went right through to the cheek. We didn't have very good dentistry the way we do now. So you see, I know what it's like." Then he shouted.

"Inge!"

Almost at once, the door opened and the young woman appeared. So much for fancy telephones.

"This is Mrs er Mrs Stevens. I am proud to say my wife and also my assistant."

She smiled at Murdoch shyly. "Don't worry, it will be over before you know it."

She went behind the Chinese screen and came back with a linen towel that she placed over his chest, tieing the ends behind his neck. She had a nice flowery smell about her that he liked. Carnations perhaps. He could hear the dentist rooting around behind him, but he resisted the impulse to turn and investigate. Then Stevens appeared on his left-hand side. He was wheeling a small cart in which sat a long metal cylinder. There was a rubber tube looped around the top. At the end of the tube was a cone-shaped piece. He maneuvered the cylinder closer to the chair.

"This is nitrous oxide. You've probably heard it called 'laughing gas.' It's a wonderful discovery, I must say. Most people feel completely euphoric and it utterly takes away pain. Two ticks of the clock and it will be over."

"I saw that stuff used at a music hall show a few years ago," said Murdoch. "It made people do really silly things. Is that going to happen to me?"

Stevens shook his head. "This gas is for medicinal purposes, not entertainment. All that will happen is that you'll go into a pleasant dreamlike state."

"And the alternative?"

"We could administer laudanum or chloral hydrate but those will need an hour or so to take effect."

Murdoch looked at Inge Stevens. Even in her severe cap and uniform there was a soft prettiness to her.

"I'll do the gas," he said.

The dentist nodded at his wife and she went over to the sink in the corner of the room, returning with what looked like a glass of water.

"Swill out your mouth with this and spit it out."

Murdoch did so. The liquid had a strong, tarry kind of taste.

Mrs Stevens dabbed at his mouth as he sat back in the chair and he was reminded of Mrs Kitchen wiping away the blood from Arthur's chin. The memory grabbed him and he sighed. Misunderstanding him, the young woman said softly.

"You'll probably think I'm prejudiced but Dr Stevens is really very good. I even let him pull one of my teeth and I didn't feel a thing."

Murdoch hoped this hadn't happened while they were on their wedding trip but he didn't comment, allowing himself to surrender to their administrations. The dentist placed the rubber cone over his nose and mouth.

"Just breathe normally."

He fiddled with a dial on the cylinder and Murdoch heard the soft hiss of the gas.

"I'm going to count backward from ten. Nice easy breaths now. Don't gasp. All right, here we go . . . Ten . . . nine . . . eight . . ."

Murdoch's head was beginning to spin as if the top part were rotating like a top. For a moment he wanted to fight it off, get back his control, but Inge touched his forehead and he relaxed. The spinning sensation stopped and he felt as if he were floating up, way up in the sky.

"Three . . . two . . . one."

He started to have a lovely dream about dancing with Liza, a waltz that he was executing effortlessly. He tried to tell her how beautiful she looked in her new white silk gown, but he had a big piece of apple in his mouth and it got in the way. He tried to roll it off his tongue but a pip stabbed him sharply. He struggled again to get rid of the fruit and suddenly it was gone. Liza was speaking to him, "Mr Murdoch, Mr Murdoch," and he wondered why she was being so formal.

"Wake up, Mr Murdoch. Wake up. We're all done."

He opened his eyes. Two rather anxious-looking faces were hovering above him. Dr Stevens had nice brown eyes he noticed, with girlishly long eyelashes. Inge's eyes were an unusual hazel colour. Both of them beamed. "They should kiss each other," he thought. He felt so happy that they were happy. Perhaps they should kiss him too. He smiled and felt something wet run down his chin.

"Oops," said Mrs Stevens, and she quickly wiped away whatever it was.

"Tooth's out," said Stevens. "Do you want to see it?"

"Why not."

The dentist had been holding the tooth behind his back and he whipped it forward and held it under Murdoch's nose. He'd used some kind of device that close up resembled a medieval thumbscrew. The ring at the end had been slipped over the tooth and then twisted. The bloody prize was firmly in its grasp.

"The infection had made the gum spongy so it lifted out like a carrot," he said. "Now you can sit there for a while longer until the gas has worn off. Told you, didn't hurt a bit, did it?"

"I didn't feel a thing," said Murdoch. He grinned broadly. What wonderful parents they will make. He wanted to put his head on the dentist's shoulder and have it stroked. Either that or curl up in Inge's lap and be rocked.

"Your gum will be sore for a few days. I've packed the hole with some absorbent cotton and you can take it out in a couple of days when the bleeding has stopped. But if it's still bad by tomorrow, come by and I'll fix it."

"Like Medusa you mean?"

121

Stevens looked puzzled, but he smiled politely and waited for Murdoch to stop laughing at his own joke.

"We'll give you some laudanum and some antiseptic to rub on it. Now I should tell you that while you were under I had a check on your other teeth and you've got some bad cavities developing. When this has healed, you should come back and I'll fill them."

"Fill them?"

"Well, I can extract them if you prefer but these days we are recommending filling. Gold is good. It'll last you a lifetime."

"Can you sit up now, Mr Murdoch?" Inge asked. He sat forward in the chair and then got to his feet rather shakily, enjoying the feeling of her cool hand in his.

"Do you want to keep the tooth?" Stevens asked.

"No, no thanks. It's never been one of my favourites."

They all chuckled, especially Murdoch, who considered he was being quite a wag today. Inge started to escort him back to the other room. At the door was a glass-fronted cabinet and he saw it was filled with shelf after shelf of denture sets. They were all grinning at him, which made him respond in kind. Outside, in the little anteroom, not even the bill dampened his good humour. He paid up, made an appointment to come in next week, and went down the stairs, armed with his bottles of medicine.

As he headed for home, he had to admit he felt happy. The experience hadn't been nearly as bad as he'd expected. Amazing what developments had happened in the last few years. He splashed vigorously through a puddle. Yes, indeed, he would recommend young Forbes to anyone that asked. No, that wasn't right. His name was Stevens. And his lovely wife was Inge. Such an adorable smile she had, such gentle hands. A wife to be proud of. Suddenly he thought of Enid. He'd have to tell her the story of the denture sets. That would make her laugh. She had good teeth, just slightly crooked on the lowers. Perhaps she would go to Stevens as well. He chuckled at such a good idea and a passerby, bent under his black umbrella, glanced over at him with some alarm. Murdoch touched the brim of his hat.

122

"Good afternoon, lovely weather isn't it?"

The man didn't respond and Murdoch continued on his way. Ahead of him was a particularly large puddle. He aimed for it and stamped through with great satisfaction. His gum was sore but the horrible white pain had gone. Hurrah for modern science.

CHAPTER EIGHTEEN

THE SILENCE THROUGHOUT dinner was so heavy, Lewis felt as if it had landed on the back of his own neck and was bowing his head. He had spent most of the time watching the lamp in the middle of the table. Janet hadn't cleaned it properly and it was smoking badly. A boy at his school had told him that one of their lamps had exploded, and hot oil and bits of glass flew straight into the face of their maid. "She was blinded from then on," said the boy. Lewis had been so frightened by this story that he sat as far away as possible from the lamps at home, irritating his mother, who could not reassure him. There was a second larger lamp on the sideboard behind him, but he thought he was far enough away to be safe.

As it was a Thursday, they had had a boiled leg of pork, carrots, and parsnips, also boiled and a pease pudding which always accompanied the pork. His mother made up the menus and they were exactly the same from week to week, unless they had company, which happened rarely. Lewis loathed pease pudding but had forced himself to eat it, knowing he would draw his grandfather's wrath if he didn't clear his plate. Nathaniel was in a bad skin, worse than usual, and he had not spoken to anybody the entire meal. Mamma and Papa still weren't on speaking terms. Augusta sent all necessary requests or instructions by way of Lewis:

"Ask your father to pass the parsnips," or "Tell your father there is no more meat."

Even Uncle Jarius, who was usually talkative, had been quiet, and Uncle Frank might have been struck dumb for all he said.

Suddenly Lewis quailed, feeling his grandfather turn toward him.

"Stop fidgeting, boy. You'd think you had worms the way you've been wriggling."

Nathaniel had a long wiry grey beard that thrust out from the sides of his chin and virtually obscured his mouth. This meant that when he spoke, the hair below his lips moved up and down in a way that made Lewis want to giggle.

Augusta intervened quickly.

"It's his new suit, father. The wool is scratchy."

She reached over and tugged the jacket collar away from Lewis's neck.

His grandfather looked as if he were about to continue with his complaint, but Janet came into the room with her tray. She put it down on the sideboard, aware that everyone was watching her.

"What's the sweet?" asked Nathaniel.

"Baroness Pudding, sir."

"I hope it tastes better than it did last week. It was a soggy mess as I recall."

Janet bobbed. "I'm sorry, Mr Eakin. I boiled it much longer this time."

The sweet was a suet and raisin pudding that had to cook for at least four hours.

Clumsy because of the criticism, Janet clinked the dishes noisily as she cleared the table. Nobody spoke and Jarius was the only one who assisted her by handing over his plate.

"I'll serve, Janet. You can bring it to me," said Augusta.

She did so and Lewis tried to catch her eye to give her a quick grin of sympathy, but she was too intent on placing the pudding dish as delicately as she could in front of his mother.

"Shall I pour the tea, ma'am?"

"No, I'll see to it."

125

Janet curtsied again and returned to the sideboard where she piled the used china on the tray. She left as fast as she could but she had barely closed the door when Nathaniel spoke.

"That girl is not improving, Augusta. Can you talk to her?"

"I do all the time, Father. I cannot make silk out of a cow's ear . . . I mean, out of a sow's ear."

"Fool," muttered Nathaniel.

Hearing him, Augusta flushed as red as her own maid had. Lewis tried to pretend he'd gone deaf and stared at the pale roll of pudding that his mother was handing him. His father had managed to withdraw his presence so completely from the table, he might as well have not been there.

Nathaniel sprinkled two large spoonfuls of sugar over his own portion and began to eat, smacking his lips. In front of him was a jug of beer that was almost empty. It was the second one he'd consumed tonight. Lewis knew that his grandfather's mood was greatly affected by the number of jugs of beer that got emptied. Usually, it was only one, but two downed, and downed quickly, spelled trouble. He looked over at his uncle Frank. He wasn't drinking anything at all, although he usually shared a carafe of wine with Jarius. Augusta only drank liquor at special occasions or if she was ill, and her husband did likewise. Lewis wished she would pour the tea. He was allowed a cup now as long as it was heavily supplemented with milk, and he enjoyed the feeling of being grown-up that it gave him. However, Augusta didn't move; instead she nibbled at her pudding. Lewis had only recently been accorded the privilege of eating with the grown-ups at the evening meal. So far he heartily wished he was in the kitchen with Cullie, even though that afternoon she had frightened him by recounting the tale of the policeman who had died. She'd heard all this from the baker's boy.

"For love. Imagine that. Shot his brains out with his very own gun. They were all over the place. That and the blood. It was so thick you'd think the room had been painted red."

This account had disturbed Lewis almost as much as the story of the exploding lamp. He wondered if the mood in the house had any-

126

thing to do with it. His father and uncle had to go and see the body. They hadn't said anything about all the blood but they must have been horrified.

He cut into the pudding. In spite of what Janet had said, it was undercooked in the centre and the suet was unpleasantly sticky. He picked out a raisin and chewed that.

Nathaniel finished eating and immediately Augusta put down her spoon. Lewis saw her exchange a glance with his uncle Jarius, who nodded and wiped his mouth with his napkin in his fastidious way.

"Stepfather, perhaps while everyone is present we could continue our earlier discussion," Jarius said. "We do owe Dr Ferrier an answer by tomorrow. As I understand it, delay will only make matter worse."

Nathaniel shook his head. "This is not a suitable subject at the dinner table. Especially not with the boy present." He took another helping of the pudding.

"I am confident that Lewis is old enough to hear," said Augusta. "If we don't broach it now, when will we? It is a matter that concerns all of us."

"You're wrong," said Nathaniel, his open mouth revealing partly masticated suet and raisins. "She is my wife and the decision is mine to make."

Jarius answered; his voice was calm, reasonable.

"No one would disagree but it is such an important matter, Sister and I thought it might be helpful to you if we discussed it more thoroughly. As a family. Isn't that so, Frank?"

"Yes," said Frank.

"And you agree too, don't you, Peter?"

"Yes, begging your pardon, Father."

"We all love and honour you, sir," continued Jarius. "However, we cannot pretend this new marriage has been easy on our household. To speak honestly, both her presence and her illness have been a dreadful disruption and created havoc for all of us." He paused. "Surely it is obvious that we cannot return to the situation as it has been. I'm sorry, I realise these are most unpleasant things to hear, as they are for me to say, but we must not put our heads in the sand like so many ostriches."

The image struck Lewis as funny and he could feel another giggle threatening to break free. He concentrated on the pattern of green squares on the tablecloth, jumping across them like stepping-stones.

Nathaniel pushed aside his dish. "You're a good talker, Jarius, and you always have been. But if you want to speak honestly like you say, let's go the whole hog. The truth is that under all this mealymouthed gabbing what my children are really concerned about is their inheritance. They're all shitting in their britches in case I get more tads." His eyes were dark under the bushy eyebrows. "And why not? She's going to be all right. It was her boy dying that unhinged her."

Lewis shrank down into his chair, trying to make himself as small as possible. He couldn't bear any mention of Charley, whom he'd loathed from the moment he'd arrived. Whenever they were left alone, he tormented the younger boy until he sobbed. When he had died so suddenly and painfully, Lewis thought it must be because of him. He'd finally confided in his mother who had been unexpectedly gentle with him. "Bad feelings don't kill us, my chuck. If they did, nobody in this household would be alive today."

"I'm still a vigorous man," continued Nathaniel, "and she'll be fertile for a long time to come yet. I could spawn five sons before I die."

"Father, please," said Augusta, indicating her son.

"You're the one said he was old enough. So let him hear."

Peter Curran stopped eating and sat staring at his plate as if he were a rabbit and the fox's snout was coming through the table.

"And any son she might drop would be a whole lot better than the one I have." Nathaniel addressed this remark to Jarius, ignoring Frank who was leaning on his elbows on the table, toying with his fork.

"We all know my stepbrother has sowed a lot of wild oats," said Jarius. "I'm not condoning that, but he has settled down now. Isn't that so, Frank?"

Nathaniel didn't wait to hear a reply.

"Ballocks. He's still up to his tricks and you know it. He's hell-bent on destroying everything I've built up."

Frank didn't look up, but began tapping the fork on the side of the dish as if he were about to crack an egg. Nathaniel wouldn't stop now.

"This woman can get me children who will have respect. I'll see to that. They won't end up scragged like he's going to. Jarius, I don't count you in this. You're not my own flesh and blood, more's the pity, but you will get a nice bequest, don't worry about that. And I know you love me like you should."

"What about Lewis?" Augusta burst out. "What about your first grandson? He deserves consideration."

"Does he? I say let him earn it. Let him earn it the way I had to."

Lewis had heard his grandfather's story many times. How, at the age of fifteen, he'd fled from a poor farm in the north of England, stowed away on a steamer to Canada, and by dint of hard work and a good mind, had established himself in a livery stable, now considered one of the best in Toronto. This history usually took a long time to relate, especially after two jugs of beer, and Lewis hoped Nathaniel wasn't going to launch into it tonight.

However, he could see his mother wasn't going to tolerate story-telling. Her mouth had gone very tight and she spoke as if her jaw were stiff.

"And what about me? I am your only daughter. Surely I matter?"

Nathaniel flapped his hand as if she were an irritating fly. "I've no time for a woman who's put a twitch on her husband's tool the way you have."

Curran didn't respond, except to stuff his hands underneath his thighs out of harm's way. Nathaniel jabbed his finger in the air.

"And I've told you time and again that you're turning your lad into a prize Miss Molly. But you, you won't listen. He's getting to be more and more soft as he grows."

This wasn't the first time his grandfather had used that term, but when Lewis asked his mother what it meant, she wouldn't tell him. Uncle Frank said it meant he would turn out like the fat gelding in the stable and Lewis added that to his other pile of worries.

Suddenly, Frank sat up straight. "Young Nephew, you probably don't know what the hell we're all talking about, do you? Concerning your new grandmother, I mean."

"No, Uncle," whispered Lewis.

"Do you remember how we had to drown Fluffy because she kept getting out and having kittens? She just wouldn't stop? Always caterwauling and carrying on."

"Frank!"

"Don't worry, Aggie. I'm only trying to educate the boy. You see, Lew, your uncle Jarius thinks Grandmother Peg should have this special operation. It's performed on women who've lost their slates. They take out their innards, their sex parts. They can't have children after that but it's said to work wonders. Dampens them right down."

"Frank, stop it. You can't talk to the boy like that."

"Why not? His future is at stake. You see, Lewis, the problem is we're not just talking about a poor woman who's gone barmy. It's worse than that. Your grandfather is in fact married to a whore who is ready to stand for any man that comes knocking."

Nathaniel cuffed his son across the side of his mouth. His knuckle caught the top of Frank's lip, cracking it.

"You piece of filth. Your mother is crying in heaven over you."

Frank touched his finger to his mouth and examined the daub of blood. "She has a lot more to cry over than just me swearing."

Nathaniel hit out again but this time, Frank was ready and he caught him by the wrist. He pushed back and they locked as if they were in a wrestling contest.

"Jarius, stop them," Augusta cried.

Gibb jumped up and came around the table. He gripped Frank's shoulder.

"Let him go."

Eakin did, at the same time pushing back from his chair so he was out of harm's way.

"I believe your father is owed an apology."

"Is he? All I'm doing is telling the truth . . . You say you'd like more sons but how could you ever be certain of her offspring?"

"Hold your tongue."

"Look at me, Father! I'm flesh of your flesh. You look into a mirror when you see me. There is no doubt who fathered me."

Nathaniel stared at him, then he said, "Don't you think I regret that every day? What I see when I look at you disgusts me."

Frank flinched and Lewis could see the movement of his Adam's apple in his throat. Jarius was still standing close to him and he stepped forward.

"Stepfather, I am afraid in the interest of truth I must take Frank's side in this matter. He did not want to tell you but she went to him as well as myself. On Friday." He looked over at Curran. "I regret to say she approached both of them."

"You're lying."

Jarius frowned. "How can you say that to me? We were trying to spare you."

"Is it true?" Nathaniel asked his son. His voice was quieter but to Lewis he sounded even more terrifying.

Frank reverted to studying his plate. "Yes, Father."

"Like she did with Jarius?"

"Yes, the same."

"And you, Peter?"

"Er, yes, sir." He glanced quickly at his wife.

"Why didn't you tell me?" asked Augusta.

Curran stared at a point over her right shoulder. "No point really."

"I don't believe you!" Nathaniel roared and slammed his fist on the table. Lewis was afraid he would hit Frank again. Jarius bent over him.

"It is true, Stepfather. I saw them bringing her back. I did not want to tell you. You had enough to contend with. And you can see how upset you are."

All eyes were on Nathaniel. Finally he spoke.

"The woman is a whore, that is clear. I must apologise to you, Frank." He held out his hand, palm down to his son.

Frank took it in his and kissed the fingers.

Lewis saw that he left behind a smudge of blood.

CHAPTER NINETEEN

———•———

SAM LEE AND his son lived in a room to the rear of the laundry. No Westerner had ever entered this place, and if they had, it would have fulfilled all their most riotous fantasies about Chinamen. Earlier the two had lit incense sticks and the smell was dense and pungent in the air. The light was a soft bluish red. Lee had draped scarves of violet-coloured silk over the two lamps, which were turned down low. There was little furniture and all of it Lee had made himself. He was a talented wood-carver, but it would have been impossible for him to find work other than in the expected laundry. However, he had built a massive hinged panel that covered one side of the room, and slowly, over the lonely years, he'd covered it with carvings of flowers, birds, and bats. The entire work was painted with gilt. In front of this panel was a red lacquered table on which stood the kitchen altar, three porcelain cups, and rice-filled bowls with their chopsticks. A brightly coloured picture of Choi Sun, the god of wealth, was propped beside these items, and tucked slightly to the back was a more subdued painting of Jesus ascending to heaven.

Against the opposite wall was a single wooden couch covered with a thin, padded mattress and a blue quilt. The evidence of Western life was an ugly iron range that served as cooker and heater. Foon had prepared boiled rice and greens for their dinner and they were having it, seated cross-legged on the floor. He finished eating, served his father the remaining rice, and sat quietly, waiting.

Sam gave a soft belch in a sign of appreciation of the meal his son had prepared.

"Shall I get your pipe, *baba?*"

The older man nodded and Foon got up, crossed to a cupboard beside the range, and took out a brown leather sack. He returned to his father, who had stretched out on the wooden couch.

"*Baba*, with your permission, I have a question I would like to present to you."

Lee was lying with his head on the pillow roll and his eyes were closed. "What is your question, *laoerh?*" He addressed his son in the traditional Chinese manner according to his birth order, number two son. Sam's oldest child had remained in Hong Kong to help support his mother and sister. Sam intended to send for them when the law changed, or smuggle them in if it didn't.

Foon opened the sack and removed the *yangqiang*, the opium pipe. It was made of bamboo with a tortoiseshell overlay. The tips were ivory and the saddle, where the bowl sat, was pewter and copper latticework studded with semiprecious stones of red and green. It was the most expensive object they owned, passed down to Lee from his uncle on his mother's side and already promised to the eldest son. Foon placed it carefully beside him and lifted the cloth that covered their eating table. Tucked underneath was a low stand of black lacquer inlaid with mother-of-pearl which he pulled out. Resting in shallow holes were four small bowls, each a different shape and material. He slid open the drawer and took out a long steel bodkin and a tiny polished wooden box. He placed them beside the pipe.

"Do you have a preference tonight, *baba?*"

Sam studied the dampers for a moment then lazily indicated an onion-shaped one made of jade with a carved dragon design around the edge.

Foon picked it up and snapped the stem securely onto the pipe. Next he unscrewed the top of the little box and dipped the end of the bodkin into the opium paste it contained. He had turned up the

133

wick of the lamp and he held the blob of dark, treacly paste in the flame. As soon as it caught fire, he blew it out and rolled it in the pipe bowl, twirling the bodkin between his fingers and thumb. He repeated this procedure twice more, then handed the pipe to his father. Sam took in a deep breath, exhaled completely, then drew in the aromatic opium smoke, holding it in his lungs as long as possible. He let go of the smoke through his nostrils. Foon watched him for a moment, until he could see the pipe was to his satisfaction.

"At the inquest this morning, you instructed me to tell them that the young woman who claimed to be Mr Wicken's fiancée was the same one that you had seen with the constable."

Sam was holding the bowl of the pipe over the lamp to heat it. He nodded an acknowledgment.

"Forgive me, *baba*, but obviously this was not the case. I too saw the woman who was walking with the constable and they were not at all like. This first one was tall as any man. Would it not have been better to tell the truth?"

His father repeated his ritual of drawing in the smoke, then he said, "Why should I give them something they do not want? If I had said no, it is not she, that is not the one I saw, they would have continued to question me, implying I am a stupid foreigner who does not know what he is talking about. It was much simpler to agree."

"Do you think then that the young constable had two concubines?"

Sam smiled slyly. "No, I do not think so. This one we saw today is a liar."

"How do you know that, with respect, my father?"

"Chinese intuition."

Foon smiled also. "Of course. But why do you think she was prepared to risk damnation by lying with God's book in her hand?"

"I do not have an answer. Frankly, I do not wish to know. It is no concern of ours. Let them kill each other for all I care. As far as they are concerned, we are ignorant savages with squirrel brains. Let them continue to believe so."

He passed over the pipe to Foon. "Here, my son, there is one draw left at least."

Foon hesitated. His missionary upbringing was at odds with his culture. His father was being generous and it was disrespectful to refuse, but he knew how the pastor had disapproved of opium smoking. He took the pipe while Sam watched him.

"All that nonsense about breaking a saucer. *My soul will be cracked like this vessel if I lie.* They treat us like foolish children."

Foon drew in a small amount of the smoke, retained it briefly, and returned the pipe to his father. Lee smoked in silence for about twenty minutes more, then he turned onto his side and stretched out his legs. Foon picked up the pipe, scraped out the bowl, and returned it to the stand. The *yangqiang* he placed back in the leather sack. Sam seemed to have drifted off into sleep and he looked peaceful. Sometimes the opium brought with it fearful visions that caused him to cry out in fear, but tonight the sensations were obviously pleasurable. Foon bent over him and gently lifted up the thick queue, untied the black silk cord that was braided into it, and loosened the hair completely. He drew his fingers like a comb from the base of Sam's skull, up to the crown, and out to the ends of the hair. His father sighed with sleepy pleasure.

"With respect to Chinese intuition, *baba*, would there be another reason you are so certain the young woman was lying?"

Sam grunted, his words were almost unintelligible with sleep. "I have seen her before. At her place of employment, a brothel on King Street."

Foon's soothing actions stopped.

Sam rolled onto his back and looked at his son. "Every man has needs of the flesh, *laoerh*. Except you, who have the mind and will of a monk. I have discovered a place where a man can find comfort. They accept a Chinaman's money with quite a good grace." He chuckled. "The whores were intrigued by me. They said they had never seen a Chinese before and they insisted I display my member to the entire band of them. I think they were a little disappointed it was not so very different from the *fangui*. The girl, Mary Ann, was one of the whores. Today I gave her thanks."

He rolled back to his side and waved at Foon to continue his

135

stroking. "Your mother would understand. I am a man." Within a few minutes he had fallen asleep. Foon rebraided his hair and tied the ribbon.

He covered Sam with another padded quilt and went to extinguish the lamps. Then quietly, he slipped in beside him. The opium had made him sleepy too, but he did not fall into dreams immediately. His thoughts were agitating to him. Lee was wrong about his son. Foon dreamed constantly of mating with a young woman and despaired of the possibility. The missionary teaching had gone deep into his soul and he was determined to remain chaste until he could find a wife and marry in the eyes of God. As this meant returning to China, he knew it would be a long time before they had enough money. He could feel a little bubble of resentment floating to the surface of his mind. His father had committed adultery and dishonoured his mother. That was sinful.

CHAPTER TWENTY

———◆———

AFTER NATHANIEL HAD gone to bed, Frank had come over to the stable, taken out a bottle of gin that he kept hidden in a box under his bed, and slowly and steadily drank himself into unconsciousness. He had paid the price today.

"What time's the green arse coming?" he called over to his brother-in-law, who was in the adjoining stall working on the mare they intended to sell.

"I told you, he said he'd be here by four."

Frank took the jar of ginger, a tin of aniseed, and a bottle of turpentine from the shelf in the tack room. He carried them over to the bench where he'd already placed the measuring cup and an enamel bowl. Without thinking, he brushed his hand across his mouth and winced as he touched his lip. But he shrugged it off. He'd had worse.

He could remember the first whipping but not the reason for it and not the actual pain, although it had hurt him so badly he lost his breath. He must have been four years old although that was hazy too. He may have been younger.

Jarius had brought him into the stable. It was winter time, he knew, because he had been outside in the yard making snowballs with Augusta. Had he thrown one at Jarius? Was that his misdemeanour? He still puzzled over it, as if knowing the transgression would make sense of the punishment. There had been many more after that, many of them severe, but it was the first one that had left the deepest scars, both physical and emotional. He had two long white marks on his right buttock where the skin had broken down.

Jarius, his stepbrother, was nineteen years his elder and Frank had always been afraid of him—his seriousness, his dark hair and skin, unlike his fairness and Augusta's, who followed after their father in looks. He didn't understand why Jarius was so different but his mother finally answered his questions.

"Your father was married before to a widow lady. She already had a son of her own—Jarius. Not too long after the marriage, the poor woman died, but Jarius was raised like his own by your father. He was thirteen years of age when I married Mr Eakin. A sombre boy even then."

Frank remembered she had sighed when she said that.

The second Mrs Eakin always spoke in a soft, anxious voice, as if she were perpetually afraid of being overheard. Her name was Harmony and she said many times how she loved to think that she lived up to her name. Much later, with some bitterness, Frank realised what this really meant: she strove to say nothing that would offend and avoided conflict at all costs. She never interceded when Jarius took him over to the stable and even when she was forced to put ointment on his bleeding buttocks, she only whispered to him to try to be a good boy in future and not cause trouble.

Nathaniel also beat him, but not as frequently and never in such a sustained way. He said Jarius was his lieutenant and ignored any protests. Not that Frank tried for very long. He soon learned that to cry to his father was to make matters worse with Jarius when they were alone. He also learned to read his stepbrother's mood the way a dog will immediately assess a potential threat. Woe betide Frank if Jarius was in a temper about something else. He would always find some excuse to vent that anger on the boy. The hardest thing was that Frank never knew how to react. Sometimes if he screamed, Jarius would stop sooner. At other times, the crying only seemed to insense him more. Similarly, if Frank bit his lip and choked back his pain, Jarius sometimes gave up in disgust; at others times, he went on until Frank begged for mercy.

He measured out a dram of ginger and sifted out two drams of the aniseed into the bowl. He added the turpentine to the mixture and stirred it with his fingers until it formed a ball.

When he was twelve years of age, the punishments stopped. One afternoon, Jarius came home earlier than usual. It was a stiflingly hot summer day and Frank was in the stable. He was so uncomfortable with the heat he had stripped off his clothes and was standing naked, pouring a bucket of water over himself. He suddenly became aware that Jarius had come in and was watching him.

"My little brother is growing up, I see," he said, but his voice was so full of repulsion that Frank there and then began to think of himself as ugly; he knew it had to do with the hair that had grown in his crotch and the changes in his private parts.

Frank hadn't been paying much attention to what he was doing but suddenly the odour of the turpentine made him retch, his stomach was already so queasy from last night's binge. Then he realised he'd forgotten the other part of the recipe. Irritated, he went back to the shelf.

"Where is the frigging stuff?" he said out loud.

"What frigging stuff?" Peter Curran was in one of the stalls, working on the horse.

"The antimony. It's supposed to be here on the shelf."

"Don't blame me, I wouldn't touch it."

"Damnation."

They were interrupted by his nephew's voice.

"Uncle Frank? Shall I feed Brownie?"

Lewis was standing in the doorway. He could have been Frank's own child in appearance, with the same light brown hair and round face, but this similarity didn't endear him to his uncle. He was too quiet, inclined to be sly, and although he would never have admitted it, Frank saw himself mirrored in that cautious, wary expression with which Lewis regarded the world.

"Of course feed him. He was purged this morning. Have you been messing with the medicines?"

"No, Uncle Frank."

"This will have to do then. Put it in the mash." He held out the ball of aniseed, dropping the sticky mass into the boy's palm. "Stir it in well."

He followed the youngster to the stall and watched while he ladled mash from a pail into the horse's pan. Brownie stepped forward and Lewis leaped away, almost knocking over the pail.

Frank yelled at him and gave him a sharp rap on the side of the head.

"What's the matter with you?"

"I'm sorry, uncle. I thought he was going to bite me."

"What a yellow-bellied little runt you are. He wanted his mash, not you. Get out of here. Go see if your father's finished."

Lewis scuttled away. Frank waited until he was sure the roan had swallowed the medicine, then followed him. Curran was in the process of blacking the mare's hooves. Earlier he had filed away the ridges in her front hooves to hide the fact she had foundered, and the blacking was to cover the signs.

"Done? Let's bring her out then. Our friend should be here soon."

Curran took the mare's halter and lead her out of the stall.

Frank beckoned to Lewis. "Now Mister Titty Suck, I want you to show the horse when the customer comes. Do you think you can do that without a big cock up?"

"Yes, Uncle."

"This man is a stupid sod, fancies himself a bit of a buck but he's a green arse. Just the kind we like. He says he wants a lively carriage horse for his new bride. Course he doesn't want to pay a top price but never mind. We have the perfect mare for him. Good thing it's raining, you'll have to walk her in here. Doesn't matter if you're nervous, that'll look good, like she's spirited."

"Oh, I'm not scared of Duchess. She's quiet."

"Any more quiet and she'd be dead," put in Curran. "I'm surprised

140

you haven't sent her to Lamb's factory. She'll make better glue than she will a 'lively carriage horse.'"

Frank laughed. "Well we have the remedy for that, don't we? Hold on to her, Lewis, don't let her run off."

The boy stood holding the lead rein. The mare showed signs of a hard life and was slightly swaybacked. Her head drooped almost to the ground.

Frank came back with a piece of clean linen and the tin of powdered ginger. He took off the lid, twisted the cloth into a tight spindle, and dipped it into the ginger. Then, clicking his tongue softly, he approached the mare, lifted her tail, and quickly pushed the twist of cloth into her anus. She jumped but almost immediately the ginger began to sting. She pawed at the ground.

"Walk her, Lew."

The boy tugged on the halter and she needed no urging, stepping forward in a prance, her tail held high as she tried to get away from the irritation in her backside.

Frank whistled in delight. "She's moving like a filly. We'll give her another little boost just before he gets here. He'll be totally satisfied. And he'll think he's bilking me into the bargain. Course in two days, she'll be near death again but that won't be my fault, will it?"

"What if he brings her back, Uncle?"

"He won't. Our agreement will be final sale. Besides, he's going away on his wedding trip. When he gets back, he can blame his own groom for overriding the horse. He's not going to admit I duped him. All right, let her walk it off a bit, then put her back in the stall."

He went over to the lantern that was hanging on a hook by the door and turned down the wick. "We can see quite well enough thank you."

Curran waited until Lewis had stabled the mare again, then he turned to Frank.

"By the way, Jarius said that Pa has made up his mind."

Eakin stared at him. "Why didn't you say so?"

"You was busy."

"Well, what's he going to do?"

Curran grinned. "I guess you persuaded him. She'll get the opera-tion."

CHAPTER TWENTY-ONE

As SOON AS he opened the front door, Murdoch could hear Arthur coughing and immediately, almost subconsciously, he assessed the sound. No worse, maybe slightly better than usual. He was hanging up his coat and hat when the kitchen door opened and Enid Jones came out.

"Mr Murdoch, I was hoping you wouldn't be too late. Your supper is almost ready."

He couldn't resist imitating her lilt.

"Is it now?"

She smiled. "Is it mocking me you are?"

"Not at all. I could listen to you all day long."

"I'd say that was a dreadful waste of time then." But her tone belied the words.

However, they were both suddenly awkward, standing close in the narrow hall.

"Mrs Kitchen has gone to a prayer vigil at the church," Enid said. "I promised I would look after you in her place."

"That's kind of you, Mrs Jones, but really I am quite capable of taking a plate out of the oven. I have done it many times before."

"Whether you are capable or not isn't the point, is it now? We both thought you could do with some tending to on a raw night like this. Especially with you having had your tooth pulled."

She scrutinised him. "Your face is still swollen. Is it hurting?"

"Very much," he said solemnly.

She stepped back. "Go get you a warm by the fire, then. I will bring in your tea."

He went into the little front parlour. The fire was crackling and there was an extra lamp on the table. The heat and light seemed dazzling after the dismal weather outside.

"Hello, Alwyn."

Enid's son was sitting at the table with some sort of games board in front of him. As Murdoch entered, the boy glanced up but he didn't look too pleased to see him.

"Good evening to you, sir."

Murdoch looked over his shoulder. "What's that you've got?"

"It's a game my mamma gave me."

"Looks interesting. *The Prince's Quest*. What do you have to do?"

Alwyn became a little more animated. "The princess is asleep and she's in danger. There are four princes who want to save her. The first one to get to the bower wins her." His face was earnest. "The path is full of dangers."

"Ah, yes, I've known it to be."

There was a silence while the boy considered his options. Finally, he said.

"Will you play then?"

"I would like to." He pulled out the chair next to the boy.

"We must first choose our pieces," said Alwyn.

He showed him cutout shapes of princes on little wooden stands. They wore flat hats, short embroidered jerkins, and dark stockings. Each had a sleeveless cloak, also short, which were of different colours.

"I'll take the purple one."

Alwyn looked disappointed. "That was the one I wanted."

Murdoch hesitated, trying to decide whether it would be better

144

for character development for the boy to take his lumps or whether he could curry a bit of favour. He elected to placate.

"Green for me then. He's a handsome fellow."

"No, it's all right. My da said it wasn't manly to complain if things didn't go your way."

"Did he now? He was right I'd say. Purple it is."

Alwyn studied the princes. "I'll take blue, no—this one, the red." He set the two chosen figures on the board, each one facing a different path. "Throw the die and move according to the number."

"Where's the princess?"

The boy pointed to a woman with extraordinarily long hair who was reclining languidly on a couch. Her eyes were closed so he assumed she was sleeping. Or waiting and full of anticipation.

Vigourously, he shook the die in his cupped hands and tossed it down with a flourish. One.

"Hm, the story of my life."

Alwyn threw a five and gleefully counted off the spaces along the path toward the prize.

"I'm beating you already."

Murdoch's next throw landed him on a square marked Shoes of Swiftness, and he was able to shoot ahead, thereby avoiding a stint of work in the dwarf's cave. Alwyn threw a four and landed in the *Garden of Sleep*.

"Oh, dear, miss three turns," said Murdoch.

"No, that's not fair," the boy wailed.

"It's the luck of the game, titch. Remember what your father said."

He was about to throw again when Enid entered. She was carrying a big tray.

He got up quickly to help her. Alwyn said something to her in Welsh, gesturing angrily at Murdoch. She answered in a soothing voice, shaking her head.

"I didn't," said Murdoch.

"Didn't what?" she said, startled.

"Cheat."

145

"You know Welsh?"

"No, but I know small boys. He landed fair and square in the *Garden of Sleep*. He has to miss three throws."

"Good gracious, that is hard."

"Rules are rules."

He wanted to add, *that is what your husband taught him*, but was reluctant to introduce any memory of her former love.

She turned to her son.

"Mr Murdoch is going to have his supper. You can finish your game afterwards."

Alwyn answered in Welsh, and picking up the die, he went back to the board. He was going to play both princes. Then he was sure to win the princess. Murdoch thought it was churlish to protest. He moved over to the place set for him.

Enid lifted the lid off the tureen.

"I made a rabbit soup," she said. "It's a popular dish at home."

The food smelled so fragrant, Murdoch's mouth watered and he was afraid he'd actually be drooling if he didn't eat soon. She ladled some soup into a bowl, handed it to him, and waited for him to take his first taste. He did so, nearly scalding himself.

"Utterly delicious," he managed to mutter.

"It's hot, be careful now."

He tore off a piece of bread from the hunk on his plate and stuffed that into his mouth to ease the pain. She watched him with gratification as he made more appreciative noises.

"I thought you'd need something soft."

Alwyn looked up. "I've got a loose tooth." He opened his mouth and waggled one of his front teeth.

"Good for you," murmured Murdoch, trying to make sure the soup wasn't getting into the gaping crater he could feel in his gum.

"I'll bring in the potatoes. I mashed them up with the rest of the rabbit," said Enid.

She went back to the kitchen, leaving Murdoch to blow air into his burning mouth.

Alwyn returned to his game, talking quietly to himself as he

146

moved his pieces. Murdoch saw him land in the Haunted Glen. He was supposed to throw a three to get out but he ignored that and moved on. Murdoch was about to call out, "Hey, you're cheating," but thought better of it. The lad needed a firm hand he decided. He studied him for a moment. He had his mother's dark eyes but he was sharper of feature and his hair had a curl to it. I wonder what it's like to see your own reflection in a child's face, thought Murdoch. Or the face of the woman you have loved? He stopped eating.

Enid came back into the room and he hastily dipped his spoon back into the soup.

"Is it all right then?"

"Wonderful."

She put the platter on the table.

"Thank you, Mrs Jones. This is very kind of you."

"Not at all. I wanted to help Mrs Kitchen."

On impulse, he caught hold of her hand, grasping it awkwardly in a semi-handshake. Then, as if his body were acting entirely on its own accord, he brought her fingers to his lips, kissing them lightly. Her skin smelled faintly of onions. She didn't pull away but he didn't know what to do next. He wanted desperately to be eloquent but found himself tongue-tied. He looked up at her. This time she did move.

"I must go fetch the potatoes."

"You brought them in already."

"So I did." She became even more flustered and reached for the soup tureen. "I'll take this out of your way and let you finish your meal in peace."

"This is peace. I'd be honoured if you would keep me company."

She hesitated briefly then sat down at the opposite end of the table.

"Very well."

He bought some time by spooning up more soup, which had cooled somewhat.

"Utterly delicious."

She nodded. Alwyn gave him a reprieve by getting up and going over to his mother.

"I won, Mama. I rescued the princess."

147

Fondly, she put her arms around him and kissed his forehead. "Well done, little one."

Murdoch was about to say that it was easy to win if you were moving both pieces but he bit his tongue. Feeling rivalrous, was he?

"If you go into the kitchen you will find a tray of lemon dumplings," she said to the boy. "You can have one for yourself. But eat it there, look you."

Alwyn took off.

"Lemon dumplings? This is a meal fit for a king."

There was another uncomfortable silence while he tackled the platter of rabbit meat and potatoes.

"Mr Murdoch, there is something I have been wanting to ask you."

"Yes?" he was hopeful.

"In church last week, the minister was preaching about the afterlife. He pointed out that if my son were to die, God defend us, the Roman Catholic church teaches that he would not go to heaven as he is not of the Catholic faith. He would be deprived of the sight of God for all eternity through no fault of his own. Can you explain to me how a person who believes in the Divine love can accept such a cruel doctrine?"

Murdoch almost groaned out loud. A theological discussion was not his notion of love talk. But she was regarding him earnestly, wanting an answer.

"As far as I am concerned, doctrine is man-made. We hope that it reflects God's will on earth but we can never know that for sure."

She seemed dissatisfied with his answer. "Yes, but . . ."

Fortunately, he was rescued by Mrs Kitchen coming into the parlour. Her nose and cheeks were reddened from the chill air outside.

"Mr Murdoch, I am so glad Mrs Jones has been taking good care of you. I won't even apologise for my absence, since I can see what a splendid meal she has prepared."

Murdoch stood up to greet her. "Splendid and plentiful."

"Are you ready for your tea?"

"I am indeed."

"The kettle is at the boil," said Enid.

148

"Good, let me just see how Arthur is doing and I'll make us all a pot. You will join us won't you, Mrs Jones?"

"Thank you but perhaps another night. I have to start getting Alwyn ready for bed."

She headed for the door.

"Perhaps I can answer your question at a later time," said Murdoch.

She nodded. "It is a discussion I am looking forward to."

Mrs Kitchen waited until she left. "She worked all day on that soup, Mr Murdoch. I would be careful if I were you."

"What do you mean, Mrs K.? It tasted quite all right to me."

She tapped his hand. "Don't pretend. You know perfectly well what I am talking about. She fancies you."

Murdoch clasped both her hands in his. "Oh, dear Mrs K., is that so terribly bad?"

"It's not so much it's bad, as that it's out of the question. Or have you forgotten she's a Baptist?"

He sighed and let her go. "No. You both seem intent on reminding me. She wanted to know how I explained limbo."

"Did she indeed? That means she's serious. She's trying to see how big the chasm is. But never you mind, some people have made successful mixed marriages. She would have to convert, of course."

He grinned. "Mrs K. here we are talking about the lady as if she and I were courting. I'm not even at the starting line."

She smiled, knowingly. "I would say you're approaching it fast."

CHAPTER TWENTY-TWO

MURDOCH PUT HIS report back in the file folder and returned it to the cabinet. Two local ministers from Jarvis Street Baptist Church had issued a complaint. An English travelling troupe of dancers had distributed bills on the street. The photographs of the young women in the troupe were completely indecent, according to the ministers. They requested the police charge them. Murdoch thought the women, although showing a length of lower leg, were suitably clothed for dancers, assuming they had to pirouette and leap about. The ministers were indignant at his defence, and it became apparent that their complaint was not only concerning the clothing, but the very existence of the troupe. He had taken their deputation, accepted the petition with a long list of signatures, and promised to investigate further.

He found it hard to muster much enthusiasm for the case. He'd been sitting for at least a half an hour with Elizabeth's photograph in front of him. He knew it was irrational of him but he was feeling guilty at the intensity of his feelings for Mrs Jones. It was all very well for Father Fair to say she was dead and in God's love and that she would be happy for him. In life, Liza had been prone to possessiveness, something he'd rather liked. It had made him feel wanted. He picked up the framed picture. *Liza, my dearest, you know that you* had my heart and if you had lived, no one else would ever have warranted a glance from me. But you left me and I cannot help myself. This is a woman you would have liked, perhaps befriended. I know she is not of our faith but oh, Liza, I do have to admit, I would dearly like to have her. The blurry image of his dead fiancée showed no expression except, he was sure, some reproach.

He and Liza were of the same faith, of course, but he couldn't remember that they had discussed it much. Religion was part of the fabric of their lives, unquestioned for the most part, the rituals so familiar. They went to mass regularly and therefore to confession. They'd laughed about that together, well aware that they were committing venial sins all the time with their mutual impure thoughts. Liza insisted her penances were more severe than his but he didn't know if that was because she owned up to worse things or because she was a woman.

He touched the photograph. It was not a very good picture. Her large-brimmed hat was shading her face too much and she'd moved just as he clicked the shutter. He returned the photograph to the drawer, feeling even more guilty that he was putting her away in that fashion.

Impatiently, he brushed off a couple of lethargic flies that were crawling over the surface of his blotter. Because of the adjoining stables, the fly population never completely disappeared. The flies just got slower, storing up energy for the spring onslaught.

He leaned back in his chair. Usually he took his surroundings for granted but today he scrutinised them with critical eyes, and his spirits sank even lower as he took in the pervading shabbiness. His desk was old, wobbly, and in need of revarnishing. He hadn't added to its appearance by constantly scratching the surface with his per-nib when he was trying to get his thoughts straightened out. There was room for only one other chair, a decidedly shabby armchair from heaven-knows-what previous life. Part of the seat was torn and some of the horse hair was coming out. He had requested a replacement, but so far nothing had happened. According to Inspector Brackenreid, there was no money to spend, although Murdoch noticed his

151

office was well furnished. Only last month, a splendid crimson velvet rug had arrived from the T. Eaton Company. So what if the roof still leaked over the stables and the sashes on the windows were so shrunken the snow drifted through in the winter? If Brackenreid met with members of the public they served, which was rare, he did so in impressive surroundings. The sweet fruits of power.

That taste was forever out of his reach, thought Murdoch, a little dismayed at his own bitterness. As a Roman Catholic, his chances of promotion were virtually nonexistent. He was considered lucky to have even been admitted into the recently formed detective department. The men who ran the police force were Protestant. Less acknowledged, but a significant factor was that they were also Free Masons and belonged to one of the numerous orders that dominated the commercial and social life of the city.

He swiveled around to face the wall behind him where there were two framed portraits hanging. One was of the chief constable, Lieutenant-Colonel Henry Grasett, the other of Her Majesty, Queen Victoria. When Murdoch had first heard a rumour that the queen insisted her dead husband's clothes, shaving water, and razor be put out every morning, he'd thought such a show of grief excessive. Since Liza had died, however, he understood completely the need to cling to any vestige of that previous life, to hold on to the illusion that death was not final.

He picked up his pen and started to run the nib along a groove in the top of the desk. Some previous owner had carved the initials I. F., and with Murdoch's help, the letters were now dark blue scars.

There was a tap outside his cubicle. Through the reed curtain he could see the large frame of Constable Crabtree.

"The inspector would like to see you at once, Mr Murdoch. In his office."

"What for now?"

Crabtree poked his head through the reed strips. "A young lady came in a short while back asking for Wicken. Said she was his friend and she hadn't seen him lately. Wondered if he was ill."

Murdoch stared at Crabtree in dismay. "That's not good, is it!"

"Sergeant Seymour directed her right upstairs to see Inspector Brackenreid but he's sent for you."

Murdoch stood up, followed the constable out to the front hall, and hurried up the stairs to the second floor where the inspector had his office. He was admitted at once.

A young woman was standing by the window, looking down to the street below. She was tall, her height accentuated by the long navy blue waterproof she was wearing. Her red felt hat with its big satin bow and curled white quill was jaunty and fashionable.

Brackenreid was behind his desk. With his heavy moustache and smart uniform with the velvet frogs down the front, he was a distinguished-looking man, as long as you didn't come close enough to see the red veins in his cheeks or the stains down his jacket. Brackenreid was a toper, something he deluded himself, nobody knew. He gave Murdoch an unusually warm greeting as he entered.

"Ah, Murdoch, glad you were available. This is Miss Isobel Brewster. She is enquiring about Constable Wicken. Miss Brewster, I'd like to present Detective Murdoch. He has, er, been, um, been involved in the case from the beginning."

The woman didn't stir; it was not clear if she had even heard what he'd said.

"I had to tell Miss Brewster what has happened," he continued. "That Constable Wicken had er, passed away. She didn't know, so she is understandably distressed at the moment. She and Wicken were friends. She was wondering why she hadn't seen him recently and came here to find out."

"I see," said Murdoch.

The woman swung around and glared at him. "What does that mean, *I see?*"

Her fierceness was startling.

"I beg your pardon, ma'am, I meant nothing by it."

He stopped, not sure how much Brackenreid had told her. The inspector gave a slight shake of his head. He pulled a watch out of his pocket. "I do apologise, Miss Brewster, but I have an appointment I must keep. Can't be put off. Why don't you just stay here a little while and talk to Detective Murdoch. I'll have some tea sent up, and when you're ready, we'll have somebody accompany you home. Will that be all right?"

She nodded and the inspector left, fast as all cowards are to leave the place of pain.

"Won't you please come and sit down," said Murdoch.

"I prefer to stand." She turned from the window but didn't come closer. She looked to be no more than twenty or so, not a beauty by any means. Her features were sharp, the nose too long, the mouth thin. She was regarding him with frightened eyes.

"He says that Oliver Wicken has died. But how? What happened? He was quite well when I saw him last."

"When was that, ma'am?"

"Monday evening."

"His body was discovered early on Tuesday morning. I'm afraid he had been shot."

She gave a quick intake of breath. "What are you saying? Shot how?"

"It appears it was by his own hand. There was an inquest and the jury returned a verdict of suicide."

She stared at him in disbelief for a moment then laughed derisively, as if he had said something incredibly stupid. "That is out of the question. When I saw him he was in perfectly good spirits. You are mistaken." With perceptible agitation now, she stepped closer. "Perhaps you are speaking of someone else. I am enquiring about Constable Oliver Wicken. He is blond-haired. He has a moustache and side-whiskers." She gestured at her own cheek.

"I'm sorry, Miss Brewster, but there is no mistake. I myself found his body. There is no doubt it was Oliver Wicken. I knew him."

She sat down abruptly on the edge of the chair, as if she could no longer trust herself to remain standing. Her manner became belligerent as shock hid itself in anger. "On what did the jury base their verdict of suicide?"

"Partly on the evidence of the post mortem examination. He had been shot in the right temple and the coroner felt this was consistent

154

with a self-inflicted wound." He almost demonstrated but stopped just in time.

"And that is all the so-called evidence?"

"No. There was a note found on his person that seemed to indicate he was in an extremely despondent frame of mind."

"What did it say?"

"The exact words were. 'Life is unbearable without your love. Forgive me.'"

He paused while she absorbed this.

"Can I see the letter?"

"It is considered part of his effects and they have been returned to his mother."

"There was nothing else? No person addressed? No signature?"

"No, that was all."

She jumped to her feet again and strode back to the window. She was virtually shouting. "I don't believe it, do you hear? Ollie had no reason to feel that way."

Sobs were threatening to break through but they were suppressed almost immediately. She came back to the chair and sat down, her back as stiff as if she were in a deportment class.

"I should tell you, Mr Murdoch, that Oliver was my . . . that is, what I mean to say is, we were betrothed. We have been for almost a year."

She caught the surprise in his face and misinterpreted it. "It was a secret engagement. Ollie was concerned about his mother. He supports her solely and he was afraid she would not approve, that she would worry about him marrying." Suddenly, she leaned over and caught Murdoch by the sleeve. "About the letter you found. . . . Are you certain it was written by Oliver?"

"It was not handwritten; it was printed. He had used a piece of paper from his notebook."

Her voice dropped. "I was always on at him about how bad his hand was. He did print sometimes."

Murdoch's heart went out to her. She had come dressed in her best, worried but never suspecting the dreadful news she would

155

receive. And that was not all of it. Suddenly, her eyes met his and he was taken off guard by the shrewdness of her next question.

"I have the feeling you are not telling me everything. Please believe me, it would help me to know all that happened. I am not going to have hysterics, I assure you. Was there something else that was said at the inquest?"

Murdoch wished he could soften the blow but he knew he couldn't. "Yes, there was. A young woman came forward who said she was Wicken's fiancée. She broke off the engagement that night, Monday, which seemed the likely cause for him to have become so despondent."

Isobel Brewster turned putty white. She could hardly form her words.

"That is impossible."

"The woman swore under oath. She said they had been engaged for the past two months."

"What was this woman's name?"

"Miss Mary Ann Trowbridge."

"I've never heard of her. I . . ."

She groaned and her lips and chin began to shake. She held her fingers to her mouth as if she could barely risk hearing her own voice out loud. Whatever she was about to say, he didn't hear because at that moment, her eyelids started to flutter and she leaned back abruptly, her eyes rolling back in her head. He jumped up and caught her just as she was about to slide off the chair.

"Put your head down on your knees."

She did as she was told and remained like that for a few moments longer, then slowly sat up. Murdoch took her right hand in his, pushed down the cuff of her glove, and rubbed the back of her wrist vigourously. The same with the left. She hardly allowed him to minister to her before she pulled away her hands.

"I'm quite all right now."

"I thought you were going to faint."

"I despise women who faint." She licked her lips. "Can I have a glass of water, please?"

"Just a minute."

He went back around to the other side of the desk. Just as he'd hoped, there was a flask in the top drawer. He shook it to make sure it wasn't yet empty and brought it over to her.

"Sip some of this."

He unscrewed the top and handed her the flask. She took a big sip of the brandy, coughing as it burned her throat.

"Good thing I'm not temperance," she said with a small smile. Her colour was better now, and satisfied she wasn't going to faint completely, he returned to his own chair. She took another drink.

"I do apologise."

"There is no need."

"What you have said is a great shock to me. It is quite unbelievable."

"The young woman has a letter from her aunt testifying to the truth of her statement and we have a witness who swore under oath that he saw the constable with Miss Trowbridge the night he died."

"What witness?"

"His name is Samuel Lee. He runs a laundry on Parliament Street. He says that Constable Wicken checked his establishment that night and he saw this young woman with him."

"When?"

"About a quarter past eleven."

"Impossible. I tell you that is utterly impossible. Oh, Mr Murdoch, please believe me. It was me he saw. I was with Oliver then. I would often meet him on his beat. We needed to catch any time together that we could. I know it was against the rules but he didn't neglect his duty in any way; he was very responsible. On Monday night, I met him on the corner as he was coming up Parliament Street and I walked with him as far as Gerrard."

"And this was at that time?"

"Yes. It was always the same time."

"Were you with him when he went into the Chinese laundry?"

"Yes. He went inside for a few minutes while I waited on the sidewalk."

"The proprietor did identify Miss Trowbridge as the woman accompanying Wicken."

"He was mistaken."

She read Murdoch's doubt. "Please believe me. I swear I am telling the truth. I went as far as the empty house on the corner. We often met there. It gave us some privacy."

"Did you go inside?"

"No. Frankly, we would have but the doors were locked. We stood in the front doorway."

"For how long?"

"About a half an hour . . ." she moaned. "We had an argument."

"What was it about?"

"I assure you, Mr Murdoch, it was not so serious. Just a tiff, a lover's tiff, the way any couple will argue."

He waited while she sorted out in her mind the implications of what she was saying. That this was the last exchange she had had with her sweetheart.

"We have been engaged for almost a year now," she continued. "I was eager to announce it and have the bans read but we could not agree. Oliver was still procrastinating. He was always afraid to upset his mother. She depends upon him entirely."

"Did you resolve the matter?"

"No. I . . . er, I have a hot temper. I told him he must make up his mind or I would break off the engagement. I walked away."

She frowned. "Wait. That is not the truth, Mr Murdoch, and it is the pure truth that we are after, is it not? I did not *walk* away, I ran. I was furious with him."

"Where was he when you left?"

"Still in the doorway."

"Miss Brewster, sometimes in a moment of imbalance we do foolish things. In your mind is it possible that Oliver was so distressed by your quarrel he took his own life?"

"He was not that kind of weakling, Mr Murdoch." She almost spat out the words. "You see, I know what I'm talking about . . . My own father hung himself when I was a child. As a matter of fact, I was the one who found him. He was in the living room when I came home from school. He had lost his job and he never stopped moaning about it. He would sit and brood all day long, talking endlessly about how terribly he'd been treated. Suicides make sure they give you plenty of notice so you can feel sorry for them. Ollie might have been distressed when I left but he was no coward. He would never desert me or his mother and sister; he cared for us too much. I can only think there must have been a dreadful accident."

Murdoch spoke to her gently. "Miss Brewster, Wicken was inside that house when I found him."

"Where?"

"In the rear kitchen."

"But the house was locked. He tried the door."

"He had a key in his pocket."

Again he waited while she absorbed this information.

"Mr Murdoch, I know what you're thinking; I can read it in your face. But Oliver was not deceiving me. We shared everything. He talked a lot about the station, the inspector, you—he liked you. Besides he had no time to be with somebody else. He has a crippled sister who requires a lot of care, and when he wasn't on duty, he was at home helping his mother. That's why I would meet him on his beat. I'd take him some supper." She plucked at the cuff on her glove. "I am certain this other woman is lying."

"Why would she do so, Miss Brewster? She came forward voluntarily."

"I don't know."

Her voice tailed off and he could see her trying desperately to sort through her memories. Was there any evidence of him being unfaithful? Small signs she might have ignored?

Isobel Brewster did not have the delicate prettiness of Mary Ann Trowbridge but there was a forthrightness to her, a promise of a passionate nature that was attractive. He believed her when she said she was engaged to Oliver Wicken. However, that didn't mean the constable hadn't been playing fast and loose.

He realised she was regarding him anxiously.

159

"I'm sorry, Miss Brewster. It is possible that Mr Lee was mistaken in his identification, but you can see that Wicken could have met with this other young lady after you left . . ."

"No!"

There was no point in continuing.

"What are you going to do now?" she asked. "You can't leave it like this surely."

"The case is officially closed."

"But you didn't like the verdict, did you? I can see it, I can see it in your eyes."

She was almost sobbing again. "Please, Mr Murdoch. Please don't leave it like this."

He hesitated, not wanting to make a promise he wouldn't be able to keep. "I must admit what you have told me changes the picture. There are some discrepancies that should be clarified. I'll see what I can do to clear them up."

Suddenly, she reached over, grasped his hand, and pressed it against her cold cheek.

"Thank you! I am quite aware that what is revealed may not be to my liking, but I would rather know the truth than not."

He hoped she wasn't deluding herself. He'd seen the truth burn like ice.

CHAPTER TWENTY-THREE

MURDOCH WALKED ISOBEL Brewster to her home, which was on Parliament Street, just below Queen Street. They did not speak at all and when they arrived, she dismissed him at the door. She said her mother and stepfather did not know of the engagement either, so there was nothing to be gained by telling them now. Murdoch could only guess at the anguish the young woman was going to go through alone. He promised to come back as soon as he had anything new to report and he left her.

Backenreid had returned from his urgent appointment and Murdoch went to tell him what had happened. The inspector was surprisingly sympathetic to Isobel's plight, muttering several "poor lassie's," but he was in no doubt that Wicken had deceived her.

"If you can get a bite on two ripe apples, why just have one?"

Murdoch murmured something noncommittal.

Brackenreid leaned back in his chair. "Do you think it's possible that one of the lassies found out what Wicken was up to and put the gun to his head? It wouldn't be too hard to write a note making it seem like a suicide. Miss Brewster could have returned, all weepy and wanting to make up for her harsh words. And lo, not only is he in the house he said they couldn't get into, he is the one weeping. It all tumbles out; you know how men like to confess these things.

She's enraged, snatches his gun from his holster and bang! She waits a few days, comes in with a good cover story."

"I suppose it's not out of the question, sir. Although it doesn't make a lot of sense that she would implicate herself unnecessarily. The case was closed. Besides, I would find that hard to believe about Miss Brewster." He remembered Isobel Brewster's grief-ravaged face and he felt bad they were even talking like this. Brackenreid hardly seemed to have heard him.

"On the other hand, Miss Trowbridge's story could have been all smoke and gammon. Maybe she saw them together. Brewster leaves, she confronts Wicken. He says yes I do have another tickler. She is enraged, seizes his gun, and so on."

Unexpectedly, Brackenreid stopped being a fool. "What you said applies just the same though, doesn't it? Why be implicated if you don't have to?"

"Yes, sir."

"However, women do the strangest things when they have their cap set on a fellow."

"Is that right, sir?"

The inspector looked at him sharply but Murdoch had kept his voice neutral.

"Regardless, there are inconsistencies. Go talk to people again. See Mrs Wicken, the Chinaman. I did wonder about his reliability by the way. The Chinese always lie. Don't understand why but they do."

He stroked at his moustache. "I hate to put it this way, but murder would be preferable, wouldn't it?"

"You mean rather than suicide, sir?"

"Quite. I don't like to think of one of my constables being so unmanly. Anyway, see what you can do."

Murdoch decided to visit Mrs Wicken first. Painful as it might be to probe this question, she had a right to know this new information about her son.

The rain had stopped and a weak sun was struggling through the cloud covering, making a patch of silver in the pervading grey sky. He was warm enough today and his abcessed tooth was now only a sore gum, but he couldn't shake the feeling of heaviness in his body. Everywhere he turned, no matter what he found, somebody was going to suffer.

When he got to the Wicken house, he paused for a moment at the gate, rehearsing in his mind what he was going to say. The place looked almost abandoned. All the curtains were drawn and no crack of lamplight showed. The branches of the tree in the front were wrapped with black ribbon, and a wreath of crepe and intertwined willow branches was hung on the door. Murdoch pushed open the gate and walked up to the door. Before he had a chance to knock, it was opened by a woman he recognised as the solicitous neighbour who was with Mrs Wicken at the inquest. She greeted him in a hushed, reverential voice.

"Good morning, sir. I'm Mrs Morrow, one of Mrs Wicken's neighbours. If you've come to call on her, you'll have to come later. She's not receiving until this afternoon. But I'll take your card if you wish."

Murdoch fished in his coat pocket and took out his card case. He handed her one of his cards.

"Please tell her I need to have a word."

Mrs Morrow frowned. "She's had a dreadful shock. I don't know if she is up to talking about anything."

"I appreciate that, Mrs Morrow, and I wouldn't trouble her if it wasn't important."

The woman shifted slightly so that she was more solidly in the doorway.

"We could all say that if we wanted to. Why, Mrs Lynch's eldest was here just yesterday and . . ."

Whatever Mrs Lynch's eldest had done, Murdoch was never to know, because at that moment Mrs Wicken herself appeared in the hall. When she saw Murdoch, she actually smiled.

"It's all right, Mrs Morrow, I would be happy to see Mr Murdoch."

The guardian stood back, allowing Murdoch barely enough room to squeeze by her into the hall.

"Mrs Morrow, will you take Mr Murdoch's hat and coat?" There was something autocratic in her manner that he thought was not conscious to her. She had been accustomed to having servants. The other woman didn't seem to mind, however, and she did as asked then went back to her post at the door, peering through the glass sidebars.

"We've moved in here," said Mrs Wicken, and she ushered him through the velvet portieres into the front room. Murdoch felt a twinge of uneasiness quickly followed by guilt at his own cowardice. He didn't want to see poor Dora. However, she was in her Bath chair close to the fire. There were two lamps lit, the wicks low so that the room was full of shadows.

"Please sit down, Mr Murdoch. It is kind of you to call."

He didn't know where to start and he procrastinated by making polite conversation. She was as well as could be expected said Mrs Wicken, but Dora had been poorly.

"She misses her brother dreadfully. You might not think it to look at her but she is quite aware of who is here. She began to be restless last evening when Oliver would usually have come in to play with her, before he went on his shift. I cannot of course explain why he is not here."

The girl made a moaning sound and turned as much as she could in Murdoch's direction, the massive head rolled too far and her neck could not control it. Mrs Wicken reached over quickly and righted her.

Murdoch could understand why young Oliver might be reluctant to tell his mother about a forthcoming marriage. It would be difficult indeed to extricate himself from the dependency of his mother and sister. He could see how distressed the child was. A man's voice, barely heard, had stirred her.

Mrs Wicken sat back in her chair and picked up the frame on which she was making lace.

"After the inquest I was hoping that the young woman who purported to be Oliver's fiancée would have spoken to me. I would have found some comfort in our mutual grief. However, she left at once without a backward glance."

She had given Murdoch his lead. "Mrs Wicken, the reason I came to talk to you today has to do with that. You said you were not aware that Oliver was betrothed."

"It was, I have to admit, a great shock to me. He was such an honest boy and he gave me no indication. I suppose he was afraid to upset me. There are very few new wives who would take on such a burden as Dora. She would have insisted they live elsewhere, I am sure."

Again he hesitated, but there was no way around it if he was going to get any information at all.

"Mrs Wicken, I was visited this morning by a young woman named Isobel Brewster. She is also claiming to be Oliver's fiancée. She says they were secretly betrothed almost a year."

"Good Lord. Am I to hear of a whole choir of fiancées?"

"I must say, she is quite credible. She says she saw him last on Monday night about eleven o'clock. They had a quarrel that she describes as trifling, and she is convinced he was not the kind of man to take his own life."

Mrs Wicken was staring at him in utter disbelief. She put down the lace. At that moment the invalid child moaned and she was distracted for the moment as she tended to her.

"I need to move her to the couch. Will you be so good as to help me, Mr Murdoch."

"Of course."

"If you will take her by the legs, I will hold her head and we can swing her over."

She wheeled the chair in closer and Murdoch followed. There was a wool rug tucked around the child's legs.

"Ready?"

He nodded and with a slight heave they moved her onto the couch. Her mother turned the large head sidewards. The girl had pale blue eyes that in a normal child would have been pretty, but the pressure of the fluid made them protrude horribly. She seemed to be watching Murdoch, although he could not be sure how much she saw. She made some more guttural sounds and her lips moved.

"She probably thinks you are her brother. She wants you to touch her," said Mrs Wicken.

"Of course, what . . . er . . . how . . . ?"

"She likes to have her hair stroked."

There was no way Murdoch could, or would have, refused. He reached out to the sparse hair, white and downy as milkweed. Gently he stroked the enormous head. The girl smiled and quite quickly her eyes closed.

"Thank you, Mr Murdoch. That was kind. She will sleep for a while now."

Mrs Wicken stood up and went back to her chair by the fire. He too resumed his seat. For a few moments, he wondered if she had actually heard what he'd said or if she was going to respond at all. She picked up her lace making and without looking at him, she said:

"It is beginning to seem as if I did not know my son at all. Not one but two fiancées. It is quite extraordinary."

"Mrs Wicken, we cannot rule out the possibility that one or even both of these young woman are not telling the truth."

She frowned. "Why would they lie? They have nothing to gain. Even if he did go without my knowledge and bequeath everything to . . . another person, with the verdict of suicide, there will be no redemption. The hope of money cannot be a motivation."

"I have spoken to Inspector Brackenreid about the whole matter and he has asked me to investigate further. To put it bluntly, to find proof."

"What can I do to help any further?"

"Isobel Brewster is the only one of the two women that I have spoken to as yet. She says that she would meet Oliver on his day off in the afternoon. Otherwise she met him on his beat. His last day off was a week ago. Did he leave the house that day?"

He could see how much she still wanted to deny it but she nodded. "Yes, he told me he was going to the lending library. He was an ambitious boy, Mr Murdoch. He thought that if he was well read, it would improve his chances for advancement in the police force."

Murdoch didn't tell her that possibilities for promotion were limited these days and depended almost entirely on attrition in the ranks above.

"I'll check if anybody saw him there. And I am going to talk to the other woman, Miss Trowbridge. Also, I was wondering if I might look in Oliver's room."

"Yes, of course, if you think it will help."

"I believe his effects were returned to you. May I see them? I particularly would like to borrow the letter."

"I burned it. His uniform belongs to the station. It was stained so I doubt it would be reused. There was nothing else of a personal kind."

She indicated a second door. "His room adjoined this one. It is not locked. When you've done, would you mind leaving by way of the hall. I don't want Dora to wake just yet; she hasn't been sleeping well. As you see, she needs care at all hours. I don't know if I will be able to manage without Oliver's support. It is quite likely that I will have to place her in the home for incurables . . . cannot think how appalling that would be for her. You perhaps think she is hardly human but it is not the case. She is very attached to her family."

Murdoch could think of nothing to say. Mrs Wicken turned back to her task.

HE STOOD IN the middle of the room, pivoting slowly, trying to get some sense of the young man who had so recently left it. Presumably for reasons of economy, the Wickens lived on the first floor of the house and rented out the second floor. This meant that Oliver occupied what would normally have been the dining room. There were connecting doors to the front room and the kitchen at the rear, both screened with tasseled chenille portieres of a rich floral pattern. The wallpaper was embossed gilt in crimson and green designs and the ceiling paper was a buff and blue glimmer. The room wasn't large and so much decoration made it seem suffocatingly small. The furnishings also would have done better in a more grand space. There was a massive wardrobe and matching bureau, both of dark mahogany. A lace-covered dining table was shoved tight against the far wall. The single concession to the actual use of the room was a mantel bed, which was alongside the window. It was neatly closed up. Wicken was tidy or had been kept so by his mother, for there was little of the debris of daily living scattered about.

What am I looking for? A diary? Love letters? Any indication into what was truly happening in the constable's life. There was no desk, but between the wardrobe and the door to the hall was a glass-fronted bookcase. Murdoch walked over to it and opened it up. On the top shelf was a small army of lead cavalry soldiers, well seasoned, and a small, cast-iron bank, brightly painted. A little brown dog was sitting in front of a slotted box while a harlequin clown held a hoop in front of it. Unable to resist, Murdoch fished out a five cent coin from his pocket and placed it in the dog's mouth. Then he pushed down the lever and the terrier jumped through the hoop, dropped the nickel into the slot, and sat down again.

The other shelves all held books, most of them seemingly left over from Wicken's boyhood. Several novels, a mix of Sir Walter Scott, Jules Verne, and Ralph Connor; the complete works of William Shakespeare in thirty-nine volumes, rather pristine. *Little Men*, a book Murdoch always intended to read and never had. A stained and obviously well-studied edition of *Clater's Farrier*. At random, Murdoch picked out a book entitled *For Boys*. There was an inscription inside: *To my dearest Oliver on the occasion of his fifteenth birthday.With fondest regards, Mother.*

Murdoch leafed through the book, which was written by a Mrs Shepherd. The tone was evangelical, exhorting the boy reader to have only pure thoughts in order to have a healthy body. Murdoch turned to the chapter entitled What is Sex? A doctor was quoted concerning one of his patients, a young man who complained of strange nervous symptoms. He suspected that the man's difficulties were due to some sort of sexual exhaustion. The patient replied, "Never, I never practiced masturbation and never had a nocturnal emission." However, he did admit to caressing his fiancée when he visited her, and afterwards his mind became occupied with sexual fantasies. "That is the source of your problem," said the doctor. Irritated, Murdoch closed the book and returned it to the shelf. As far as he was concerned, these sort of teachings were worth piss, the nattering of priests and women with no experience.

What else was here? Nothing remarkable. Ah, a book on etiquette that he himself had pored over years ago. He took it out with a little grin at the memory. Shy and awkward in social settings, Murdoch had tried to teach himself the rules, which unfortunately tended to make him even more self-conscious. It wasn't until he met Liza that he'd relaxed. She'd showed him what to do and laughed him out of his stiffness.

He was about to abandon the bookcase all together when he saw that there was one book tucked away at the back of the shelf. He took it out, wondering if it had been hidden or had just fallen back there. *The Heart of Midlothian* by Sir Walter Scott. The cover matched the others in the set and this too was inscribed lovingly by Mrs Wicken. A twelfth birthday this time. He was about to replace it when he saw that there was a thin piece of muslin pressed among the pages. He took it out. Inside the cloth was a lock of dark brown hair. Murdoch stowed the find between the covers of his own notebook. There was nothing else he could see that might be relevant, and the overfurnished room was beginning to close in on him. He went back to the hall.

Mrs Morrow showed him out, and as soon as he was on the street, he took a long, deep breath. He had quickly developed respect for Mrs Wicken and he could only feel compassion for her loss. However, he sensed that beneath the gracious manners there was a will of iron. He could understand why her son might have chosen to keep certain matters from her.

CHAPTER TWENTY-FOUR

—————◆—————

HE DECIDED TO go straight over to the lending library, which was situated on Toronto Street, to the rear of St James's cathedral. He wanted to see if he could find at least one definite confirmation of Isobel's story. Needing exercise, he walked briskly down Sackville to King Street where he could catch a streetcar. This far east, the stores were smaller, not as classy. There wasn't a line of carriages waiting outside any of them the way there always was nearer to the fancy stores on Church and Jarvis Streets.

A streetcar was clanking toward him and he signalled to the driver to stop. He stepped on board into an almost empty car. The oil heater at the rear had been lit and inside was warm, smelling of the straw that was scattered on the floorboards to soak up the mud. In the middle of winter, the snow made everything a brown stew, but today the straw was still relatively fresh. Murdoch took a seat near the front and the ticket collector was on him at once, rattling his box.

"Fare please, sir."

He dropped in his ticket and the collector moved on. For a moment Murdoch almost envied him. His job seemed so clear-cut and defined. His only challenge was to keep a sharp lookout for cheaters, men who only went a couple of blocks then, when he was busy, got off without paying. He was a young fellow, good-looking in a bold way. Destined to go far up the ranks of the Toronto Street Railway Corporation. He looked like the kind of man who would push for Sunday service. Murdoch thought the fuss about this issue was an utter waste of time. Some councillors were adamant that to have the streetcar running on the Sabbath was to propagate the work of the devil himself. Logically, this applied only to the streetcar workers, as all taverns and hotels and places of entertainment were closed on Sunday. Murdoch himself would like to have seen the cars running, taking people out to Sunnyside on hot summer days, for instance, or church even, if that's what they wanted. He sighed at the thought. He had long hated the dead space of Sunday when the entire city went into a kind of slumber.

"Church Street. Who wants Church Street?" the conductor bellowed out. Murdoch got to his feet, the conductor pulled on the bell rope to alert the driver, and the streetcar halted at the corner.

On the northeast side of King and Church was St James's cathedral. Murdoch had passed by many times without paying much attention, but now he actually looked at it. The slender copper spire, gleaming from the recent rain, soared into the pewter sky. The buff-coloured brick was warm and inviting even on this dull day. From the outside, it looked like a Roman Catholic church. The same cruciform design, the same dignity. If he had more time, he could go in and see what the inside was like. For one reason or another, not the least being a primitive superstition, he had never disobeyed the Catholic church's teaching about the dangers inherent in the abodes of the nonbelievers. As he walked up to the library, he chided himself. It wouldn't hurt if he started exploring.

It was so quiet in the library that entering it was not unlike stepping into a place of worship. He almost looked for the holy water font.

The newspaper reading room was to the right and he decided to start there. At the far end was a high counter, and behind it, a young woman waited patiently for requests. She was wearing a white waist with a stiff high collar and a rather masculine tie. Her fair hair was pulled up into a severe knot and she was wearing gold pince-nez. She looked highly efficient. Nonetheless, her smile was friendly as she acknowledged him.

"Today's *Globe* is the only one available at the moment, sir. Would you like that?"

Murdoch assumed the rush on the daily papers was because of the shipping disaster everybody was caught up in.

"I'm not a customer, I'm afraid. I'm a detective with the police force, number four station." He handed her his card and she took it gingerly. "I'm trying to trace the movements of one of our constables. I have reason to believe he was here on Saturday last, in the afternoon. Were you on duty at that time, Miss, er . . ." He checked the brass nameplate that was on the counter, ". . . Miss Morse?"

"Yes, I was."

"Perhaps you remember him? A tall fellow, about twenty-four years of age, with a blond moustache, fresh complexion."

"Does he have a name?" she asked, reaching for a small file box in front of her.

"Oliver Wicken."

Surprisingly, she looked a little flustered. "Yes, I do remember the name. He was here about three o'clock. He took the *Huntsville Forester*. It isn't often I get a request for that newspaper, so we had a little chat about it . . . that's why I remember him so particularly."

Murdoch felt bad. Wicken was an attractive young man and probably not above a little harmless flirting. At least Murdoch hoped it was harmless and he wasn't going to unearth yet another fiancée.

The librarian looked at him with curiousity. "May I ask why you wish to know? He isn't in any trouble surely?"

They had both been speaking in hushed tones, but even so, an elderly gentleman wearing check knickerbockers who was at one of the nearby stands hissed at them.

Murdoch sidestepped her question. "Was Mr Wicken alone?"

"Yes, he was."

Murdoch sighed. Did this mean Isobel Brewster had lied? A man came up to the counter. His clothes were shabby and he smelled

172

stale. Murdoch knew he had come in because the library was warm and dry.

"*The Globe*, if you please," he said to Miss Morse.

She took the rolled up newspaper from one of the cubbyholes behind her, where they were stashed, and handed it to him.

"There's a free space in the far aisle at the back," she said.

Murdoch liked her for not discriminating against the man, who more than likely couldn't read a word.

From where she was sitting, the librarian had a good view of the entire room and who came and went. Murdoch turned back to her.

"Did you notice if Mr Wicken spoke to anybody while he was here?"

She frowned. "I believe he did. He must have met an acquaintance. They did talk briefly as I recall."

"Could you describe the gentleman?"

"As a matter of fact it was a lady."

Several men were standing in front of the long easels where the newspapers were hung, but as far as he could see there were no women. He didn't expect anything else. Most women were still doubtful about the propriety of being in a man's domain.

He leaned forward. "Miss Morse, you have been very helpful and I'm sorry that at the moment I am not at liberty to tell you why I am making these enquiries. However, it is very important. Can you describe this woman?"

"I barely paid her any attention."

"Anything at all that you remember would be helpful. Her age, her colouring, her costume."

"Very well." She wrinkled her forehead in concentration but he knew she was pretending. She had paid a lot of attention to Wicken's acquaintance but didn't want to admit to it.

"I believe she was quite dark, with an olive complexion, and tall. Almost as tall as Mr Wicken himself. Perhaps a few years older than myself . . . I am twenty-two. She was wearing a long water-proof, a rather smart scarlet hat with a white feather and navy ribbons."

Murdoch dragged at his moustache, relieved. *Sorry Miss Brewster for doubting you.*

"Did they leave together?"

"Yes, now that you mention it, I believe they did."

"Did Mr Wicken seem distressed in any way?"

"I don't understand what you mean."

"Was their exchange amicable would you say?"

"It appeared to be," unconsciously the young woman sighed. "He looked quite happy to see her."

Murdoch could almost read her thoughts, the doubts that his questions were raising, but he still couldn't stomach telling her what had happened. Perhaps he could come back at a later time near the end of the day. He suspected Miss Morse might be harbouring more passion in her breast than her white starched shirtwaist might indicate. Fortunately, the knickerbockered man intervened as he returned his newspaper. Murdoch whispered a quick good-bye and left. It was time to get back to Isobel Brewster. At least one part of her testimony seemed to be true.

ISOBEL HERSELF ANSWERED the door and he knew she had been waiting, jumping at every knock. He asked her to get the exact clothes she was wearing on Monday night, which she did at once. He could hear a fretful child in the background and the rather sharp hushing of a woman's voice. Isobel joined him quickly. She had put on her long waterproof and a sensible black felt hat, which had only a single piece of blue ribbon for trimming. They set off up Parliament Street and he told her that the librarian had confirmed that she was with Wicken last Saturday. She made no comment but he could see how relieved she was.

At the corner of Queen Street, he stopped and took the piece of muslin from his notebook.

"Is this your hair, Miss Brewster?"

She hardly looked at it but he could see she was affected. "Yes. I gave it to Ollie at Christmastime as a memento. At his request. He snipped off a piece himself when we were walking in the park."

Unasked, she took the curl and placed it close to her own hair. It was an exact match. Another point on her side.

They soon reached Sam Lee's laundry and Murdoch asked her to stand where she had been on Monday night. She did, taking up a spot close to the curb.

Murdoch pushed open the door and entered. Almost at the same time, the door at the rear opened and Foon Lee emerged.

"Can I be of assistance, sir?"

"Detective Murdoch, again, Mr Lee. I wonder if I might speak to your father for a moment?"

The young man stared at him, not recognising him at first. Then he gave a slight bow of recognition.

"Certainly. I will fetch him simultaneously."

Murdoch was about to correct his English usage, but thought it might seem rude and he let it go. Foon went back through the rear door.

He heard a murmured conversation and Mr Lee came out, his son close at his heels.

He put his hands together and bowed in the Chinese greeting.

"Mr Murdoch?" He pronounced it "Mulldot."

Murdoch addressed Foon. "Will you tell your father that I am still concerned about the death of the constable. Some new evidence has come to light that I am investigating. I have a witness outside and I would like to see if he can identify her."

Foon translated. Lee nodded.

Murdoch went to the door. "I am going to stand here, the way the constable did that night. Will your father come close to me? If he looks out over my shoulder he will see a young woman. I would like to know if he has ever seen her before."

Lee moved forward before his son was in mid-translation. They stood in the threshold of the laundry, the door partially open behind them. Lee was considerably shorter than Murdoch but he peered around the detective's arm and looked at Isobel.

The Chinaman shook his head and spoke to his son. Murdoch thought he was agitated.

"My father says not. He has never clapped his eyes to this woman before in her life."

"Is he positive she was not the one walking with Wicken on Monday night?"

"He is certain of that. He has made a positive identification of that woman during the inquest . . . He wonder why you are asking him to retract his statement. A statement he made under oath."

Murdoch sighed. "Please tell him that's not it at all. I just wanted to make absolutely sure."

"I do not know this person," interjected Lee. "I have never seen her before."

Murdoch could not tell if he was speaking the truth or not. Both of them were watching him. He was disappointed. He had put a lot of stock in this meeting.

He thanked them and went outside.

Isobel stared at him anxiously as he approached her.

"Well?"

"I'm afraid he denied it. Says you are not the woman he saw."

"Damnation. How is that possible? Of course I was. He saw me, I know he did. I'll talk to him . . ."

Murdoch caught her by the arm. "No, Miss Brewster. It won't do any good. He's adamant."

She looked as if she were about to burst into tears.

"Then you don't believe me?"

"Of course I do. I think he was too afraid to change his sworn testimony." He let her go and she stood in front of him, her shoulders slumped.

"What are you going to do now?" she asked.

"I am going to talk to Miss Mary Ann Trowbridge."

He thought she was going to grasp his hand again, but she didn't, and they headed back to her house.

CHAPTER TWENTY-FIVE

———◦———

JARIUS GIBB WAS not at work. He had sent Janet with a message to say he was ill and would not be in for a few days. In a way, it was true. He felt as hot and restless as if he had a fever. He had been this way since dinner on Wednesday and nothing calmed him. Finally, he forced himself to sit at his desk, his ledger open in front of him. Janet had brought him a mug of strong coffee, milky and sweet, which he laced with a good dose of brandy. He made himself drink it slowly and deliberately before he took up his pen.

I want to fill up this page with obscenities and blasphemy, to pour out the vilest and crudest words I have ever heard, but it will not help me. He says, "You are not my own flesh and blood but you will get a bequest." As if I should be grateful, should rejoice in the pew over his generosity. He has betrayed his promise to my mother which he made in my presence. "I will treat him as my own son, my own flesh and blood. I will give him my name." And he has never. Not when he first married her, swelling with lust, he said it then. "The boy will be like my own." LIAR. And he said it at her most solemn deathbed. "He shall have my name." LIAR AGAIN. He could never love a son who did not reflect his own face back to him. I almost feel pity for Frank, who takes so markedly after his mother. But he will bypass me because of the accident of blood. No son of his flesh would have behaved better than I. How many hours did I listen to him weep and complain at the loss of his wife, as if she had died on purpose to thwart him. He cared nothing that she was also my mother. And then to marry again without any consultation! It serves him right. He married weak blood and he threw weak blood. And now he would set up for more spawn. And with such a woman.

He stopped writing. He was pressing so hard he was in danger of bending his nib. He got up, went over to the fireplace, and picked up the poker. He prodded one of the lumps of coal that wasn't burning.

Fortunately, Nathaniel had agreed to have the woman spayed. Presumably that would occur soon. He hit a piece of coal hard, splitting it in two. Flames jumped up to lick at the new fuel. He pounded another piece and another until the coal was completely fractured.

Miss Trowbridge had given her address as 106 Jarvis Street. Murdoch took his second streetcar of the day and set out to talk to her. He was certain now that Mr Lee was mistaken in his identification but afraid to admit it. However, he thought it was odd Miss Trowbridge had made no attempt to negate Lee's statement. On the other hand, witnesses often had blinkers on about matters other than their own. She must have met up with Wicken after Isobel had left.

As he headed back down Parliament toward Queen Street, he probed the hole in his gum with his tongue. His jaw was practically back to normal, as long he didn't let in too much cold air and chewed on the other side. Mrs Kitchen had resumed her duties and sent him off with a couple of hard-boiled eggs and a jar of milk sops for his luncheon. It didn't come close to the rabbit stew that Enid had made for him, the memory of which made his mouth water. He hadn't seen her this morning but he could hear her at the typewriter quite early. Perhaps tonight they could continue the interrupted talk she so obviously wanted. Not that he was any closer to coming up with an answer, but he didn't just want to spout the church's doctrine without thinking about it.

There was a woman walking ahead of him. She halted at the corner and he saw her lift her skirt decorously to avoid a puddle as she stepped off the curb. Nevertheless, her hem dragged through the water and he suddenly had a vivid memory of himself and Liza, sitting one evening in her kitchen. She took care of her widowed father, and when he went off to bed, they had some rare and precious privacy. On this particular occasion, she was trying to clean the skirt of her best walking suit. The hem was covered with mud. "Wretched thing. It is always dirty." If she had lived, he knew she would have become an agitator for many reforms for women, including the adoption of what was currently called Rational Dress. "Why shouldn't I be able to wear a sensible shorter skirt without being leered at, or insulted?" she'd demanded. He'd stupidly tried to make light of the issue with a lewd joke and she was angry with him. "How can you be so clever about some things and so nocky about others? I wish you'd open up your mind."

They'd eventually worked their way to a reasonable talk about her point of view, but her words had stung and he still thought about them.

He was checking the house numbers now. One hundred and six was a big house of yellow brick, gables painted in the popular hunter green. Shrubs filled the large front yard, held in by a very fancy wrought-iron fence. The gate squeaked when he opened it and on closer inspection, he could see the shrubs were shapeless and too bushy. There were weeds in the cracks of the flagstone path. The house might be grand but it looked neglected. He tugged at the bell-pull, hearing it clang inside the house. The bay windows to his right showed more care than the grounds. They were curtained with white lace, hung half way up the window in the fashionable style. So far, nobody had answered and he was about to ring again when the door creaked open. An elderly woman stood at the threshold, scrutinising him with a distinctly unfriendly expression. She wore a black silk dress and a white mobcap. There was a chatelaine at her waist which jingled slightly. He was somewhat surprised that the housekeeper had answered the door, but he gave her a polite smile and tipped his hat.

She frowned. "What do you want?"

"I'd like to speak to Miss Trowbridge."

"Who?"

"Miss Mary Ann Trowbridge. I understand she lives here."

"Who are you?"

Murdoch handed her his calling card. "Acting Detective Murdoch."

The housekeeper, if that was who she was, studied his card, even reversing it as if there were more information on the back.

"She isn't here."

She handed it back to him.

"When will she return? It is important I speak to her."

"She won't."

"Won't what?"

"Return."

"Do you mean she's left the city?"

"No, I mean she won't return, seeing as how she's never lived here."

Murdoch bit back a retort. If the woman needed to play games with him, he wasn't going to give her the satisfaction of getting riled up.

"Ma'am, this is an important police matter and I would appreciate your cooperation. Does a Mrs Avison live here?"

"She does, but you can't talk to her because she hasn't finished her breakfast yet."

Murdoch reached inside his coat and fished out his watch, looking at it ostentatiously.

"My, it's half past two in the afternoon. Is your mistress an invalid then?"

She scowled at him and was about to close the door but he got his foot in just in time. He summoned as stern an expression as he could, although he had no desire to act the bully with such a tiny shrivelled old woman.

"I repeat, this is a police matter. If you don't go this minute and tell your mistress I would like to talk to her, I will be forced to come in and find her myself."

The servant stared back at him and he thought there was a glint of amusement in her eyes. *The old crow. She actually enjoyed that little contest.* He stepped into the hall.

"I'll wait here."

With a loud sniff of disapproval, she shuffled away down the hall. He watched her draw back the portieres in front of a door to the right, tap, and enter. He looked around. The hall was unusually spacious, large enough to accommodate several chairs, an imposing coat tree, and a fine marble fireplace, which was still protected by a brass screen as if it were summer. The place felt cold and gloomy. The only natural light came through the door windows, and although there was a splendid chandelier of crystal glass, none of the candles were lit. There were so many paintings on the wall, the crimson flock covering was almost obscured. As far as he could tell, they were all portraits. In spite of the grandeur of the house, there wasn't a sign of any other servants. No butler came hurrying out to take charge, no maids on route to some task. The silence, the cold musty air, made him feel as if he were in a mausoleum. It seemed an old-fashioned, gloomy house for a young, pretty girl like Mary Ann to live in.

The rear door opened and the housekeeper emerged. She beckoned to him and he approached her.

"Mrs Avison will see you. She doesn't hear so good so make sure you speak up and don't mumble."

"I make a point of never mumbling," said Murdoch, but any irony was lost and he felt petty for even attempting it.

"Good," she said and moved a few inches out of the way so he could enter.

Like the hall, the room was dark but at least there was a cheerful fire going in the fireplace. A woman was seated close to it in a large armchair. She was wearing a man's maroon silk dressing gown and her white hair was in a loose braid down her back. As he came in, she reached for a hearing trumpet and held it to her ear.

"What is it you want, sir? I couldn't make head nor tails of what Beulah was saying." She waved her hand at the chair opposite her. "Sit down for goodness sake. Beulah, go and fetch another cup. I'm sure he'd be glad of some coffee; it's perishing out there." Her voice was strident.

Murdoch did as he was told, putting his damp hat beside him on the floor. In spite of her white hair, Mrs Avison was by no means an invalid, nor elderly; more likely she was in her late middle age. He decided her unorthodox dress and willingness to receive him the way she was must be cultivated eccentricity. She didn't wait for the housekeeper to leave before she said, "Beulah's been with me since we were both children. She started out as the nursery maid. She fusses over me in exactly the same way she did then." She aimed the trumpet in his direction. "Go on then, explain yourself."

He leaned forward. It was rather like playing a trombone in reverse.

"I want to speak to your niece, Miss Mary Ann Trowbridge. I apologise for intruding at such an unhappy time but I would like to ask her a few more questions concerning Oliver Wicken."

Mrs Avison heard perfectly and she looked at him puzzled.

"I don't know what in Hades you are talking about. There's no such person here. I'm a widow and I live alone except for Beulah. You've made a mistake."

It was Murdoch's turn to be taken aback. "You don't have a niece named Mary Ann who testified at the coroner's inquest on Tuesday?"

"I certainly don't. Neither niece nor nephew. Thank goodness for that, I might add."

"The young woman gave this address and produced a letter purporting to be from her aunt, Mrs Avison."

"What sort of letter?"

"Corroborating her statement that she was engaged to a young man named Oliver Wicken."

"It certainly was not I who wrote the letter."

The housekeeper came back in carrying a china cup and saucer that could have belonged to a child's tea set.

"Beulah, listen to this story."

"Just a minute." She went to the sideboard, poured out some coffee from a silver pot, and brought the cup to Murdoch. He had only drunk coffee on three occasions in his life and then it came liquid from a bottle and was loaded with milk and sugar. Cautiously, he sipped at the dark fragrant brew.

"We always serve it black," said Mrs Avison. "It's an abomination to do otherwise. You like coffee, don't you?"

"I do now," he said.

"So, tell Beulah what you just told me."

The housekeeper, who might also have been hard of hearing, didn't wait for him.

"I remembered while I was getting the cup. We used to have a servant here named Mary Ann. She was the upstairs maid. About ten or eleven years ago it was. But her last name wasn't Trowbridge, it was Trotter. What's this woman look like that you're after?"

"She has light brown hair, fair skin, rather dainty features, grey eyes. Probably about twenty or so."

Beulah nodded with satisfaction. "Same one. She always looked young for her age. I'm not surprised as a policeman is after her. She only lasted a couple of months with us. Got the shoot on account of immorality."

Mrs Avison had been trying to follow the conversation but she couldn't and said in exasperation, "What are you blathering about, Beulah?"

The housekeeper shouted everything into the trumpet. Murdoch drank more of the delicious coffee.

Mrs Avison nodded vigorously. "I recollect the girl now. Why in Hades is she pretending I'm her aunt? She was the maid here."

"I don't know the answer to that, Mrs Avison. I wish I did."

"Looked like butter wouldn't melt in her mouth but she was as sly a minx as ever I did see."

"What exactly did she do to be dismissed?"

"Got herself in the family way, that's what," Beulah answered. "She was barely sixteen. Wicked."

"So, she married then?"

Mrs Avison heard that one. "She did not. One of our gardeners was quite willing to take her but she refused."

"Was he the father?"

She clucked her tongue in disapproval. "He said he wasn't but she wouldn't tell us who it was. She probably didn't know."

"Did she marry anybody? I might need to seek under her married name."

Mrs Avison waved her trumpet at Beulah, who answered for her. "As far as we know she did not. She left. The gardener's name was Crenshawe but he married somebody else soon after anyway, so there's no sense talking to him."

"Is the name Oliver Wicken familiar to you?"

She shook her head. "No. Never heard of him."

"You said they were engaged," interrupted Mrs Avison. "Why is that of concern to the police? Has he abandoned her?"

Murdoch explained as succinctly as he could what had transpired. They listened attentively.

"Did Mary Ann stay in touch with any of the other servants? Is there anybody here that I could talk to?"

"No. I told you I live by myself with Beulah. I let them all go. Servants are an expense and a bother as far as I'm concerned. Any extra help we get in from time to time. We manage quite well, don't we Beulah?"

The housekeeper ignored the question, intent on pursuing the more lascivious topic of Mary Ann Trotter.

"One of the maids did run into the girl the year after she'd left us. She told her the child had been stillborn. Whether that was true or not it was certainly convenient. But Agnes said she didn't look respectable at all."

"What did she mean by that?"

"She'd become a fallen woman," Beulah said in the tone of one who takes pride in calling a spade a spade.

CHAPTER TWENTY-SIX

MURDOCH WAS BEHIND his desk, Constable Crabtree seated in front of him.

"George, what's your opinion? Why'd she give us the run around?"

"My guess is she's still in the game and doesn't want anybody to know."

"Do you think she really was engaged to Wicken?"

"Hard to tell. She might have said that to pretty it up. She wasn't about to come right out and say he was having some dock on the side and paying for it."

"Would a man kill himself over a prostitute giving him the shove?"

"Some men are stupid enough for anything. The doxie hands him a line about how he's the only one she's ever loved, all other men are as eunuchs compared to him. He makes her happy. What man wouldn't like to hear that? He believes her, gets besotted, starts to make a nuisance of himself. She's bored, says that's it, no more, and he thinks life is over. Bang."

Murdoch stared at the constable. Crabtree was a happily married man with five small children, one a newborn. He spoke with such authority, it made him wonder.

"What is puzzling me, George, is why she came forward at all. Wouldn't it have been better for her to keep quiet? She could assume nobody knew about her." He drummed his fingers on the desk. "On the other hand, we could be maligning her. We don't know for certain that she's a doxie or ever was."

"She just happened to lie under oath for no reason."

Murdoch grinned. "A point, George."

"She said she read about his death in the newspaper. Maybe she's one of those women who just want to make mischief, or get in on the limelight. She could adapt her story to whatever circumstances revealed themselves. If he'd been married she could have said the same thing. 'Oh, he loved me but I sent him back to his lawful wife.' Cow leavings like that."

"You're saying maybe Trowbridge didn't know Wicken at all."

"Yes, sir. Made it up."

"What about the letter from her aunt?"

"We haven't seen the woman in person and she certainly isn't Mrs Avison of Jarvis Street."

"Hm. I'm wondering if Wicken was the father of the child she conceived when she was fifteen."

"That'd make him fourteen at the time."

"It happens, George. Let's say she revealed this to him. He is overcome by remorse, and after she leaves, he mulls it over to the point of despondency and takes his own life."

"That wasn't the wording of the note."

"You're right. Cancel the fathering theory. Having been in Wicken's home, I can't imagine he'd have been allowed within ten feet of a girl when he was fourteen."

"Maybe we dismissed the inspector's speculations too soon, sir."

"You mean that one of the women shot him?"

"Yes, sir."

"I have to eliminate Isobel Brewster. If she's lying to us, I'm going to throw in the towel on policing because she's convinced me."

"Be careful what you say, sir. You always were a softie for a girl in a faint."

"Do you think so?" Murdoch asked in surprise. He rubbed his hands hard over his scalp.

186

"Let's go over this again." He took a piece of paper from his drawer and drew a square.

"Here's the house at the corner where we found him. Isobel Brewster has walked up Parliament with him. The timing as she told it to me fits. They stay on the porch because for some reason, Wicken hasn't let on he has a key."

"Perhaps he didn't want her to linger. He's got an assignation with Miss Trowbridge."

"True. Anyway, they stand here for at least a half an hour, maybe longer. She is threatening to break off their relationship unless he sets a date for the wedding. A half an hour is plausible isn't it, George? Especially if they've talked about it before."

"You can have a barney in less time than that, sir. Take it from me."

"All right, Miss Brewster leaves. Wicken now encounters Miss Trowbridge. They go inside the empty house. She is still in the game but wants to go respectable. They quarrel. She wants to marry, he spurns her, says he already has a respectable sweetheart. She grabs his revolver and shoots him. Then she prints a note that suggests suicide and cool as a cucumber comes to the inquest to reinforce her story that he was the rejected one. What about that?"

Crabtree grinned. "I'd say that's a good one, sir. 'Course, it does depend on a slip of a girl being able to get the better of a healthy, six-foot-tall man."

"She took him by surprise. This would also be some explanation for the position of the gun. She was in a rage with him and stuffed the revolver in between his legs in some sort of symbol."

"You've got a good imagination, sir."

"And it's getting us nowhere. We've got to find the mysterious Miss Trowbridge. First off, I want you to go round to all the newspapers. Put an advertisement in the personal columns. Give them her description, say we'd like to get in touch with her further to the death of Oliver Wicken. Anybody knowing her whereabouts should contact us at once."

"Are we offering a reward?"

"Probably not. There's no money. I'm going to go back to his beat; do all that again. You can join me after."

At that moment, they heard somebody coming down the hall to the cubicle.

"Murdoch?"

The reed strips were shoved aside and Inspector Brackenreid came in. He couldn't go too far with Crabtree sitting where he was and they sashayed for a moment as the constable tried to stand and get out of the way. Murdoch groaned to himself. If Brackenreid came looking for him instead of having him brought up to his office, it usually meant trouble. He, too, stood respectfully. Crabtree managed to squeeze against the wall and it was too awkward for the three of them to all be standing. The inspector took the chair. Murdoch sat down again.

"Yes, sir?"

"I was wondering how you're getting on with the Wicken case?"

"I was just going over the possibilities with Constable Crabtree."

"Go over them with me."

Murdoch related his visit to Mrs Avison. Brackenreid looked gloomy.

"I see. That's all we need, a Jezebel mixed up with one of our officers."

"None of this is proven, sir. The housekeeper was relating another servant's judgement on the young woman. However, this has cast doubt on her testimony."

"It's beginning to look like it was a pack of lies. Our young buck must have got himself mired in some tail. I've seen it before. Men who get wet-eyed over a fen, promising to give them a better life. As if they ever want it!"

Murdoch tried not to look at Crabtree. The inspector was notorious for his cynical statements about human nature. *"I've seen it before,"* was a covert catchall phrase among the officers.

Brackenreid tapped the piece of paper in front of Murdoch.

"You fancy drawings, don't you? You should have been a general.

But you can sit here and draw pictures until the cows come home and it won't get us any closer to knowing what the hell happened. You need to find that Trowbridge girl."

"That's a good idea, sir."

Crabtree winced. Will was at it again.

Brackenreid glanced up sharply at the detective, but Murdoch was a master at the blank look when he needed to be.

"I think you're on to something. It's not unlikely we are, in fact, looking at a murder."

It was a tidy proposition but even though he was the one who'd presented it, Murdoch knew the danger of prejudice. Mary Ann Trotter may have been a prostitute at one time in her life. It didn't mean she still was or that immorality and murder were always bedfellows.

"I want a report on my desk by tomorrow afternoon."

"Yes, sir."

The inspector got up. He obviously wanted to leave in a commanding way, but it was impossible as he had to press himself past Crabtree with uncomfortable intimacy.

As soon as he was out of earshot, both men grinned at each other.

"You'll go too far one of these days, Mr Murdoch. He's not as thick as he likes to pretend."

"I know. It's the only thing that keeps me from asking for a transfer. He hasn't completely lost his wits."

He reached for his sealskin coat. "You get off to the papers. I'm going to see if Miss Trowbridge-Trotter was noticed by anybody, anywhere, anytime."

CHAPTER TWENTY-SEVEN

FRANZ LIEPMAN WAS eating his breakfast. He'd toasted two slices of bread in front of the fire and made a pot of strong tea with lacings of sugar and a tot of rum against the damp. He yawned. For more than ten years he had not had a complete night's sleep. Four hours in the evening before he went to the Foresters building where he was the night watchman, sometimes a nap there in the back room but he had to be careful. Occasionally an hour or two before he went to his second job, sweeping floors at the general hospital. He was used to it, probably couldn't have slept an entire night through if it was offered. He did this all week long and never took time off unless he was sick.

Once at the hall, he'd overheard two of the men talking about him. "He's a bit simple is what it is," said one of them. Franz had been hurt by this remark, but his mother was alive then and she had scoffed. "Let them think it. Clever people are noticed and you don't want that. Not as you're German." And she made him a nice apple cake to make up for the hurt. "I've told you, family is the only thing you can rely on. Blood is what counts."

For as long as he could remember, there had only been the two of them and now she was gone, there was no family, no blood ties to turn to. However, the necessity to have two jobs when she became ill had turned into a habit. He continued to live frugally and the extra money that accumulated he kept in a strongbox under his bed. There was a lot of it by now and sometimes he wondered if he should do anything and he'd take out a few dollars. But then he'd sit and think about it, and realise he could make do. His trousers got a good brush and his boots another blacking. So, most of the time, he put the money back. His mother taught him that. "Don't let any women know how much you have or they'll try to seduce you and take it all." He never quite knew what it was to seduce but he could tell it was bad. His mother had been born in Germany and had come to Canada just after he was born. She wouldn't talk about his father no matter how much he begged, and although she had received occasional letters for a while, they hadn't come for years now.

Even though force of habit had kept him up, he'd not gone to work at all since Monday night. He sent the neighbor's boy with a note to Mr Tweedie saying as how he regretted but he was incapacitated for work. It took him almost an hour to write those two lines, but in the end he was proud of his big word. He didn't go the next day either.

"You'd better go tell the police," the secretary had said when Franz spilled out his story. But he wouldn't consider it. The police were always on the lookout for culprits, and they didn't care who they got, especially if they were foreigners. He could end up in jail for the rest of his life and nobody would be the wiser. No, he was very sorry he'd spoken up at all.

It was only because the cries he'd heard were so disturbing that he'd told Mr Tweedie about them.

DARKNESS WAS WELL settled in and the street lamps were struggling without much success to throw out some light in the gloom. A few passersby, bent under their black umbrellas, hurried to get out of the drizzle that had started up again. Murdoch had started at Queen Street, knocking on every single door, and it had taken him almost two hours. He was tired and disheartened and his mouth felt dry from too much talking. Almost all of the people he spoke to had heard about Wicken's death, and they were eager to discuss it with him. Much as he would have expected, there was not much sympathy for the dead man, who was considered to be a disgrace and a coward to boot. Opinion ran cool toward Mrs Wicken and the word "unfeeling" was said many times, even though for most of them this opinion on her conduct was based on hearsay. Enthusiasm was high for Mary Ann, and his questions concerning her engendered a great deal of curiosity, which he tried to diffuse. The Lees were mostly referred to as "the heathens" and he knew that if he had introduced them into the investigation at all, speculation would have run riot. He was, in turn, asked questions, most of them prurient. He had no answer to "was it true there was blood and brains splattered all over the walls?" Sometimes the question was asked as bluntly as that, sometimes with more subtlety, but the reason was the same—they wanted to feast on the morbid details. However, so far, he had no more information than when he had started out. If Mary Ann Trowbridge had met up with Wicken anywhere along this section of his beat, nobody had seen her. He gave out Isobel's description as well but with the same result. At least he didn't have to worry about the nocturnal habits of Toronto citizenry. They all seemed to enjoy the untroubled sleep of the righteous. And Mr Lee was unusual in that he worked late into the night. No other business owner had. Murdoch groaned to himself. At this rate, he wouldn't get home until ten o'clock, certainly too late to visit with Mrs Jones.

On the southwest corner of Parliament Street and Gerrard, directly across from the vacant house where Wicken had died, was the imposing Foresters Hall. Lights were burning in the downstairs windows, and hoping to find a caretaker who might have been awake on the night in question, he went in. The double front doors were unlocked and he entered a large foyer. There was a fine brass and crystal chandelier suspended from the ceiling, all the globes extravagantly lit. A splendid staircase curved in front of him and there was an imposing line of portraits ascending to the second floor. He assumed these were depictions of officers of the order.

There was nobody in sight, but to his right was a half-open door and he could hear the now familiar tapping of a typewriter. A plaque on the door said H. TWEEDIE, SECRETARY. He knocked and a strong male voice called, "Enter." Murdoch complied. A young man, presumably Mr Tweedie, was seated behind a long desk. Several bound ledgers were piled around him like a barricade, and he seemed to be copying something from one of them. There was an electric light suspended above his head and he wore a green eyeshade to protect himself from its brilliance.

"Yes?"

"My name is Murdoch. I'm acting detective at number four station and I'm pursuing some inquiries concerning the death of one of our constables. No doubt you've heard about it?"

The secretary pushed back his visor. "I'll say. Did himself in, didn't he? Don't understand that, I must say. I mean we all have our trials and tribulations don't we? But we've got to keep going. As far as I'm concerned, suicide is a coward's way out. However, I digress. How can I be of assistance?"

"The investigation isn't completely closed and I was wondering if you employ a night watchman at all. If so, I'd like to talk to him."

"Yes, we do. Fellow by the name of Franz Liepman. Didn't he get in touch with you?"

"No. Should he have?"

"I told him to. But then again, I'm not surprised he didn't. He's a strange bird, bit slow on the uptake, German. He came in here on Tuesday with quite a story. I'd heard about the constable from one of our members so I thought it might be relevant. Told him to get to the station right away."

Murdoch stared at him. The green eyeshade made his face look sickly but his brown eyes were keen enough.

"Well, he didn't. What was his story?"

"He claims he heard somebody crying. Pitiful was the way he described it. Like this, he said." Tweedie put his head back and cried in a falsetto voice, "Don't leave me, please don't leave me."

"A woman?"

"Oh, no, it must have been the constable. He was beseeching his lady-love." Tweedie looked as if he were about to howl again. Murdoch cut him off.

"Did he say where the cries were coming from?"

"The vacant house."

"What time was this?"

"Franz was on his way here and he usually arrives about half past midnight, so it was shortly before that."

"Do you have this man's address?"

"Matter of fact, it's right here," The secretary propelled his chair toward the end of his table and rotated a card file that was sitting beside the telephone box. He rolled back and handed a card to Murdoch. "He hasn't been in since Tuesday. Sent a message to say he's ill. Too much of a coincidence if you ask me. He looked like he'd shit his britches, begging your pardon, when I said he should speak to the police. Like I said, he's a strange sort of fellow. But he's been with us for years, no complaints. First time he's been off sick for six years. Hasn't missed a day."

Murdoch checked the address. "I'll go and have a word with him. Thank you, Mr Tweedie."

"You're welcome I'm sure." He regarded Murdoch with keen curiosity. "Do you mind if I ask why the investigation isn't closed? I popped down to the inquest myself, my own backyard as it were. The verdict was unequivocal, wasn't it?"

"It was but there are a few discrepancies in some of the testimony that we need to clarify."

"The Chinaman's? What a pair they were."

"I'm not at liberty to go into it at the moment."

"Well, any time I can help, just drop in. Oh, by the way, I recommend you take a deep breath and hold it when you go into the fellow's place." He made a gesture of pinching his nostrils. "He doesn't believe in soap and water."

"Thanks for the warning."

Murdoch took his leave and left. The typewriter soon resumed its rapid clacking.

MR LIEPMAN LIVED at number 375 Gerrard Street, just east of Sackville. The house was a tall semidetached with a narrow strip of

194

paved front yard and a brown painted door that needed freshening up. The front window was dark, but slits of light came through the blinds at the second- and third-floor windows. There was an outside bell and the clapper was fastened to a frayed rope. He rang it as loudly as he could, given that the casing was cracked. He expected he'd have to repeat this several times before somebody heard him, but surprisingly, there was a response almost immediately. Through the glass, he saw light from a candle drawing closer. The door opened and an elderly man stood there, his candlestick held aloft.

"The room's taken," he said before Murdoch could speak.

"I'm not here for the room, I'm looking for Mr Liepman."

"He's on the third floor."

The old man didn't wait for Murdoch to introduce himself or express any curiosity; he turned around and began to shuffle back to his lair. He took his candle with him.

"Wait a minute," Murdoch called but the man ignored him and entered a door on the left. Murdoch heard a bolt shoot closed. The hall was completely unlit and there was a strong smell of raw onions hanging in the air. On the other hand it could have been skunk. Cussing at the old man for his rudeness, Murdoch stood for a moment to get accustomed to the darkness. There was a staircase to his left and the room at the landing was occupied. Enough light came from beneath the door for him to make his way up. The stairs were uncarpeted and creaked loudly but nobody came out to see who he was or what he was doing. He didn't hear anything—no voices, no sounds of life behind the closed doors.

The stairs to the third floor became narrow and steep and again the only light came from beneath a door at the top of the landing. He slid his hand along the railing and more or less felt his way to the top. Here there was some sign of life, a man's voice speaking rather softly in a language he didn't understand but assumed was German. It sounded as if he were reading aloud. Murdoch rapped hard on the door. The voice stopped abruptly but there was no movement. He knocked again.

"Mr Liepman, I'm a police officer and I would like to talk to you."

No response. Murdoch was getting thoroughly annoyed. He thumped hard with his fist on the door. "Mr Liepman, please open up."

A squeak and scrape of a chair, the door opened a crack and a frightened face peered out at him. Murdoch had expected an older man but Liepman was of middle age. His hair was long about his shoulders and he had a full, untrimmed dark beard. He was wearing a red flannel combination suit under a pair of loose trousers.

"Mr Liepman, I'm Acting Detective Murdoch from number four station. I have just come from the Foresters Hall. The secretary told me you had some information concerning the death of one of our constables."

Liepman stared at him for so long, Murdoch wondered if he had understood anything. He was about to repeat himself when the man said. "I have been ill. I couldn't have come." He had a pronounced German accent, turning his *v*'s into *f*'s.

"I'm not here to reproach you or charge you with anything, Mr Liepman. I'm pursuing an inquiry into the death of this officer."

"I thought the verdict was for self-murder."

The man wasn't as ignorant as he first appeared. "Yes, but there are a few matters I'd like to clear up. Can I come in?"

Reluctantly, Liepman stepped aside and Murdoch went into the tiny attic room. Tweedie was right about the smell. It was far worse than the odour downstairs. He tried to breathe lightly.

"I was just having my tea," said Liepman and he indicated a pine table tucked underneath the window. There was a cup and the remnants of a meat pie on a plate. A black book was turned face down beside it. Could have been a Bible.

"I won't keep you."

Murdoch had been annoyed with the old man who let him in, but this one's lack of manners was more forgivable. It seemed less deliberate and more as if he simply wasn't used to company. Unexpectedly, there was the sound of birdsong, a cascade of trills and chirps. At first, Murdoch couldn't see where it was coming from, then he noticed a small cage in the corner of the room, next to the hearth. Inside was a dainty yellow and black finch. It shook out its feathers, raised its beak, and let out another series of whistles. Liepman grinned. "She likes to show off."

"That's a beautiful song."

"Yes, we've won competitions. Her name's Jenny Lind. She's named after the singer. My mother heard her when she did the only show she ever performed in Toronto. Fifty-three it was. I was only five years old but she took me too. It cost Müder a week's wages but she didn't care. It was worth it. I name all my birds the same now. This is Miss Jenny Lind the eighth, or is it ninth?"

The little bird preened herself then took a sip of water from the dish inside her cage, for all the world like a diva warming up for her performance.

Murdoch glanced around the tiny room. The furnishings were spare but whether that was from penury or from choice, he didn't know. The walls sloped and there was only one small window. It must be hot as Hades in summer. At the moment, however, it was comfortably warm and, in contrast to the rest of the house, well-lit and cheery. There was a fire going in the fireplace and a kettle was steaming on the hob. This was obviously where Mr Liepman cooked his meals. He hadn't invited him to sit, but Murdoch pulled out a chair and sat down at the table.

"Mr Tweedie said that you heard the sound of somebody crying on Tuesday night. Can you tell me more about it?"

"What would you like to know?" Liepman had plumped himself down in the single armchair by the fire but he jumped up again, went over to the cage, and shook out some seed for the bird.

"Could you describe this sound?"

"Oh, yes. Piteous, it was. Made my blood run cold."

"Were they words or just cries?"

"Words."

"What were they?"

"'Help me, help me.'"

That wasn't what Mr Tweedie had said.

"Mr Liepman, could you swear an oath that those words were exactly what you heard?"

The other man looked frightened.

"What I mean is that we often recall things differently from the way they actually happened. I may for instance insist that a friend said to me, 'We must have a chat,' when in fact what they said was 'I'd like to get together for a talk.'"

Liepman was staring at Murdoch. He tried again. "All I am asking, sir, is if, to your recollection, these were the precise words. Mr Tweedie has reported it rather differently."

"Has he?" He scowled. "Well, he can go stuff himself in his filing cabinet for all I care. I heard plain as you're talking to me, 'Help me. Help me.' And that's the gospel truth, may I be put on the rack and not change my mind."

"Were the words repeated several times or twice like that?"

"Only twice."

"What made you think it was the constable?"

"Eh?"

"Mr Tweedie said you thought it was the officer who died."

"I didn't say that. It was him who said it must have been."

"He imitated the sounds for me and they could have come more from a woman."

"I did think that at first. That it was a woman, but according to Mr Clever, it couldn't have been."

"Did the cries come from the empty house?"

"Thereabouts." Liepman clicked his tongue at Jenny Lind but she didn't respond, just continued to dig into her flight feathers.

Murdoch sighed. "I must repeat what I said earlier, Mr Liepman, you are not in any kind of trouble. But it would be more than helpful if you could be exact. You were walking by on your way to the hall; at what point did you hear the noises?"

"Just as I was going past the livery." He turned around and faced Murdoch. His face was tight with anxiety. "Mr Tweedie said sound at night is difficult to pinpoint, travels around. He's the one convinced it was coming from the house. I'd have said it was behind me rather than in front. But he knows best."

"Did you hear a gunshot?"

Liepman was emphatic. "No. Not so much as a pop. Just the cries."

"And what time was this?"

"About twenty minutes past twelve. I get to the hall at half past."

"That is your regular route to work, I presume? Have you ever seen the constable on his beat? Tall fellow, blond whiskers and moustache."

"I see him most every night. He's regular and so am I."

"Did you see him on Monday?"

"No. I did wonder at it."

"Have you ever seen him accompanied by anybody else?"

"Once or twice he was with the sergeant."

"On Monday night, did you notice a young woman on the street?"

"No, it was too late for women to be out."

"You're certain?"

"Absolutely. Everybody is in bed by the time I go to work. I'd notice if it was different."

"When you heard these cries, did you see anything? Did you look up at the windows, for instance?"

Liepman shook his head emphatically. "Müder said never to look at devils. If you did, you would go up in a puff of smoke."

"You thought these cries, piteous as you describe them, might have not been human?"

"Devils can take all kinds of shapes."

"Indeed they can."

He focused on the little finch again. "I don't want to get anybody in trouble. I won't, will I?"

"I don't think so, Mr Liepman. You have been very helpful."

Murdoch looked at the book that was on the table. It was a Bible. There didn't seem to be any other books in the room, as far as he could see. He stood up. That was probably all he was going to get out of the man. Realising they were done, Liepman cheered up. He took the lamp from the mantelpiece.

"I'll see you down. Mr Henry won't leave any candles out. He's afraid of fire."

As they left, the finch let loose with a glorious torrent of song.

An image had leaped into Murdoch's mind. A young woman tied to a chair, trying to reach out to him, whispering, "Help me, please help me."

CHAPTER TWENTY-EIGHT

SHE FELT AS if she were recovering from an illness, a fever that had distorted her view of the world. The strict routine of the asylum, the orderliness, was actually helping to bring about clarity. However, this served to intensify her fear and her isolation. She could see only too well what she faced and she was threading her way like a cat on a mantel.

During the day, there was little to distract her from her thoughts. Mrs Foster was coherent but childlike, and she soon gave up on any attempt to communicate with the other women. Trying to hold on to their sanity was like catching a bird in cupped hands. The attendants had a lot to do and were still wary of her. Fortunately, Miss Bastedo had made sure she was given some tray covers to embroider and it helped to while away the time. When she was in the orphanage, she had been taught fine sewing and she had become adept at it, enjoying the praise she garnered for her neat stitching. After Harry died she tried to support herself and Charley by doing dressmaking. Unfortunately, there was a plethora of skilled dressmakers in the city and she never had enough work. It was at this point Nathaniel Eakin had entered her life, by chance, looking for someone to sew for his ailing wife. Peg couldn't really understand why he had been so smitten with her but it was clear he was. After his wife's death and when he was scarcely out of mourning, he had proposed marriage. Seeing no alternative, she accepted.

On Friday Miss Bastedo announced that the Lippincott choir was coming to sing for them that evening. Peg felt a surge of excitement at the prospect of contact with the outside world. Then the reality of her situation rushed in on her. Nobody had visited her yet and she was still wearing the institutional clothes, cotton drawers and chemise, a petticoat, grey woollen dress and a stiff white pinafore. They were the regulation apparel worn by all the charity patients and she felt ashamed to be seen by normal people. Briefly, she considered begging off as being unwell, but after the plates were taken away, the attendants ushered all the women into the sitting room and she filed in with Mrs Foster on her arm.

The Lippincott church choir was already there. Seven of them, five women and two men. They were used to the asylum and didn't gawk or pay any attention, instead sorting through their music sheets or chatting to each other quietly. There were four rows of chairs for the patients set up in a semicircle in front of the piano, but the rear seats were already occupied. Peg's hope of sitting inconspicuously at the back was dashed.

"Who are those women?" she whispered to Mrs Foster. They were all in the asylum clothes, many of them with white mobcaps. There was an air of restless energy surrounding them, as they fidgeted and looked around them. Various looks—bewilderment, fear, suspicion.

"They're from second floor," replied Emma. "It's not fair of Miss Bastedo to bring them in but she always does. Says it calms them down. Which it doesn't in my opinion. They don't pay attention and shout out at the most inappropriate moments."

Peg felt afraid of the strangeness of these women and made sure that she was one row removed as she sat down. That put her in direct line of vision with the women of the choir, but it was the lesser of two evils. She scanned them quickly, relieved that there was nobody she knew in the group.

Mrs Foster leaned up closer and spoke into her ear. "Whatever

202

you do, don't get too close to the woman who's sitting at the end of the row at the back. The one in the bonnet."

Peg glanced quickly behind her. The woman in question was small and thin with haggard features. She was sitting quietly but her lips were moving in a conversation only she could hear.

"She's had ringworm. It's very contagious. She shouldn't be here but matron is always letting the old-timers get away with things. She's been in this place for twenty-two years."

"My Lord. She doesn't look much into middle age."

"She was twenty-six years old when she was admitted."

"The same age as me."

"There you go then," said Emma ambiguously. "I've been here seven years, three months, and fourteen days tomorrow."

That wasn't what she'd said before but Peg didn't challenge her. "Wouldn't you like to leave?"

Mrs Foster shrugged. "I have left more than once, but I've had to come back."

"Why?"

"I didn't get along with my daughter-in-law." She hesitated and began to pleat her skirt, nervously.

"Why didn't you?" Peg asked.

"She said I stole things."

"Oh, I see."

The other woman looked up at Peg in confusion. "Sometimes I take things that I know people would give me anyway. That's not so wicked, is it?"

"I don't think so but perhaps it would be better to ask them first."

"Oh, no. They wouldn't give them to me then." Mrs Foster's eyes filled with sudden tears. "She's a good girl, is Letty. I miss her so much. She's been like a daughter to me."

She began to weep with increasing fervour. Miss Reid, who was talking to the choir leader, came over.

"What is it, Mrs Foster?"

"Hurt," said the old woman in a child's voice and touched her chest.

"Did you say something to her?" the attendant asked Peg.

She shook her head. "No, I did not. She mentioned her daughter-in-law and that seemed to upset her."

Reid took a handkerchief out of her pocket and wiped at Mrs Foster's face. "Come on, where's my sunshine smile? We want to set a good example, don't we?"

Emma sniffed away the tears and gave her a wan little smile.

"Lovely. That's what I like to see. Now I need to have one more word with Mrs Greenwood. Shall I ask them to sing 'Annie Laurie' for you?"

"Yes, please."

Reid straightened up, gave Peg a warning don't-do-anything-else glance and returned to the choir mistress.

Emma examined the handkerchief, which was of good linen with a deep black border.

"Poor Reid's brother died this year. She was very fond of him."

She put it in her pocket.

One of the choir members was at the piano. She struck a note; the others hummed to get the right pitch. Then Mrs Greenwood faced them, lifted her arms, and they all rose, music held straight out in front of them. A patient from the rear seats shouted out, "Hurray."

"And . . ."

They burst into a boisterous rendition of "Bringing in the Sheaves."

Peg felt a surge of grief that tightened in her throat. If only she could get up and walk across that small patch of floor and be with them, the normal ones, the ones who could leave when they wanted to; the ones who could go to a home where they were safe.

CHAPTER TWENTY-NINE

———•———

IT WAS REMARKABLE that the real business that occurred at the house on Sydenham Street was undetected. Clara Doherty told her neighbours that she was a music teacher who lived with her four orphaned nieces and her housekeeper. She was strict about secrecy. Customers entered the house by way of a lane at the rear and were accepted by referral only. The whores were available at certain times and no other. Most of the men came directly after working hours, some few before work, although only Rose was willing to do that, the other girls preferring to sleep in.

The setup of the house was simple and practical. The four bawds shared the top two rooms, something they unfailingly grumbled about, as the attic was unbearably hot in summer and cold in winter. Clara only allowed them a small coal allowance. On the second floor were three well-furnished bedrooms which were used only for business. Clara had a private suite on the first floor that she shared with Emily Dawson, the housekeeper, who was also her long-time lover. Across the hall was the parlour, a good-sized room where the men could wait and have a drink of spirits and smoke a pipe if they wanted. However, they were rarely permitted to linger through the entire evening, and Clara was always there to ensure they obeyed. Sophie, the oldest whore, referred to this policy as, "Get up, get in, get on, and get out." The premises were closed at midnight and woe betide any man who presumed otherwise. Drunkenness was frowned upon and those leaving late were expected to be quiet. The Sabbath was always a day of rest.

On the whole, Clara treated the girls well. She let them have short holidays every so often, food was plentiful, and she performed abortions herself when necessary. She would have been comfortably off by now, except that with dismaying regularity, she lost her heart to some young doxie and lavished such gifts on her that her savings were seriously jeopardised. This blatant favouritism created havoc in the house, but fortunately the infatuations never lasted long, and the girl disappeared to Montreal or America, where Clara had friends who also ran ill-reputes. Later, the others would hear her sobbing in Emily's arms, begging for forgiveness, promising it would never happen again, and then the house would settle down for a little while.

Every afternoon the girls were invited into Clara's sitting room and Emily served them lemon junkets and cakes as a treat. Here they would sort out petty quarrels, receive their allowances, and discuss their customers. Clara encouraged them to unburden themselves. The information gave her ammunition if she needed it at a later time.

She yawned. The others had been having a lively discussion of their toms, ever a popular topic.

"Personally, I like the fast-trigger ones the best; the grunters, no words, next; and the shouters the least. You could go deaf with some of them yelling in your ear," said Nellie, licking the last of the junket off her spoon. "You had one of them Friday, didn't you, Rose? The greenhead. I heard you."

"Ha! That humper wasn't a greenhead. He said he was sixteen, a virgin and the son of a bishop. The closest he's ever been to a bishop is his own cock."

"It's wicked to say things like that," said Sophie. She had been brought up in an orphanage run by the Sisters of St Joseph. Although she had become a prostitute at an early age, she suffered from regular attacks of guilt that sent her scuttling off to confession at St Michael's Cathedral. She was so oblique about her sins, however, that the priest never understood what she was referring to, and she always got off with a light penance. She compensated by wearing a piece of sacking next to her skin for the next week and refusing her favourite delicacies. Behind her back, the others referred to her variously as Mother-of-God, Saint Sophie, or Jesus-Wept, which she said often.

"He was wild for it," continued Rose. "'Oh, another one, my dear, that was so bad, oh, say that again, I'm coming, I'm coming.' You'd think he was a delivery boy. I was running out of words by the end."

"That's not what it sounded like to me," said Nellie. "I thought you could have gone on for another half hour and not repeated yourself."

Rose scowled. She was notorious for her vulgarity, but she hated the scorn of the other women.

Clara intervened before a squabble could develop. "Now dears, let's get on. They'll be arriving soon." She picked up a small wooden pail of candies and offered it around. "Everybody take one for now and one for later. They're lovely and fresh; Emily just bought them."

The women started to help themselves.

"I just wanted to reply to Rose," said Mary Ann, her mouth full of the candy. "The one I had, friend of your gull, he was the opposite. He whispered lovely things in my ear the whole time, 'You're so lovely, your eyes are extraordinary.' Never repeated himself and he was spent twice."

"How many times were you?" asked Nellie. The other two snickered. Nobody liked Mary Ann, whose childlike body appealed to a lot of customers. She milked the attraction for all it was worth—wore her hair down, kept her skirts short, and flounced and pouted like a spoiled child.

Mary Ann wasn't offended. She enjoyed stirring up the other whores. "All men are the same. They need to think you are really enjoying yourself, that they are therefore great lovers."

"I think about the taste of the dollars they're going to leave," said Nellie. "I must look happy."

Emily came in. "Hurry up girls. Time to get dressed. Nellie, don't you have anything cleaner to wear?"

"My other dress isn't dry."

"Well, you've got a stain all over your bodice; it's disgusting. Wear a shawl."

She clapped her hands as if she were shooing away geese. "Come on. We're late tonight."

One by one the girls started to leave. Emily went over to the dresser, pulled open a drawer, and took out a corset.

"You'd better get ready," she said to Clara. "There's a man here. Wants to talk to you."

"Who?"

"Mr Smith."

"Which Mr Smith?"

"One of the older ones."

"Damn. Did he say anything else?"

"No. Come on, stand up."

Clara got to her feet and Emily helped her off with her dressing robe. She held the corset so that Clara could step into it and started to tighten the laces.

"Not so tight, Emmie, I can't breathe."

"It's no tighter than usual; you've been eating too many candies."

"You're the one who bought them."

Emily planted a kiss on Clara's shoulder and grinned. "True, I like to see you enjoy them so much. It's like watching my little piggy at her trough."

"Emmie!"

"Don't get frosty. You know how much I love that pig."

She gave Clara's plump buttock an affectionate squeeze. "There you go. All done. What dress do you want to wear?"

"The pearl grey."

Emily came around and looked Clara in the face. "Be careful what you say, dearest. This man smells like trouble to me."

"I know. But we've managed this long, I'm not going to let any gull sink me."

THE MAN CALLING himself Henry Smith was sitting in the front room. Clara had furnished it according to her idea of a well-to-do family parlour, and it was so crammed with furniture there was barely room to enter. There were two Turkish couches upholstered in purple velour with gold fringes, four Morris chairs, and taking pride of place, a so-called courting couch. It was S-shaped and a man sat on one side and a woman the other. The notion was they could converse quite intimately without physical contact. Rose particularly liked this couch as she could whisper lewd things in her customer's ear and have him squirming in no time. There was a piano in one corner on which Emily stoically played popular songs like "Peg of My Heart" and "Home Sweet Home," which were always in demand. The piano invariably needed tuning and she added fancy chords that changed the melody, but nobody would dare voice an objection. There were two sideboards on either side of the door, heavy and ornate with burled walnut moldings. This was where Clara kept the more lascivious tools of her trade. Plush vellum albums of special photographs, books to make a man as randy as a goat. A stereoscope sat on one of the sidetables. Just in the unlikely event that a neighbour came to call, the photos on display were innocent: a view of the Nile, a girl on a giant lily pad, children sitting on a wall. In the sideboard were the other pictures. The three dimensional nature of the stereoscope made these pictures particularly startling. They were twenty-five cents a viewing.

Smith had been a customer of Mrs Doherty's for seven years, following her whenever she moved to a new location for safety. Sometimes he visited once or twice a week, sometimes he would stay away for a month or more. There was something in his disdain that made the women uncomfortable. He wouldn't take liquor, ignored the books and photographs, and was never tempted by the latest special novel. They were glad when Mary Ann took him over.

Nellie was sitting on one of the Morris chairs. She had a bad cold and was hawking copiously into her handkerchief. Clara came out of her room. The man immediately took a gold watch from his waistcoat pocket and consulted it.

"Good evening, Mr Smith. Sorry to keep you waiting. Nasty

209

weather, isn't it? Can I get you a hot gin in the meantime, warm you up?"

"No, thank you. I'd like to speak to you in private."

"Of course. We can talk in my sitting room."

He followed her to the door, where she paused and looked over her shoulder. "Nellie! If you have to blow out that much snot, can you do it more quietly? The customers are going to vomit."

The girl coughed. "I can't help it. I've got a bad cold."

"Go back to bed then or you'll give it to everybody. It looks like it's going to be quiet tonight anyway."

Gratefully, Nellie got up, pulling down her skirt, which had been hitched to her scrawny thighs. She wasn't wearing any drawers.

The man's face contorted with contempt. "I must admit, the mere sight of female private parts has never aroused me."

"Each to his own," said Clara with a shrug.

She showed him into her sitting room. It too, was crammed with furniture, and every surface was covered with crotchet work, each piece lovingly made by Emily. She'd left the lamps lit and the fire was cheery.

Clara took one of the armchairs close to the hearth and indicated he should take the other.

"Were things satisfactory with Mary Ann?" she asked.

"They were indeed. She was most credible. And adroit. There was a witness we didn't expect. A Chinaman. He'd seen the constable with a young woman. Fortunately, he couldn't tell the difference between one devil woman and another and swore it was Mary Ann. It made our case even more convincing."

"So I understand. The joke is that Mary Ann knew him. He has been one of our customers."

"Is that so?"

"She is sure he recognised her and decided to help her out."

"I doubt it. He was probably just confused. Nevertheless, this leads precisely to what I wanted to talk about. Mary Ann must go somewhere else. I would like you to send her away. You have places she can go, I know you do. Wait . . ."

He held up his hand to stem the protest Clara was about to make. "I will pay for any inconvenience to you and her."

"She is one of my most popular wenches."

"I realise that, Mrs Doherty, and in a way I am asking this as a favour. It would be better if she were not available should anyone come looking."

He had not told Clara the reason he'd wanted Mary Ann to appear at the inquest and perjure herself, and she had not asked. She'd long operated on the premise that what a person didn't know couldn't hurt them. Any suspicions she pushed far away from her consciousness. Life was easier that way.

"Well . . ." she pretended to think about his offer but she'd already accepted. It was true Mary Ann was popular but she created trouble with the other girls. She'd also had the temerity to laugh when Clara had approached her full of tenderness when she'd first arrived. It was time she visited Montreal.

"As I say, this is going to cost me a lot of money."

"Name a figure."

"I won't be able to get another girl for at least a week, that's thirty dollars lost income right there. Then there's the train fare to Montreal . . ."

"I said name a figure. I have no interest in the particulars."

Clara had been about to inflate the expenses but she thought better of it. This man was too fly.

"Forty dollars."

He took out a wallet and counted out the money. "I'd like to see her gone tonight."

"Tonight!"

He added another five-dollar bill. "This will cover your losses. I'll wait and accompany her to the train station myself."

"I don't even know if there is a train tonight."

"There is. She can stay in a hotel until you have a chance to notify her new . . . employer."

He stood up. "Thank you for your cooperation, Mrs Doherty. I'll wait in here while she gets ready."

Clara took up the bills and put them in a porcelain box on the mantel. "It will take at least an hour for her to pack her belongings and to say good-bye."

"Make it half an hour and she and you get another two dollars."

"Very well."

Clara left. She closed the door behind her and rested against it for a moment. Then she spat into the cuspidor that was provided in the hall. Sometimes not even money could sweeten the shit she had to eat.

CHAPTER THIRTY

———•———

THE YOUNG MAID answered Murdoch's second knock. She was wiping her hands on her apron and gaped at him in a flustered way. Her eyes and nose were reddened. He wondered if she had been crying and if this was what happened to her every day. He smiled and touched his hat politely.

"Hello Janet. I'd like to speak to Mrs Curran."

"She said she's not at home, sir."

"Did she? I'm afraid I have to insist. It's police business. Would you mind telling her that I'm here? I'll make it right for you."

"Yes, sir."

She scuttled away, leaving him on the threshold, afraid to be so definite as to invite him in. He gave his feet a good wipe on the mat for her sake and stepped into the hall. The far door opened and Augusta emerged, Janet hovering anxiously behind her.

"Mr Murdoch, we were about to go in to dinner."

Murdoch tried to appear suitably apologetic. The house was quiet, but the way she spoke, you'd think the mayor and council were lined up two by two.

"I insisted on seeing you, Mrs Curran. Your maid did her job very well." Janet looked so alarmed at his words that he was afraid he'd made things worse for her.

"I'll get back, ma'am," she said.

Augusta fanned her hand dismissively and the girl hurried off.

"What is it you wish, Mr Murdoch?"

Tonight, she was wearing a black silk dress with grey satin trimming down the bodice and skirt. From what they'd told him before, he assumed this mourning attire was for her mother. Devotion or defiance?

"There have been further developments in the Wicken case. I wondered if I could talk to Mrs Nathaniel Eakin?"

"Oh no. She is still . . . she is no better."

"Is she able to receive visitors?"

"I believe not. We haven't seen her ourselves yet."

At that moment, a man came into the hall. He was of medium height, stocky, with a thick grey beard that jutted from either side of his chin. He was wearing a burgundy velvet smoking jacket that even from a distance appeared spotted and stained along the lapels. Although there was no physical resemblance whatsoever to Murdoch's own father, he was immediately reminded of him. It was the air that some men acquire when they have undisputed command over their domain.

"Augusta, bring the detective into my study. What are you thinking of?"

He held out his hand to Murdoch. "I'm Nathaniel Eakin. We haven't met before."

"No, you were indisposed when I came last."

"That's what they told you, was it?"

"Father, you were . . ."

He interrupted her. "I think you keep me from too many things that go on in this house. I'm as well as the next man."

He didn't seem that way to Murdoch. His face had an unhealthy, shiny flush to it, and his eyes were carrying enough baggage underneath to fit a traveller.

"Come this way, Mr Murdoch."

The study wasn't large but the walls were panelled in the English style from floor to ceiling. There were glass-fronted bookcases on two sides and in one corner was a closed, rolltop desk. All the wood was a dark hue; the chairs brown leather. However, instead of conveying the snug respectability of a gentleman's library, the room was gloomy and oppressive. It reeked of cigar smoke.

Eakin followed him in with Augusta close behind.

"Have a seat, Mr Murdoch," she said.

Murdoch took one of the big armchairs, Eakin the other. Augusta came behind her father and stood with her hand on the back of his chair. Murdoch couldn't quite tell if she was using that as a shield or if she wanted to ensure her father was within reach. Eakin picked up a cigar that was on the table next to him. The ash was long on the end and he scraped it off against the dish. He obviously wasn't concerned about tobacco smoke damaging his books, but Murdoch had the impression they were for show anyway. He waited until the cigar was relit and drawn, the end disappearing into the thicket of Eakin's beard. Murdoch almost coughed. He liked a pipe himself on occasion, but this smoke was vile.

"You were asking after my wife?"

"Yes, I was wondering if I'd be able to talk to her."

"She's in the loony bin."

"I know. Does she have any rationality at all?"

Eakin studied the tip of his cigar. "Depends what you mean. She can form sentences, say words in English. But she's gone mad. Why the hell would you want to talk to her?"

"There are one or two things we want to clear up. We have a new witness who says that on Monday night he heard the sound of a woman crying. He thought it was coming from your house and it was roughly in the same timeframe that Constable Wicken died. At the very least, it indicates somebody was awake at that hour and may have seen or heard something."

Nathaniel frowned. "You think it was my wife?"

"Possibly. The witness described the sound as cries for help. When I was here on Tuesday, I saw Mrs Eakin. She cried out to me for help."

"She did not!" burst out Mrs Curran.

215

"She didn't shout out loud, ma'am, but she did speak and what she said was, 'Help me.'"

Nathaniel put down his cigar, took out a large red handkerchief, trumpeted into it, then stuffed it back into his trouser pocket.

"Well, it's true, she moaned often enough."

"You can understand why I'd like to pursue this matter," said Murdoch.

"No, frankly I don't."

"Two reasons. Perhaps Mrs Eakin saw the constable going by. She could corroborate whether or not he was alone. Secondly, if he did hear these cries, he may have come to investigate . . ."

He left the rest of the sentence, not wanting to fill in too much, waiting to see what would be their reaction.

Eakin looked up at his daughter. "Well?"

"Nobody came here."

"Is it possible you wouldn't have heard, ma'am? Your chambers are on the third floor. You didn't hear your stepmother calling out and it does seem that she was."

She thought for a moment and he had the feeling she was searching for the safest answer.

"It is possible but not likely."

Nathaniel poured himself a generous amount of wine from a decanter on the sidetable and took a good swallow. "I don't see the point of this, sir. Even if the officer did come to this house, which he didn't, what does it matter? It don't overturn the coroner's verdict. The man took his own life and that's all there is to it."

Murdoch decided to change tack. "As I said there are one or two loose ends to the case. The more I know about Wicken's last movements, the better."

Eakin took another drink of wine as if it were water. "You're wasting your time here."

There was the merest slur to his words. Murdoch knew the signs, and in spite of himself, his body, which had its own wisdom, grew tense.

"I'll be able to determine that myself after I've spoken to Mrs Eakin personally. And may I ask, what is wrong with her?"

Augusta shifted uncomfortably and involuntarily smoothed the antimacassar that was on the back of the chair. Her father made a show of staring at Murdoch as if he were a likely candidate for a freak show.

"She's been taken up the loop, that's what's wrong. She's gone batchy, barmy,"

"Insanity has many faces, doesn't it? My question has more to do with the form that your wife's lunacy has taken."

"I thought you were a police officer, not a physician."

"Father ..." Augusta tried to place a placating hand on Nathaniel's shoulder. He immediately shrugged it off.

"I would imagine Mr Murdoch wants to know if Stepmother is a danger to herself or anybody else. Isn't that right, sir?"

Murdoch hadn't actually been that clear in his mind as to what he wanted, but he nodded.

"Is she?"

Nathaniel drew deeply on the cigar; the end glowed red through the ash. He didn't reply, his thoughts suddenly pulled away. His daughter answered.

"Unfortunately, Mrs Eakin suffered a tragic loss not too long ago. Her son by her previous marriage died suddenly of peritonitis. The doctor feels that the grief has caused a temporary derailment of her faculties."

"Derangement. You mean derangement, fool."

Nathaniel had come out of his daydream as vicious as a ferret from its hole. Murdoch smiled falsely. "I can see you've been a schoolteacher, Mr Eakin?"

"No, I have not. But any fool can use words properly if they want to. She's had more education than I ever did. I never had the opportunity to continue past standard two even if I wanted to. I had to work. The family needed my wages."

Mrs Curran attempted a feeble retaliation. "I hardly think he needs to know our personal history, Father." Her fair skin flushed with humiliation but she continued to address Murdoch.

"She began to suffer from delusions of persecution. She became convinced the child was poisoned and that she herself was in danger."

"Speak to the physician if you don't believe us," said Nathaniel. "He wrote the death certificate. Boy died from a burst appendix. Nothing could be done." He gulped down the last of the wine. Then he leaned forward toward Murdoch, fixing him with eyes that were fast becoming bloodshot. "The thing is, Margaret knows this lot is against her and she mulled that over in her mind until she went batchy."

His daughter fluttered nervously. "Nobody is 'against her,' as you put it, Father. I, in particular, have tried to be welcoming. She would have none of it. She was so hostile from the very beginning."

"She was afraid. Stands to reason she would be. Here I was, a widower. Children grown. My daughter here is used to running the house. You know what women are like when another hen comes into the barnyard." He made pecking motions with his fingers. "Cluck, cluck, cluck. Fact is, they're all afraid she's going to get one under her apron and claim their inheritance."

Murdoch was beginning to feel sorry for Mrs Curran. She turned her face away and moved over to the hearth. There was no mourning crepe or festoons of black ribbon in this room, Murdoch noticed.

"What was the name of the doctor who attended your wife?"

In spite of what he'd said, he wasn't at all sure this inquiry was going to yield anything, but Eakin was such a vile-tempered old sod, he didn't want to let him off too easily. Nathaniel didn't reply but began to puff on his cigar again. Murdoch knew the procrastination was a further attempt to intimidate him, to put him in his place, and he could feel his own temper rising. This man might have money and fancy himself a gentleman, but he had the temperament of a pugilist, and if he wasn't careful, he, Murdoch, would take up the challenge, old man or not.

Augusta answered for him. "Dr Ferrier. He lives just across the road. Number 312."

Murdoch took out his notebook and wrote down the name and number.

A gong started to mark out the hour and he saw that there was another clock on one of the shelves that was identical to the one in the parlour. The coins around her bosom gleamed in the firelight.

He folded up his notebook, returned it to his pocket, and stood up.

"Are you going out to the loony bin?" asked Eakin.

"Yes, I'll go tomorrow."

Nathaniel got to his feet and came over to him. He was a good head shorter than Murdoch, which meant he had to look up and Murdoch could smell the cigar and the wine on his breath.

"What they should tell you is that my wife suffers from erotomania. Do you know what that means?"

"No, I don't."

"Well, you should write it down in your little notebook. It means as soon as she sees a pair of trousers, she's going to lift her tail for you. She went for Jarius in the same way. And my son-in-law, her husband . . ." he jerked his thumb in Augusta's direction. "I wouldn't recommend you take her up on the offer. She'd do it for the butcher's boy if he came by."

"I'll take that into advisement," said Murdoch.

"Yes, I would if I were you."

Sullenly, he backed off. With a nod to Mrs Curran, Murdoch left.

CHAPTER THIRTY-ONE

MURDOCH JOG-WALKED ALL the way to Ontario Street in an attempt to dispel his anger. His head was filled with fantasies, all of them violent, of what he would do to Nathaniel Eakin. When he'd finished smashing the man's head against the floor for the second time, he slowed himself down. Yes, the old geezer was a horse's arse but Murdoch knew the rage he'd stirred up didn't totally belong with him. His memory of his father shouting about his mother was a tight pain in his chest and he felt short of breath. "She's a whore, a tart, cheap as a dish clout." And more, words that he didn't want to recall. She, silent as always, going about her task, head bowed in a way that made him, the boy, want to scream out. "Look up! Don't lower your head down like that." But when he spoke to her afterwards, she wept, and his feelings of fear and pity became overlaid with contempt for her and a burning rage toward his father that even now made him hot. According to the local magistrate, his mother had died accidentally, while she was gathering shellfish on the beach. A slip, a hard knock on the head that rendered her unconscious and she drowned. Murdoch had gone to the shore afterwards, trying to find the pool where she'd died. He couldn't place it exactly but it didn't matter, they were all shallow, no more than splashing deep. That made her death even more meaningless.

"Evening, Mr Murdoch." His next door neighbour, O'Brien, was going by. He had a sailor's duffel bag slung over his shoulder and Murdoch assumed he was off once again to some exotic place. He turned and waved in the direction of his house and Murdoch could see his wife and children were crowded into the window. They all waved back with varying degrees of enthusiasm. Murdoch thought O'Brien had probably once again impregnated Mrs O'Brien and they could expect to see child number nine.

All the little faces were watching Murdoch now and he tried to give them a cheery smile. He resolved to pick up some more barley sugar sticks from Mrs Bail's confectionary as soon as he could.

He let himself into the house and was greeted by the sight of his landlady and landlord.

Arthur was walking slowly down the hall, Beatrice close behind as if ready to catch him. They both turned around to welcome him.

"Evening, Will," said Arthur.

"What are you doing out here?"

"Taking in the sights. I'm getting corns on my rear end from sitting so much. I thought I'd take a stroll. I'm pretending this is King Street. Any minute now I'm going to go in one of the fancy shops and spend a lot of money."

"Good thing you've come, Mr Murdoch," said Beatrice. "He always overdoes it and he won't listen to me. We've done quite enough for one night."

Arthur had dressed himself in trousers and a flannel shirt for the occasion. In the candlelight, with a brighter energy in his face, he looked almost healthy. Murdoch felt a rush of affection for him and would have embraced him if he hadn't known it would embarrass everybody. He tapped his foot on the floor. They had rolled up the hall rug to make walking a bit easier.

"This is perfect for doing a schottische. Mrs K., we can practise whenever you're ready."

"I've forgotten how. Here, let me take your things," said Mrs Kitchen, abandoning her husband. "It's been so miserable all day. I've got your dinner warming."

221

"Thank you. As usual, I'm famished. Will you join me, Arthur?"

"Why don't you eat first. I'll have a rest to satisfy my wife and then we can have tea."

"You can go right into the parlour," said Beatrice. "I'll just see to Father."

"No, you won't," said Arthur and he flexed his arm to make a muscle. "I am strong as the Borneo Wild Man. I will go myself and sit in my chair until called."

He was speaking jokingly but his frustration was evident. Before he became ill, Arthur Kitchen had been highly active, a keen bicyclist and walker. According to his wife, he was an excellent dancer, speciality the polka, something Murdoch was still aspiring to.

Beatrice went on down to the kitchen and Arthur into the middle room. Murdoch stood for a moment, blowing on his cold hands, but really trying to listen for sounds from upstairs—the typewriting machine, or Enid talking to her son. He was just about to go into the parlour when he heard the stairs creak. Mrs Jones herself came down the stairs. She was holding her son's hand and they were both dressed for the outdoors in long rubber waterproof coats. There was something in her expression that he couldn't quite read. Guarded, not altogether happy to see him. He felt a rush of disappointment. Back to that again, were they?

"Mrs Jones, Alwyn. Where are you off to on such a dreary night?"

"There is a special meeting at the church. A speaker has come up from Wisconsin. He is just returned from our mission in Nigeria. Apparently, he is most inspirational." Her voice was full of enthusiasm and Murdoch felt jealous. It made him sharp.

"I sincerely hope he is worth braving the rain."

She was aware of his tone and her face clouded. "He will be I am sure. He has worked for Our Lord for many years."

Murdoch stepped back so she could pass him. He tapped the boy playfully on his cap but the child shrank away as if he had dealt him a blow. That irritated Murdoch as well. The boy was a mardy tit most of the time. At the door, Enid hesitated and turned back to him.

222

"I really don't expect us to be late, Mr Murdoch. Perhaps you and I could have a word together if you're still up?"

"For that I'll wait till midnight."

He'd meant to be gallant but the words came out angry.

"Good evening, then."

She opened the door, letting in a surge of cold, wet air. Murdoch went into the front room, chastising himself for being such a boor. Mrs Jones seemed highly devout to him. Not likely to change her religion. He caught himself. If it came to that, what about him? Could he denounce his faith, which is what he supposed he would have to do if . . . again he stopped. Look at him, racing ahead of himself like a fanciful girl. Marriage on his mind and they didn't even use each other's first names! He went over to the table and sat down at the place set for him. Does any of it really matter? Our Lord didn't declare himself a Baptist or a Catholic for that matter. He'd started out his life as a Jew. Who was he anyway? Murdoch had asked that question once when he was being taught his catechism. The priest had slapped him with the holy book on the side of the head. "Those sorts of heathen questions sound too close to blasphemy, young man. Go kneel down in that corner and say your Paternosters until I tell you to move."

Murdoch had stayed there until his knees screamed with pain but he had not begged for release.

He rubbed at his face hard. This seemed to be his day for chewing over old grudges. Father O'Malley was one. A big, tough priest, he had both a brogue and brain as thick as an Irish bog.

Murdoch knew his mother would have liked to have seen him enter the priesthood, but he couldn't imagine it. However, his sister Susanna had gone into a convent school and took her final vows at the age of eighteen. She lived as a cloistered nun in a convent in Montreal and he hadn't seen her for a long time. He was allowed to write and received one letter a year. Hers was impersonal, full of devout phrases. The playmate he had loved, argued with, and ultimately protected had vanished behind a veil of platitudes.

"My, you are looking very fierce, Mr Murdoch."

Mrs Kitchen came in carrying a tray.

He grinned at her, glad to be brought out of his thoughts. "You're right. I was thinking about the Church."

She gave him a shrewd glance. "The Church or people in the Church?"

He helped unload the dinner plate. Tonight she had cooked his favourite dish, sausages and mashed potato and baked rutabaga.

"Your sweet is an egg custard. Mrs Jones made it. She insisted. She said your gum was probably still sore. Arthur even tried some. Very tasty too."

"Can I start with that?"

"Don't you dare." She smiled at him. "I find Mrs Jones is a woman who grows on me. Quiet. I thought she was standoffish at first but she's just reserved. Wouldn't you agree, Mr Murdoch?"

"I do indeed."

"I particularly like the fact that she teaches her boy proper manners. She won't take any nonsense."

Murdoch nodded noncommittally.

"She's a good mother, I'd say. Not one of these flighty women who'd stuff their children into whatever purse suits them."

He looked at her but she wasn't giving anything away.

She removed the tray to the sideboard. "I'll leave you in peace then. Ring when you're done."

When she'd closed the door, Murdoch slowed down on the gusto with which he'd approached his meal. The potatoes were cold and lumpy, the rutabaga bitter, and the sausage had turned hard as a rock. But he didn't live here on account of the food and he would never want Mrs Kitchen to know what a dreadful cook she was.

HE MUST HAVE been asleep for more than an hour. The last he remembered was sitting in the armchair by the fire and putting his head back. He had the hazy impression of Beatrice covering him with a quilt, but he couldn't let go of the sleep that was pulling him down. What finally woke him was the sound of the front door opening. He sat up, groggy, trying to grab awareness. The candle had burned low in the holder and the fire was down to embers. The clock showed eleven.

He heard footsteps on the stairs and yawning, he got up and went into the hall. Enid Jones was struggling to negotiate the hall furniture. She was carrying Alwyn who was fast asleep.

"Here, let me." He held out his arms for the boy. At first he thought she was going to refuse but her only other choice was to put Alwyn down.

"Thank you."

Awkwardly, she passed him over, heavy with the relaxation of sleep. His head dropped against Murdoch's shoulder and he tucked him in under his chin.

"I'll hold the door," said Enid, and she whisked up the stairs ahead of him.

At the entrance to her room, he paused for her to light a lamp and pull back the coverlet from the bed. How warm and solid the boy felt in his arms, his breathing deep and regular. Murdoch gently kissed his cheek, still cool from the outdoors.

"Let me take off his waterproof." She manoeuvred the boy's arms out of the sleeves while Murdoch held him up. She was so close, he could see the shape of her mouth, a faint down on her upper lip.

"Lie him here if you please."

He did so and Alwyn immediately rolled onto his stomach, knee bent.

"I'll have to take off his boots, but I don't have the heart to disturb him now. I'll wait."

"Surely you didn't carry him all the way from Jarvis Street?" asked Murdoch in a whisper.

"No, just from the top of the street, but by the time we got here, he felt heavier than a sack of potatoes. I would never have managed the stairs. Thank you so much, Mr Murdoch."

"Not at all. It was my pleasure." And he meant it.

She hesitated. "I was hoping we could talk for a few moments. If you're not too tired, that is."

225

"I'm wide awake. We can go down to the parlour if you like. I don't hear anything from the Kitchens so I'm assuming they are asleep."

"I am much later than I expected."

"The speaker had a lot to say then?"

"Yes. He was quite wonderful and people had many questions for him."

She took off her waterproof, unpinned her hat, put it on the dresser, and quickly smoothed back her hair.

"Shall we go downstairs?"

NATHANIEL COULD NOT understand why Jarius was not answering him. He had told him twice that he wanted to get up. He had vomited on his bed, on the pillow, and the sour smell was in his nostrils. He wanted to move his face away but he couldn't. He tried to talk again but the words he heard coming out were garbled, not what he wanted to say. He could see Jarius frown uncomprehendingly. *My arm has gone to sleep, help me roll over on my back.* Somebody must have put the rug over him because he could feel the weight. It was far too heavy. He was cold though, the fire must have gone out. Had he tripped when he was going to put on another piece of coal? He wanted to turn his head to see but no matter how hard he tried, he couldn't. He could hear somebody talking gibberish. *What idiot is that?* he wondered.

"Father? Father?" Jarius was kneeling beside him, and he slipped an arm under his shoulders to hoist him into a sitting position. Nathaniel made an anguished effort to tell him what was happening but all that came out were grunts.

"Augusta!" yelled Jarius. "Augusta, come here quick!"

CHAPTER THIRTY-TWO

———•———

MURDOCH HEARD FOOTSTEPS coming down the corridor toward the cell. The heavy tread could belong only to Constable Crabtree. The tiny panel in the cell door was pushed aside and he could see his eyes peering in. They looked amused.

"You can come in, George, I'm awake."

Crabtree entered. He was carrying a mug of something, presumably tea.

"Thought you'd like this, sir."

Murdoch scratched his leg under his trouser legs. "Who was in here last?"

"Old Joe Baxter, I think."

"He left a lot behind."

He took the mug and drank some of the tea. It was strong and tasted as if a cup of sugar had been dumped into it. It was also scalding hot and he winced.

"Did you get any sleep at all, sir?"

"No. But at least it made me more sympathetic toward our guests. I'm going to requisition a new pallet. Some rocks have wandered into this one."

He yawned and looked around the small cell. There was a narrow bed, which had a straw mattress and an iron-hard blanket, a stool, and a bucket "What do you say to a couple of pictures on the walls, George? Tasteful. I'll donate my portrait of Colonel Grassett. Cheer the place up a bit."

"The prisoners might want to stay on if we do that."

Murdoch scratched again. "Highly unlikely even with decorations."

He twisted his head, trying to get the kink out of his neck. "I'd better get out of here before the others start wondering what the hell I'm doing."

"You're not the first officer to doss down in one of the cells and you probably won't be the last."

"I should have gone to the Avonmore but this was the first place I thought of."

Crabtree nodded. Ever tactful, he hadn't yet inquired why Murdoch had come to the station in the middle of the night looking for a bed to sleep in.

"George, how did you and Ellen meet each other?"

If the constable was surprised by the question, he didn't show it. "We've known each other since we were kids. Our parents were good friends. We played in each other's back yards."

"So, when did you know you were in love with each other?"

"In love? I can't say exactly. We just sort of took it for granted that we would get married."

"And you're both Methodists aren't you?"

"Yes, sir."

"Do you believe in mixed marriages, George?"

"You mean if the parties are of different religions?"

"Yes. What if one was, say, Roman Catholic, and the other was, say, Baptist? Do you think such a marriage would work?"

"That would depend, wouldn't it?"

"On what?" Murdoch almost shouted out the question.

"I suppose on how important religion was to each person and how much they were prepared to compromise."

Murdoch groaned. He felt as if he'd been drinking for two days, with his thick tongue and head. Enid and he had gone downstairs to the parlour but he knew, he could tell, he was not going to like what she had to say. And he hadn't.

"I've been thinking and thinking, and difficult as it is for me to come to my conclusion, I have done so."

"Yes?" his heart sinking.

"You would want me to convert to Catholicism and I could not do that. I would be disloyal to my husband's memory and the solemn promise I made to him to rear Alwyn with Jesus as his Saviour. Therefore, I'm leaving. I've found another boardinghouse closer to the church."

"And further away from St Paul's, I suppose?"

He had to admire her, she'd shown more honesty than him. Then, for the first time, she called him by his Christian name and the sweetness of it was almost obliterated by the hurt of what she was saying.

"Will, I must admit, I am growing very fond of you, but for both our sakes, it is better that these feelings do not continue.

Murdoch fingered his bristly jaw. He needed a shave.

"I have been turned down, George."

"By Mrs Jones, sir? The Welsh lady?"

"That's the one. She doesn't think she can overcome the obstacle of our different religions. She also said, and I quote, 'We have both suffered loss of a loved one. It is lonely we are. We must not mistake these feelings for real love. They may have been created by mere proximity.' As if it would have happened with any man."

Crabtree cleared his throat. "Forgive me, Mr Murdoch, but she does have a point. Perhaps when she is living somewhere else, you can determine if you have found true love or not."

Murdoch had to laugh at the solemnity with which his constable delivered this speech. "You're in the wrong line of work, George. You should have been a minister."

"I did consider that at one time, sir. But Ellen didn't fancy being a minister's wife. Too much scrutiny on you. I am assuming, by the way, sir, that you do intend to see Mrs Jones when she is not under the same roof?"

"I don't know. I hadn't got that far."

They heard steps outside and one of the young constables came to the door.

"There's somebody here to see you, Mr Murdoch. A Scotch lassie."

"Who?"

"The boy with the braid down his back."

"The Chinaman's son?"

"That's the one."

"Did he say what he wanted?"

"Och, no." He gave a dreadful imitation of Foon Lee's accent.

"Give me a few minutes then bring him down to my office."

"Yes, sir." He looked around the cell curiously. "Are you doing an inspection, Mr Murdoch?"

"Something like that."

He stood up and felt a sharp twinge in his lower back. "George, remind me from time to time will you that I am a grown man and I do not have to behave like a child in a temper."

He'd yelled out at her, "If you consider I am too proximate as you put it, I will go somewhere else."

Crabtree grinned. "Why don't I see if I can dig out a razor for you? Nothing like scraping at your face to make you realise you've grown up."

LIFTING THE STRANDS of reeds, Crabtree ushered Foon Lee into the cubicle. The young man bowed. Murdoch didn't quite know how to respond but he sort of bobbed his head.

"Have a seat, Mr Lee."

Foon took the chair in front of the desk and immediately put his hands in the wide sleeves of his tunic. He was in his working clothes today, blue linen tunic and black wide trousers. Murdoch thought he seemed ill at ease, and was trying hard not to show it. Probably it was the first time he had ever been inside a police station. Murdoch suddenly had the sense of how it might look to the young Chinaman. Strange people, strange ways. He smiled, trying to put him at ease, then got self-conscious. Perhaps in China, it wasn't considered good manners to smile.

"You wanted to talk to me, Mr Lee?"

The young man nodded or bowed, Murdoch couldn't tell which it was. Maybe both.

There was an uncomfortable silence while they both looked at each other; Murdoch tried to appear encouraging.

"I have come concerning the matter of the constable who recently met with his death. On later reflection, my father has decided he is not utterly positive in his identification of the young woman accompanying the constable on that fateful night. In fact, on later reflection he has determined that the woman you, yourself, presented was more likely to be the one he had first seen standing behind the officer." He paused to await Murdoch's response, who, sensing there was more to come, didn't say anything. Foon looked away and addressed the rest of his remarks to the wall behind Murdoch's shoulder. "In the interests of helping the police officers in their quest, my father is however able to offer some information concerning the other woman. The ladyship who appeared at the inquest and said she was betrothed to Mr Wicken."

"Is he now? And what might that information consist of?"

"Her name is Mary Ann Trowbridge as she stated but her address is a deceit. She does in fact live on Sydenham Street. Her profession is of ill-repute."

"I see. How does your father come to have that information?"

Foon coughed politely but still spoke to Her Majesty's portrait. "This ladyship and my father had acquaintance at a previous time. Of an entirely chaste nature of course."

It wasn't easy to read him through the thick dialect and the apparent lack of expression on his face, but there was a hint of resentment in his tone, a tightening of his lips.

"When was this chaste encounter?"

"A few months ago, I believe."

"Did he mention at what number on Sydenham Miss Trowbridge lives?"

"Yes. She resides at 334. The house with a blue door."

Murdoch fiddled with his moustache. Foon was corroborating what Beulah had said. Apparently Miss Mary Ann was still active. It might make matters even harder for Mrs Wicken and Isobel if this came out.

The Chinaman finally met his eyes. "Mr Murdoch, would it be correct for my part to assume you will not need to mention my father? We are at the mercy . . ." His voice tailed off and Murdoch realised what a serious thing it was for him to come to the station.

"Does he know you have brought this information to me?"

Foon looked at him and his expression this time was revealing. "Can I say that my father would no doubt have approved, but I have not yet had the occasion to inform him. I chose to encumber myself with this errand."

Murdoch held out his hand. "Thank you, Mr Lee. You have performed your civic duty. I will follow up on this."

Foon shook hands somewhat hesitantly. His fingers were cool, slightly damp.

CHAPTER THIRTY-THREE

———◆———

ALL THE CURTAINS were drawn at the house with the blue door. A cast-iron lantern was fastened on a bracket to the side of the porch. It was placed so that no direct light fell on the person who might be standing there. Cunning. Murdoch opened the gate, which screeched a warning, and walked up to the door. There was a heavy brass knocker he thought at first was carved in the shape of a lion's head. As he lifted the ring, however, he saw that the design was that of a woman's face with snakes writhing from her brow. He thumped hard.

Almost at once, the curtain across the windows to his right lifted slightly. He couldn't see who was looking out but he smiled pleasantly so as not to frighten them. After what seemed a long wait, the door opened, barely a crack, only sufficient for him to glimpse a tiny woman, soberly dressed and sharp featured.

"Yes?" She scowled at him.

He touched the brim of his hat politely. "I was wondering if I could speak to Miss Mary Ann Trowbridge. I understand she lives here."

"Who are you?"

Murdoch hesitated, not sure whether revealing his identity at this point would get the door closed in his face. He felt squeamish at the idea of pretending to be a customer, however.

"My name is Murdoch. I'm an acting detective at number four station. I'm pursuing an investigation and I would like to talk to Miss Trowbridge."

She didn't look impressed or alarmed. "What sort of investigation?"

"I'd prefer to discuss that with her."

"She doesn't live here anymore." She didn't relent from the frown.

"Where is she?"

"I don't know. I'm not the post office keeper."

The woman's hair was pulled up tightly into a knot at the top of her head, accentuating her rather prominent ears. What he could see of her dress was a drab brown. She made him think of an elf, but without the endearing qualities one usually associated with the fairy world. She also was a kindred spirit to Beulah.

"Is there anyone else I can speak to then?"

"No."

Fortunately, he was saved from more aggravation by somebody speaking from the hallway.

"Emily, you are letting in the worst draft. Either invite the gentleman in or close the door."

The woman addressed was obviously about to follow the second injunction but Murdoch quickly got his knee in the way. He pushed his way forward across the threshold.

A young woman was standing at the bottom of the stairs. She was full fleshed and her white diaphanous gown was cut to reveal a considerable amount of bosom and bare arm. Her abundant brown hair was loosely pinned, her lips and cheeks rouged. She was Murdoch's idea of a whore.

She smiled. If the doorkeeper was a bad-tempered elf, this young woman was a flower fairy. At least in the dim light. He touched his hat again.

"Excuse me, ma'am, for disturbing you, but I am a detective and I would like to come in and ask a few questions."

The smile vanished and she looked alarmed.

"I, er . . ." She glanced over her shoulder for help and yet another woman appeared. The hall was becoming crowded. She was older, statuesque in build, magnificently corseted into a pearl-grey silk gown. The ivory satin draping her bosom would have done credit to any mantelpiece. Her full chin was pushed into further roundness by the high lace collar. Exactly what he imagined a bawdy house mistress would look like.

"Emily, what is the trouble here?" She spoke with complete authority and the gatekeeper stepped back a pace. The young woman also moved halfway up the stairs but stayed to watch.

Again Murdoch introduced himself. "I would appreciate some of your time, ma'am."

He saw her consider all of her choices, then she smiled. Her teeth were startlingly white, and faultless. He was reminded of Dr Stevens's denture display case. She held out a mittened hand, leaning across Emily as if she were a piece of furniture.

"How do you do? I'm Mrs Clara Doherty."

He took her hand, a little uncertain as to what was expected of him. She was wearing a large emerald ring on her index finger and the gesture was almost papal. He refrained from kissing it however and half squeezed, half shook the palm.

"Please come in. We can talk in my chambers." Her accent was quite English.

He wasn't sure how he was going to get past the recalcitrant servant without embarrassment to both of them, but Mrs Doherty saved him.

"Emily, I'm sure Mr Murdoch needs something warm. Bring us some Turkish coffee. Is that agreeable to you, sir?"

Murdoch nodded appreciatively. His search for Mary Ann Trowbridge was introducing him to some exotic culinary tastes.

"Give me your things," said the housekeeper and he obeyed, struggling in the confined space to divest himself of his sealskin coat. Finally he was free and she took the coat and hat and trotted off down the hall, where she dumped them on a tall oaken stand. The young woman, who had giggled prettily during this transaction, was still watching, but with a quick nod of the head from her mistress, she too left, ascending the stairs with a certain degree of melodrama and her dress lifted well above ankle height. The effect was marred, however, by her need to sneeze violently. She didn't let go of her skirt but sniffed back whatever snot she could.

"Mr Murdoch?" Mrs Doherty said.

He blushed, annoyed at himself for being distracted.

"This way." She pulled aside a red velvet portiere to the left, opened the door and ushered him in. He immediately banged his shin against the corner of a low table that seemed to be placed directly in the doorway. Mrs Doherty sailed ahead, navigating an astounding amount of furniture—lamp tables, plant stands laden with large potted ferns, purple plush armchairs. She took a seat on one of the couches by the fireplace and indicated he should sit across from her. The carpet was thick, fawn coloured, patterned with large pink and yellow roses. Mrs Doherty glanced at his feet and he was aware that his boots were wet and he shifted like a schoolboy. He'd conducted many interviews in his career but he didn't remember feeling so ill-at-ease and clumsy. He didn't know if it was his own consciousness of his lack of sexual initiation or if Mrs Doherty had perfected the art of keeping the male half of the population off balance.

"I know that Mary Ann Trowbridge lives here. I would like to talk to her."

His harsh tone apparently startled Clara, who had obviously been intent on keeping up pretences as long as she could. She frowned.

"I'm afraid she's moved out."

"When?"

"Yesterday as a matter of fact. But I must insist you explain yourself, sir. Why do you want to speak to her?"

Her voice changed, the false English intonation dropped away.

"As you no doubt are aware, Miss Trowbridge testified recently at an inquest into the death of a young constable. The investigation is not complete and I would very much like to ask her some questions."

She chose to look affronted at his lack of manners.

They were interrupted by Emily, who without a knock or any other warning, opened the door and entered the room. She was carrying a silver tray on which sat a silver coffeepot and two cups and saucers. They were delicate but normal size, unlike the ones at the Avison house.

"I've just took out some plum cake, shall I bring it in?" she asked Clara.

"No, this is quite adequate."

Murdoch would have dearly liked some plum cake as his stomach had been growling for the last hour, but he had offended Clara by his lack of tact and she was punishing him. There was a stiff silence while Emily put down the tray on the sideboard, shoving aside a porcelain lamp that tinkled musically as the crystal droplets shook. She poured out some dark, thick liquid into the china cups and handed one to Clara, the other to Murdoch. Then she herself took a seat on the couch beside Mrs Doherty, who immediately sipped avidly at her drink. Murdoch tried his. The brew smelled all right, but tasted so harsh and bitter he almost spat it out. He was aware Clara was watching him.

"Hm . . . hm."

Surprisingly she smiled her perfect smile. "I prepare the essence myself. I have heard there is none quite like it."

Murdoch nodded in acknowledgment, not sure how he was going to swallow the rest of the poisonous brew. He felt as if he had lost a layer of skin off his tongue.

"Horrible stuff," said Emily. "Burn a hole in your stomach."

Mrs Doherty ignored her and he wondered again what the status of the bad-tempered elf was in this household. Not servant surely. She took too many liberties.

His hostess opened a drawer in one of the plant stands that was on her right. She took out a small silver flask, unscrewed the top, and held it out to him. "A little brandy, Mr Murdoch. It is a very dull morning."

He wouldn't have broken the fragile truce even if he'd taken the Pledge.

"Thank you, ma'am. A spot would go down well."

Emily snatched the flask from Clara's hand and poured a generous shot into his cup. She then added a much smaller amount to Mrs

Doherty's cup. Murdoch tasted the coffee again. The brandy definitely improved the flavour and he managed to gulp back most of it.

He heard the faint sound of a bell ringing from the rear of the house. Emily immediately stood up. "I'll leave you to your business," she said, and she gathered up the two cups, put them on the tea tray and left. As soon as the door had closed, Mrs Doherty bent over, fished beneath the skirt of the couch, and pulled out a wooden pail. She took off the lid.

"Would you care for a sweet?"

"No, thank you, ma'am."

She paused, scrutinised the contents of the pail, and selected a bright pink, egg-shaped candy.

"Now, sir. You were saying?" asked Clara. The English inflection was back in place, slightly muffled by the crackling of her chewing. He decided to come in on a more oblique tack.

"Are you acquainted with Mr Sam Lee, a Chinaman?"

She didn't speak until she'd finished off the candy egg. "No, I am not."

"He says he has been a visitor here."

"Is that so? Unfortunately, Mr Murdoch, as all of my friends will tell you, I have a most appalling memory. In my capacity of music teacher, I see many people but I could not tell you who they are. If we were ever to meet on the street, I do not acknowledge them. I regret to say, I will probably forget you, yourself, tomorrow."

So that was going to be her line, was it?

"But you do remember Oliver Wicken? He was engaged to Miss Trowbridge."

"How extraordinary. But these days young women are so independent. They don't share their lives at all, not the way we used to when I was a girl."

Murdoch was certain she had never been young, that she had sprung fully dressed and bejewelled out of her father's head.

"You are saying he never came here to see her?"

"No, he did not."

"What is your relation to Miss Trowbridge?"

238

"She is my niece by marriage."

He leaned forward, trying to force her to look him in the eyes.

"Mrs Doherty, at the inquest which is under the jurisdiction of Her Majesty, Queen Victoria, Miss Trowbridge produced a letter supposedly from her aunt. She named her as a Mrs Avison. That good lady has informed me that they are not related and that, in fact, Miss Trowbridge was her maid some years ago. Her name then was Trotter. It seems that the poor girl was got in the family way and was dismissed."

"How unkind of her employer."

"Madam, I must remind you we are dealing with the law. This is very serious. It seems that your niece produced a document which was a forgery. She will be open to charges."

"I understand that."

Frustrated, Murdoch stood up, although there wasn't very far to move.

"You are saying, unequivocally, that you have no knowledge of a constable named Oliver Wicken or any engagement that existed between him and Miss Mary Ann Trowbridge?"

She shrugged and delicately probed underneath her dentures to remove a fragment of icing. "I am saying that with such a bad memory as I have, I am utterly unreliable as any sort of witness."

He knew he would not shake her. Even in such ridiculous lies she was imposing.

"Why did Miss Trowbridge leave your house?"

Again the shrug. "She was a little bored with Toronto. She has relatives in Montreal and it seemed more exciting to her, I presume. She rarely confided in me."

He returned to the couch, sat down, and took out his notebook.

"Where is she staying in Montreal?"

"Alas, Mr Murdoch, I don't know. She never said."

He closed the notebook with a snap. "Was Miss Trowbridge at home on Monday evening?"

"Yes, I believe she was."

"All evening?"

He'd made a move she hadn't expected. She bought time by sifting through the candy pail.

"I cannot say for certain. I was rather unwell; I retired early."

A yellow egg was popped into her mouth. More crunching.

"Did you say good night to your niece?"

"Yes, of course."

"What time was that?"

"I cannot be precise."

"Just within an hour would help. Eight o'clock? Nine?"

She hesitated, trying to sort out the least compromising answer. "Perhaps closer to nine. As I say, she is an independent young woman. She must have slipped out not wanting me to worry."

"Would you have forbidden her if you had known?"

"Of course. Which is why she was probably so cautious. I doubt anyone else would have seen her."

"In other words, nobody will deny or corroborate her statement?"

"I suppose you could put it that way."

She offered him the candy pail.

"Can I tempt you?"

"No, thank you." He waited for her attention. "Miss Trowbridge said under oath that she met with Wicken the night he died."

"Indeed!"

"But I have a witness who says he saw the constable in the company of a different woman at that exact time. His fiancée."

"Really? Another? Is he setting up to be a bigamist?"

"I don't think so. I believe he had only one, the young woman who met him on his beat. You see, according to my witness, Miss Trowbridge is a prostitute."

He'd wanted to shock her but she was ready.

"There are always people ready to smear a young woman's reputation."

"And yours then, ma'am. My witness says that you run a bawdy house here and that Mary Ann Trowbridge is one of your doxies."

She smiled, she was on safe ground here. She'd dealt with this

240

before. "As I already said, I am a music teacher. I run a music academy for adult students. People are only too ready to gossip."

As if to validate her statement, a piano started up from somewhere in the house. The sound was execrable, out of tune and spasmodic.

She was as implacable as the stuffed couch she sat on. Murdoch sat forward.

"Mrs Doherty. At this time I am not too interested in how you earn your living. I am more concerned with trying to find the truth about what happened to Oliver Wicken. Let me put it this way. I will give you until tomorrow evening to locate the current whereabouts of Miss Mary Ann Trowbridge. If I receive that information in good time, I will not proceed any further with the complaint we are going to receive about you and the music academy. Is that clear?"

For answer, she reached over and pulled at a bell rope that hung beside the fireplace.

"I will ask Emily to see you out."

He didn't move and they faced each other like two opponents across a chess board. She lowered her gaze first. "I'll think about what you have said, Mr Murdoch. If I do obtain the information you need, I will send a messenger to the station."

"Number four, the northwest corner of Parliament Street and Wilton."

The door opened and the housekeeper came in carrying his sealskin coat and hat. He took them from her and headed for the door, negotiating his way around the chairs. Mrs Doherty and Emily both watched him.

THERE WAS A lamp beside Nathaniel's bed, the wick turned low. The old man's face was dark with shadows, but there was a glisten of saliva dribbling from the corner of his mouth. His eyes were open. Jarius leaned over the bed, placing his hands on either side of Nathaniel's head as if he would embrace him. He stared into the unmoving eyes.

"I don't know if you can hear me or understand what I am saying but I don't care. Listen to this Nathaniel. It is time you died. You

241

should have gone years ago. You won't recover from this, don't even hope that you will. So it is time to make right some wrongs. You are going to make a new will."

The old man made grunting sounds in his throat and his eyelids flickered.

"Does that little fart mean you understand me? I dearly hope so. I want you to make your last journey knowing the truth. You can take it to hell with you because that is surely where you are going." Jarius picked up the cloth that was on the pillow and wiped away the dribble. Then he bent down until he was so close, it was almost a kiss.

"I hate you! You think I loved you but you fooled yourself. I have never for one moment felt any feelings toward you other than disgust. You destroyed my mother, my dear mother, as surely as if you had put a revolver to her temple. She wanted to die because her life here was unbearable."

He caught Nathaniel by the chin and jerked his head higher.

"You do understand. I can see that you do. You looked shocked. I don't know why you should be. We reap what we sow. You are fond of proverbs aren't you? *Spare the rod and spoil the child. Waste not want not.* Lots of them, all impressed on my bare backside."

Nathaniel made a feeble attempt to move his head away but it was impossible. Gibb squeezed his chin even tighter. "Frank hates you too but you probably know that. The surprise must be me."

He let go and stepped back, pulling aside the quilt. "You stupid, revolting old man. At your age, to think you could still stop your beak in some poor woman." With a tug, he lifted the nightshirt. "Look at you. A chicken gizzard has more life in it than that." He leaned over him again. "Listen to me good, Nathaniel. Your little jade was as light heeled as they come. She wanted to hump with me from the moment she came in the house. And she did. She slipped between my sheets many a night when you were snoring. Oh, she is as willing a tit as I've ever had. She was spent over and over. Quite wore me out. I only told you the half of it."

It was all lies of course. Peg had done no such thing. Except for the single desperate visit to his room, she had kept her distance. Jarius had enjoyed contemplating which course of action he would take. Tell the truth and make the old man face his mistake, or send him to eternity with a lie to make him squirm. The latter had seemed more likely to inflict pain.

The gurglings from Nathaniel's throat were louder. Jarius smiled. "Don't like to hear that, do you? She'd almost convinced you she was innocent, hadn't she? Well, take it to your grave, dear Step-father. May it torment you for all eternity."

He reached inside his waistcoat and took out a folded sheet of paper. "This is your new will. I have written it out according to your instructions. I'll read it to you."

He opened the paper, shook it in mock seriousness. "*This is the last will and testament of Nathaniel Joseph Eakin Esquire of 295 Gerrard Street in the city of Toronto and the county of York. Being of sound mind . . .*" Debatable, but never mind, I'm going to predate it. "*I hereby bequeath my goods and chattels in the following manner. To my beloved children,*" I call that a poetical conceit, "*To my beloved children, Francis John Eakin and Augusta Louisa Curran, I leave the sum of one thousand dollars each.*" Not what they are hoping for, of course. "*To my wife, Margaret Eakin, I leave likewise the sum of one thousand dollars, to be used for her care and maintenance as long as it is necessary.*" Don't worry, she won't need that much longer. "*I leave to my faithful servant, Janet Cullie, the sum of two hundred dollars.*" See how kind you are in your dotage, Nathaniel. Now here's the nub. "*To my dearest stepson, Jarius Gibb, whom I have ever loved and been loved as a son of my own flesh and blood.*" That's good isn't it? Another poetical conceit. "*To Jarius, I hereby leave my estate and all money that does acrue from the same, my insurance policies, and savings bonds.*" A goodly sum, Stepfather, thank you. Nobody would have sus-pected you had such a fine dowry. I welcome it, and as we both know, it is only fair and just that it go to me. Augusta has her own husband to take care of her, Frank would piss it away on whores and horses within a month, and dear stepmother won't have any need. So there we are."

He had brought in his scribe's lap desk and he opened the lid, took out a pen, and dipped it in the inkwell. Then he lifted Nathaniel's flaccid hand and wrapped the fingers around the pen.

"Sign here."

Slowly, he drew the old man's signature on the paper. "Good, that will do nicely."

He blew on the ink to dry it, then replaced the paper in his pocket. "I know what you're thinking, Stepfather, but I have taken care of that. The date on the will is two days ago. Before you became incapacitated. How fortunate for us that you had the foresight to take care of your affairs. And it is witnessed by both yours truly and Frank. Or will be. No, he won't balk. How can he? He will get one thousand dollars. That is better than a rope necklace."

He bent over and kissed Nathaniel on the cheek. "Good night, Stepfather. Sleep well."

He left, closing the door as softly as if he were leaving a nursery. Good. He was fairly certain the document was watertight, but just in case, there was one more thing to take care of. It was time some member of the family went to visit the unfortunate Mrs Eakin.

CHAPTER THIRTY-FOUR

THE BRANDY MURDOCH had drunk at the bawdy house was racing through his body, and there was a jauntiness in his step as he headed toward Queen Street to catch the streetcar.

When he took his seat, however, the false energy left him abruptly. The car clattered along, and before he knew it, his head drooped forward on his chest and he began to doze off.

"Sir! Sir!" the conductor was shaking his arm. "Here's your stop. The Provincial asylum."

He was speaking in a hushed voice as if it were impolite to say the name out loud.

Murdoch scrambled to his feet, and conscious of the curious gaze of the other passengers, he made his way to the front. The car slowed down and halted in front of the gates. He was the only one to get off.

He hadn't been here before and didn't know what to expect. However, at first sight the asylum appeared imposing and dignified rather than frightening, although he could see the windows were barred and there were sharp-looking railings on top of the surrounding wall. The building was long with two wings, each four stories high, and a higher central block. There was a cupola over the centre pediment that gave the building an ecclesiastical appearance, but which he'd heard actually housed a water tank. Although there was currently a lot of gossip about the bad air and need for repairs, originally the asylum had been designed with pride and care and it still showed through.

The tall iron gates were open and he walked in and along a winding path to the front doors. In the garden were two fine marble fountains, now turned off for the winter. Probably in summer the aspect was as pleasant as a public park.

He had telephoned the asylum earlier to see if it was all right for him to come, and the matron herself said she would meet him in the receiving area. He was relieved at that. As he entered the building, a uniformed doorman with impressive grey side-whiskers greeted him.

"Good day to you, sir. What is your business?"

"I am Acting Detective Murdoch. Miss Bastedo is expecting me."

"Ah, yes. Come this way if you please."

He lead Murdoch across the marble-tiled hall and up a flight of stairs. The place seemed deserted and Murdoch remarked on it.

"On a day like this we don't get many visitors," answered the doorman. "Pity really. Makes a change for the inmates to have some family company. They like variety same as everybody else."

At the top of the stairs was a wide corridor with windowed rooms opening onto it. A sign said FEMALE PATIENTS ON LEFT. MALE PATIENTS ON RIGHT. He glanced into one of the rooms on the right. A man, head bent to his chest, was seated between a woman of middle age, quite well dressed, and a younger woman. They must have been mother and daughter by the similarity of their posture, and they were staring ahead of them, not speaking or touching the man, each lost in their own misery.

In the centre of the corridor was the matron's office. It rather reminded him of the bridge on a ship. Windows on all sides gave her a view of the comings and goings in the reception rooms. She was writing at her desk but she looked up at their approach and came out at once to greet them.

"Mr Murdoch, I'm Miss Bastedo. We can talk in my office. Thank you, Landry."

246

The doorman bowed slightly and left them. Must have been a butler in his earlier employment, thought Murdoch. The matron, however, had none of the polite airs of a lady of leisure. She held out her hand as straightforwardly as a man might and her grip was firm indeed.

"I have arranged to have Mrs Eakin brought down. She will be here shortly."

She indicated he should sit down and she went behind her work-table, a severely plain piece of mahogany that took up most of the space in the small office. She opened a clothbound daybook.

"I thought we should talk about her condition beforehand. This note was completed by the attendant this morning. I'll read it to you. 'Mrs Eakin continues to show signs of improvement. She is keeping herself clean and is generally pleasant to the staff and other inmates. She has agreed to do some light sewing and has already completed two tray covers. She is eating well and taking her tonic without complaint.' Good."

She paused. "One of the reasons Mrs Eakin was committed to the asylum was because she was convinced somebody was trying to poison her and she had not eaten in days."

"Who is it that Mrs Eakin thinks is trying to kill her?"

Miss Bastedo frowned. "That is the terrible thing about illusional insanity, Mr Murdoch. The poor lunatic fears and suspects everybody. She said at first her entire family was involved, then she suspected the doctor and even perhaps the staff here, although that suspicion seems to have disappeared."

"I suppose it is not entirely impossible—that somebody is trying to poison her, I mean."

Miss Bastedo smiled at him. "That is a detective talking, Mr Murdoch, not a physician. Many of our inmates sound quite convincing because they are sincere in their own beliefs. However, Mrs Eakin's family has shown great concern for her well-being. It is a rather unusual situation as perhaps you know. She is a good deal younger than Mr Eakin and his own children are her age or even older. I would think there might be some tension brought about by this inequality. Her only son by her first marriage died suddenly and it was after this that she began to show the first signs of instability."

So far, what the matron was saying concurred with what he'd heard from Mrs Curran. "I understand the boy died from peritonitis."

"That is the case. Dr Ferrier was in attendance. The poor boy's appendix burst and nothing could be done."

"I was told by her husband that she could also be suffering from what he called erotomania."

She glanced at him sharply. "Did he now?"

"What is that exactly?"

"The patient will approach men in a lascivious and seductive manner, or express an inordinate sexual appetite often manifesting in self-abuse."

She spoke as if she were quoting from a medical textbook. It was quite different from Eakin's, "She will lift her tail to any man."

"We understand there was some inappropriate behaviour toward a family member, but she has not shown any evidence of that here. There is a possibility of surgery," she continued. "Her doctor is recommending a hysterectomy but Dr Clark likes to proceed conservatively. We will keep her under observation for at least a week or so longer."

"Not speaking as a detective, Miss Bastedo, but simply as a man, is such an operation effective?"

She wasn't happy about the question but she was an honest woman. "Some doctors believe so, others do not."

"And you?"

"On a conservative estimate from witnessing several female patients who have been so treated, I would say it is too early too tell. Dr Clark himself is a great believer in fresh air, regular exercise, and a calm setting."

Murdoch was about to ask her about the efficacy of that particular treatment, but she consulted the large gold watch that hung from her belt. "I have to do my rounds shortly. You can interview her in this office. There is always an attendant within call. Please try not to overly excite the patient, Mr Murdoch. She is just settling here." She sighed. "I should tell you that we received a telegram this morning from the senior member of the family. Apparently, Mrs Eakin's husband has suffered a severe stroke. The doctor does not think he will recover. We have not told her yet. The daughter is planning to come in later today and we will tell her then. So, please, Mr Murdoch, don't upset her. I suggest you make no comment if she does bring up any of her delusions."

Murdoch wondered what he should do or say if she displayed signs of erotomania, but he didn't quite know how to ask the matron about this.

She stood up and looked through the window. "Ha, here they are."

He turned and could see one of the attendants leading in a patient. Small and thin, her hair in a long braid, Mrs Eakin could have been taken for a child.

"Excuse me a moment, Mr Murdoch," said the matron and she went out to meet them. She had a short conversation with the attendant that he couldn't hear. He realised the glass windows of the office were a double glaze, giving some measure of privacy. Mrs Eakin was looking toward him the entire time. There was something about her expression he couldn't quite identify. An eagerness perhaps, again reminding him of a child. The matron brought her into the office. He got to his feet.

"Mrs Eakin, this is Detective Murdoch. He is conducting a police investigation and he would like to ask you some questions. You don't need to be alarmed in any way. It is simply a matter of routine. Miss Shelby is outside if you need her. Sit here." She pulled forward a second cane chair. "I will return in one half an hour."

She smiled at Peg, patted her arm, and bustled off. Both Murdoch and the young woman remained standing until, hesitantly, she sat down in the chair the matron had indicated. Murdoch resumed his seat facing her.

She was watching his face anxiously and he had the impression that she was straining every sense to read his countenance. "I beg your pardon, sir. Miss Bastedo did say your name but I did not quite register it."

Her speech was quite rapid but the words were enunciated precisely, as if she were holding them tight in case they slipped away. Her accent was English.

"Murdoch. Acting Detective William Murdoch. I am pursuing a police inquiry and I hoped you might be able to help." He hesitated, searching for the right words. How could he ask her bluntly if she were awake and crying out the night Wicken died? She was sitting very still, watching him. She did not seem insane to him or in the least irrational but she was expecting something. Keeping his voice low and even, he continued.

"The matter concerns one of our constables."

Unexpectedly, her eyes lit up and she interrupted him. "Thank the Lord. He has spoken to you, then?"

"About what, ma'am?"

Murdoch had no idea why what he said was so distressing to her but the brightness on her face disappeared, replaced by something else, a look of such despair he wanted to reach over to her and make it go away. Her voice dropped so low he could hardly hear her.

"Why have you come to see me, Mr Murdoch?"

There was no way around it. "Last week one of our officers, a Constable Wicken, was found dead in the vacant house on the corner of Gerrard and Parliament, close to your house. The circumstances of his death are not completely clear. I thought you might help me with my inquiry."

He thought she had been sitting still before but now she seemed to freeze.

"What do you mean, he was found dead?"

"He was shot. Apparently by his own hand."

"When?"

"Monday night last."

"Was this constable fair-haired?"

"Yes, with a full moustache. Constable, second-class, Oliver Wicken. He was on duty."

She moaned and began to rock slightly back and forth in the chair. Suddenly, he had an image of a young cougar that a sailor had brought into the village when he was a boy. For five cents you could go into the hot musty tent and view the animal. For a further five cents, the sailor handed you a stick and you could poke her through the bars of the cage and "make her roar." The expression in the eyes of Mrs Eakin and the tormented animal were the same.

He glanced out of the window wondering if he should send for the attendant.

"Can you tell me what is the matter, ma'am? Did you know the constable? Did you see him?"

She didn't answer and he tried to find a way to reach through her fear. "What did you mean just now when you asked if he had spoken to me?"

"They must have killed him after he left. So he wouldn't talk." She was whispering as if she had no energy left to propel her voice.

"I'm afraid I don't understand. Talk about what?"

Suddenly, she jumped up and rushed at him. She was so fierce he involuntarily put up his arm to shield himself, expecting a blow, but she stopped short and caught at the lapels of his coat.

"They murdered him . . ." Her voice was high pitched and tight in her throat but her grip was strong.

Murdoch forced himself not to back off. Her pupils were dilated, there was some froth at the corner of her mouth. "Who did? Who are you referring to?"

Before she could answer, the door to the office opened and the attendant swept in.

"Now, now, Mrs Eakin, calm yourself, please. Leave the gentleman alone."

She grabbed Peg by her wrists and snatched her away from Murdoch. Peg pulled back trying to twist herself free.

"No, you've got to believe me . . ."

251

Shelby spun her around so she could pin her arms to her sides but as she did so, Peg arched her back and her head jerked upward. She caught the attendant under the chin, causing her to bite through her lower lip.

Another attendant rushed in, sized up the situation at once, and ran over to a cupboard near the door. She took out a restraining jacket.

"No!" shrieked Peg. "I'll be good. I swear. I won't fight." Miss Shelby ignored her and forced her arm into the sleeve of the jacket. Murdoch could only watch helplessly while the other attendant assisted, and within moments, Peg was fastened into the restraining jacket and the strings tied behind her back. She was crying now, tears she could not wipe away. "Please, please let me out. I'll be good, I promise. I'm sorry."

"Bit late for that, isn't it?" said Miss Shelby grimly. Her white bib was spattered with blood from her bitten lip and Murdoch pulled out his handkerchief and gave it to her. He felt dreadfully responsible and wished he had never attempted the interview.

"Come now, Mrs Eakin," said the attendant and they began to lead her away. Peg looked at him beseechingly over her shoulder, just as she had that morning. "Help me," she said.

Augusta Curran seated herself in the reception room of the asylum. There was another woman visitor in the next room who was talking to an elderly inmate. Augusta tried not to look at them, although she glimpsed some affectionate exchange. Another woman, who was wearing the institutional uniform, was down on her knees by the door, scrubbing the floor. There was a sharp smell of carbolic in the air. Augusta hoped she wouldn't meet up with anybody she knew. She had hired a cab to bring her to the asylum, but she'd got him to let her off two blocks away so he wouldn't know her true destination. As a result, her cloak was wet and the hem of her skirts was muddy from dragging through puddles on the way. She sat, chilled and miserable, clutching her basket on her lap, staring ahead. She thought it was most unfair that she was the one sent to deliver the bad news, but Frank flatly refused and Jarius claimed the sight of him or Peter might inflame Peg's already unstable mind. "Do your duty,

Aggie. There's a good girl. And why don't you make her one of those lemon cream tarts she likes? It might make the visit go a little easier."

Jarius had sent Cullie off on some silly errand which meant Augusta had to do the baking herself, and although he kept her company and tried to soothe her with sweet words and compliments, she resented it.

She had been waiting about ten minutes when the door to the reception room opened and a woman in the severe blue dress of a nurse came in. She was dark-complexioned, strong-featured, and had an indisputable air of authority.

"Mrs Curran, I'm Miss Bastedo, the matron."

"How do you do?"

The matron sat down in the chair next to her. "I regret to say that Mrs Eakin has had a bad spell. She is still quite unsettled and we think it better if she doesn't have visitors at the moment."

"What sort of bad spell?"

"A police detective came to interview her. Unfortunately, I had no idea it would upset her as much as it did. She became quite hysterical and she has had to be restrained."

"I knew he shouldn't have come. He insisted. He doesn't realise how unstable she really is."

"I am of the opinion that any mention of death completely unnerves her," said Miss Bastedo. "It brings back her memories of the sad demise of her son. We must be very careful what we say to her and only discuss the most cheerful topics until she is much stronger. It will be wise not to mention the illness of Mr Eakin at this point."

"Yes, of course."

"Perhaps you could come back in two or three days? We have every confidence she will be quite improved by then."

"Yes, yes, I will." Augusta was eager to make a good impression on the matron, as she had an uneasy feeling Miss Bastedo did not approve of her. She took a cake tin out of the basket.

"I brought her a lemon tart."

"You can leave it with me. I will make sure she gets it."

Augusta thanked her and took her leave. She was only too glad not to come face to face with Peg. The woman terrified her.

CHAPTER THIRTY-FIVE

In part because detective Murdoch had declared the blow to the attendant was an accident, Peg was released from the restraining jacket and had been given only a mild chloral sedative. She had fallen into a restless sleep where images surfaced and sank and surfaced again. Shelby dabbing at her cut lip, glaring at her; Mr Murdoch in his long coat, brown eyes troubled as he talked to her; Miss Bastedo, grave-faced, telling her that Augusta had come to visit, although Peg was certain she hadn't actually seen her.

She could hear somebody moaning, *oh, oh,* but she couldn't sort out what the sound was. The cry was sharp and Peg sat up in bed.

Emma Foster was also sitting up. She was clutching at her stomach and it was she who was moaning. Suddenly, she vomited on the coverlet.

"Oh, oh," she groaned and another spasm gripped her. The vomitus was mixed with blood. She cried out and rolled onto her side, the violent momentum sending her crashing to the floor. Peg jumped out of bed and rushed over to her.

"Mrs Foster! What is it?"

The old woman couldn't answer but lay thrashing in spasms that shook her entire body. A rush of watery diarrhoea came from her bowels. The smell coming from her was vile. Peg looked around desperately for something to use, and as she did so, she saw the cake tin sitting on the bedside cupboard. It was black with red and white flowers painted on it. The last time she had seen it was in the kitchen of the Eakin house. The knowledge stabbed at her chest so that for a moment she could hardly breathe. Hurriedly, she pried off the lid. Inside was a cream tart, one large piece missing. Panting now, she bent over the sick woman.

"Mrs Foster, did you eat the tart?"

But she knew she had. One of the attendants must have put the tin in Peg's cupboard and Emma had stolen it in order to help herself to some of the delicacy.

Both Miss Anderson and Mrs Mallory were sitting up.

"One of you, bang on the door for Reid."

Miss Anderson started to sing "We Will Gather by the River" and Mrs Mallory pulled the quilt over her head, whimpering.

Peg got up and ran to the door. "Miss Reid! Help!"

She heard footsteps outside the door, saw the attendant's alarmed face in the window, and the key was turned in the lock and the door flung open.

"What on earth . . . ?"

She saw Mrs Foster's plight and rushed over to her. The floor was slippery with vomit and blood and she gasped as she trod in it.

"She's been poisoned," cried Peg. "She ate some of the tart. Look!"

Reid waved her hand. "Never mind that now. Go and fetch Miss Corley as fast as you can. She's in the sitting room."

"It was meant for me."

"Nonsense. Please do as I ask, Mrs Eakin."

Suddenly, Peg felt as if her mind were functioning on its own with no connection to her body. The fragile sense of security that had been growing while she was tucked away in the asylum shattered like glass. She was safe nowhere. She had to escape.

She ran from the bedroom. Outside in the corridor, the wooden warning flag in the ceiling dropped down. Reid must have pressed the electric button in the room to signify there was trouble. Peg knew an attendant would be coming soon. The only place to go was the dining room directly across from her. She tried the door and it was unlocked. Quickly she slipped inside and leaned against the door, listening. The blood was pounding in her ears, making it difficult to hear anything else. She tried to will herself to be calm. She didn't have a lot of time before Reid realised she hadn't done as she was told.

Even through the closed door she could hear Mrs Foster's cries.

The dim room was unlit but she could see sufficiently to make her way over to the dumbwaiter, which was in the far corner. She slid open the doors and pulled hard on the rope that brought up the lift. It was light and came up easily. For a moment, as she gazed into the small cupboardlike space, her resolve almost failed. *Now! Do it!* She climbed in, hoping desperately it would hold her weight. There was barely enough room but she curled up tightly, and except for a slight shaking, it held. She pulled the doors closed. As soon as she did, she was in pitch darkness. A wave of fear grabbed her but she forced herself to concentrate on the task. She caught hold of one of the ropes and began to pulled hard, hand over hand. With a creak, the lift began to descend. There was another access on the second floor but she pulled steadily past it, her arms aching in the cramped space. *Just one more floor to go.* At last, with a bump, she reached the kitchen level. There was no handle on this side of the doors and she scrabbled at the wood, trying to open them, breaking her fingernails. She was sweating, fighting back panic. She couldn't get out. Could she breathe? Was there enough air? There was a sharp pain in her back from being bent over but there was no room to move around. Finally, the doors yielded sufficiently for her to make a space wide enough to get her fingers through. Then she wriggled her hand in and she could push the doors back.

She had gambled on the fact that there would be nobody working in the kitchen at this hour but she didn't know for certain. However, the place was in darkness. Stiffly, she climbed out of the lift and immediately fell to the ground as her knees gave way. She knelt on the floor, listening. There were no sounds of racing footsteps, no voices calling an alarm. She stayed where she was, crouching like a dog. She had no idea where she would go even if she did manage to get out of here. She'd seen all too clearly the expression on the detective's face. He had been kind but she knew he thought her mad. She should have been calm, talked reasonably, but the shock of what he said was too much. She had been waiting for Wicken to come and she was sure he was investigating her accusations as he had promised. She sank even lower to the floor. She couldn't struggle anymore. It was all too big for her. They were too powerful.

Probably only a minute elapsed but she felt as if she had been lying here on the flagstones for a long time, her cheek pressed against the cold surface. *If only she had some proof. Something more than the word of a deranged woman against that of a respectable family.* Bitterness was like bile in her mouth. They were hypocrites all of them. Nathaniel, Frank the cheater, and especially Jarius Gibb. She sat upright. Jarius's diary! Shortly after Charley died, desperate, she had started to prowl around the house whenever she had the opportunity, looking for evidence. She already knew of the existence of Jarius's journal, because one evening she went to call him to dinner and accidentally interrupted him. He was writing in a ledger and he closed the book at once. "I do value my privacy, Stepmother." Words said in a tone so biting, she had shrunk away. After that, she'd observed him and his habits. She knew how often he left late at night, how furtive he was. Not too long ago, she had decided to risk going back to his room. She'd found the key under his chair and unlocked the scribe's lap desk. The ledger was his private diary and what she read there made her face burn with shame. He had recorded the events of her entry into the household and had not tempered his utter contempt for her or his dislike of her son.

She had the sense he wrote down everything that happened. Surely there would be something there that would help her, something revealing she could show to the detective who had come today.

She got to her feet, shivering. None of the ranges were lit, waiting for the early morning workers to rake them out and start them up. It was easier to see now, and frantic, she looked around for something she could use. She was barefoot and clad only in her nightgown. *Thank God.* Over by the door was a row of hooks for the kitchen workers to hang their coats and hats. There were two things, a pair of felt slippers and a rubber waterproof cloak. She thrust her cold feet into the slippers which for that moment seemed as luxurious as anything she had ever worn. The waterproof was too long for her and dragged on the floor but she had to use it.

Hurry, hurry. She ran over to the window and pushed up the sash. There were no bars. Encumbered by the heavy waterproof, she climbed over the sill, dropping quickly to the ground, soft and muddy from the unrelenting rain. She almost lost one of the slippers in the dirt and she took them both off and stuffed them in the pockets of the waterproof. Barefoot, she ran toward the path that was just visible in front. She knew it must lead to the stables and the far end of the garden. Not too distant, there was a dark tree, leafless now but broad and thick-branched. She halted here, panting and gulping for air. From the shelter of the trunk she peeked toward the building. Lights were lit on the east wing where she'd come from but so far, the rest of the institution was in darkness. They wouldn't want to sound an alarm yet. They'd search the ward first. She might have at least an hour before they realised she had got out. She set off again. She had to be careful as she approached the stable, because she knew there would be one or two men sleeping there. She got past without incident and then she was at the wall. There was a low iron railing along the top making the entire height about eight feet. She stopped again, breathing hard. *A ladder. There must be a ladder.* She turned around and jog-trotted to the shed that was at the edge of the vegetable garden. Against the wall she could see a tarpaulin that was draped over some long object. Almost crying with the hope of it, she fumbled with the rope that was tying down the end. Her fingers were clumsy with cold but she finally undid the knots and was able to pull back the covering. There were three ladders underneath and she tugged at the one uppermost. It was heavy and difficult to move but her fear gave her strength and it finally slid free. She dragged it to the wall, hoisted it up, and climbed up. The top rung reached just

258

below the iron railings that surmounted the wall. Here she hesitated, looking down the steep drop. But she had only one option. She held onto the railing, hoisted herself up and swung one leg over so that she was balanced astride on the narrow toehold. For a moment, she swayed dangerously but she clung to the railing and began to lower herself until she was dangling. She let go and landed awkwardly on the muddy ground. She had to wait a moment to get her breath, then she got to her feet and put on the slippers. They were useless for protection against the wet but they would make her less conspicuous. Head bent into the pelting rain, she set off as fast as she could manage around the outside of the wall toward Queen Street.

The macadam pavement was black with rain and the streetcar tracks glistened in the flickering gas lamps. There was not a soul abroad. She pulled up the collar of the waterproof to hide the fact that her hair was unpinned and began to walk away from the asylum. She could not allow herself to think what would happen if her plan didn't work; if Jarius was at home. Her teeth were chattering uncontrollably and her entire body was trembling. But she was out.

CHAPTER THIRTY-SIX

———◆———

EDDY TINGLE BLEW hard into his glove trying to get some warm air into his fingers. His thoughts about his passenger were becoming decidedly un-Christian. She must have been gone for a good ten minutes by now. Had he been conned, he wondered? She didn't look too respectable but she spoke good, sounded like a lady's maid, which is what she said she was. She'd flagged him down on Queen Street, practically weeping with the relief of seeing him.

"I was afraid I would have to walk all the way home," she said. "I've been watching my sister, who is poorly from childbed, but I've got to get back. My mistress doesn't even know I'm out. I'll be dismissed without a letter if she finds out. But what could I do? She's my only sister and all alone except for the one girl to tend her."

This had poured out of her, unasked. Tingle hadn't really hesitated. He was going that way home anyway and another fare was gravy on the pie. Not that he completely believed her story. She was a bedraggled scrap of a girl without hat or gloves. More like she was visiting a sweetheart, had a quarrel, and ran out all of a huff.

"Where do you want to go?"

She gave him an address on Gerrard Street east of Parliament.

"It's extra charge after midnight you know."

"That's all right."

"Hop in, then." And she had jumped right fast into his cab. He got a bit of a trot out of Blackie and they were up at Gerrard in about a half an hour. Just as they were approaching the number she had given him, she opened up the small trap in the roof of the cab.

"Cabbie, I've just discovered I have left my purse at my sister's house. You will have to wait while I go in and get some money. How much is it?"

"It's fare and a half after midnight and you were also in the second zone. That makes it three dollars."

He pulled up in front of the house. It was set back a bit from the road and looked quite grand. His passenger got out of the cab and scurried off, her long cloak dragging on the wet pavement.

She went through the gate, walked quickly down the path, and disappeared around the side of the house to the servant's entrance. Tingle waited. He gave her enough time to get in, go to her room, which would be on the third floor, get her money, and come right out again. He tucked his hands between his knees under the beaver throw that covered him. He was ready for a kip. He didn't like night fares, but earlier, he'd picked up a gentleman outside the National Club on Bay Street and brought him out to the west end of the city. Swell of a fellow, evening dress, cloak, but full as a soldier. He'd delivered him to a house on Jane Street and left him to the not-so-tender mercies of his wife. Tipped well but it made for a long night. So this girl's fare had seemed a bit of a blessing. Until now. Blackie shifted restlessly. He wanted the comfort of his stable. Stiffly, Tingle climbed down from his perch. Time to investigate Miss Lady's maid.

He followed in her footsteps through the gate and around to the back of the house. There was not a light to be seen, the household was asleep. He tried the back door but it was firmly locked. He banged hard on the door. "Anybody at home?" Bang, bang. "Hey, in there!"

He saw a light flare in a second-floor window and he knocked again. In a few minutes, the door opened and an elderly man in a flannel dressing robe appeared on the threshold.

"What the devil do you want at this time of night?"

261

"My fare, that's what. I just delivered a young woman to this house. She's your mistress's maid and she owes me three dollars."

The man leaned forward and ostentatiously sniffed the air. "Are you drunk? You've come to the wrong house. There is no mistress, only my master and he doesn't have a maid; never did nor never will."

"What are you gabbling about? She said she lived here. She came through the gate. Said she had to get her money. She was watching her sister over on Queen Street and left her purse there."

"She's told you a nailer, my lad," said the butler with some satisfaction. "The only person of the female persuasion in this house is my wife, Mrs Bezley, and she's in bed, until a few minutes ago, enjoying a well-deserved sleep."

Tingle looked around him. "But where'd the girl go then?"

"She's done a bunk. Must have been trying to avoid ponying up."

He went to close the door but Tingle stopped him. "What about the neighbours? Anybody close by have a lady's maid?"

"Not on the right nor the left. The Eakins, two houses down, have a general servant that's a girl. What did your one look like?"

"A titch. Spoke good."

"That's not Cullie. She's a big lass. Anyway, no sense in me catching my death standing out here. You've been bamboozled and that's all there is to it. Good night to you."

He closed the door.

"Arse crawler," said Tingle. He was tempted to knock again but knew it wouldn't get him anywhere. The girl must have gone through the rear gate to the laneway at the rear of the house. She'd be well on her way now.

He made his way back to his cab. Sod it. He was going to make a report to the police. He hated his good nature being taken advantage of and this girl had gulled him. He climbed back into his seat, clucked to Blackie, and they turned around and headed off down Parliament Street toward the police station.

Peg had done exactly what Tingle surmised. She had run along the laneway, which ended at the Eakin property, two houses down. Here, she crouched by the gate, afraid to move until she was sure the

262

cabbie wasn't going to pursue her. She could hear him banging on the door and shortly after, the sound of voices. Silence, only the soft patter of the rain, until finally, she heard the clop of the horse's hooves as the cab moved off. As soon as the sound had faded completely, she opened the gate and ran across the cobblestone yard to the rear door of the house. She was inside at once. The door opened into a small passageway at the end of which was the back staircase. She knew this was the way Jarius went when he left at night. For these excursions, he always wore a shabby overcoat of dark English tweed, quite unlike the formal black business coat of the day. She could barely make out the coat stand that was beside the door, and feeling almost more than seeing, she checked whether the tweed coat was there. It was not and the flood of relief she felt made her dizzy. Jarius had gone out.

Immediately, she took off the cumbersome waterproof and hung it on the stand. There was an old green cape belonging to Augusta on the peg and she slipped it on, burying her face in the soft fur trim and hugging herself tightly to feel the warmth of the flannel lining. She knelt down, searching for the boots that were usually kept on a rack beside the stand. There were four pairs, one of them her own, a pair of red kid. She kicked off the soaking felt slippers and pulled on the boots, not stopping to button them. The warmth from the cloak and the boots gave her renewed strength, and she hurried as quickly as she could up the stairs to the second floor. Here, she waited briefly but there was no sound in the house, nobody had been disturbed. Carefully, she pushed open the door that led onto the landing. There was a candle burning in the hall sconce and she could see another faint light shining beneath the door of Nathaniel's bedroom. Her heart lurched. Was he still awake? She stood still, listening. Faintly, she could hear his windy snores. He must have fallen asleep with the candle lit. She crossed the landing, pressed her ear against Jarius's door, and hearing nothing, she went inside.

The curtains were closed and the room was dark. She would have to risk lighting a lamp. Forced to move more slowly, she felt her way to the mantelpiece. Here she fumbled for the box of matches, found them, and struck one. Jarius's bed was made and tidy. The room smelled like him. She lit the lamp, turning the wick low, and crossed over to his chair where the key was hidden. For a moment she couldn't find it and almost panicked but there it was in the leather pouch. Rationally, she knew she had only been in the house a very short time, but her fear was mounting. She had to hurry.

The lap desk wouldn't open at first and she fiddled desperately with the key. Finally, the lock yielded. The ledger was inside and she took it out, hugging it to her chest as if it were a beloved infant.

She had already started toward the door when she heard a footstep on the landing outside.

The door opened and Augusta stood in the threshold. Her hand flew to her mouth in shock. "You! What are you doing here? Where's Jarius?"

For a second, Peg stared at her, transfixed.

"Why are you wearing my cloak?" gasped Augusta.

Peg bolted. Augusta was taken off guard and the force of Peg's charge sent her reeling to the floor, so that she dropped her candlestick. Peg raced back the way she had come, out to the yard. She was heading for the front gate when she saw a man coming along the street. A tall man in policeman's uniform. She swerved away and ran toward the barn, the only place she could hide.

Murdoch was dreaming he was in his childhood bed. Somehow, his mother had got herself locked out and she was knocking on the door. *Wake up, Will! Wake up, I've got to get your father's tea going.* He was trying to open his eyes, straining to see, but the room was too dark. He had to get up and let her in before his father came home, but he couldn't move.

Suddenly, he was awake and in the present. Somebody was knocking at the front door.

"Mr Murdoch! Mr Murdoch!"

He jumped out of bed, grabbed his trousers from the chair, and pulled them on over his nightshirt.

Again the persistent knocking and the half-hissed call. "Mr Murdoch!"

He opened his bedroom door and at the same time, Enid Jones appeared on the landing. She was holding a night candle and in spite of the circumstances, his heart jumped at the sight of her. She was dressed in a red flannel robe and her hair was down, loosely braided. She looked still soft from sleep.

"What is it? Who's knocking?" she asked.

"I'm just going to see."

He hadn't waited to strike a light and she held out her candlestick. "Take my candle."

He did so and hurried down to the hall. Mrs Kitchen emerged from her room.

"Who on earth is here at this time of night?"

Murdoch opened the door.

A tall, gangly young constable was standing outside, his dark lantern pointed downward.

He touched his forefinger to the rim of his helmet in greeting.

"Constable Dewhurst here. Sorry to disturb you at this hour, sir, but Sergeant Hales thought I should fetch you. We've heard from the asylum that the lunatic lady, Mrs Eakin, has managed to run away. It seems like she's come back to her home."

"Good heavens! Have you got her?"

"Not yet, sir. The matron had only just telephoned. She wanted us to go and notify the family. The sergeant was about to send me over there when up shows a cabbie, name of Tingle."

The constable's words were rapid and excited. The drama was spicing up an otherwise dull evening. "He came in right at that moment to report on a fare who had gammoned him. We knew from his description it was one and the same woman. He'd picked her up on Queen Street not far from the loony bin and dropped her off right near the house."

"Did the matron give you any more information?"

"Only that the woman has lost all of her slates. One of the inmates was taken ill in the night, gastritis probably, and Mrs Eakin

265

took it as a sign she was being poisoned. The matron thinks she could be dangerous. To herself or to her family. Sergeant Hales decided to go over himself. He wanted me to get you, seeing as you know the woman in question."

Murdoch was already dragging on his boots.

"Here!" Mrs Kitchen, who had heard all this, handed him his hat and coat. "Please be careful." He gave a quick glance up the stairs and saw Enid was still standing on the landing, watching. The concern on her face warmed him.

"The cabbie's waiting outside," said Dewhurst. "We requisitioned him."

He led the way.

"Did you telephone the asylum?" Murdoch asked.

"Yes, sir. They're sending somebody right over."

Like the constable, Eddie Tingle was finding this quite an adventure and he grinned at Murdoch as he climbed into the cab.

"Where to, sir?"

"Corner of Gerrard Street and Parliament. Can you get that nag of yours to at least trot?"

"Looks are deceiving. He can run like a thoroughbred when he needs to."

"This is one such occasion then."

Dewhurst got onto the step, holding on to the door handle.

"Scorch it, Tingle," said Murdoch. The cabbie cracked his whip over the horse's head and they lunged into a gallop up the sleeping street.

CHAPTER THIRTY-SEVEN

———•———

SERGEANT HALES PUSHED open the gate and went into the yard. As he did so, a man and a woman in night clothes appeared at the rear door. He recognised Peter Curran from the inquest. When the woman saw him, she cried out.

"Officer! There's a mad woman on the loose. Did you see her?"

"Yes, ma'am, I believe I did. She has just run into the barn."

Mrs Curran gasped. "My brother is in there. You must do something. She'll kill him."

She made as if to run to the barn and Hales caught her arm. "Hold on, ma'am."

At that moment, another man came through the gate behind him. It was Jarius Gibb. He went over to the woman.

"Aggie, what on earth is the matter?"

"She was here, Jarius. In your room. She knocked me down."

Mrs Curran was almost incoherent with fear. Her husband made no move to comfort her and stood like a simpleton, staring at the sergeant.

"You mean Stepmother?"

"Yes. Oh, she's quite mad, Jarius. She was standing there, in my cloak. She ran at me."

Gibb turned to Hales.

"Officer, what is going on?"

"We've had a telephone message from the asylum, sir. Apparently, Mrs Eakin has run away."

Augusta interrupted him. "Oh, what a shock she gave me. I thought it was you in there, Jarius. She stole your ledger, Jarius. Why would she want that? And my cloak?

"Hush. Peter, is Frank in the barn?"

"S' far as I know. He went over there at midnight, same as usual."

"She'll kill him," repeated Augusta.

"Ma'am, try to calm yourself," Hales interceded. "She's a slip of a woman and he's a strong grown man. I doubt she'll hurt him."

"We can't count on that, Sergeant," said Gibb. "My brother often drinks himself into a stupor. There are many knives available to her if she wants to do him harm. And a shotgun. It is still there by the door, isn't it Peter?"

Curran nodded. "S'far as I know."

Gibb turned to Hales. "I'm going to go into the barn, Sergeant. We must do something."

"Begging your pardon, sir, but I don't think that's a good idea. A doctor is on his way from the asylum. He's better to handle it."

"She's terrified of doctors. He will only make her more disturbed. I'm the one who should talk to her. She knows me and trusts me. Isn't that so, Aggie?"

"I, er . . . oh, Jarius."

"I'll come in with you then, sir."

"No, Officer. Absolutely not. She fears police even more than she does doctors. You can wait outside. If I need help, don't worry, I'll call for you."

"Jarius, what about Frank?"

"Be quiet, Aggie. I'm doing what I can." His voice was sharper, impatient. "Officer, may I take your lantern?"

Rather reluctantly, Hales handed over the light. Leaving the Currans at the door, he and Jarius hurried across the wet cobblestones to the barn. When they reached the doors, Gibb stopped, cocking his head to listen. There was no sound from inside except the soft snicker of a horse, no indication that the sleeping Frank had awoken. With a nod at the sergeant, Gibb swung open the door and stepped inside.

Hales heard the sound of the bolt being closed behind him.

Jarius waited for a moment, swinging the lantern high above him.

"Peg? Stepmother? Don't be afraid. You can come out." Gibb wanted to make his voice pleasant and reassuring, but even to his own ears, it didn't sound that way. He walked over to the corner of the barn where Frank slept in a partitioned-off room.

His brother was fast asleep, face-down on his bed and fully dressed. The room reeked of stale beer. Jarius shook him awake, hard and roughly.

"Get up, you sot. Come on, rouse yourself."

Frank blinked into the light. "What's the matter?"

"Our dear stepmother has escaped from the loony bin. She's hiding in the barn somewhere."

"In here?" Frank was still stupid with drink. "How'd she get in here?"

"Never mind that now. Get on your feet. There's a police sergeant outside. I said I'd bring her out nice and quiet."

He put the lantern on a wooden box beside the bed, took off his overcoat and threw it across the bed, and went over to a shelf where Frank kept his shotgun.

"Where are the shells?"

"Why? What are you doing?"

"You know damn well what I'm doing. I'm going to save your arse for the second time. Where are the shells?"

"In that box."

Jarius snapped a cartridge into the shotgun. "You look in the stalls. I'll do the tack room."

"Jarius—"

Gibb swung the gun around so that it was pointing at Frank. "It will be quite easy to have two accidents instead of one. She aimed this gun at you, you struggled, boom. You both die."

269

"My God, are you going to shoot her?"

"Do I have a choice?"

"She doesn't really know what happened."

"It's got nothing to do with that."

"What then?"

"For Christ's sake, Frank. Why are you always so stupid? You know the woman is in the way."

He tucked the gun under his arm and gave his brother a shove. "Come on. We don't have much time."

PEG SAW JARIUS come into the barn and heard him call to her. She had run into the carriage room and was crouched in the far corner. He must have gone to wake up Frank because she heard voices. She crept to the edge of the partition that separated the carriage room from the rest of the barn. She peered through a crack in the wall. Frank and Jarius emerged and Jarius was carrying a shotgun.

She ran for it.

In front of her was the ladder to the loft and she was up it in a flash.

"There she is," Jarius shouted.

Peg tripped and sprawled on the floor. She knew Jarius must be close behind her and she turned, cowering against one of the hay bales. She heard somebody climbing up the ladder and Jarius's head and shoulders appeared.

"Please don't shoot me. You can have the book. I won't tell anybody." But she wasn't even sure she had spoken out loud. If she had, the words made no impact on Jarius. He turned sideways, leaning against the ladder so he could take aim. There was a terrifying deliberation in his movements, as if he were on a duck shoot and preparing himself.

Frank came up close behind him holding a lantern.

Peg tried to press herself into a bale. Jarius raised the gun and she heard the click as he cocked the trigger. She covered her head with her arms.

CHAPTER THIRTY-EIGHT

———◆———

TINGLE HAD JUST pulled up his cab in front of the Eakin house when Murdoch heard the boom of the shotgun. Sergeant Hales was standing in front of the barn doors with Augusta Curran and her husband. He saw Murdoch.

"This way," he shouted, and he started to run along the side of the stable. Murdoch raced after him, Constable Dewhurst at his heels. They were at the side door in a moment and into the barn. Horses were screaming and the air was thick with the smell of cordite. Frank Eakin was lying on his back close to the wood stove. Jarius Gibb was almost on top of him. Somebody was moaning dreadful sounds of pain. As Hales and Murdoch approached, Jarius tried to get to his feet but his leg splayed out at an angle, and with a cry, he fell forward.

Murdoch felt rather than heard the whisper from above his head. Peg was looking down at him.

"Here. I'm up here," she said.

PEG WAS NOT injured but in such a state of terror, she was unable to move. Murdoch hoisted her over his shoulder, fireman style, and carried her out of the stable, while Hales tended to Gibb and Frank. He sent in Tingle to calm the horses and ordered the Currans into the

271

house under the supervision of Constable Dewhurst. Augusta was weeping ceaselessly, her antagonism for her brother apparently forgotten. Her husband said nothing.

Peg was seated on the bench in the yard and it took several minutes before she could stop a kind of dry, choking sob. She kept repeating that she had dropped Jarius's diary in the barn, and it was only Murdoch's firm insistence that he would get it that calmed her down. He chafed her hands and kept talking to her and finally she was able to tell him what had happened. When she tried to relate how Jarius had stood and aimed the shotgun at her as if he were at a hunt, she broke down again and Murdoch had to wait patiently for her to recover. She was not entirely sure what had happened next, but she had the impression Frank had grabbed Jarius to stop him and they had both fallen from the ladder.

At that point, Dr Ferrier arrived with two burly attendants from the asylum. Fortunately, he was a sensible man and when he saw how Peg was with Murdoch, he made no attempt to interfere. Murdoch accepted responsibility for his charge and the doctor hurried into the barn to tend to the injured men.

As SOON AS Tingle had dealt with the horses, Murdoch persuaded Peg to go with the cabbie to the Kitchens'. He made her promise she wouldn't try to run away but he knew she wouldn't. She was still dreadfully shaken, but as far as he could see, she was quite sane. He knew that Mrs Kitchen would take very good care of her, and if Peg needed anything, it was some motherly attention.

That done, he went into the barn.

DR FERRIER HAD just finished administering morphine to Jarius Gibb, who was propped up against the knee of one of the attendants. Sergeant Hales had brought out more lamps and the scene was bathed in light.

"Mr Gibb has dislocated his hip," said Ferrier when he saw Murdoch. "We can take him to the hospital, momentarily."

"And Mr Eakin?"

"He cannot be moved. I fear his back is broken."

Frank looked dreadful. His skin was ashen and his face was already swollen, his eyelids puffed to the point of closure.

Murdoch crouched down beside Jarius Gibb. "Can I ask you what happened, sir?"

Jarius scowled. "I've already talked to the sergeant, I'm not going to repeat it."

"As you wish." Murdoch stood up and pointedly beckoned to Hales, drawing him off to one side, out of earshot.

"According to Mrs Eakin, she was up there in the loft and Gibb climbed up and was about to shoot her. She thinks Frank saved her bacon by grabbing Gibb and they both fell. What did he tell you?"

"He said she was the one with the gun and that he climbed the ladder so that he could talk to her. Persuade her to come down. She aimed at him. He managed to wrest the gun from her, in the process of which it went off. Then he lost his balance and fell off the ladder, taking his brother with him."

"Is that likely, do you think?"

"Dog droppings, if you ask me. Look over there." Hales pointed to a low, splintered hole in the next partition. "I'd say the gun hit the floor and discharged and I'll wager it was him was holding it when he fell. He intended to kill the woman, I'm sure of it. When I got to the house, I saw Mrs Eakin running into the barn. Just then Gibb came up. Said he could look after it." Hales frowned in chagrin. "I shouldn't have allowed him to go in but he was soft as shite. I've seen lunatics before and I know how riled up they get at the sight of a uniform. So I let him. But as soon as I heard him throw the bolt behind him, I knew something wasn't right. I'd have gone after him at once but Mrs Curran got all hysterical and I had her to deal with."

"There's some kind of diary of Gibb's that Mrs Eakin came to get. She thinks she dropped it in here somewhere. I'll have a look."

Gibb had been watching them while they talked, but he was distracted by the pain of Dr Ferrier trying to immobilize his hip with a makeshift splint. Murdoch crossed in front of him and went into the tack room. A black, official-looking ledger was lying in the straw. He picked it up, opened it, and glanced at the contents. He saw enough to think that Peg was right. Holding the journal, Murdoch returned to the doctor. One of the attendants had laid out the stretcher and they were about to lift Gibb onto it. He scowled at Murdoch.

"That's mine, I believe. May I have it?"

"I'm afraid not, sir. Police property until this case is cleared up."

"What case is that, Officer? You saw her. She's insane. Can't help herself. I won't press charges."

"That's not what I'm referring to," said Murdoch, and he tapped the ledger. "Let's see if this gives us some answers."

"Lie down if you please, Mr Gibb," said one of the attendants. "We're going to lift you."

Reluctantly, Jarius obeyed and the two men heaved him onto the stretcher. Although the movement must have caused him great pain, Jarius only grunted. He had expressed no concern for Frank, or Peg for that matter. He lay looking up at the ceiling but Murdoch knew there had been fear in his eyes and he was glad of it. The attendants carried him out to the ambulance.

Murdoch turned his attention back to Frank Eakin.

"How is he?" he asked the doctor.

Ferrier shook his head for answer. He took a small bottle out of his bag, unscrewed the top, and held the vial underneath the injured man's nose. Frank opened his eyes, flinching. He couldn't move his head away from the stinging smell.

"Can you get this weight off my chest?" he whispered. "I can't breathe."

Dr Ferrier shook his head. "Mr Eakin, there is not a weight, you have been injured."

"I can't seem to move my arms. Have you tied them down?"

"No, we haven't, sir."

A look of panic came into Frank's eyes. "I must have hit my back on the stove. Jarius was on top of me."

He licked his lips. "Could I have a drink of water?"

"I'll get him some," said Hales.

"Am I dying?" Frank asked; his breath was raspy.

Dr Ferrier was a decent man and his voice was gentle when he spoke. "If you wish I can send for a minister immediately."

"No. I thought I heard that detective. Is he here?"

"Yes, I am." Murdoch knelt down, leaning in close.

"I must talk. Tell you the truth."

Hales had returned with a dipper and a bowl of water. The doctor dribbled water on Frank's mouth. Murdoch bent over again.

"Mr Eakin, Frank. Do you want to make an official statement?"

"Yes, I do."

"I am sorry to say this, but for such a statement to be valid in a court of law, I must ask you if you are fully aware of your present circumstances."

Frank blinked. "That I'm a goner, you mean?"

"Yes. That you realise you are dying and that what you are about to say is a true statement on your deathbed?"

"I understand."

"Sergeant Hales, please write down what Mr Eakin says."

Murdoch waited for the sergeant to take out his notebook and pencil. "According to Mr Gibb, Mrs Eakin had the shotgun and was about to fire at him. Is this true?"

Anger seemed to give Frank strength. "No! Other way around. He's a cold-hearted devil as ever walked on the earth and I ain't going to die without him getting his comeuppance, same as me . . . He was going to shoot her. I stopped him. I couldn't bear seeing her like that. Scared witless. I suppose you might say, the worm turned. He didn't expect that. I grabbed his legs and we fell." He managed to meet Murdoch's eyes. "Is he hurt?"

"Yes. He's smashed his hip."

"Too bad it wasn't worse. And her?"

"She's in good hands. She will be all right . . . Frank, Mrs Eakin says Constable Wicken came to the house the night he died . . ."

"Yes, he did. We'd all had a terrible barney the night before. Cooked up by Jarius, of course, and she was barricaded in the upstairs

275

room. She'd called to Wicken from the window and he'd come to see what was the matter."

He gagged and yellowish spittle ran from his mouth. Ferrier took a sponge from his bag and wiped him.

"Joke was, the three of us, Peter, him, and me, had been having a talk about what to do with her. Jarius kept saying as how she was a loony and should be shut away. Didn't seem like that to me but he was pushing it. Then in comes the frog and she starts to tell him she was being poisoned . . ."

"Was she?"

"Not by me, nor Aggie, I'm sure. But I wouldn't put anything past Jarius. He hated her from the first moment she come here. Thinks she's going to whelp and cut him out."

His breath was so harsh Murdoch wondered if he could keep on. He glanced at the doctor who put his fingers on Eakin's pulse. He used the vial of ammonia again and Frank continued, his words faster, as if he were trying to outrace death.

"I could tell the frog was swayed. Told her he'd look into it. Then she said other things. About me and the horses. Fiddling. He said he wanted to see the stables. He insisted and we all marched over. When he examined the horses, he got his dander up, cos he saw what I'd been doing. Him and me had words. It made me hot. I hit him. Hard. Side of the head . . . He fell down."

Tears started to spill from under the swollen eyelids. "He was just a young fella . . . I didn't mean to do for him . . . Will I go to Hell for it?"

Murdoch winced. "Our Father is ever merciful."

He wasn't sure if Eakin even heard him but his urgency pushed him on. "Jarius took over as always. 'You've killed him, Frank,' he says, but did I? Did I? He looked bad, white as paint, but maybe he wasn't dead, I don't know. Jarius made us wrap him in a blanket and carry him over to the empty house. He had the key. 'I'm doing this for your sake,' he said, and he got Peter to prop him up. Then he shot him with his own revolver . . . he aimed it at the place where I'd hit him. He said it would be easy to make it look like suicide. He wrote the note and he got one of his whores to testify. The one you saw."

His voice died away and Dr Ferrier wagged his finger at Murdoch, warning him.

Murdoch took the sponge, wetted it, and bathed Frank's face and mouth. That seemed to revive him sufficiently for him to continue.

"That bastard shouldn't get away with it. He kept saying he was protecting me but he wasn't. It meant he had me good then, forever. He made me put the revolver in between the officer's legs. He thought it was a good joke. I'm sorry I did that; it wasn't right."

Again the tears spilled out and down his cheeks.

"Funny ain't it. Papa's up there not able to move and I'm down here in the same way. Like father like son. What a laugh. Well, at least he can say I'm following in his footsteps now."

There was a sob that couldn't get past the paralysed walls of his chest and Murdoch could see the light was leaving his eyes.

"I think you've got all you need, Mr Murdoch," said the doctor. "His sister should pay her last respects now."

Murdoch stood up. He wanted to say something to the dying man, something that might ease his soul into the next life, but even as he looked down at him, he saw it was too late.

Dr Ferrier put the back of his hand under Frank's nose to check for breath. After a moment, he shook his head.

"He's gone."

He lifted Frank's wrist to confirm there was no pulse and then laid the dead man's hands across his chest. "Sergeant, will you be so good as to bring in Mrs Curran and her husband."

Hales put away his notebook and with a nod at Murdoch he left. The patrol sergeant was a man vindicated.

"We'll need to send for a coroner and gather a jury," continued Ferrier.

"I'll see to that."

There was no more to be done here, and he thought Augusta was owed some privacy in her grief. He'd wait until she had done before he spoke to Peter Curran.

He went outside to the yard. After the brightness of the barn, the night seemed dark. He took a deep breath, shivering in the cold air. A horse whinnied softly nearby. Tingle had brought two of the horses out of the barn and they were tethered to the hitching post. Murdoch went over to them. The mare turned her head to look at him and he patted her neck.

"What a piece of work we men are, my girl. But you don't care, do you? You just want some mash and a warm stall." She tossed her head.

As for him, he felt sick at heart with the awareness of how much pain human beings were capable of inflicting on each other. He, too, wanted to get home as soon as he could. He needed some evidence that love could have as much power as hatred.

For Wil with love

Acknowledgments

With thanks to the Port Phillip Sea Pilots, Queenscliff, Victoria. Thanks also to the Victoria Police Film and TV Unit and to Dr. Simon Young, Royal Children's Hospital, Melbourne. All these people gave generously of their time and knowledge.

A note on Point Nepean

Much of this story is set in and around Point Nepean at Portsea on the Mornington Peninsula. If you go there you can see many of the landmarks mentioned in this story: the Harold Holt memorial, the quarantine building, the cemetery, Pearce Barracks, the old cattle jetty. I did take some liberties with distances within the Point Nepean National Park, but apart from this the setting is real.

"And nothing I cared, at my sky blue
trades, that time allows
In all his tuneful turning so few
and such morning songs
Before the children green and golden
Follow him out of grace"
　　　　Dylan Thomas, from *Fern Hill*

Kip

If you stand on Cheviot Hill at Point Nepean, you can see the ocean on one side and the bay on the other. The bay is protected by the headland: it's calm and blue like a photo in a travel brochure. The ocean looks wild because . . . well, because it's an ocean—it's Bass Strait. It might be close to the bay but they're so different it's hard to believe that only a five minute walk separates them.

Still, on that day, that night, it felt as if they weren't separate, as if the ocean didn't stop where it was meant to, it came right on over and swept into the bay.

Annie

When Grace got lost, I had to go with her. Grace would never have found her way out, not when it was starting to get dark.

But, as it happened, neither of us found our way out. I couldn't find it either.

Grace, she's my sister. She's exactly eleven months older than me. That means that for one month every year, we're the same age. That month is June, and it was June when Grace got lost. June the twenty-fifth, when we were both twelve.

In my opinion, winter at the beach is almost as good as summer. I wouldn't know what Grace prefers because

Grace isn't the sort of person who likes comparisons, or lists of your five favorite things to eat, or anything like that. You can't pin Grace down on anything.

In winter we play tracking. Two people wait and the rest go and hide in the dunes. You have to leave markers, like arrows made of sticks, to show where you've gone. You've got half an hour to hide and then the others come to find you. You can leave tracks and markers that are straightforward, or you can try to trick the finders. You can leave tracks to the water and then walk along the water's edge so that there are no footprints to follow. Sometimes I walk backward really carefully in my own footprints.

Grace got lost because she saw a penguin. She loves animals and she wants to be a vet. I don't mind animals. Basically, I can take them or leave them, but Grace would never leave an animal anywhere.

That was what got us into trouble.

We were playing tracking at Point Nepean. It's a thin strip of land that stretches out into the sea. It's a peninsula. Mum had walked home with our little brother, Simon, but I wanted to hide without him tagging along. So Dad, Grace, and I were having one last game.

Point Nepean used to be called Fort Nepean, and the army still uses it for training. There are cyclone fences everywhere and signs that say DO NOT TOUCH ANYTHING—IT MAY EXPLODE AND KILL YOU. Those signs make me laugh. Nothing's going to kill me, but Grace always gets this worried look on her face when we pass one.

"Don't be stupid, Grace," I said. "Nothing's going to get you." I made an arrow with three sticks pointing in the wrong direction, to trick Dad, then we went down along the beach all the way to the end.

Kip

I remember the date—June the twenty-fifth—the first day of the school vacation, and just after my birthday. It was winter but the afternoon was warm, almost as if summer were about to begin. It was the sort of day when you look at the water and want to dive in, the sun's sparkling on it, and it's welcoming and you can't imagine that it would be cold.

I was walking down to the beach. I had my headphones on so I saw the whole thing with no sound. I mean there was sound, just not natural sound. What I really mean is that I saw the whole thing to music. It was a bit like a video clip, the way I saw it: you know when you've got headphones on and you feel disconnected from the world—you're putting one foot in front of the other but you can't hear your footsteps.

Still, when I remember what happened, I don't think there were any other sounds anyway. I went along the road and there was this kid, and he jumped out of a car while it was moving. It wasn't going that fast, it was slowing down outside the shops, but this little kid got out and he stumbled and then he ran. He ran right across the road with cars going by. He wasn't looking at me, he wasn't seeing anything, and he ran straight into me. His face was screwed up, angry. He looked at me for a second, probably less, and I had this feeling. It was as if he wanted to ask me something, wanted me to give him some kind of answer. Maybe he even spoke, but all I heard was music in my head. I didn't do anything. I didn't even take off my headphones. It all happened so quickly. And then he ran off through the trees toward the foreshore.

I could see this lady in the car, and I thought it was probably his mum. But she didn't get out or call to him. She kept driving, slowly at first then a bit faster, staring straight ahead at the road. She looked in a complete daze. She wasn't doing anything at all about the kid. She was just letting him go.

I headed over to the foreshore and then down onto the beach. I couldn't see that kid. Not anywhere. He'd disappeared.

Annie

At one end of the beach there's a rock shelf and then the Heads. The water there is only as wide as a river, and it looks shallow. You can see Point Lonsdale on the other side. It seems really close. If you were a good swimmer you could probably swim across.

Even though the water in the Heads is flat, there are currents and whirlpools under the surface. It's because there's so much water pouring through such a narrow gap. Grace and I watched a ship go through the Heads. Then we left an arrow for Dad and walked back the way we'd come. I was walking fast, but Grace wasn't keeping up. She's always wandering along, not concentrating.

"What's that?" she called out. "Annie! A penguin."

I turned around. It was a penguin, a little fairy penguin in the water.

"It's all on its own. It's lost," said Grace. "Look, it's swimming in circles."

We followed it along the water's edge. It struggled in the current. Grace wouldn't take her eyes off it. Water lapped at her sneakers but she didn't care. We went with the penguin all the way down the beach, past the spot where you go up to the parking lot. We walked over the rocks around a point and when we'd nearly reached another point, a wave washed the penguin toward the shore. It collapsed on the beach at Grace's feet. Its little body was going in and out, in and out.

Grace knelt in the wet sand. "I bet it's got oil on its wings," she said. "We have to help it."

There was no point arguing because Grace was not going to leave this penguin. I'm used to Grace and her animal rescues. She talked to it gently. Then she tried to pick it up but it made a squawking noise and squirmed out of her hands.

"Watch out, Grace," I said. "It'll peck you."

After about twenty minutes, she managed to get it into the backpack. She zipped it up nearly to the top.

"We can take it home and wash the oil off," Grace said. She lifted the backpack as if it were a newborn baby. "We can look after it till it's better."

I stood up. The tide had come further in. The weather had changed quickly and I hadn't noticed. Half the sky was covered with a long, dark cloud. We'd forgotten about the tracking, and we'd come a long way—right past the quarantine station. "Are we even allowed up this far?" I asked Grace, but she was only interested in the penguin.

At the point, waves washed over the rocks that jutted into the bay. "We'll have to get around here quickly," I said. Grace didn't think we could.

"No, Annie," she said, still nursing the backpack, "let's go back the way we came. We've been so long, Dad might have gone back to the car."

The air had become cold. I didn't want to walk back the way we'd come when we could take a shortcut.

From here we would be near the car park if we went up and over the hill. It was too steep on this side, but if we got around the point we could climb up where the land looked lower. It would only take a few minutes.

I looked at my watch. "Grace," I told her, "it's nearly four thirty. It'd take us half an hour at least to walk back that way. And look, a storm's coming."

She frowned at the sky.

"Come on," I said, "I helped you with the penguin. Dad won't find us this far up because we stopped leaving tracks. If we get around these rocks we can go up over the hill to the car park. We don't need to go back to the track, we can climb up here."

"Look at the water—the tide's come right in," Grace said.

"Hurry up, then," I said. The low dark cloud had broken up and was moving over the sea. I took the backpack from her. She didn't want to hand it over. I grabbed it. "Let me carry it."

She let me have it because she knows she's uncoordinated and I'm a good rock hopper.

"Put it on your back," she said. "Be careful, Annie."

I slung the backpack over my shoulder and off I went, jumping from one rock to the other around the point. The penguin tapped my back. Farther out to sea it had already started raining.

Waves washed up and covered the black rocks ahead, then they pulled back and the rocks appeared again. They glistened. Cold wind was coming from the water. I had to time my jumps for when the waves went back. I knew not to jump on the smooth, sloping rocks. But my sneakers were wet and I slipped. I grabbed on to a rock, but the backpack slid off my back. I almost fell in, too. One of my new sneakers was full of water.

"Annie," Grace called out. "The penguin."

I scrambled onto the rock. I almost grabbed the backpack; I touched the strap with my fingertips but the sea was pulling it.

In the backpack were the keys, Simon's jumper, my Roxy wallet, Dad's cell phone, and the penguin.

I jumped onto another rock and reached for the backpack. A wave came over my feet. The wind was getting stronger, quickly.

I went farther out. This rock was taller and steep. I grabbed the tip of it and stood up with my arms out, balancing.

There were no more rocks left. I was standing on the only one not covered by water.

I could see the backpack moving away in the current.

"I told you we shouldn't have come this way," called Grace from behind me. "Why don't you ever listen?"

Kip

I walked out along the pier. At first, the water was clear and shallow. I could see dark patches of swaying seaweed. A ship had come in through the Heads. It was quite close. There were others farther out—weird shapes as still as statues. I could see the car ferry coming over from Sorrento, a few people standing on the top deck: clean, sharp silhouettes, as if they'd been cut out of tin, leaning against the railing. The sun shone on them but there was a dark cloud behind. When I looked back at the beach I could see some of the big houses toward Point King. But the kid wasn't around.

The houses along the cliff have signs: SECURITY SERVICE. NO BEACH ACCESS. KEEP OUT. PRIVATE PROPERTY. They're great big houses with views right over the bay. You don't see too many people around during winter—except for staff: pool cleaners, builders, gardeners with leaf blowers and riding mowers. A security car.

I leaned on the rail at the end of the pier and watched the ship head toward Melbourne. I like watching the ships.

When you think about it, the only way out of Australia is across water. And here, in Port Phillip Bay, you can't get out unless you go through the Heads. Across the bay I could see the faded shapes of city buildings on the horizon—Melbourne. A long dark cloud was coming over the western sky, but a patch of sun was still shining on the city. It made me think of that famous convict William Buckley, who escaped from the settlement at Sorrento. He got in a boat and thought he was heading north toward Sydney. But he wasn't, he was just going around the bay. If Melbourne had been there in those days, he would have gone straight past it. As it turned out, he ended up at Point Lonsdale, just across the Heads from where he started.

William Buckley got lost. He should have gone through the Heads, out to the back beach, the ocean side, because the other side of that horizon is the rest of the world.

I walked back to the shore and past the jetties. The wind had changed direction. It had become colder, stronger. Farther up I could see two people wading in the water. They were so far away I couldn't tell if they were kids or adults.

I watched the tiny waves breaking on the sand—like surf beach waves, but miniature.

The dark cloud was moving in fast, its ragged edge looked torn against the blue sky. I was thinking I should probably go home. I was just wondering where that kid could have got to when I saw this guy wearing a red and yellow jacket, sitting on a jetty and dangling his feet.

"G'day," he called out.

I wasn't sure if he was talking to me but there was no one else around.

I noticed the sign on the jetty. PRIVATE PROPERTY. KEEP OFF. He saw me looking at it.

"I'm allowed to sit here. It's a free country."

I don't think he was allowed to sit there if the jetty wasn't his property, but I didn't say anything. I nodded and kept walking.

"I suppose you recognize me."

He said it in an aggressive way, as if he were confronting me with it.

I stopped. It was an odd thing to say. I didn't recognize him. I wondered if he had been on one of those reality TV shows. He had a dark face and black hair and really green eyes. He looked a bit like that singer Nick Cave, whom I'd seen on music videos.

"No," I said, shaking my head.

He shrugged and took a swig from a can of drink.

I started to walk off again.

"See those clouds? I gotta watch them."

I stopped, looked toward the Heads. The bank of heavy gray cloud was moving along the horizon above Point Lonsdale. It looked full, like it would burst.

"Why?" I asked.

"Severe weather, that's what that is."

I nodded. "Are you going out on a boat?"

The guy acted as if he hadn't heard what I'd said.

"People get lost in severe weather. All the time," he slurred, "they're getting lost."

That reminded me of the kid I'd seen. I wondered if he was lost. I was about to ask the guy if he'd seen anyone when he hopped off the jetty and into the water. He had bare feet. He was wearing black pants and they got wet but he didn't seem to notice.

"Thought you might have recognized me from the TV." He stumbled slightly in the deep, damp sand.

"Oh, right," I said, "I don't watch many of those reality shows. Sometimes I watch *Big Brother*, but—"

He interrupted me. "No, not those deadbeats." He waded out of the water. His legs were skinny. His jacket was faded corduroy and it fell around him, taking on the shape of his body, which was bony. He looked up at me and smiled, as if his mood had suddenly changed. His skin was weather-beaten, his face hollow, but he had a turned up nose that made him look younger than he might have been.

"I'll give you a clue." He stood there and played air guitar for a minute. When I must still have looked blank, he started to sing. His voice was deep and husky, breathless, but in tune.

Time held me green and dying
Though I sang in my chains like the sea.

It sounded like a sad song, the way he sang that bit, but it didn't really clear things up for me. The guy looked as if he'd get angry again if I didn't know who he was.

Maybe he'd been on *Australian Idol* or something? But he didn't really look the type. I said, "You look a bit like Nick Cave." Was this what he wanted to hear?

The guy snorted, as if Nick Cave were a complete amateur.

"I had two number one albums," he said crossly. "Don't you recognize the tune?"

Suddenly, he swore and lifted his foot. Bright red blood spilled down between his toes and dripped on the sand.

"Are you okay?" I asked.

"Cut my bloody foot, didn't I." He took his foot in his hands and hopped around, nearly over-balancing.

I had a look at it. I could see the cut. It was a deep gash in the shape of an eyelid.

"Maybe you stepped on a shell, or some glass," I said. "Hang on, you've got something in it."

He toppled over and sat in the sand. "Where?" He lifted his foot again and peered at it. "Get it out, can you?"

I held his foot still. It was white and cold. Blood ran onto my hands and on the sleeve of my shirt. I ran my finger along and felt the jagged glass. I pulled it out quickly. He flinched. I held it up—it was a piece of beer bottle. Then the guy's foot bled more.

"Better wash it," he said, hobbling to the water's edge.

I followed him and washed the blood off my hands. It was still on my sleeve, and I'd got it down my front as well. Red threads trailed off into the icy water. The guy winced.

Spattering rain blew in from the sea and formed tiny, perfect circles on the sand. I wanted to walk off, to leave him. I didn't like him and I didn't want to help him anymore. He limped back up the beach.

"It looks like a pretty bad cut," I said. "You might need stitches." He was making little groans as if his foot really hurt. "I better get going." I started to walk away.

"The number one albums," he muttered, ignoring what I'd said, "can't you remember? 1990 and 1996."

That explained things. "I was born in 1990," I told him.

"You look older than that." He said it like an accusation, as if I had deliberately misled him. "You don't look like a child to me."

"I'm not a child," I said, "I'm fourteen."

"Yeah, well," he said sulkily, "you look older."

That's not my fault, I felt like telling him.

A cold breeze came across the water. The little waves overlapped each other and sounded more urgent. The clouds now covered half the sky. I couldn't see Melbourne anymore.

I decided to head home. Then I remembered the kid. Maybe he'd gone up the beach the other way.

"Did you see a kid around here?" I asked. "There was a little boy on his own, he ran out of a car, down to the beach."

He looked at me strangely, and it dawned on me—I realized that by the way he was sprawled on the sand, the way he was speaking and falling about, it wasn't just that he'd hurt his foot. He was drunk. Completely drunk at four thirty on a Monday afternoon.

"A kid?" he asked, and then he smiled.

Annie

It wasn't my fault. I was only trying to get back the quickest way.

I had to step down into the water. It was getting too deep. It was freezing. It almost pushed me over. The rocks were sharp through my Converse sneakers. They were getting wrecked. The backpack was floating farther and farther away. I could still see it. It wasn't going out to sea—it was bobbing alongside the rocks in the water.

The tide had come right in. There was no beach, the rocks had disappeared; there was just water.

Grace was coming out after me. She was stumbling. Her arms and legs looked stiff, like a wooden doll.

"We can't get it," I called. "It's too deep."

She stopped. The water ran past her and over her and around her.

I started to come back toward her. "I can't get it," I said again.

Grace stared at me. "I told you not to go around on the rocks," she said. "The poor little penguin. It'll die in the backpack. It won't be able to get out."

I knew what Grace was thinking. She was thinking that I killed that penguin.

I looked each way. I was more than halfway around the point. We had to keep going to the other side.

"Come on," I told her, trying to pull the wet legs of my jeans up over my knees. When she reached me, I took Grace's hand and we waded through the freezing water. We got around the point, but it wasn't the longer beach that I had imagined. It was a little cove at the base of a cliff. There was hardly any sand left, and no sign of the backpack. There was no way we'd be able to get around to the main beach. I looked up. "We'll have to climb up here," I said, pointing to the cliff.

But she refused and wanted to head back.

"You won't be able to do it, Grace," I told her.

"I'm going to get Dad," she said. "He can take me

in the car around the other way to find the backpack. The current will take it to the main beach."

She stumbled through the water, back the way we'd come.

"Grace, don't be stupid, the tide's even further in. You won't be able to get around."

I started to climb the cliff, thinking she'd follow me.

"Come back, Grace."

I climbed up. It was much easier than the rocks.

I got to the top and stood there kicking at small stones. The sky kept changing. Half of it was gray and the other half the deep blue that comes just before nighttime.

Wind blew my hair against my face. I couldn't see Grace anymore.

I knew she'd come back.

I waited.

Even though Grace is older than me, half the time I feel like I'm the one who's older, like I'm the one who should be protecting her. It makes me mad, the way I feel I have to take care of her.

And now I couldn't see her at all.

Kip

The guy gave me the creeps, so I left him waiting for his foot to stop bleeding and walked along the beach toward the point. I could go up to the track and then home along the road. The rain had stopped but I knew it would start again. The sky was so dark. It was cold, too, the wind was quite cold.

I don't know why, but I was worried about that kid. I couldn't work out why the woman in the car hadn't called out to him. Maybe if I hadn't had my music up so loud, I might have heard what was going on. Had he said something to me? I tried to remember if I'd seen his lips move. Maybe he'd needed help. Maybe he'd screamed and I hadn't heard him. That's what his mouth had looked like—a small dark cave in the shape of a scream. I couldn't get it out of my mind. I was looking out for him, and I thought I saw him up toward the point—someone was up there, but so far off that I couldn't see clearly.

It wasn't normal to be worried about a kid who I didn't even know. But then, I worry about lots of things. Big things and little things. I worry that terrorists will blow something up in Australia. I worry about the future, the drought and global warming and things like that. I worry that I'll never get a girlfriend. I worry that I can't be bothered doing things like I used to. And I was worried about the kid. Other people wouldn't have even noticed him. Then I started to worry about the fact that I was worried about some kid who I'd never met.

I'd come as far as the cliff track. I could see a pilot boat going out, moving easily through the waves. The sea pilots go through the Heads, then they climb up a rope ladder on the side of a ship and they guide it into Port Melbourne or Geelong. They do this any time that a ship is coming in or going out—day or night, and even if there's a storm.

Sometimes I think I'd like to do a job like the sea pilots. That's real work. Not like my dad's job—sitting at IBM, working on a computer inventing ways to sell more computers. Some people think that my dad's job is great. Lots of kids want to get into I.T. But I don't know what sorts of jobs there'll be when I finish school. At the beginning of this year, when we started eighth grade, the principal told us that most of the jobs we'll be doing when we leave school haven't even been invented yet. He said that the world will change in the next ten years more than it has in the last forty. I don't know what the others think—most of them aren't listening in assemblies, and it might be better if I tuned out as well, because I don't like that kind of talk. It makes all these questions appear in my mind. What do they mean the jobs haven't been invented yet? How can we learn to do a job if it hasn't been invented? And what's the point of learning the way we do at school if the world is going to change that much? But then I think, who said it will change that much anyway? People used to say that by the year 2000 we'd all have robots to do the housework and we'd have cars that could fly and all sorts of things. And that didn't happen, did it.

I watched the pilot boat till the cliff blocked my view. A sea pilot—that was a job where you really did something. A computer couldn't do that job. Not properly. Not yet. I wondered what the new jobs might be. The ones that no one's invented yet. One job I reckon you could always do is sports. Even if all the other jobs "fall by the wayside," as Mr. Sweet, our principal, says. (Everyone calls him Sour, which he is.) People will always want to play sports and they'll always want to watch it, too.

I could have been a swimmer. Actually, I am, I was a swimmer. It's pretty simple. All you have to do is swim as fast as you can. I used to like that about it—when I was younger. It was a rhythm in my life; thinking about swimming stopped me worrying. You can just concentrate on breathing and it blocks out everything else. It was easy to focus on improving my time. I could name it and then aim for it and reach it. But more than that, I used to like the feel of water. Water holds you up, it balances you.

Then, for some reason, I started thinking What's the

point? I mean, training is okay but basically it's pointless. You get to the end and all you can do is turn around and swim back again. That's why I gave it up. I was a state swimmer—backstroke—but last term I stopped. That feeling of the water all over me—it didn't seem as good anymore. The times and the clock had taken over, and then I lost it. I lost the feeling of water. Now I only get it back when I'm in the sea, because there's no time, no clock, no wall at the end.

Once you start asking what the point is, it's difficult to keep trying so hard. Dad told Mum, "Kip hasn't got what it takes." He's right. I mean I still wanted to get faster and better and I knew what I had to do, but I didn't have what it takes to do it. I wanted to compete for Australia, I really did, but I think I lost the will to swim. I don't know where it went—my drive or ambition or whatever it was—all I know is that it's gone now. The water stopped balancing me. I started to think that it was suffocating me. Swallowing me. That I was drowning.

I don't know if that's normal or not, but my parents and coach were really disappointed. They said that I was throwing away my gift, that I'd regret it.

I knew my parents were still mad with me, even though I made the decision to quit two weeks before the end of the term. They said "It's your decision," but it's not really, because I know I've hurt them and they'll punish me without meaning to. I can see it already— their disappointed looks, the fact that they're having to change what they believe about me. I always thought I was swimming for me—it was only when I stopped that I saw how much I was also doing it for them.

Then they said, "Take the holidays off and think about it." They say to their friends, "Kip's having a break." Not "Kip's given up" or "Kip's stopped swimming." Now they're not mentioning it to me, but they're being really nice and reasonable about everything else. Don't they see it's not going to change my mind if they let me turn up my amp or go to the movies in the city? I don't regret giving up. I don't miss swimming at all, but I feel they had these dreams for me and I've wrecked them. I've closed a door. I've started closing doors on my life already. I think they're worried about me. And that's the worst thing: to know that people are worried about me. Because that makes me worry, too.

The light was eerie now, bright where the sun lit up the water against the dark sky. It reminded me of an eclipse. I was about to turn up to the cliff track when I heard something. I turned my head. A beeping noise was coming from the water. I went down to the edge. Something was floating, and there was a light, flashing on and off. It was only a little way out so I took off my sneakers, rolled up my jeans, and waded in. As soon as I stepped in I felt a current. Cold waves lapped at my knees.

It was a black backpack floating on the water. I reached over and grabbed it. I lifted it out and unzipped the front. The top part was still quite dry. It mustn't have been in the water very long. There were car keys and in the outside net pocket there was a phone. That was the light I'd seen. I took it out. It had stopped ringing. There was no name on the backpack. Just as I got out of the water with it, the phone rang again. Without thinking, I answered.

"Hello?"

"Who's this?" It was a man's voice. "Where are you?"

"It's Kip."

"Who?"

"My name's Kip. I just found this phone in a backpack in the water down here at the beach . . ."

"In the water? Are Grace and Annie there?" He was puffing.

I looked around. "There's no one here," I said. "The backpack was floating around the point. There's a strong current from there."

"Have you seen two girls? Sorry, what did you say your name was?"

"Kip."

"Who?" He sounded angry, too. My horoscope must have said, "Monday: watch out for angry people."

"Like Kipling, the writer."

"Can you see anyone else on the beach? The phone belongs to me. My daughter had it."

I couldn't see all the way around because there was a small sandy cliff in the way.

"Hang on," I said. I climbed halfway up the cliff and looked toward the Heads. "I think I can see someone, way down near the next point."

"Two people?" he snapped, as if I were only telling him half the story.

"I can't be sure, I think it's only one."

"Where are you?"

"I'm at the point at the end of the beach."

"You mean at Point Nepean?"

"No, I'm on the main beach. Do you want me to go up the path to the road?"

He paused. "No, wait where you are. Stay there. If you see my girls, tell them to wait with you. I'll come down. They're my daughters. Annie and Grace. I think they're lost. Please, just wait where you are with the bag till I get there."

I hung up. It was really getting dark now. I had to wait on this cold beach until he showed up. The cloud was charcoal gray and I could see more rain, far off, hanging like a flimsy curtain. Mum would be wondering where I was. I'd told her I was just going out for a walk.

The rain came quickly. It was heavier. I went up the path a bit to take cover under some trees.

I looked at what else was in the backpack. Maybe there was a slicker or something that I could put on. I lifted out a jumper. Underneath it I felt something slick, warm, and moist. I turned the backpack upside-down. Something tumbled out onto the wet dirt—a small, dead weight. It gave me a fright; it was a penguin.

Why would anyone keep a dead penguin in their backpack? I picked it up by its wing and lowered it back in. Maybe this guy was a vet or a scientist, collecting dead penguins for research.

It was raining harder now, loudly, spattering and dripping through the tea tree I was crouched under. I could see the beach from here—water tumbling into water.

I didn't even know the name of the person I was supposed to be waiting for.

Annie

I stood on top of the sandy cliff and waited to see if Grace would give up and come back. It was raining again and I was cold. I just wanted Grace to hurry up so we could find Dad and go home. I went to the edge to see if Dad was on the beach but I couldn't see him. Clumps of soft rock tumbled down so I moved back. He could have been waiting for us on the path to the parking lot, where we started the tracking game. He could have gone back to the car because it was so wet. The tea trees rustled. Where was Grace? Behind me was a tall fence with more signs. DANGER. KEEP OFF. UNSTABLE CLIFFS. The DO NOT TOUCH ANYTHING notice was there, too. The stupid thing is, I never want to touch anything till I read that sign, and then, all of a sudden, I want to start touching things.

Dad would be mad with me. He'd be angry about the backpack, but it was only an accident.

I was getting saturated. Through the rain I could hear music playing, like a flute. Far off.

Stupid Grace. I always had to wait for her. Where was she?

Then I heard her calling. I went over and looked down. Grace was at the base of the cliff. I couldn't see her but I could hear her.

"I can't get back that way," she called. "The tide's up too far."

"I told you, Grace," I yelled. "I told you that would happen."

I moved to the edge again. It felt soft under my feet. Then I saw a color. Her pale pink jacket moved. "I can see where you are. Come on," I called. "You'll have to climb up here."

"Can you see the backpack?"

"No. There's nothing we can do about it now. It must have floated out to sea."

She started to climb up, then stopped.

"But the penguin," she shouted, "it's in the backpack. The oil destroys their natural waterproofing. If it doesn't drown it'll die of the cold."

Then, of course, she started to cry. I don't think she was scared; it was because of the penguin. I bet if it had been a person we couldn't reach she wouldn't have been so upset. But because it was an animal, tears were pouring down her face.

"We could come back tomorrow and see if it's been washed up by the tide," I told her.

"But the penguin will be dead!"

"We could still get the keys and my wallet."

The rain was getting heavier. The water was right around the base of the cliff, making pools in the rocks and clay.

It had been easy for me to climb the cliff, but now I was wondering whether Grace would be able to do it.

She tried, but she can't climb or anything. Like I said, she's uncoordinated.

"Come on, Grace, it's not that hard. Once you're on the cliff it's easy. It's just sand," I called down to her.

Slowly, she came up the cliff. She grabbed at jutting rocks and grasses.

Then she got stuck halfway. "There's nothing more to hold on to," she called out, looking up at me. "I'm slipping, Annie." Rain fell on her face, making her blink.

"Come on Grace," I yelled, "come *on*."

I stumbled. Something moved.

Then the sand shifted.

That's when Grace fell backward.

That's when she went under.

Kip

That guy was right about the severe weather, anyway. I sat under the tree. Luckily tea trees grow out, not up, so it wasn't a bad shelter. Still, it had become really cold. I wanted to go home but I'd told the guy I'd wait. I stood up and went down the path a bit. The rain got heavier. I was completely soaked. Nobody on the beach yet. A crack of fork-lightning gave me a fright. It split the sky and lit up the horizon.

I was thinking that if I'd left the backpack floating

in the water, I could have been home by now, not out in the middle of a storm.

I could see houses set into the cliffs. It would be a great place to have a house. In summer, you could just run down the track to the water. It was a secluded sort of area—there are places like this all along the beaches at Portsea and Sorrento. A real estate agent would call it "direct beach access." The house we stay in isn't like these at all. It's a clapboard bungalow that belongs to friends of my grandparents. We rent it; they let us have it cheap.

Most of the houses that have direct beach access are hidden behind tall hedges or fences. I went to shelter under a bigger tree beside a hedge, and passed a concrete fence that was split and cracked. The gate had fallen off and I could see a white house. It wasn't old, but it was run-down. The windows were foggy with salt spray. It looked out of place because the other houses were well kept. Not mansions like the ones up around Point King, but interesting, nice houses. A rusting yellow RX 7 with pop-up headlights sat in the long grass, one headlight up and one smashed, winking sadly as it sank further into the weeds. The car wasn't that old— probably a nineties model. If you had such a good car why let it rust away like that, I thought. Bamboo had pushed the fence over and was spreading across the garden. It was competing with the ivy that had completely covered a shed in the corner.

Over the splattering rain, I could hear music. I think it was flute music, wafting in and out with the wind.

"Come in out of the weather," someone yelled. I looked around, and there was that guy again. He was standing on a concrete veranda, his long hair hanging around his shoulders, all straggly and wet. His feet were still bare, but he'd wrapped some sort of bandage over the cut. It was loose and messy. Blood seeped through it and mixed with the puddles gathering on the concrete. He was drinking a can of beer. I realized he must live in this house. A big sub-woofer speaker sat on the empty veranda, which looked like it had never been finished. His neighbors must really hate him, I thought.

He was the last person I needed to see. All I wanted to do was give the owner of the backpack his things and then go home.

"I can't," I called back to him.

"Why not?"

How could I explain it to him. "I have to wait for someone," I shouted.

His head went to one side. "Do you?"

"Yeah, I found a phone in the water and it belongs to someone. I have to wait here."

"Why don't you come in?"

"No, that's okay," I replied quickly. "No thanks."

"Why not?"

I'd just told him why not! "Because I have to wait for the guy who owns the phone and this backpack."

The rain was easing a bit. I came out from under the tree.

"Don't ever go into a stranger's house. That's it, isn't it? But we're not strangers, pal, we're old friends!"

"No we're not. I don't even know your name."

He stepped out into the rain, and held out a shaky hand. "Ted. Ted Atwood. Pleased to meet you."

I shook his hand. Both our hands were wet and cold. It was like shaking hands with a fish.

"And you are?"

"Kip. Like Kipling, the writer."

He hobbled over and sat on a solitary, dirty director's chair that leaned to one side. Rain dripped down from rusted gutters.

"Know all about Kipling, do you?" He motioned for me to come under the shelter of the veranda.

"Only *The Jungle Book*, and *Just So Stories*."

There was a crash of thunder and the rain came down hard again. Ted's green eyes flashed and he put on this unnaturally deep voice. "The great grey-green, greasy Limpopo River, and the inquisitive child who pays the price for asking one question too many."

I didn't understand what he was going on about. I told him that I didn't know the story that well. "My parents called me Kip because Kipling was my mum's surname. It wasn't because they were big fans of Rudyard Kipling or anything."

I looked toward the beach but I still couldn't see anyone. I squinted. There was so much rain, I could hardly see anything.

The water and the music were loud together. Ted turned the sound down. "Do your parents know where you are, Kip?" he asked quietly, from close behind me. He handed me a can of Coke, already open.

I hesitated, then took it. "No. My mum knows I went for a walk, but they don't know that I'm here." I took a sip. It tasted odd.

"In this weather, you could get lost. People do, you know."

I nodded dumbly. What was I supposed to say to that?

"You know about Harold Holt?"

"Sort of," I said, because I had heard about Harold Holt. He was the prime minister who drowned when he was swimming at Cheviot Beach. It happened when my parents were little kids.

"He got lost," Ted chuckled. "He got so bloody lost that he could never get found. A big, strong, grown-up man, a prime minister, lost! Come on, drink up, get it into you, you look freezing."

Since when did a can of Coke warm people up?

For some reason, this guy thought that a prime minister drowning was a great joke. I wasn't even listening to him anymore. I just wanted to get away. I kept trying to see through the rain to the beach. I needed to watch out for the man coming to get the backpack. No sign.

Ted kept talking. "I reckon it was the kelp. Have you seen the kelp down there at Cheviot? Seen how thick it is, the way it's heaving in the water?" He took a long swig of beer. "Dense. Harold Holt could have got caught up in that kelp." He nodded to himself. "I reckon that was how he got into trouble."

"I better go and see if the owner's down—" I began, but Ted interrupted me.

"Don't you think you should phone your parents and tell them where you are? How old did you say you were?"

"Fourteen."

"Only fourteen! Jesus Christ, I could be your father."

Thank Him that you're not, I thought.

Lightning turned the sky silver. For a second it crackled and hissed like a fire.

He pointed to the khaki pants I was wearing. "You a soldier?" he snickered.

"No," I said. This guy was a real joker.

I wanted to leave but the rain was really pelting down.

A boom of thunder made me jump.

"How far away do you reckon that is?"

"What?" His conversation leaped all over the place.

"For every second you count between the lightning and the thunder, the strike's three hundred meters away. I reckon that was four seconds, so let's say . . ." He took a swig and wiped a hand across his mouth, "twelve hundred meters. Not good to be outside when there's so much lightning about. Your parents will be worried."

"I'll go home as soon as that guy comes for his backpack."

"You can't go out in this," he said. "That bloke you're waiting for, he's probably sheltering from the storm. Blowing a gale out there now. He might be ages." He stood up. "Didn't you hear the warnings?"

"What warnings?"

His answer was not to my question. "Parents always like to know the whereabouts of their children."

It would have been a good idea to phone my parents, but I didn't have my cell phone. I didn't want to use the one in the backpack, and I didn't want to go into this weird guy's house.

"I haven't got my phone," I told him, taking another sip from the can. "Is this Coke?" I asked. It tasted funny, as if it were warm as well as cold, burning my throat.

"Of course it's Coke. Go on, have a drink."

I took another gulp. It made me cough, and I spilt some down my front. It wasn't Coke. It had Coke in it but it wasn't only Coke. "I'll just go back down to the beach and see if I can spot him." I started to walk away.

"No you won't."

I turned back. He was still sitting in his rickety chair. Was he going to stop me from leaving?

"I can't let you go out in this. That would be totally irresponsible. I insist that you use my phone. Go right ahead." He motioned with his hand for me to go in his house. "I'm not going to do anything to you!" He laughed. "Go on, I'll mind your backpack." He took it from me and held it on his lap, as if he were on a bus. He smiled at me again—I was really beginning to dislike his smile.

"Can you get it for me? Can you bring it out here?"

He took a swig on his beer and looked out at the rain, as if I hadn't said anything.

"Can I bring the phone out here then, so I don't miss the guy who's coming?" I asked.

He didn't answer.

"Can you tell me where your phone is?"

No answer again. Was he really concerned that my parents wouldn't know where I was? Why would he care?

"Look, I think I'll just go—"

"Get the phone," he said again, almost threatening, so I ran in, thinking the phone would be on the bench or the wall or something and I could grab it and bring it outside again. It was like one of those nightmares when you're trying to get somewhere but you keep being stopped. All I wanted to do was forget about that little kid who'd run into me, forget about this Ted, get out of the rain and go home. But here I was, in the wrong place at the wrong time, soaking wet, babysitting a backpack with a dead penguin in it, and a strange guy was insisting that I use his phone.

Inside, I had to move slowly because although there was hardly any furniture, there were heaps of junk. The carpet was light-colored, quite new looking, but dirty and stained. There was stuff everywhere— magazines piled up and old records and things. It looked like a teenager's bedroom. Even for a teenager's bedroom it was messy. He had two pretty good guitars, by the looks of things. A Gibson Les Paul and a Fender Strat. They weren't in cases, but lying amid the junk. On the walls were posters and pictures from the news- paper. They showed storms—storms at sea, in the bush, in paddocks, in cities. Lightning, purple skies, huge heavy banks of cloud all lit up—tornadoes, cyclones, wild storms like nothing I'd ever seen. There was a tripod with camera gear littered around it, and battered electrical equipment.

I tried to find the phone. On the bench I noticed a framed photo with no glass in it. The photo was faded—it was a picture of the guy and a woman with long dark hair.

I couldn't see the phone in the kitchen. I went further, into the hallway. Water-stained curtains had come off their hooks and dangled onto the floor. Rain must have got in at some time. Everything in the house was quite new but wrecked. There was a big square mirror, thick with dust. I noticed a smear of blood across my forehead and my eye where I must have wiped it with the back of my hand.

I found the phone in the living area, under a fluorescent-purple Boogie board that was leaning against a computer table piled high with papers and maps. I took the phone outside because I felt safer in the open.

I rang Mum. It took me ages to explain it to her.

"Kip, it's getting dark. There's been a storm warning on the radio. You can't walk home in this. I'll come and pick you up."

"Don't worry," I told her, "I'll give the man his bag

and then I'll come straight home. The storm will probably have passed by then. If it hasn't, I'll borrow his phone and call you."

There was a pause. Normally she would have insisted on coming to get me, but because they were on the be-nice-to-Kip campaign, she let it go. As I walked back through the room I noticed other things around the computer. They were magazines, and not the type you'd share with your mum and dad, if you know what I mean. I glanced down for a minute, I couldn't help it. They were pretty hardcore, I'd say. Women in all these poses and things. I felt my stomach lurch. This guy Ted, he didn't hide them away or anything—he had them on the table the way normal people might have a book about houses or the Great Ocean Road. I wondered if he cared whether people saw them. Maybe no one ever dropped by, so it didn't matter.

Maybe he'd wanted me to see them, because when I got back he had this weird smile on his face.

I handed him the phone. "Thanks," I said, "see ya." I turned up my collar and ducked my head to go out in the rain. Water flooded from the gutters, streaming into wide puddles.

"Hang on, hang on, don't go yet." He stood up. "You haven't finished your drink."

I don't know why I didn't just leave. I suppose you get so used to obeying adults who tell you what to do.

He went to his stereo and turned up the volume. It was a jazz track, as loud as the rain. I stood there. His stereo looked top of the line. Bang & Olufsen, I think. Streamlined and brushed steel, surrounded by clothes thrown about, cans and cups, and leaning piles of books.

"Do you like this music?"

"It's okay." We had to shout.

"What's wrong with jazz?" he asked accusingly.

"Nothing," I said. "I suppose I just don't really get it." Although on this system, through these speakers, I was beginning to think that anything might sound good.

He snorted with contempt and turned it down, then pointed through the grimy glass door. "See my guitars?"

"Yeah." I nodded. "They look pretty good."

I sipped my Coke.

"Do you play guitar, soldier?"

I hesitated. I wished he would stop the stupid "soldier" stuff.

"Well, do you or don't you?"

I nodded. "Yeah, sort of."

"What sort of music do you like?"

I didn't know what to say. He might get angry. I answered him like it was a question, as if I were asking whether it was okay to like what I liked. "Nirvana? Kurt Cobain?"

He nodded. At least I wasn't going to get abused for liking Kurt Cobain.

Ted went over to a huge pile of CDs on the floor. This guy's stuff was completely out of control.

"I've got one here," he said, coming back out again. *Unplugged.* He took out the CD and handed me the cover. "Okay until he was nine years old, then the parents split and, wham, there goes his life. Poor old Kurt." He shook his head sympathetically. "Played a Fender Strat. I've got a book about him somewhere in there." He indicated the bomb site inside. "All my books are cataloged."

He had to be joking! Cataloged! I couldn't help smiling.

"What's so funny?" he demanded suddenly.

"Nothing." I stumbled over the word.

"Listen, let me give you some advice, soldier. Never trust a person with a tidy house." He came really close. His breath stank. "You know what that means? Lack of imagination. Order is really dull, man." He staggered toward the sound system, CD trembling in his hand.

There must be some sort of happy medium, I thought, looking at the chaos.

He put the CD on. I'd never heard it—it was a live recording.

"Warming up, soldier?"

I nodded. "Yep."

He sat on his chair and looked around. "This is nice, isn't it?"

What? Standing in the freezing cold drinking Coke that tasted odd and listening to Kurt Cobain with a complete lunatic?

I didn't answer him.

Annie

"Grace!" I kept screaming out for her. The rain came down harder. "Grace!"

It was darker now and I couldn't see her. I couldn't hear anything except the rain and wind and thunder. I slid down the cliff to the rocks at the bottom. Part of the cliff had given way. I didn't know if she was in the water. I was half in the sea and half out. It was crashing on me, making me stumble and crawl. I called out her name but the wind and the rain were making more noise than me. I climbed back up again.

Where was she? She'd gone so quickly. I ran. I ran through the scrub and past the signs and the cyclone fence. I came to the track and the car park. Dad's car was the only one left. But he wasn't there.

"Dad," I called out. "Dad!"

I ran back to the road and the Visitors' Center. It was closed and I couldn't see anyone. So I ran back to the cliff and tried to get down, but I couldn't.

Kip

One song, I thought. I'll stay for one song and then I'm out of here, storm or no storm.

We listened. It was "Pennyroyal Tea," but a really different version.

"That Coke," said Ted after a few minutes, "it might be Gulf War Coke."

"What?"

"They reckon that half the American Gulf War vets got sick when they came home because the Coke had got too hot in storage and gone a bit off. Collateral damage!" He laughed. "Yeah, soldier, maybe you've got yourself a can of genuine Gulf War Coke."

I didn't know what to say.

"Oh well," he muttered, annoyed that I didn't share his sense of humor, "you're probably too young for the Gulf War."

The rain pelted down. Trees swayed in the wind and water was sloping in under the veranda.

"Look," I said, "I have to go down to the beach to find that guy."

"Have a look through this. Save you getting so wet and cold."

He lifted a telescope on a tripod from behind a couch and stood it on the veranda. I looked through it.

Tea tree, rain, gray-green branches swirling wildly. Looking close up always gives me a sense of expectation, as if I'm about to discover something, to see something that I'm not supposed to see.

Ted was fiddling with it and the trees moved in and out of focus. He steadied the tripod.

"Have you got the beach? Can you find the Couta boat? See the brown one? That's my boat. I might take it out later."

I looked at him. "You what?"

But he was too busy studying the bay that looked nothing like a bay. "Boy, they're getting blown around a bit!" He seemed to think it was funny that all the boats were being tossed like toys in a bath. "You can look out for him and when you see him you can go down." He put his eye to the telescope again. "Check it out, man. Check out the tide! There'll be no beach left tomorrow." He turned to me. "Lucky you're safe and dry here."

The song had finished. I wished the storm would ease a bit so that I could go. I don't know what kept me there—maybe I was afraid that he'd get violent if I told him again that I had to leave. He seemed pretty high-strung.

He went inside and waved his hand around the room, like some sort of demented magician. "See if there are any others you like. Try this." He took off

Kurt and put on another CD. "Acid jazz. Can you get into this, soldier?"

It was like a cross between grunge music and jazz. I'd never heard it before.

I stood for a moment, half inside and half out. The music had a kind of swinging beat. You couldn't help moving to it.

"You know Jamiroquai? They started out as an acid jazz band. James Taylor?"

He picked up the Les Paul and came over to me. He held it out gently, as if it were a large glass ornament.

"Go on, have a play. It's a special edition. Custom. 1934."

"Look, I better not. I better go." I glanced down at the guitar, thinking it must sound great, a custom-made guitar, it must have cost him thousands.

"Come on, there's no one on the beach. Wait till the storm passes. Should only be a few minutes." He shoved the guitar at me. "Playing's the most important thing, man."

I hesitated, then put down my drink and took the guitar in my arms. I hadn't been allowed to bring mine on vacations because Mum and Dad said it would be too loud in a small house. I strummed it. Picked out a few notes. I played a bit of a Nirvana song. Felt the sound go through me. It was a beautiful instrument. I'd never played anything like it. Whatever I did sounded good, almost as if someone else were playing, or that it were playing itself. I mucked around for a minute with a few things I'd been doing with my own guitar—a really crappy one—back home.

"You're not bad," said Ted. "Keep your hand curved, thumb behind the neck of the thing." He stood behind me and put his bluish hand over mine, moving my hand to a different position. "Did you learn classical?"

"Yeah, I did when I was in elementary school."

"You can tell." Although his hand was shaking, he sounded lucid. He'd stopped stumbling around, as if he were suddenly focused.

"That'll really help you, classical training," he said. "Elton John, Bowie, Sting, Radiohead, they all had classical training."

He seemed to know a lot about music. For someone who must have been nearly as old as my parents, he did, anyway. My parents don't know much about music. Music isn't in their lives much at all.

That reminded me, my mum would really panic if I didn't get home soon.

I put down the guitar. Ted turned the acid jazz up loud. He stood there swaying, closed his eyes and moved his head to the uneven, jarring beat.

This guy was beginning to freak me out. I really had

to go. "Look," I told him in a break between tracks, "I think the rain's eased up a bit. Thanks for the drink. I'm quite warm now." I had to finish the Coke so I could get out of there. I perched on the arm of the couch and downed it quickly. Blood rushed to my head as I staggered up. "I better go."

He was still leaning against the doorway. He opened his eyes and started to say something, but I had to get out of there. "See ya," I called, and I ran. I went back to the beach. I stumbled on the uneven track. I felt quite sick. Maybe it was those magazines. Whenever I look at that sort of stuff, I half want to but then I feel sick.

There was still no sign of the guy who was coming for the backpack. It must have been twenty minutes since I'd spoken to him. Maybe longer. Maybe he hadn't been able to find me so he'd left. I went up to the point, to the rocks and the sandy cliff. The rain was steady. Wind blew my clothes against me. They were wet and heavy.

Around the point is out of bounds. There's a cyclone-wire fence and a sign that says AUSTRALIAN ARMY, PROHIBITED AREA, KEEP OUT. There's an old quarantine station there. It's not used anymore—it hasn't been used since the 1970s. It's deserted. If someone really wanted to, they could easily get around the fence. All you had to do was climb up from the cliff or over the rocks at the base and wade around. I decided to go a bit farther, to see if the man or his daughters were around the point. I waded under the cliff.

There was a smooth sandstone cave, tiered into three steps. I sheltered there for a moment. I rested my head against the sandstone. When I stood up, I felt dizzy. The stepping-stone cave looked like a path into the cliff, as if you could walk right inside it and keep going.

I couldn't get very far because the tide was high, but I could see that on the other side was a rocky beach— well, there was hardly any beach, just rocks and water. I couldn't see anyone, and was just turning back when I thought I heard shouting. I looked around, toward the top of the cliff. I might have seen something, a patch of blue, a figure move, I don't know. My head was spinning. At that moment I heard someone calling from the beach side of the rocks. I clambered back and saw a man coming from the other direction, running along the beach toward me. "Stop!" he yelled. Maybe he thought I'd seen him and I was trying to get away from him. But there was no need to run, no need to chase me. As he got closer, I realized that I was pleased to see him, even though I'd never seen him before. He looked like a regular, normal guy. Not like Ted. This guy looked like a father.

"Kip?" he puffed.

I held up his stuff. At last, I could give it to him and go home. "Here's the backpack." He took it.

"I was taking cover out of the rain," I explained. It was hard to get my tongue around the words. "I was looking out for you." The sea was getting wilder. I felt cold in my body but my face was hot. He started to open the backpack. I though I better explain about the penguin, otherwise he might get a shock. "There was a penguin in it. It was dead." I fiddled with the zipper, undid it and the penguin flopped on the sand like a small, weighted sack.

The man bent down and touched it with his finger. He looked up at me as if he didn't understand. He looked so sad, like a kid who'd lost a pet. I felt I had to say something. "Poor little thing," I said. For some reason, right then I thought of the boy I'd seen. The man didn't say anything. I didn't want him to think I meant he was the poor little thing, so I added, "Poor little penguin."

The hood of his blue slicker slid off. "What happened to it?"

"I don't know," I said. "It was dead in the backpack when I found it."

He stood up, shaking his head. "Okay." He seemed agitated. "It's just that my girls are lost," his face creased up, "and you've got the backpack, with," he poked at the penguin with a stick, "with this in it."

I looked up and saw Ted through the trees, his red and yellow coat. He was still standing on the veranda, watching. The guy with the backpack hadn't seen him. I could faintly hear the music, the acid jazz, but the other guy didn't seem to be hearing it. He was looking out toward the sea and the sky, which had become one. A heavy violet cloud had come down right over us.

"Where are they?" he said quietly, evenly. Then he turned to me, shaking his head again. "Where are they?"

Annie

I didn't know what to do, so I ran all the way home. The rain spattered on my face. The road gleamed. It was slippery. My jeans were sodden and they clung to my thighs. They were cold. They were stinging from the salt. Only one car came past. I waved for it to stop but it didn't. Trees swayed in and out of the headlights.

All the way back, I imagined cliffs collapsing. Maybe it had come down on top of her. That was why I couldn't see her—she was under the sand and the rock. I ran faster. I saw lights on in houses. I wanted to ask someone for help, but I didn't see anyone except for a man standing in his driveway. I stopped running and walked toward him. I had this terrible stitch in my side, so bad that it hurt to breathe. I only saw him because he was under an outside light—a single bulb sticking out from the wall of his house. He was wearing a funny old-fashioned coat and he had bare feet. I was going to ask if I could use his phone but he looked at me in this strange way and I got scared.

When I reached home, there were no cars in the garage. I banged on the front door with my fists. I called out. No one was there. Not Dad or Mum and Simon. I couldn't even get inside because I didn't have a key. There was nobody home next door.

I stood on the front step, out of the rain, shivering.

What was I supposed to do now?

Kip

The guy on the beach was rummaging through the backpack, taking everything out.

"Do you want me to show you where I think I saw them?" I said.

He looked up. "What? You saw them? Where?"

He was such a nervous guy. "I told you before, I saw some kids up the beach, when the tide was a bit farther out. Around from the point. It might have been them."

"Okay," he said, pushing at his forehead with his hand. Then he looked at me as if he had only just no-ticed I was there. "Thank you," he breathed out, "yes, that'd be good. But hang on, Point Nepean will be closed now. How can we get around?"

"We can go over the top," I said, pointing to the cliff. Then I had to sit down. I almost fell down.

"Are you okay?" the guy asked.

I stood up, wobbling like a newborn calf. I didn't answer him because I had this sudden feeling that I was going to be sick. I took a deep breath of cold salty air and felt a bit better. We went to the cliff at the end of the beach. The KEEP OUT sign loomed over us, but what the hell, we needed to get around.

We climbed over the rocks. When the waves washed right up to us, we climbed up the side of the cliff, along the top and down to the beach on the other side.

"Tide's right in," the guy said as we stepped onto the sand. He looked worried. Then I forgot that I hadn't introduced myself.

"My name's Kip," I told him, and I held out my hand, like my dad had taught me to do when I meet someone.

He looked at my hand. He shook it as if he didn't want to.

"Andrew," he said slowly. "When did you see them?"

I looked at my watch. The glass had fogged up. The numbers were hard to make out. I couldn't remember what time I'd left home. I think my watch said

5:42. Why was it so dark? Why had day ended in the afternoon? "I don't know," I told him. "I saw them before . . ." but I had to stop because I felt sick again.

"We were playing a game," he said, as if this might help me to tell him something. "A tracking game. At Point Nepean. They were hiding. They must have gotten lost."

We'd reached the old quarantine station. The cliffs had become small dunes and behind them scrub and grasses. I'd never been here before. It was different from the rest of the bay. It seemed fuller, swollen; the silver-green water was swirling around at all angles.

"I'll go along the dunes and you stay on the beach," Andrew said. He stopped. "Are you sure you're okay?"

I nodded.

I called out. "Grace! Annie!"

Andrew shouted out to me. "How do you know my daughters' names?"

I stopped. He was standing in the grasses.

"You said their names before," I told him. "On the phone. Grace and Annie."

"You've got a good memory." He didn't say that as if it were a compliment. He was looking at my hands, my shirt with the blood on it.

"This mark, this blood," I said, trying to make things better, "a man cut his foot and I helped him."

Andrew looked at me. I didn't look back.

"Right," he said. "Okay."

I felt as if I'd said the wrong thing.

Up ahead, through the rain, I saw a four-wheel drive. It was a security car parked at the end of a track. Someone was sitting in the driver's seat. A man got out as we came closer.

"This guy's probably picked them up," Andrew said, sounding relieved.

"Have you seen two girls?" he asked when we reached the car. The man glared at us. He was probably angry that he had to get out of his nice warm car and into the rain that was falling in a steady rhythm. I noticed a gun and handcuffs hanging over his stomach.

He shook his head. "What are you doing here?" he asked. "This is government property."

I waved my arm in the direction we'd come from. "We came from up the beach," I told him.

"Yeah," he snapped, "I saw you hanging around here earlier."

Andrew turned his head quickly to me.

"Called out to you to get off the land. You're lucky the police haven't come to arrest you. This is property of the defense department."

Did he think we were some sort of terrorists?

"I'm sorry," said Andrew. "Let me explain what's happened. I knew the gates would be closed and I think my daughters are lost in here." He stopped. "They're young, they're only children."

"I don't know about any children. I'm ordering you off this land. Go back to the track and leave the park immediately. This beach is closed. Don't ever come down here again." He spoke to us as if we were naughty school kids.

"Will anyone be at the Visitors' Center? I want to know if they've been taken out of the park," said Andrew.

The security guard relaxed a bit, or maybe he just wanted to get rid of us and out of the rain before we could ask him to help out. "I'd say that someone driving the transport would have picked up your kids. They're pretty careful about getting everyone out by closing. They've probably been dropped home by now. I'd advise you two to get on your way as well. It's a very high tide, you'll need to go back on the track. It's about a hundred yards up."

Andrew walked toward the track. I followed. The sand gave way under my feet. "We'll go to the Visitors' Center and see if anyone's there," he said. He rang his wife on the cell phone to check if they had come home. When he'd finished, he shut the phone and turned to me.

"Were you around here earlier?" he asked.

"No."

"The security guard said that he saw you."

"Oh, I was only a little way around the point."

We'd almost reached the old cattle jetty when I saw something at the water's edge. I thought it was a towel on the wet sand, a wave washing over it.

I went over and picked it up. It was heavy, dripping—a piece of clothing. It was a pair of jeans, with one leg completely ripped up the side.

Andrew grabbed them from me and his face crumpled up. "These are Grace's jeans," he cried out.

I could see a dark streak down the torn side. I didn't want to say anything to Andrew, but he knew, too. He knew what it was, by the way he was looking at it.

It was blood.

Annie

I stood on the porch until Mum and Simon came home.

Mum slammed the car door as I ran to the garage.

"Annie, thank God." She rushed over to me. "Where were you? Dad phoned me. I was just out getting fish and chips for dinner." She spoke too quickly.

"I couldn't find Dad. I didn't know where he was."

"I better call him back and tell him you're here. How did you lose the backpack? Where's Grace? Is she inside?"

Simon was getting out of the car. She handed him the phone, and held the warm parcel. I could smell salt.

"Quick, phone Dad and tell him they're okay," she told him.

"Mum," I said loudly, then more quietly. "Mum, Grace isn't here."

She turned around quickly. "What?"

"Grace is still back there." I pointed in the direction of the rain and the dark and Point Nepean.

Mum's voice got higher. She dropped the fish and chips on the garage floor. They fell with a thump. "Is she all right? Why did you leave her?" She held my shoulders, almost shaking me. "Annie, what happened? Where's Grace?"

"She found a penguin and we had to rescue it, then she got stuck on the rocks and the cliff. We didn't know where Dad was. A storm came. I ran all the way home . . ."

I could feel my voice tremble. I pushed my dripping hair off my face, wiped my eyes.

Mum grabbed the phone from Simon.

"We've got Annie," she said, "but not Grace."

Kip

Andrew was on his cell phone, calling the police. He was telling them that his daughter was lost, and that I was there with him. He looked over at me and then I heard him say, "About seventeen."

"I'm not seventeen," I told him. "I'm fourteen." But he'd turned his back.

I didn't know whether to hang around or head off home. The tide was so far in now that it would be impossible to get back the beach way. I decided to take the road. I started off, but I felt so sick. I threw up on the sand.

Andrew came over.

"I threw up," I said, wiping my face on my sleeve. "I think I need to go home."

"You need to wait here till the police come," he told me.

We stood there, getting buffeted by the wind. "They'll be okay," I said. "They've probably found some shelter. One of the old concrete forts. The police'll find them."

"Shut up," he told me.

The rain came again, suddenly, falling down in straight silver lines. I looked out toward the horizon. The bay was lifting like an ocean.

Andrew led me under a tea-tree in the scrub behind the beach. "Will the police see us here?" I asked.

He didn't answer me.

I didn't want to sit under the tree. I stepped out

toward the old cattle jetty. Lightning turned the sky silver and I could see big drops of rain flying at angles across the light.

There was a swell. The sand was all uneven rises and falls, like a lopsided hill going into the sea. The water swirled and rocked—it looked full to bursting. It made me feel dizzy.

"Was it around here that you saw them?" he asked, coming to stand beside me.

"I don't know." I had no idea. I'd completely lost my sense of direction.

"I thought you said you saw them?" He sounded angry.

"It could have been them. I don't know."

"We better get up to the road so the police see us."

A narrow track through the bush took us up to the road. Above the rain I could hear the ocean crashing on the other side of the peninsula. Andrew held the sleeve of my shirt. We took cover in an old concrete bunker. The wind howled through the openings. Both of us were totally saturated. I felt exhausted and completely lost. After a few minutes, the police car lights appeared in the dark.

"Right," said the first policeman out of the car, "we'll put some waterproof gear on you and you can show us where you found the jeans."

They gave us each a flashlight and we led the police back to the spot. Then they started asking me questions.

"Where did you find the backpack?"

"Floating in the water."

"And there was a dead animal in it?"

I nodded, still watching the sea. "A penguin."

"What's that on your shirt?"

Lightning struck again. "Hang on," I told them, swinging my flashlight around. I'd seen something in the water.

"No you hang on," said the policeman. "We've got two kids missing. You've already been reported loitering in the area, you stink of alcohol, your shirt's covered in blood and so are these jeans."

"Two kids?" said Andrew. "Annie's okay, she's with my wife."

The policeman nodded. "There's your daughter, plus we've just had word that a young boy went missing this afternoon."

I took a quick breath. The little boy. The policeman looked at me, his face dripping water. "Someone fitting your description was seen in the area."

I should have taken the headphones off. I should have listened to him.

"Do you know something about that as well?" He shone the flashlight at me.

"No," I said quickly. I shook my head. They both looked at me. They knew I was lying. Police are trained to spot liars. Why did I say no, when I *did* know something?

"Listen," I said. I felt like crying. "This blood on my shirt is from when a guy up the beach hurt his foot." But I didn't say it as if I meant it because somehow I knew they would think it wasn't true, as if I wasn't sure myself whether it was the truth or not. How had I got myself here, in this storm, in this state, with this blood on me?

More police arrived. One guy was telling them to get flashlights and start looking. I heard them call the coast guard, and the policeman with me went over to talk to them on the phone. "Stay here," he said, "we'll need to call your parents." He left me for a minute. I went out onto the broken-down jetty to get a look at the water again. I balanced on the posts and shone my light. There was something out there. It was a board, being tossed around, moving in and out of the light. It was chipped across the top. It was purple.

I turned back to tell the police. The wind was so loud that they didn't hear what I said. I couldn't make my voice louder. I wanted to go home. I didn't want them to call my parents. I didn't understand why they seemed so angry with me—the way they looked at me—but it made me feel terrible. It made me feel guilty for not helping that kid. I kept seeing his face. But why should I have felt bad? I didn't even know who he was.

The waves threw the board up into the beam of flashlight. A Boogie board. I was sick again, I was wet through and the wind was screaming.

Wait—someone was clinging to it. It must be those girls. Or did he say he'd found one? I called out. I nearly overbalanced on the rickety jetty.

"There's someone in the water. Annie!" I yelled. "Grace!" But nobody heard me. Nobody at all. It was as if I had my headphones on again. Police were moving across the sand, a line of lights jostled in and out of my eyes.

And then the wind and the rain and the storm were like music. And it came to me. The sky was moving, it poured down and the storm picked me up, making me part of it. And of course I knew what I could do. It was simple. I could save whoever was clinging to that board. I could get away from that man and the police who didn't believe me. I could swim. I had this moment of focus, when everything became clear. I never ever felt sick in the water. I'd feel better, and then they'd know that I was the old Kip, the young Kip, the Kip who was sure and knew what he was doing. I started to fall.

The water hit me and all my breath went out. It was stinging cold, but I didn't mind. I was away from the police and the man on the jetty, away from Ted. Now all I had to do was reach the purple Boogie board.

I saw silky lights over the water. I felt the strong current, like a surf undertow.

I knew it now: they didn't trust me, they thought I'd done something terrible, but I was going to do something fantastic. I was going to use my gift. Each time my head came out of the water, I could hear rain pelting down; I could hear shouting, then I went under, and their voices disappeared. Sound became muted. I was alone. It was me and the water. I was going to save that man's kids.

I reached the board. But the water was churning and the wind was blowing so strong. There was no one clinging to it anymore.

There was a current. I was being pulled away from the jetty. But this was the bay! This wasn't the ocean side, I kept thinking. I should have taken my jeans off—they were so heavy. I couldn't breathe. I couldn't swim. I was being swept out and away from the lights. The sea grabbed the board and flung it into the darkness. I turned on my back to do my best stroke, the backstroke, but the waves broke over my head and crushed me. I rolled over and over in the water, my legs curled up to my chest. I was floating, in a whirlpool. Even though I was strong, I could feel that the water was a million times stronger than me. The bay had never been so wild. It was like a giant undertow. It was taking me away. I kept struggling and fighting it. I was gasping and throwing my arms up. I fought for ages and then I didn't have it in me anymore. It was true—I'd lost the will to swim. This wasn't a bay. This was a massive river, it flowed so fast. I couldn't get up to the surface to take another breath. My lungs would blow up, they would burst. I was floating. This giant sea-river was taking me with it. My mouth opened and the water poured into me. And I had the strangest thought. I thought, that guy Harold Holt, the guy Ted told me about, this must have been what happened to him.

Annie

Inside the car I could still smell the fish and chips. Mum drove to Point Nepean with Simon and me. The rain made it hard to see, even with the windshield wipers on fast. Mum leaned right over the steering wheel and peered ahead, scrunching up her eyes. She asked me what happened and then didn't listen when I told her. Then she asked me what happened again.

A police car was waiting and they let us in through the gate at the entrance to the national park.

The policeman's raincoat glistened. Water hit it and made a pattering sound.

"Drive down to Gunner's car park," he told Mum.

He peered in at me and Simon. "You're Annie?"

I nodded.

He stood back. "Okay, we'll see you in a minute."

Mum parked the car next to Dad's. The policeman came over. Mum grabbed coats from the trunk. "Put this on," she said, handing me one.

I took off my soaking wet jacket and put on the dry one. It was Dad's. It was too big.

"Can you show us where you both were?" the policeman asked. Everyone was shouting because the weather was so loud.

Another police car pulled up near the jetty. They grabbed flashlights and we walked on the beach toward the point.

"She got stuck climbing up," I shouted as we walked, "then a bit of the cliff came down and she fell. I couldn't see her." It was hard to breathe with the wind blowing in my face. "I couldn't get down to her."

"How much of the cliff came down?"

"I don't know. It was getting dark."

"Can you give us an idea?"

"It was some sand. Some sand went down with her."

We reached the point. Suddenly the sky went white with lightning. It was like a strobe light. For a split second I saw the whole landscape, like a negative photograph. The cliff looked completely different, a pile of rocks and sand with the water rushing over and around it, making new shapes, a new point.

"More of it has come down," I told them, as the thunder roared. They leaned forward, straining to hear. "Much more has come down," I said, louder. "It looks like a different cliff."

"Call SES. Call search and rescue," said the policeman, staring straight ahead. I didn't know who he was speaking to, but people behind him had their phones out.

"Are you sure this was the place? It wasn't farther around?"

"No, this is it. This is where I left her."

Dad came running up.

Mum's voice shook. She wiped her hand across her eyes. "The little cliff . . . this cliff," was all she could say.

Simon started to cry. I stood beside him, but I didn't cry.

Mum was pointing. Then she dropped her arm as if it were too heavy to lift. "She could be there, Andrew, under there, under the sand."

Dad put his arm around Mum. He shook his head. "This could have happened after she fell. If the sand came down on her, she could have been pushed farther out. Pushed off."

The policeman turned to us, nodding.

"She could be in the water."

Kip

Then I saw a light.

Sharp silver streaks of rain hit my face. The light came down and blocked out everything else.

Someone was shouting. My head went under and up again. An orange metal hook came toward me. I knew what I had to do. I had to grab the hook, but my arm wouldn't work. It was numb—I couldn't feel it. Then it lifted up because the waves pushed it. I held onto the hook and they pulled me toward a boat. Waves hit my face, my body rolled.

A hand, thick and warm, grabbed at my arm. I was hauled up.

I was only half aware. They took me inside the cabin and closed the door. All the noise stopped. I heard a voice say "nearly swept clean out of the Heads." I couldn't stand up, my knees gave way. I could hardly breathe. I think I vomited up a whole lot of water. I couldn't speak. My body was shaking, not shivering, but the way a really old person will shake. The hand that I'd held the hook with was still gripping the air. A man pulled my jeans and jacket off. He dried me and wrapped me in a big towel and then a blanket that looked like foil. You'd think it was embarrassing having a stranger rip your clothes off, but all I remember thinking was that my legs were blue.

One of the men put his face to mine. It was glistening wet. His breath was warm and smelt of mints. "Hello there. Hello."

I pulled back a bit. "Hi," I managed.

"What's your name?" he asked. It was a strange question, but I think he was trying to work out if I was all right.

"Kip."

"Well, Kip, a few minutes later and we would have had the helicopters looking for you out in Bass Strait, I reckon."

I started to breathe in a funny way, almost panting, as if I might start to cry.

It wasn't the police or the coast guard who had picked me up. It was the pilot boat.

"I'm John," said the guy who'd pulled me out. "You're going to be okay, Kip." He took off his beanie and pushed it down on my head, right over my ears, as if he were dressing a snowman.

I nodded, feeling too weak to do anything more.

"What happened?" asked the guy at the front. He was steering. It wasn't a big boat but the engine sounded deep and strong and even. "Did you fall overboard?"

"I was looking for someone," I managed to tell them.

The guy looked out at the night. "Funny place to look, mate. Bloody lucky, you are. We're not usually this far over. Ebb tide, southeasterly . . ." He looked out again, shaking his head. "Unbelievably lucky."

In the light from the boat I could see waves, big savage waves like the surf. I closed my eyes. How long had I been in the water? Was it the middle of the night?

The guy steering eased down the throttle. I found out later that his name was Gary. The boat stopped rocking so much and ploughed through the waves.

I said it again. "I was looking for someone. In the water."

John looked at me for a moment, then put his fingers on my wrist, taking my pulse. "*You* were in the water, mate, and we've got you now. You're safe."

Why didn't he understand what I was trying to tell him? I went to stand up, but he stopped me. It was like a strange, lurching dance we were doing. My voice got louder. I could hear the other guy talking to someone on the radio. I held onto John's arm as the boat went over a wave.

"There was someone in the water. Not me. A man on the beach, he's lost his girls." I was really thirsty. I thought of the Coke and threw up again. It probably went all over that poor guy.

He held my shoulders. "Listen mate, you're in shock,

the only person in the water was you." He sat me back down again. "It's okay. We're going to get you home."

My head rolled back.

John squinted out the window. He sighed, shaking his head. He looked at his mate.

"What do you reckon?" I heard him say.

"There's a tug waiting out there for us to bring him in."

"I saw them," I said, trying to make them understand. "That's why I was in the water. I was swimming out to help them."

Gary turned around. "You saw someone?"

I nodded.

They talked quietly to each other. One of them said, "Look, the kid's been drinking."

I didn't have the energy to explain. I rocked on the seat. I smelt diesel. The foil blanket crinkled.

"If anyone else is out there, we won't find them," said John. "It was pure luck I spotted you."

"A great night for everyone to go swimming," Gary muttered. "I'll call the Lonsdale lighthouse."

"There was a board," I managed. "A purple Boogie board."

Gary sighed loudly. Rain hit the windows. "I can call the coast guard," he said, "but by that time . . ." He looked at me, then shook his head as if he were trying to make up his mind. I closed my eyes. I heard him say,

"We'll go up as far as the first point. Then I'm turning around."

The boat slowly followed the line of the coast. Each time the hull hit the waves I felt a jolt go through me. I couldn't work out in which direction we were going except there was a light on the headland, and I could see luminous sand when the searchlight at the front of the boat swept the coast.

"Stay here," John told me. He opened the door and the storm noise filled the cabin. John held onto the side and shone a big light on the sea. Waves leapt up, grabbing at the light. The boat kept moving through water. John made a signal and Gary slowed down. The motor went quiet and all we could hear was the storm—the wind whipping the water and the water slapping the boat.

Then I saw it: the Boogie board, being tossed in and out of the light. It flew right up in the air and down again. John leaned forward, peering into the rain. The boat lurched like a carnival ride. John tilted his head, frowning, holding still. And then I understood what he was trying to do. He was trying to distinguish the sounds. The wind from the rain, from the sea, from any human sounds. He was listening for sounds of life.

After a few minutes, the boat moved forward again.

Gary radioed the coast guard. "We've picked up a kid here." He frowned at me. "He seems to think there's someone else in the water."

I rested my head against the spattered window and looked out. Then I heard John yell. I turned around. Gary looked up from the radio.

I was dazed. I felt sick. "What?" I said. My heart was racing. "What is it?"

Gary put the engine back into neutral. John yanked out a metal lock that let down a platform at the back of the boat. It went up and down like a horse at a rodeo.

A shape rolled over a wave. A neon arm. My breath came out shuddering, as if I were going to cry.

It was terrible: a blue face, blue lips.

But it wasn't a girl.

It was the little boy.

Annie

A truck came toward us along the beach. SES workers in bright orange uniforms got out. Doors slammed. They all had spades. Men set up lights on stands. It looked like a movie shoot.

Mum wanted Simon to be taken home. There was nobody to do it, so I had to look after him.

They'd driven a police van right down onto the beach. I sat inside with Simon and watched.

The radio was on. The ABC. The announcer was friendly and calm, as if he were chatting to someone in his living room. "It's coming up to seven o'clock," he said. Seven o'clock. I thought it'd be later by now. I wasn't hungry even though it was dinner time. I leaned into the front to turn off the radio. It was giving me a headache.

On the front seat was a clear plastic bag. In the bag were Grace's jeans.

Mum stood outside. She rested against the van.

I opened the door a bit.

"Mum. Mum, they've got her jeans here."

She nodded. "Dad found them on the beach near the cliff."

"How come? How come they were on the beach?"

Mum didn't answer me. She opened the door wide and let the rain in. She sat on the back seat and hugged me and then she hugged Simon. She touched our faces, kissed our heads, both of us at once.

Dad came over.

"Annie, the police need to ask you a couple more questions. Can you hop out of the car?"

"Stay here," I told Simon, and I got out.

Dad held a wide umbrella, while the policeman talked to me.

"Did you see a boy on the beach?"

"No, we didn't see anyone."

"What about afterward? Did you see anyone afterward?"

"At the car park?"

He nodded.

"No, there was nobody there."

"And on your way home, did you see anyone?"

"No, only one car."

"Do you know the color of the car?"

"I think it was white."

"Could you tell us what type of car it was? The make?"

I shook my head. "I don't know."

"Anyone else?"

"No."

"Are you sure?"

"There was a man out in front of his house."

"Do you think you could remember where that house was?"

"Yes. There was a light bulb on, without anything around it. I can remember that."

"Did he say anything to you?"

"No. I was going to ask him to help me."

"Did you ask for help?"

"No, I didn't."

"Why didn't you?"

I thought for a minute.

"He gave me the creeps."

The rain got heavier. "Let's get in the van," the policeman said. The windows were fogged up inside. He switched on the heater. I put my hands out to the vent.

"Anything else you can tell us about him?"

I pictured him in my mind.

"He was soaking wet, his jeans were all wet, and he had bare feet."

The policeman opened the door to get out of the van.

I wanted to ask him something. "The boy who found the backpack," I said.

He looked around. "Yes?"

"Was the penguin alive?"

He shook his head.

"Oh." Poor Grace.

He turned to go.

"Will Grace be all right?" I asked, sitting forward on the wet seat.

But he didn't hear me. He closed the door and walked away. I sat with Simon. He was crying but I couldn't comfort him.

I was only trying to help Grace, to get her up the cliff.

But I couldn't, I didn't.

Kip

John moved quickly. He got the orange hook around the kid's waist and pulled him toward the platform at the back of the boat. We rocked wildly.

"I've lost him," shouted John. "He's underneath us."

Gary swore and stood at the front, swaying.

John yelled again, this time from the side. He dipped the hook back in the water. He struggled with it as if someone were pulling the other end. "Okay," he yelled, nodding to Gary, who used a remote control to raise the platform.

On it lay the little kid. It was the boy I'd seen earlier, the one who'd run from the car, I was sure. He was crumpled, blue. Still.

"He's not breathing," I said. I felt as if I were choking. I really panicked. "He can't breathe."

"Sit down!" Gary yelled.

John lifted the boy in his arms and carried him into the cabin. The door slammed shut and the outside sounds faded. "He's got a pulse," he said quietly.

"But he can't breathe. Make him breathe again," I screamed. I felt crazy, as if that kid belonged to me, was my responsibility. "Make him breathe!"

Gary drove the boat and John lay the kid across the seats and gave him mouth-to-mouth. John's face was calm and concentrating. Gary kept turning around and checking how they were doing.

After a long time, John looked up at both of us. "He's breathing," he said. "It's okay, mate." He turned to me and smiled for the first time. "He's breathing now."

He didn't look okay to me. "But he's unconscious."

John didn't answer. He put the boy on his side, wrapped him in a blue blanket and checked his pulse.

"He's breathing, mate. It's okay, see, he's breathing now."

John sat on the floor beside the kid. The boy half woke up and started to cry, sort of whimpering. I was so relieved. I slid down and rested my hand across his blanket. He closed his eyes again.

They took us across to the sea pilots' headquarters in Queenscliff. An ambulance was already there. John carried the boy inside. The sea pilots' place was like a house, a low, modern house with a warm living room. The carpet felt soft and the whole building was quiet. I think the windows were soundproofed or something. In the hallway, John put the boy straight onto a stretcher. Then the ambulance guys took over. He was able to talk now; I heard him tell them his name was David. A lady who was the sea pilots' cook gave me a warm drink. It was sweet and tasted like Ribena. She put her arm around me and I nearly cried again.

"Is he your brother?" she asked.

I shook my head. They gave me dry clothes that were too big and the lady helped me into them. When I came out they were on the veranda, wheeling the stretcher to the ambulance that had been backed up to the house. It was still pouring. Rain hit the roof like stones.

The little boy was propped up.

"What were you doing out there?" I asked him.

"Looking . . ."

"Like your friend here," said Gary, holding the door open for the ambulance guys. "Everyone's out looking for someone. King tide, biggest storm I've seen in years—you picked a good night."

"For my dad," the kid finished weakly.

"Who's your dad then," Gary muttered to himself, "a dolphin?"

Then they pushed the stretcher into the back of the ambulance. Just before they closed the door, the boy looked straight at me, like he had earlier that day, although it was hard to believe it was still the same day because it felt so long ago.

"Remember this guy," John said, nodding toward me, "because he's your bloody guardian angel."

Annie

The rain didn't stop. People had to shout to be heard. Simon and I sat in the police car. Inside it smelt like mold. He fell asleep against me. I got out and he crumpled against the door. The wind was pushing and pulling the trees. Mum and Dad were standing on their own, all bedraggled. I went over to them. "Why can't they dig faster?" I asked. "Why can't they use a bulldozer?"

Mum didn't answer.

"A bulldozer might hurt Grace," said Dad. His voice was all on one note.

I looked at the sand, where it had come down. Rain was making waterfalls and tracks down it. If Grace was under there, couldn't she dig her own way out? I could do that.

Then I looked at the sea. It was black. It was lifting up and coming down. "Why aren't they looking in the water?"

"They can't," said Dad. "It's too rough. It's too dangerous."

Too rough? If it was too rough for the police then it was even rougher for Grace. "If she's in the water, she needs their help right now," I said, but no one heard me.

After hours and hours, Mum took Simon and me home. The police said that if Grace had been in the water she might have got out and made it back to the house. Two policemen went with us—one drove us in our car and the other one followed in a police car. It felt wrong to drive away from Grace, to leave her outside in the night. But they said there was nothing more we could do. They said they'd start a sea search at first light. But for how long could someone tread water?

Dad stayed behind. I felt better knowing that he was going to be there. I looked out the car window as we drove back to the house. I was thinking she's somewhere, but where? Where is she?

I wanted her to be sitting on the steps like we do if we forget our keys after school and Mum and Dad aren't home yet.

Mum picked up the fish and chips from the garage floor. They'd made a big oily mark on the concrete. She dumped them straight in the bin. Then she put us both to bed.

"Grace said we had to follow the penguin," I told her. "She said we had to rescue it. That's why we got so far along the beach."

Mum nodded.

"What are you going to do now?" I asked.

She sat on the edge of my bed. She didn't answer for quite a while, as if I'd asked her a really hard question.

"I'm going to wait for Dad to call or to come home," she said.

"And for Grace to come home," I reminded her.

She nodded again.

She gave us each a hot-water bottle. When I held mine I hated the sound the water made inside. At the beach house, Grace and I share a room. I put the hot-water bottle in the middle of Grace's bed, under the covers. I smoothed it back down. I was thinking she could have gone looking for the penguin. That would be typical of her. When I wake up she'll be here, I said to myself. I looked across at the little bumpy shape that the hot-water bottle made. I watched the shape and waited for Grace to come home.

Kip

They said that I was lucky because of all the swimming I'd done.

Mum took me to the doctor the next morning to make sure I was okay. He told me to rest and to keep warm. Apart from that I was fine. All of that day, I stayed inside, watching TV and listening to music. My sister, Sarah, even bought me a magazine with her own pocket money. Mum must have told her to be nice to me because I'd had a shock.

In the afternoon, Mum rang the hospital to ask about the boy in the water. They told her that he was all right and would be going home in a day or so. I wanted his number to phone him myself but they wouldn't give it to me. It was their privacy policy, they said.

One of the girls had walked home. But the other one was still missing. It was on the news. There were volunteers out looking for her. It was the older one. Grace.

The police came around. There were two of them— a man and a woman.

"We're interested to speak with you because you are the last person to have seen the young lady on the beach," the guy said.

But had I even seen her? I had seen two figures a long way off.

They sat opposite me on the couch. "Let's go through your movements yesterday, Kip."

It was hard to remember anything much. I told them about going for a walk. I didn't mention the boy running across the road because they'd found him so they didn't need to know that. But they got really interested when I told them about Ted.

"Did he say anything to you that you haven't told us?" the policeman asked. "He invited you into his house. He gave you something to drink. Did he touch you in any way?"

"What? No," I told them, "he didn't do anything."

"Did you see anyone else on the beach, on the cliff, anywhere at all? Did you see anything in his house?"

I shook my head.

"And later, you dived off the jetty. I think you'd been told to stay where you were. Is that correct?"

I nodded. "But I saw someone in the water."

The policeman rested back on the couch. "Probably the best thing to do would have been to tell the police. They could have handled it without people getting into life-threatening situations."

Nobody said anything. I wondered if the police would have found the boy in time.

The policeman sat forward again. "Don't you think?"

"I yelled out," I said, "but nobody heard."

"Well, you're lucky nobody drowned."

"Yeah," I said. "I s'pose I just didn't think."

"Mmm," said the policeman, nodding.

I was going to say something about the Boogie board I'd seen in the water and the one I'd seen at Ted's house, but I didn't mention it. The policeman was writing something in his notebook and I didn't think I should interrupt him. And anyway, I felt uneasy. I mean, what were they trying to suggest? Was that guy some sort of deviant? Did they think *I* knew something about the girl who was missing? They never came out and said anything like that, they just gently asked all these vague questions.

I wouldn't even know what to do with a girl. I think about girls. I worry that I'll never get a girlfriend. I've never even kissed a girl, except Sarah. And of course I don't think of Sarah in that way, or my mum. But even when I kiss Mum now it's different, it feels uncomfortable. Sometimes I want to hug Mum but I don't like the feeling it gives me. I mean I like it, but at the same time I don't.

The police, they're really good at profiling. I wonder if they think I'm strange. Odd. Like that guy Ted.

I thought I'd better go over and tell him, warn him because the police would come to speak with him as well. I felt a bit bad about mentioning him to the police. I don't know why. I was only answering their questions. But I didn't want him to get into trouble or think that I had turned him in or anything. Even though he was strange, he was kind of friendly; he had sheltered me in his house from the storm. I decided to drop by quickly and let him know. I was thinking he should probably put those magazines away before the police got there.

I went over in the afternoon when Mum and Sarah had gone for a walk. Music was soaring out of the speakers on the concrete. Beethoven. I don't know much about classical music but I know that one piece that everyone recognizes. The "Moonlight Sonata." It's gentle music but it sounds triumphant in some way. It was such a great sound system—almost as if a real piano were there, you could sense the fingers hesitating just before they came down on the keys.

I knocked against the pane of glass.

Ted was sitting cross-legged on the floor, facing the sea, surrounded by papers and books.

"Hi, soldier!" He jumped up and slid open the door. I was relieved—he seemed pleased to see me.

"How's your foot?" I asked.

He looked blankly at me, then down at the thick socks he was wearing. "Oh yeah," he said, "I cut my foot," as if he'd forgotten all about it.

"Listen," I said as I came in, "I thought I should let you know, the police came over this morning."

He frowned.

"Because of those girls. The guy with the backpack, it's one of his daughters that's lost."

He looked a bit blank.

I tried again. "There's a girl they can't find. Didn't you hear it on the news? The police talked to me about it, on the beach and at my house."

He nodded.

"It's just that I told them I'd met you, so they might come and see you, too."

"Fine, mate, that's absolutely fine with me." He paused. "Moonlight Sonata" soared. He turned the volume down a bit. "Listen," he said, "don't ever trust the police, man. Don't trust anyone in a uniform."

That canceled out quite a few people. Pilots, school kids, everyone in the armed forces, football players, chefs, people in choirs who wear those long robes.

"Like a chip?" he said, shoving a bag at me.

They weren't chips, they were pretzels. I took the bag and tasted one. It was spicy.

"All natural ingredients," he said. "You don't want to put all that other crap into your body."

I ate another one. It was hot, stinging my tongue.

"You know, meat, animal products."

"Are you a vegetarian?"

"Vegan. No animal products. Tread lightly on the earth, man."

"Oh, right, yeah."

He helped himself to a few pretzels.

"Isn't it hard for vegans to get protein or iron or something?"

He snorted. "Some people think so. Never trust a doctor, man. In fact, never trust a health professional."

Looks like I had to add health professionals to the list.

I looked at the wrinkled papers and books all over the floor. I noticed a small white card that said Victoria Police on it. "Have the police come to see you already?" I asked.

He ignored my question, but said, "So who do you reckon we could have done without, soldier?"

"What?" I didn't know what he was talking about.

He pointed to the mass of papers on the floor.

"Beethoven or Captain Cook?"

No one had ever asked me a question like that before.

"Captain Cook came to Australia the same year that Beethoven was born. If we had to have one or the other, which one do you reckon the world needs more? The worst thing a bloke can do is spend his life taking up food and space and energy and then do nothing with his time. Which man could we have done without?"

I thought about it for a minute. "Maybe Beethoven was the one we needed?" I asked. "Sooner or later someone would have come across Terra Australis."

Ted smiled. "We might all have ended up speaking French, or Dutch. Chinese—people reckon they were here in the 1400s." He stopped to hear the last note of the "Moonlight Sonata." "But this guy, no one could have written his music, ever." The CD finished. "Some people reckon Beethoven was the perfect composer. That he had a tuning fork to the universe."

"Didn't he go deaf?" I asked.

Ted didn't answer. He went on with his own train of thought.

"You can't be perfect, soldier. But I reckon Beethoven was pretty bloody close. See, the thing about being *imperfect* is that it means that so much is still possible." He jumped up. "It's all here." He indicated the spread-out papers. "I'm working on a theory. The Theory of the Imperfect."

From the looks of things he seemed to be mastering his theory pretty well.

I sat on the edge of a worn armchair. He hadn't asked me anything about what had happened with the guy and the backpack. "After I left last night," I told him, "I met that guy and then we went looking for his girls. I thought I saw them in the water, so I dived in."

He was sitting on the floor again. He nodded, as if it were perfectly normal to dive into the bay during a storm in the middle of winter—unlike everyone else, who thought I was mad.

"A tugboat picked me up."

"That was lucky then."

"Yeah, I was getting swept out."

"That'll be the tidal flow. Moves at ten ks an hour sometimes. And this time of year, the tides are big, they're king tides."

"There was a little kid in the water, too. A little boy. That was who I'd seen."

"A kid in the water? Probably gone fishing and fallen out of his dad's boat."

"Yeah, he said he was looking for his dad." I wasn't sure if Ted was following me. As if anyone would have been out fishing in a storm.

"You must have got home pretty late after all that."

"Mum came to collect me. We had to wait till the wind died down, then they took me over to Sorrento and she picked me up from there."

"Mum worried about you, was she? Lost in a storm like that?"

"Yeah, she was."

"What about your dad? Have you got a dad?"

It was a strange question. "Yes," I said. "He works for IBM."

"Good for him," said Ted.

"He's in Sydney on business right now. He's coming down tomorrow."

Ted didn't say anything.

"He used to be in the air force. He can fly planes."

"Really? Fly planes?"

"Yeah. Do you have any kids?"

"Me?" He shook his head and went back to his theory on the floor.

"Well, I better head off," I said. "I just wanted to let you know about the police and stuff."

"Yeah, thanks for that, soldier," he said vaguely.

I was about to open the glass door.

He stood up, hesitated.

"Do you want a drink?" he asked.

"No thanks."

"Like to have a go on the Fender?"

"I really better get going, Ted. Mum doesn't know where I am."

"Come on." He was already reaching for the guitar. "You need to compare the Gibson to the Fender, man."

"Okay, well just for a minute."

He picked it up. "Where's the bloody lead?" he muttered.

We looked around for it. I noticed that the Boogie board wasn't by the phone. I saw again the purple one in the sea, being thrown around in the night sky.

"What happened to the Boogie board?"

"Here it is." He held up the lead.

"Ted?"

"What?"

"There was a Boogie board here yesterday."

"How should I know?" he said, anger starting up in his voice.

"Did you move it?"

"I must have, mustn't I, if it was here yesterday and not today."

He handed me the Fender. It was black, too—not all polished up but pretty shiny, especially compared to everything else in his house.

"Vintage 1968 Strat," said Ted.

I couldn't believe it. These were absolute classic guitars. He must have spent all his money on them.

My worries about the Boogie board melted away for a moment. This instrument felt so great in my arms I shivered.

"You like music, don't you, soldier," he said.

"Yeah." I played a G chord. It went right through me. Just a simple G chord sounded like something new and original. Each note vibrated and rang in the air.

"Never trust someone who can't enjoy music," Ted said, turning up the amp. He smiled. "You can guarantee that they're only half alive."

I handed the Fender back to him. I wanted to play it so much, but it was wrong to be back in this guy's house. "I better go," I said. "I really just came around to let you know about the cops. To . . . to warn you."

He didn't take the guitar so I leaned it against the wall.

"Don't you want to stay?" he asked, as if he were a little kid I was letting down because I couldn't play at his house anymore.

"Yeah, I do." It was true, part of me did want to stay. I really did want to play that guitar. "But I better go."

"Listen, borrow the Nirvana *Unplugged* if you like." He held out the CD case. "Take it."

"That's okay, I can always download it when I get back to Melbourne."

But he thrust it into the pocket of my jacket and wouldn't let me give it back.

I left quickly and ran down the road. Four police cars passed me on the way home. How long had I been at his house? It was getting late—the sun was lower than the trees. I guessed it must have been around five. Mum and Sarah would be back from their walk. Mum might be worried. But she needn't be. It wasn't as if I wanted to get any more involved with that guy.

That was another worry I had. Lately I seemed to be getting myself involved in things I couldn't help. Like in the last week of school we did something really stupid. This girl Abbie was getting changed and we went into the girls' locker room and grabbed her bra from under the stall. I don't even know why I took part in it—it was so dumb. We threw the bra over the fence near the tennis courts. Abbie came out and acted as if nothing happened, but she kept her arms crossed in math class that afternoon. When the bell rang, the guys got the bra from where they'd thrown it. All the way home they kept snickering. When I asked what the joke was, they wouldn't tell me.

Luckily, Mum and Sarah were still out when I got back to the house. I was really tired. I lay on the couch, half falling asleep, and watched the sports channels. Then I switched over to music videos. They were having some eighties and nineties retro show. Mum and Sarah came home, and Mum recognized just about every song. Some of the bands are still around now. U2. David Bowie. The Cure. AC/DC.

The phone rang. I heard Mum tell someone about what had happened—the storm and me "falling in the water," as she put it. I hadn't fallen in, I'd tried to help someone. I *had* helped someone and I wanted to feel good about myself, but I couldn't because I sensed all this disapproval. Anyway, I can't believe how much people gossip, because after dinner, everyone started calling me up. A couple of girls from school called my cell. Michaela was one of them. She'd heard about the girls who'd gotten lost. It had been on the TV news.

"Do you know that girl who's missing? Are they friends of your family down there or anything?"

"There were two girls. They got lost at Point Nepean. I don't know them," I told her. "I've never even met them."

"There's no need to bite my head off, Kip," she said. "I was only asking."

Girls like Michaela annoy me sometimes. They make me feel bad. Hopeless. About myself. With those girls, you're always saying or doing the wrong thing, or saying something in the wrong way.

People sent me text messages, too. They wanted to

know what happened and how I'd fallen in the sea. I didn't text anyone back. I went to bed early and slept for a while but then I woke up. It was about one or something. I went to the living room and turned on the TV. We didn't have cable at home so all these shows that people at school talked about were new to me. I found another music show. There were lots of old bands I hadn't heard of. Some of them were pretty good.

I got my quilt, lay on the couch, and watched the show, half asleep and warm. A clip came on. There was a guy with long black hair. He looked like a dark Kurt Cobain, but taller. It caught my eye because the clip was set on a cliff by a beach. It was one of those really basic videos that they used to make—just a bunch of guys standing somewhere and occasionally the camera would zoom in on one of them.

"I sang in my chains like the sea . . ."

That line sounded familiar. I was thinking that someone recently must have done a remake of this song, maybe a heavier version or something because this one was pretty unplugged. Then the camera zoomed in on the singer. He was playing a Gretsch guitar, a black Falcon. I'd seen Robert Smith from The Cure play one. They were such cool guitars—all rounded, such a great shape, with the big brass tremolo across the front.

A shiver went through me, and I realized who it was. The green eyes. Ted. They were the words that he'd sung when I met him on the beach. It was a song about time and about the sea. I went closer to the TV, sat on the floor, and stared. Through the tiny dots on the screen, it was as if I could see through Ted, into his whole personality—singing like this, everything that he was came together and he had this energy, even on television. Like Kurt Cobain. A power. It was a pretty good song. They must have been a great band to see live. Stupidly, it made me want to see Ted again. To have a proper go on his guitar. I could understand why the song had been a hit, why he had been a hit. The song was called "Still."

Annie

We couldn't find her—no one could find her. She had been gone for two nights and a whole day. She didn't have warm clothes and she had no food or drinks, or anything like that.

The police organized a search. I wanted to go on it but Dad wouldn't let me. There were SES volunteers, he said. People from the CFA were helping. All day and part of the night people were looking for Grace. They worked in shifts. Men from the army came in green trucks. They looked all around the national park. Police divers were going in and out of the water. They kept having to stop and wait when the weather got bad. Their boats were tied up at the pier at Portsea. Every time we went down the street we saw police cars.

It was terrible. Mum cried. She looked as if she had the flu. She'd start doing something and then stop it and start something else. Day and night were the same. There was always someone up, staring at the TV. There were lights going on and off, voices, the teakettle whistling and waking me up.

Stupid Grace. Why did she fall down? Why did we have to follow the penguin? The penguin had died anyway. She hadn't even saved it. And now school vacation was completely wrecked. We were supposed to be going to the chairlift and the maze and to the movies, as well.

I kept telling them that she'll come back, because I really thought she would. The reason I thought this is because things like this don't happen in normal families. I just wanted Grace to be found, and we could go back to Melbourne and school and we could forget all about it. I could forget any of it had ever happened.

I even wanted to forget about the penguin. But they'd left it on the beach. I wished that someone had buried it. Dogs might get it, I thought. Or crows.

Simon and I watched a lot of TV. I watched the cooking shows. I like them. I could be a chef when I leave school. I could be heaps of things—a chef, an architect, a singer, I could design my own clothes, anything.

Kip

It was in the paper on Wednesday: "Fears held for safety of Grace as storm lashes Port Phillip Bay."

Extreme weather conditions and wild storms battered the Mornington Peninsula on Monday evening. King tides and storm surges produced local flooding in several areas and winds up to 35 knots and a two-meter swell in the bay wreaked havoc with small craft, many of which sustained major damage. Police fear for the safety of a twelve-year-old girl missing at Point Nepean National Park since the storm hit Portsea late on Monday afternoon. The area includes many quarantined areas where public access is denied. Hampering the search are continued poor weather conditions and the possible presence of unexploded ordnance in the area, making it essential that only members of the armed forces conduct painstakingly slow ground searches in much of the terrain. Point Nepean will be closed to the public until further notice.

I read the article a few times.

Mum kept asking me how I felt, as if it were a casual question. Dad phoned and asked the same question. He said he was trying to get on an earlier flight from Sydney. On the surface they sounded calm. But underneath, they were worried about me.

I wanted to get rid of the Nirvana CD, to give it back to Ted. I decided to drop it in his mailbox first thing. Then I wouldn't have to go inside his house again. I wouldn't have to see him at all.

The trouble was, he didn't have a mailbox, or I couldn't find it. I was looking around his fence, pushing aside the overgrown ivy, when he came out.

"I'm just returning your CD," I said. "I was trying to find your mailbox."

He smiled. It was sunny and bright, as if the storm had washed away the dirt. "No need to leave it there, mate. Come in. I'm not busy, I've got a bit of time."

He seemed really pleased to see me. I felt a bit sorry for him. Compared to the clip I'd seen, he looked old, haggard. All that amazing energy had been lost. "Look, I better not come in," I said. "My parents—" but he interrupted me.

"What did you think of it? The *Unplugged*?"

"Good," I said, although I hadn't listened to it because I was worried Mum would ask me where I'd gotten it.

"I've got another one. Some of the same songs, and some others. A bootleg. From Hong Kong. Come in and I'll get it for you."

I stood there, unable to think quickly enough.

"Can't download this one in Melbourne, mate." He grinned.

"I saw a clip," I mentioned, trying to change the subject so that I wouldn't have to take more of his CDs. "I saw a clip of your band."

His eyes lit up. "Did you?"

"On cable. Last night. It was that song about the sea." I paused. "I think you were playing a Gretsch."

"Still got it, soldier!" He beamed. "Come on, I'll show you."

I hesitated.

"Come on," he smiled, knowing he had me. He beckoned with his hand as if I were a puppy.

As soon as I got inside he had the guitar in his hands. He held it out to me. It shone as he moved. It was shaped like a human form. It reminded me of paintings I'd seen in the art gallery—paintings of women, full of curving lines. I held it in my arms. It was heavy, round, and smooth. My heart raced. I couldn't wait to play it. Ted turned the amp up full bore, and the sound went through my body. He got his Les Paul and we actually ended up playing a few songs—Nirvana, Radiohead. I tried to play a Cure song. We even played AC/DC, although Ted said he hated that band. We just mucked around with the two guitars. He also had a Fender 1962 Jaguar and he let me play that, too. I started to relax. I had to admit it was good, once we were playing. Actually, it was really great. He did the solos and then he did the backup and got me to do the solo. To play a Gretsch was just fantastic. Heaps of great bands use them—U2, the Red Hot Chili Peppers, even the Beatles played them.

We played that Everclear song, "Santa Monica." But Ted did this great grunge version of it, really heavy. He played these wild chords where the drumbeats would usually be. He was fantastic, brilliant. We both knew the words and we belted them out together. I'd never played so loud or with such great equipment. Ted's amp was a massive Marshall cab. Sometimes we'd play the same note and it didn't sound like two instruments but one guitar, one fantastic guitar that took up all the space and the sound and the time. It was almost like dreaming. I didn't have to think of what note to play, my fingers had a memory, they found the perfect place on the fretboard. The feeling of sound surrounded me and I felt alive, like when I used to swim—where it's deep and you're not touching anything except water. I was swimming in sound, drowning in it, losing myself in this fantastic way. When I play on my own I have to stop and start and it doesn't flow. With Ted it was easy; I didn't have to stop at all. He drew me through the music. It was so effortless to play on this guitar. I sounded so much better. For the first time I thought this was something else I could do.

When we finished I sat in the armchair, exhausted. Morning sun came in through his smudged glass doors. Ted poured himself a drink and leaned against the wall. "If you really wanted to, you could be a musician," he told me.

"Do you reckon?" My parents just tell me to turn it down.

"Yeah, you've got it, man."

"You're a great guitarist, Ted. And you've got such great equipment," I said. "It must have cost you heaps."

"You should come and see me play," he said suddenly.

"I thought you didn't play anymore."

"I don't, but it's a favor for a benefit gig. A fundraiser. For the national park people."

I'd seen posters around the place for a fundraising day at Point Nepean.

"Yeah, so it's this Saturday, starts in the afternoon. Got a rehearsal tomorrow."

"That's nice of you," I found myself saying. "To help them out."

"Yeah, it's real nice of me."

Even though I hardly knew Ted, even though I'd

only just met him, playing that music together had made me feel better. I think I was starting to like him. I know that I wanted to like him. I wanted to believe that he was a nice guy, a nice person.

He took a long drink. "Yeah, they gotta look after it. I mean, the value of this land, it'd be worth hundreds of millions. It's got to be protected or some joker will build a bloody cliff-top resort."

"But if it's government land, if it's a national park, they wouldn't let that happen, would they?"

He shrugged. "Some people'll do anything for money, sell anything at all. Listen, soldier," he said, shaking his head, "just make sure you get something for your soul. You got to get something for your soul, man." He finished his drink. "Because I got nothing for mine."

I wasn't sure how to take his advice. "Okay, thanks Ted," I said, standing up. I'd been there for an hour or more. I hadn't even meant to come inside.

"I really better get going."

This time he let me go.

As I left, I noticed he had written something on the wall, stuck up on a big sheet of torn butcher's paper, above one of the storm posters. I thought it might be lyrics.

So when the last and dreadful hour
This crumbling pageant shall devour

The trumpet shall be heard on high
The dead shall live, the living die
And music shall untune the sky.

"Did you write that?"

He chuckled. "No, not me, mate. John Dryden. Restoration poet."

I must have looked blank.

"You know, the restoration period. New ideas. Celebration of the possibilities of life!"

I opened the sliding door. It had been really good, jamming with him.

"You're pretty smart, Ted," I told him.

He snorted. "Course I'm bloody smart."

I relaxed for a moment. I may even have laughed. "I always thought that smart people had jobs and families and lived in nice houses."

Ted laughed, too. Meanly, right in my face.

Annie

That afternoon, the whispering started. Our beach house is small, so I could hear everything. And they couldn't send me outside because there were reporters from the TV stations out front with cameras and vans. Mum and Dad whispered about a "person of interest." Of interest. Did that mean someone who was interesting? Interested?

Different police came over and took us to the police station. I had to tell them everything that happened. I had to tell them many times. There was a woman and a man. The man was called Geoff and the woman was called Lynette.

I had to tell them about the music I'd heard. I said it was flute music, or pipe music. They asked me if I'd seen anyone apart from the man wearing the colored jacket under the light. They wanted to know whether I'd seen someone younger than him. A teenager. "A young person" was what Geoff said.

But I hadn't seen a young person.

Then they asked me about the penguin, and whether I thought Grace was upset, whether she might be someone who would run away. I said that I didn't think she was that sort of person.

Back home, Mum put her arms around me and said, "This is tough, isn't it? How are you feeling?"

I was feeling that I wish it hadn't happened.

Dad said, "Do you have any questions you need to ask us, Annie?"

I said, "No."

But then I did have a question. My question was: "Why do they keep asking about the man under the light and the young person? And what about her jeans on the beach? Do they think that someone has taken Grace away?"

Mum shook her head. I wasn't sure what it meant.

I sat on the couch with Simon. He had a question, too.

"Why didn't you look after Grace?" he asked me.

"I did. It was her fault that we got trapped at the point. She was following the penguin in the water."

"I bet you bossed her around. That's what you always do."

"Shut up, Simon," I told him.

Kip

When I got home, I was sick of the TV, so I went to get a book from my school bag, and that was when I found it. A white bra. In the zip-up part on the side.

Those dickheads. That's what they had been laughing about. They'd put Abbie's bra in my bag.

I know where I stand at school. I stand on the edge of the cool people. Most of the time I'm one of them, but sometimes I'm the one they pick on if there's no one else around.

I held the bra in my hands. It was very white and had a bit of lace around the edges. It looked new. Sometimes you can see a girl's bra strap if she's got the top buttons of her school dress undone. The white looks really good against the girl's skin, especially if she has a tan. But what would I do with it now? I held it to my face. It smelt of girl, of Abbie.

Abbie's a nice girl. Why did they have to do that to her? Why not Michaela or one of the others, the ones who wear really small bikini tops when we go swimming and they look so good and you can't stop staring but then they say, "It's rude to stare" and "That's sexual harassment" and "You're so sexist" and things like that. Then they laugh and walk off.

Guys can hurt you, but those girls can hurt you so much more.

The girls at school, I hate some of them. But sometimes the ones I hate most are the ones I'd like for a girlfriend. When a girl acts all snobby and superior, when she ignores you, I don't know what that means. I used to know what it meant—that she didn't want to know you. Now I don't know what it means.

I hate those girls, but I want them.

I didn't know what to do with the bra, so I shoved it right to the back of my closet.

I felt so bad. I felt bad about Abbie and about the comment I'd made to Ted about smart people living in nice houses and stuff. It was supposed to be a joke, but I think I really hurt his feelings. I kept thinking about it. He'd let me play his guitar and everything. He told me I was good enough to be a musician, when the only thing I'd ever thought I was good at was swimming. Then I'd wrecked it all with that stupid comment. I don't even know why I said it.

That evening I went to the video shop. I could see the police boat by the pier. The sea was calm and although it was cold, there was no breeze. I could see lots of seaweed in black, still clumps on the sand. Driftwood and rubbish had washed up in the storm. On the way back I dropped in on Ted to apologize.

The music was opera or something. I knocked on the door. I could see him lying on the couch. Cans were strewn around the floor, some drink had spilt on his Theory of the Imperfect notes. I thought he was asleep. How anyone could sleep with that opera going I don't know.

The TV was on with the sound down. So the music I heard was opera, but what I saw through the dirty glass door on the TV was Nirvana. It was a clip where they were smashing up their guitars. Part of it was in slow motion. It was just Kurt slamming into the drum kit, repeated over and over.

I slid the door open.

"Ted? Ted?"

He half opened his eyes. "Piss off!" he yelled.

He lurched up, half falling over, and started to come at me, as if he might hit me, so I left.

Annie

Night came again. It rained and Simon started crying. Usually, Grace reads him a story before bed. He was okay in the day—he wouldn't even talk about it. But each night at the same time he started to cry and he didn't stop until he fell asleep. No one could make him stop—not me or Mum or Dad.

"I can read you a story if you want," I told him, standing in the doorway to his room. He shook his head and kept crying.

I heard Mum crying, too. At our beach house the walls are thin, like cardboard. I kept getting woken up. Sniffing, talking, people moving around, then more sniffing. Muffled sounds. I wondered if Simon got woken up, as well. I lay in the dark and didn't want to hear. The words came through anyway.

"I can't bear it," Mum sobbed. It didn't sound like her. "It's happening again . . ." Then she was really crying, not even trying to keep quiet.

I pulled the comforter over my head and pushed it against my ears. I didn't understand what it meant. All I could think was, why did Grace have to wreck our family, to hurt us all so much? She couldn't do anything! I mean she could think and write, she could read long books and play piano but she couldn't do anything useful. She couldn't see that we should have just left the penguin and gone back to Dad. Then she couldn't see that we should have just climbed the cliff. If I hadn't had Grace with me, none of it would have happened.

We were in the newspaper and on television. No one asked us, they just took photos. Mum and Dad hid the papers. They weren't lying around like usual.

Simon and I weren't allowed outside. Reporters were on the median and in the garden and sometimes right outside the door. The phone rang all the time. It was Dad's work and Mum's work and friends. Someone came to the door with a camera.

"Would you like to make a plea for help?" a voice said.

When we went out in the car, there was a camera on me. Mum didn't let us watch the TV news. She came and switched it off. Normally I'd complain but I didn't.

I've always thought it would be good to be on TV. On an ad or something like that. But seeing myself on TV now was like having someone spy on me. Whenever Dad went out they came and talked through the door at Mum. "We understand how difficult this must be for you," they said. "Is there anything we can do to help you find your daughter?"

"Yes," said Mum. "You can go away." But they didn't.

"Would you like to make a public statement?" someone said. "We know how hard this must be."

How did they know? Had their sister disappeared, as well?

The police said that we could make a public statement if we wanted to.

Dad said no, he didn't want to do that. Not yet.

I started to feel sick. The sick feeling came in waves. Wave after wave after wave.

The next morning, I went outside. It was early and I felt locked up. It was like the signs at Point Nepean—if you're not allowed to go outside then all you want to do is go out there.

A lady came up to me across the grass. She had a lot of makeup on.

"Annie," she said quietly.

"Yes?"

"How old are you, Annie?"

"I'm twelve," I told her. "The same as Grace, except that she's nearly thirteen."

"You must be feeling very worried about your sister."

"Yes." I nodded.

"She's been missing for two days now, hasn't she?"

I nodded again.

"Where do you think she is, Annie?"

I shook my head.

"Do you miss your big sister? Do you want your sister back again, Annie?"

The woman moved closer toward me.

Dad was suddenly behind me. He grabbed my arm. He was still in his pajamas.

"What are you doing? Don't speak to them," he told me. He turned to the lady. "Leave her alone." He made me go back inside. He stood on the veranda and faced them, the people with their cameras. "How dare you." His voice shook. "She's just a child."

My dad hardly ever gets angry, but he was angry with that lady. He closed the door. "Don't go outside again, Annie," he said quietly.

Dad went out later and I asked Mum about it. I actually wanted to ask her about what I'd heard through the walls but I didn't do that. I didn't know how.

"Why was that lady talking to me?" I asked. "Asking those questions. Do they want to help find Grace?"

Mum closed her eyes and shook her head.

"And what's hypothermia? It was in the paper. They said that Grace might have it."

Mum told me what hypothermia is. She's a doctor so she knows things like that. Then I got out the first-aid book. For more information. It was listed.

Factors that contribute to hypothermia:
1. Cold temperatures
2. Being wet
3. Not wearing the right clothes
4. Not having food or drink

At the end of the chapter there was another heading: "Death from Hypothermia." I didn't read that part, but the list had given me an idea. I went to my room and wrote it down. Step by step, what had happened.

1. Tracking
2. Find penguin
3. Lose backpack
4. Climb cliff
5. Grace falls off

Step by step, where Grace might be now.

1. Under the cliff
2. In the water
3. Somewhere else

The cliff had been dug up and they'd found nothing. Helicopters were looking for her, and divers were in the water. That left number 3. Somewhere else. But where else? There was a search party looking all around the beach and right through to Point Nepean, in case she got out from the cliff or the water. In case she was hurt somewhere. In case she was lost.

I went out to show Mum and Dad what I'd written. Mum looked blank. Dad looked sad. He rubbed his forehead. They said that the police were interviewing people, they were interviewing the man I saw in the driveway.

"If only she hadn't seen that penguin, none of this would have happened. If only we hadn't gone tracking. If only we'd all gone back together instead of playing the last game, if only I hadn't—"

"It's no good thinking like that, Annie," Dad said.

Grace

I hear water on my skin. It's wet. I can't see. It's blacker, darkness that is thick.

No one can hear me. I've heard them, but I can't call anymore.

I can't move. I can't look at my leg.

Kip

The police came again. This time Mum and I had to go with them and they drove us around. I had to show them exactly where I thought I'd seen the figures on the beach, where I was walking, which direction, and how far. I had to show them where I sheltered on the path near the houses set into the cliff.

I was doing my best. I was telling the police what happened. I was pointing out where I had been waiting with the backpack.

"How long were you waiting, would you say?" one of them asked.

I looked up, thinking.

Through the stringy gray tree trunks I saw him, behind his telescope. I didn't know if I should say anything to the police. I felt uncomfortable. I looked away, then back again. The policeman was staring at me.

I bet Ted could even see my lips moving through that thing—he could get up so close.

That night Dad arrived. He asked me what had happened. He said, "Was it an accident, Kip? Did you fall into the water?" I said yes. I was so sick of talking about it. I hated the look on his face: disapproving.

He'd brought the mail down from Melbourne. "There's a note from Lindsay," he said, "about the squad this semester."

Lindsay is my swimming coach. The squad is the elite squad I used to be in.

"Maybe now is not the best time," said Mum. "Kip is pretty tired."

I agreed. I was tired. I went to bed but I couldn't sleep. I kept seeing Ted's face all screwed up. And I was worried about Abbie's bra. In the middle of the night I got it out of the closet and sat on my bed in the semidarkness. I needed to get rid of it; I couldn't stop thinking about it. I picked it up, put it to my face. What was I? Some kind of pervert? I shoved it away and got back into bed.

Much later, I went out walking. Some kids at school would sneak out at night—they'd told me about it. Now I understood why people might need to do that.

I didn't mean to go to his house, I didn't even mean to go out in the middle of the night. I just wanted to walk, to clear my head. The air was really cold. I had this energy, like when I used to swim, like I could keep going forever. Tiredness would never come.

Maybe I was lonely. I wasn't used to having time. Usually, I'd be at squad, even during vacations, with kids I knew, guys I swam with every day. But not anymore.

I went down the road. I wouldn't have gone in, but his lights were on. Every single one of them. I wondered if he was still pissed off.

I stood outside the glass door. Just to look in. I didn't know what to expect, whether he'd shout at me again. I could see him sitting calmly, cross-legged on the floor. He was wearing a cap and reading a book. I recognized it. Terry Pratchett. One of the Discworld series. I'd read some myself.

"Hi there, soldier," he said, opening the door for me as if two o'clock in the morning was a regular time to drop by. I liked that about Ted. Although he was completely unpredictable, he didn't seem to make judgments in the same way that other people did. It made me smile, even though I'd been so stressed out.

"Hi," I said quickly, and went in. It was really warm inside, as if he had the heater up too high. I started to sweat.

"Ted, I'm sorry about yesterday."

He looked blank.

"You know, what I said about smart people."

Still blank.

Was he doing this to annoy me, to make me squirm and have to keep begging for forgiveness? I sighed. "It was a stupid thing to say . . . I didn't mean to hurt your feelings . . . you know how you yelled at me to piss off when I came back."

Utterly and completely blank.

"Ted?"

"Oh, right," he said vaguely. "Yeah, well that's okay."

I decided not to mention that I'd seen him looking through the telescope. I didn't want to fight with him. I wanted to say that I hadn't meant to get him into trouble, to rat on him or anything, but I didn't want any more misunderstandings.

"How was your rehearsal?" I asked. "For the benefit gig."

He didn't answer. He sat back down on the floor. I wanted to tell him about Abbie and the bra. I needed to tell someone. But I didn't know how to start, or even whether I should.

He picked up a large photo of a storm and studied it. "You know, the eye of a tropical cyclone can be calm—sometimes you can even see blue sky." He looked up at me and grinned. "But it's not over, man," he pointed at the picture, "the other half of that cyclone is still to come."

"Oh," I said, "right."

"Tonight it's calm." He picked up a small thermometer from the coffee table. "Not a bad night tonight. Fifty-four degrees Fahrenheit."

"I only know Celsius," I told him.

"Easy! Just take thirty-two from the temperature in Fahrenheit, divide it by one point eight and your new temperature, my friend, is now Celsius."

I nodded.

"Thirteen degrees." Ted looked pleased. "That's mild, for winter. Come and sit out in the garden with me, soldier. Beautiful night. You can see the moon over the bay."

I followed him outside. We sat on wooden chairs that sank into the earth. Rain had made the ground soft beneath them.

I leaned back and my chair sank deeper.

"How's your guitar going?"

"Remember, I said I wasn't allowed to bring mine to the beach house."

"Feel free to borrow one of mine, soldier. Do you want me to lend you the Gretsch?"

I smiled. "Ted, it's a classic guitar. A one-of-a-kind. It must have cost you at least fifteen grand. You don't want to lend it to people, to a kid."

He shrugged. "Any time, any of them, take the Fender, the Gibson, take one home with you tonight if you want. I remember what it was like not to have your instrument." He breathed out and shook his head.

"Thanks, Ted, that's really nice of you," I said, thinking it was also really stupid. Imagine my parents if I appeared with a fifteen-thousand-dollar guitar under my arm.

"Are you chilly, soldier?" He jumped up. "Hang on, I can light a little fire."

He pulled over a rusty Weber barbecue. One wheel had come off so he balanced it on half a brick lying nearby. "Right," he muttered to himself, "gotta get some charcoal." He went over to the shed and pulled at the door that was only held on by ivy. The whole thing nearly came off in his hand, and he stumbled back as if that was how you normally opened doors. I smiled. He was such an odd and funny guy. The door fell back on one hinge.

The charcoal was damp and I didn't think it'd light, but Ted got some starter to get it going. "Just be careful," I told him as he splashed it around.

He got the fire going and sat back down, pleased with himself.

"I like my garden," he told me.

"Yeah," I said, "gardens are nice." I don't really have an opinion on gardens.

"Never trust anyone who doesn't like gardening, soldier."

Had he forgotten that I'd seen this place in the daytime—it was an infestation of weeds.

"But you don't like gardening!"

"So," he chuckled, "don't trust me!"

He went inside and came back with another beer and a small radio. He turned it on. "Mustn't wake up the neighbors," he said, adjusting the volume.

I was feeling a bit calmer now. The fire was warm. I was glad that he'd got it going. I was glad he wasn't mad with me. "Maybe I'll have a beer with you, Ted," I said. "Maybe a lite beer."

"Great!" He leaped up and went inside. "Sorry, no lite," he said, coming back. He dropped a cold can in my lap and sat down again. I opened my can and took a sip. This was okay. Things weren't so bad.

"We're just two guys," he said happily, looking really pleased with himself. "Two guys having a beer." He seemed relieved in some way, not so jumpy or aggravated. We sat there, we talked about the Terry Pratchett books that we'd both read. They were pretty funny. We talked about school.

"I hated school," Ted told me.

"How come?"

He shrugged. "Just different."

What was different? Him? School? What?

"So, tell me about your family, soldier. Your mum and dad, are they together?"

"Yeah," I said. I sipped my beer. "I think they're pretty happy."

"That's good, soldier. That's really nice. I bet they were childhood sweethearts, were they?"

"I don't think so." I took another swig. "But I know how they met. They were in line to get ice cream at a beach on some Greek island. Her ice cream fell out of its cone and then he gave her his."

Ted nodded. "Lovely," he said. "That's lovely."

I suppose it was lovely, but it was strange to hear Ted speak like this. I would have thought that he'd scoff at this sort of thing, but he was in such a mellow mood. I thought of Mum and Dad, the way they have this secret smile when they talk about that ice-cream cone, as if just for a moment they are back there being young and suntanned, before marriage and me and Sarah came along.

The news came on. It was three o'clock. Ted flicked the radio dials. We heard a bit of that pop song, "What About Me?" He turned it down, suddenly angry. "Never trust anyone who listens to this sort of crap, mate." Then just as quickly his whole face relaxed, and he grinned at me, a little boy's smile, sparkling and cheeky. "They've *gotta* be a jerk."

We laughed. Yeah, Ted and I, we were into real music. He didn't know me as the swimmer who'd wasted his chances. I was just Kip, a guy who could play guitar, who might even be good enough to become a musician.

He changed the station to some jazz, and closed his eyes.

I closed mine, too. I was starting to get it.

The track finished and the announcer said the name of the saxophonist and the piano player.

I opened my eyes. Ted's were still closed.

Now there was just talking on the radio.

"They still haven't found that girl," I said after a few minutes.

Ted said nothing.

"Still searching Point Nepean."

Ted opened his eyes suddenly. "Wild place, Point Nepean."

"What do you mean?"

"Don't get me wrong, soldier, I love it. I walk around there all the time. But it's a wild place, it's got an ancient history." He leaned forward and his chair did too, sinking again. "Thousands of years ago the whole bay was a giant floodplain"—he spread his arms wide and nearly toppled over —"with the Yarra running right through it to the Heads." He took a swig.

"And there were settlers," I added. "I've seen their graves around Sorrento."

"Yeah," he said casually, "reeks of death, I reckon." He waved his hand vaguely. "The whole place. Graves everywhere." He pointed in the direction of Sorrento. "Those settlers, they came with convicts, and they reckon there's no fresh water and the soil's no good, so off they go to Van Diemen's Land."

"Except for William Buckley," I added, glad that I could add something, so he didn't think I was totally ignorant.

"Yeah, but then he disappears and turns up thirty years later, wandering along the Yarra speaking another language altogether." Ted chuckled, shaking his head, as if William Buckley were a wayward personal friend of his.

Another jazz tune came on. Ted leaned back and downed his can.

We didn't talk for a while. The night was still and the sound of waves lapping drifted up from the beach. It was so different from the other night. The night of the storm.

"So how come they built the fort?" I asked. "And all the cannons?"

"What do you reckon, soldier? Defense. Guarding the Heads from invaders."

"Is that from World War Two?"

"No, built way before that. Hasn't your dad told you? He'd be a military man."

I shook my head. "I've never been there with Dad."

"Eighteen eighties. They thought the Russians were coming. But you know what, soldier? Nobody came." Ted laughed. "Then in World War Two they get this idea to put an infrared beam across the water, between Lonsdale and Nepean. If the beam was broken it'd ring an alarm, so they'd pick up any subs coming in at night on the surface of the water."

"Don't subs go under the water?"

"You couldn't stay submerged in the Heads, soldier. Too wild."

"So did it work? The infrared beam?" It sounded like a pretty modern invention for World War Two.

He crushed his empty can. "Nope! Because bloody birds fly around at night, don't they?" He laughed out loud. "Their great invention, their infrared beam, it wasn't detecting Japanese subs, it was picking up seagulls!"

I drank more of my beer. Smoke from the Weber rose up, drifting, and I could see stars behind the haze.

"And it was where Harold Holt was lost. And now that girl, Grace."

Ted nodded, opening another beer.

That made me think. "She could be in one of those buildings. Those old forts. You know, for shelter."

"Who?"

"That girl. Or she could be in the quarantine station or somewhere. Is the search party allowed to look for her in there?"

"They would have looked in all the buildings, soldier."

"Will your benefit gig still be on if they haven't found the girl?"

He shrugged.

Thinking about the missing girl had made all my worries come back again. We'd been talking for ages. Suddenly, tiredness had come. My mood was shifting. I started to feel vaguely cross and uneasy. Ted didn't seem to care about that missing girl at all. I wanted to go home, but he never seemed to let me go when I wanted to. I didn't want him to get angry again.

I stood up. "It's really late. I need to go, Ted. My parents could freak if they woke up."

He'd been concerned about my parents before. Now he looked annoyed that I was leaving.

"Want another beer before you head off?"

"No thanks." I headed toward the side of the house to the front gate.

He stood up as well. "Might go for a bit of a walk myself." He slipped a pair of old sandals over his black socks. "Want me to walk you home?"

I stretched. "No, that's okay." We both yawned.

I worried about him wandering off into the night. I was going home, I was heading somewhere. But going for a walk at nearly four A.M.? Where was he going?

"Maybe you should get some sleep, too," I said as we went out toward the road.

"Who are you," he snapped suddenly, "my bloody father?"

I shook my head, too tired to answer him. Too tired to argue.

"See ya, Ted."

He wasn't looking at me. He wandered up the road in the other direction, toward the Heads.

"Yeah, see ya," he muttered.

Why was he suddenly so pissed off? All I'd done was suggest that he get some sleep. We'd had a good time and then he'd ruined it.

I arrived home just after four. I crept inside, took off my shoes, and got into bed.

Eventually I got to sleep and had a dream. I dreamed that Abbie was walking in front of me at the beach, wearing her school uniform. Then she turned around and it wasn't Abbie at all, it was that missing girl, Grace. I had seen her face in the paper, but it wasn't as if I recognized her; I just knew it was her, the way you do in a dream. And she was wearing Abbie's clothes. Ted's voice was somewhere, yelling at Abbie, yelling at me, laughing then yelling again, abusing me over and over.

The next morning I slept in. When I got up, everyone had gone out. I took a plastic bag from the kitchen and put Abbie's bra in it. I went out to the garbage bin around the side of the house and shoved it in, right down under the bags that were already there.

"What are you doing there, Kip? Putting out the garbage for your mother?"

It was the policeman.

Grace

The sun comes and I want to feel it. I hear breathing.

I see a bird.

My head is heavy on my arm. My eyes close. I want to drink the water.

A man follows a bird. Covers me. I shake. He won't take me with him.

Water comes right up to me.

A man will get my dad.

My dad . . . a man is speaking to me.

He's come in with the bird.

Annie

Now it was Friday. My auntie and uncle had come down. My auntie and Mum kept whispering and holding onto each other. Dad was going out and coming back again, but nobody was doing enough.

My auntie said I could help by looking after Simon. But that's Grace's job. She's the one who looks after Simon.

In the house everything piled up. It took Mum ages to fold the clothes because she sat very still on the couch, staring at the pile of washing. When she stood up, she'd sigh as if folding the clothes needed more effort than anything. Mum is a doctor. She's always busy. It made me nervous to see her sit like that.

And when Mum and Dad talked, they murmured quietly. In our family we used to talk normally. Even loudly. When I came into a room, they'd stop, or they'd start talking in these fake voices about what to have for dinner, or did we need more milk. But I heard things they said.

I heard, "I can imagine it. She wouldn't have stopped to think. She never thinks."

But Grace always thinks. Grace thinks more than anyone else I know.

I went to my room. I sat on my bed. What would things be like if Grace never came back? It would be only me and Simon. I wondered if I would get Grace's room. All her clothes, her certificates for writing stories and essays. I wondered what people would say to me. I would be the girl who used to have a sister. We'd remember a time when we were a real family, with everyone in the right order; with everyone who was supposed to be in it. Grace was the special one, anyway. The oldest child. The first. But if she never came back, then I would become the first.

I decided to write a new list. I'd come to some conclusions.

People don't just disappear. I don't believe that people disappear, anyway. Grace must be somewhere. This is what I wrote down:

Places to Search –
Beach
Point Nepean
Top of cliff
Road between our house and the beach
Somewhere else

No one cared what I did, so in the morning I went out. I folded my list and took it with me. I walked right past the people with the cameras. They clicked and called out but I looked straight ahead and ignored them.

I walked to the beach. There were groups of people, searching: I counted three. They were the volunteers. One person in each group wore a bright orange jacket. None of these people knew my sister. Still, they were looking for her.

I wondered if Mum and my auntie would be worried about me. It was cold and I wasn't wearing a jacket. The wind made my eyes water. I went up a track that led to the houses on the cliff. I called a couple of times. "Grace, Grace." But there was no point. It wasn't like tracking; it wasn't as if she were hiding and about to jump out and surprise me.

I could hear music that I'd heard somewhere before. I came down onto the sand again, and that's when I saw it.

The penguin.

It was very dead. Its body was open. Its eyes weren't there any more and bits of feathers had been pulled out.

Something crawled across it.

"Oh, Grace," I said, starting to whisper like my parents did.

It had turned gray. I didn't want to look at it. I dug a

hole with my hands and pushed the penguin into it. I covered it over and stood up to look around for something to make a cross with, like she always does. I looked among the trees for sticks. The bushes made a scratching sound. And through the trees I saw a color. Red.

A man was standing there. He was very still and quiet. He was wearing a red and yellow coat. He smiled.

I knew who he was. He was the man I'd seen the night Grace disappeared. The man with bare feet, under the light. The person of interest.

He took a step toward me. He held out his hand. It was white and it shook from side to side. Then he spoke.

He said, "Do you recognize me?"

Kip

I'd told the police the truth—I *was* putting out garbage.

But they came back before lunchtime. I felt sick because I'd hardly had any sleep. Mum answered the door. "I'm glad you're at home," one of them said. They were in the hallway. "Are you aware that your son was in possession of some clothing that doesn't belong to him?"

They came into the living room. Mum looked horrified. Sarah glanced up from her Gameboy. "What are you talking about?" Mum said. "Kip? Have you got someone else's clothes?"

"No." I didn't know what to say. "I haven't . . . it's not . . ." I saw the green plastic bag in the policeman's hand. He opened the bag to show Mum. He didn't touch what was inside, as if it were too filthy to pick up.

I stood up, knowing I had to explain. "It was just some guys from school. They put it in my bag. It belongs to Abbie, a girl in our class."

Mum looked so confused, disappointed. As if she'd never imagined that a son of hers could end up doing such stupid things. How could I explain it all properly? "It was a joke," I ventured weakly. "We took her bra when she was changing."

"That's not a very nice thing to do, is it?" said the policeman, as if he were talking to someone in second grade.

"No," I said, stating the obvious.

"In fact, I'd call that sexual harassment, myself." He nodded at me. "I'll take this, and we'll need to get your friends' names and phone numbers. In the meantime, I understand you saw Mr. Atwood yesterday."

I looked across at Mum. "Yes," I mumbled. How did they know I'd been there? Did they know I'd also visited in the middle of the night?

The policemen exchanged glances. "Did he mention to you that he was going away?"

"No."

"He seems to have headed off somewhere. No car, no sign of him around the house since early this morning. Apparently he told a neighbor he was going away for a couple of days. Let us know if you see him or if he contacts you again."

When they left, my parents had a talk with me.

"It's really important that you tell us everything you know. You lied about having this girl's . . . clothes," Dad said. It was almost funny, as if Dad couldn't actually say the word *bra*. The cops already thought I was a liar because I told them on the beach that I hadn't seen that little kid, David.

"We didn't know you'd been to see that man again," said Mum.

I didn't say anything.

"Your friend Ted . . ."

"He's not a friend!" I shouted.

I felt confused, I felt exhausted. I didn't even know why I'd gone over there. I felt angry. "He's just some guy I met on the beach. He's got this guitar—"

"Listen," said Dad, "you've had a shock, a bad experience in the water. Are you sure you saw those girls?" He stood up, rubbing his forehead. "What happened that night in the water? I don't get it, Kip. Did you fall or did you dive? Did you think the girl was in the water?"

It was such a blur I couldn't remember clearly. "I thought I saw something, or someone on a board. I jumped in to help them."

"But why didn't you alert the police? They were there with you by this stage, weren't they?" He shook his head because he couldn't work it out.

"I tried to but they couldn't hear me. I thought I could . . . swim . . . but I wasn't strong enough."

He gave me a knowing look, which really pissed me off. He probably thought that if I hadn't given up swimming I could have managed in the water. But he didn't see the water that night.

"Dad," I said, "I nearly drowned."

"Exactly, Kip. Can't you see how reckless you were being?" He shook his head. "And this other child, this boy—"

"If I hadn't dived in they would never have found him."

"That's true and everyone, I'm sure, is very grateful about that. Still, I don't know why you didn't just tell the police immediately. They could have gotten the child from the water without all this fuss." He sighed angrily, shaking his head again. "I mean are you telling us the truth? What really happened?" He sat down again, exasperated. "It was a freezing cold night. *Why* were you in the water? It's so impulsive. It's just not logical. Were you running away from someone?"

Was I? I was running away from Ted because I was scared of him. I was running away from Andrew because he didn't trust me. I was running from that security guy and the police.

"Yes," I said, "I was running away."

"From Ted?"

"Yes." Now were they satisfied? I was so tired and sick of them harping on at me.

Mum and Dad looked at each other. "Is there anything else you saw?" asked Dad. "Anything in his house? Anything that might help the police."

"Or that poor girl," added Mum.

I was completely over their crappy talks that went nowhere. Anyway, why was I protecting Ted? He *was* a weirdo, he was crazy, always mad with me for no reason. And half the things he said made no sense. Sitting out at three o'clock in the morning as if it were a summer's afternoon. It had seemed like a good idea last night, but now it seemed stupid. I felt like such a fool.

"He had magazines in his house," I said. I heard Mum gasp, as if I'd said he had ten dead bodies in his room.

"Pornographic magazines?" asked Dad.

I almost laughed, the way he said it so seriously.

"Did he show them to you?"

"No."

"But you saw them."

"Yes, I saw them."

We sat in silence as if I'd committed a dreadful crime, as if my whole life had just been ruined.

It was great timing, because the phone rang. It was the policeman. Dad spoke to him, then came back. His face was white.

"This Stephen from school, apparently he's told the police he's got no idea what you're talking about."

That bastard. That absolute gutless bastard. I could just imagine him panicking when the police called and saying anything to save his skin.

"And this clothing, you're telling us it belonged to a girl at school?"

"Oh, God," I sighed, "yes, we played this joke on a girl."

"It's not a joke, Kip."

I felt like yelling at him. Of course it's not a joke! Did I think it was funny? Was I laughing?

"Are you sure this isn't just something you've invented? I mean it's all a bit hard to believe if you ask me."

All of a sudden I felt furious. "Phone up Abbie's parents, then. Ask them. Ask her. Check up on me. What do you believe?" I shouted.

"To tell you the truth, I don't know what to believe about you anymore. Mum tells me you're wandering around on your own, you disappear for hours at a time, you're being uncommunicative." He paused. "First you give up swimming—"

I knew that was coming. "*Why* is it always about swimming?" I shouted. "Will you just get over it! I'm sorry that you can't feel good anymore about having a champion son. But I can tell you now that I will never, ever take up swimming again."

Dad looked stunned, as if he'd been hit.

"I got sick of it, okay?" I shouted. "I got sick of getting up at four every morning. I lost it, I just—"

"Listen," Dad shouted back, "it wasn't only you who made sacrifices. We put in a lot of time, a lot of money, your mother drove you every morning, Sarah had to adjust her schedule, and now you decide on a whim to give it all away. Then there's this . . . this blaring guitar every time I walk in the house and now you're in some sort of trouble with the police."

"So I've given up swimming and become a criminal. Do you think that's how it works? Do you think that me, your son, Kip, the champion swimmer, do you think *I've* done something to that girl?"

"Of course not!" gasped Mum. "Kip, you're tired, you're overreacting."

"But admit it! You think that the bra belongs to that girl who's missing. You don't believe me, so you must think that I got the bra off the girl."

"No," said Dad, slowing down, shocked, as if he'd only just realized that we'd both lost control. "Kip, stop."

I stopped. We had always been a calm family. We had never shouted at each other like this before.

"You need to tell the police everything about your meeting with this Ted. You mustn't try to protect anyone." Dad went back to his usual straightforward self. It came from being in the air force.

"I've told the police. Just because he's some lonely drunk doesn't mean he's done anything wrong."

"Do you think he's that type of man?" asked Mum, as if she were terrified of what my answer might be.

"What type of man?" I put my head in my hands. Was Ted a good man or a bad man? What had he done? Did they think I was that type of person, that I'd become that type of man? I didn't even understand what type of man I was talking about. A man who's given up? A man like Ted.

I tried to think clearly. After a moment, I looked up at my parents. "I think he's angry."

"Angry?" said Dad. "What's he angry—"

I didn't let him finish. "What do *you* think," I yelled at them, feeling a sudden rage myself, "tell me what you really think about me."

I stormed out, went to my bedroom, and slammed

the door. I stood on the other side. I felt like screaming, I felt like kicking something. I sat on the bed. I stood up again, paced around, restless. I knew what I had to do. Somehow, I had to find that girl. Grace. It was up to me to find her, wherever she was. Then I could prove that I had nothing to do with it. The awful thing was, I was almost starting to believe that maybe I *had* done something bad; that I *was* something bad, that there was something about me, some secret, that I'd hidden even from myself. Why did I want the girls that I hated? Why did I help steal Abbie's bra? Why did I even hang around with guys who do that sort of thing? Why did I lose the feeling, the great feeling of water against my skin? Why did I tense up when I hugged my own mother? What was happening to me? I couldn't tell anyone any of the things that worried me. They were the things I had to hide.

Annie

When I got home, Geoff, our policeman, was there. He was asking Mum if Grace wore a bra.

Grace does wear a bra, but she'd be really embarrassed if a policeman knew that.

I told them I'd seen that man again, that he'd spoken to me.

"What did he say?" Geoff asked.

"He asked if I recognized him."

"And what did you say?"

"I didn't answer him," I said. "I came home straight away."

"Good girl, Annie," he said. "That was the right thing to do." The policeman seemed more interested in this than my own mother. She was just looking past me, staring at nothing at all.

"Does that man know where Grace is?" I asked the policeman.

He looked at my mother. She was still staring. He turned to me. "We're all looking for Grace," he said. "Lots of people are helping, Annie. Lots of people are looking for her."

This didn't really answer the question, but I couldn't ask any more because he left.

I went to my room. This is how things will be if she never comes back, I thought. Asking questions that will never be answered properly.

I closed my eyes and imagined her. How can she just disappear? She's my sister! She's Grace! Clumsy, dreamy, stupid, clever Grace. The oldest child in our family.

I opened my eyes. It was raining again. The sky was bright and dark. The TV vans parked on the street had lights on inside. It looked cozy. They'd packed up their deck chairs and one of them had come back with McDonalds for everyone, as if they were all friends at a picnic. The volunteers would probably go home again because the weatherman had said strong winds overnight. Gale-force winds. But they shouldn't stop searching. We can't stop searching—ever.

Grace had been sick when she was a baby. She'd been really sick. That's why people watched out for her. Once a baby has been as sick as Grace had been, no one can quite believe that she will be as healthy as other people. Maybe she always carried something from that sickness with her. Sometimes her face was pale. Maybe it left her weaker. She had nearly died. They had to take out her kidney and everything—she's still got the scar around her tummy. Even by the time I was born, Grace was still sick. If I got this hypothermia, maybe I could last longer than her. I've always been really healthy. I'm the strong one in our family. That's why no one needs to worry about me. I'm never sick.

I wondered if Grace might die more quickly than normal people.

Die. I'd said that word in my mind. I'd heard it. It's a very short word, only three letters. It's strange that this word is also a person's name. Like Diana. Diane. Di.

I never got to make a cross for the penguin. Grace

would think that was important. It's easy to make a cross. You just get two sticks and tie them together with string. I went outside to find some sticks. Someone called out to me, asking me what I was doing. I turned away from them. They were so annoying, they drove me mad.

I picked a few flowers to put with the cross. I could see Mum staring out the window. She had a cup in her hand. She didn't come and yell at me for going outside when I wasn't supposed to, for being outside in the rain. She didn't do anything.

A man came right into our garden with a camera. He pointed it at me. "Leave me alone!" I yelled at him. "Go away!" I ran inside and back to my room. The room I share with Grace. I refilled the hot-water bottle. I'd been doing it each day so it would stay warm for her.

Mum was cracking up. Maybe I was cracking up, too. Would I go back to school without Grace? Teachers say things to me, like, Are you as smart as your sister? Some say, You're nothing like Grace, are you? I don't know.

When she was in sixth grade, Grace used to eat lunch by herself. It annoyed me that she did that. It was embarrassing for me. I bet she does it in high school, too. She doesn't even care that she looks like a loser.

But she's Grace, she's my Grace.

I put the cross on my bed. Four nights had gone by and nearly four days, too. Dad came home and they told me again that I wasn't allowed out.

The TV cameras stayed outside, and inside, all I did was watch TV.

Kip

Point Nepean was closed to the public but I didn't care. In the afternoon I went there anyway. I didn't tell Mum and Dad where I was going. Too bad if they'd worry. I just left.

The Visitors' Center was full of police. They had set it up as their command post. The volunteers were out again, searching. The lifesaving club had sent people, too. I wanted to go and tell them that I could be a volunteer but I didn't know what they'd say. Helicopters had been flying low along the ocean side.

I went along the road, then right down to the tunnels and forts at the end. She could have been anywhere. It would be so easy to get lost here. There were signs all over the place, telling people where they couldn't go. All along the road in, there's this tall black cyclone fence, with thick scrub behind it. The tea trees twist and curl, their ends are gnarled like an old woman's hand. They look like ghosts of trees, their branches dried out bones. WARNING, say the signs. DANGER.

I headed toward Cheviot Hill. It was very quiet. I listened to my sneakers hit the blacktop. I passed more signs. COMMONWEALTH OF AUSTRALIA. TRESPASSING AND OR SHOOTING IS PROHIBITED. UNEXPLODED ORDNANCE. LIVE FIRING IN PROGRESS.

I could see small pockets of people deeper in the scrub. The tea tree along the ridge is so exposed that it's grown sideways, as if it's blown over. Even when there's no breeze, it's shaped like that. If you took a photo on a still day, the picture would look like it had been windy.

It was cold. The sun would be out one minute, then a shower would come across. Four seasons in one day—that's what they say about Melbourne. As I made my way up the track to Cheviot, there were more KEEP OUT signs, this time with a picture of some sort of missile. I thought I could hear a car engine up ahead, over the rise. The wind lifted through the trees, shaking the she-oaks, making them quiver. A rush of cold air came over the hill. I got up to the top and I realized the noise hadn't been a car at all. It was the roar of the ocean.

Ted was right. It was so wild, it was so beautiful, but you have to keep out, keep off, go away.

I saw the monument for Harold Holt, standing over

Cheviot Beach. They never found his body. The water below was deep blue, there were shelves and rocks and water pouring, pounding in and out and over them. Wind blew into my face. I closed my eyes.

When I opened them I saw the man Andrew with a policeman. They were standing on the track. I don't know if he saw me or not. He looked in my direction, then turned his back.

I'm helping, I felt like shouting, I'm trying to help.

I walked all the way down to the Heads, where the wind blows across the ocean to the bay. I saw a boat going out, churning through the rip. The sea at the Heads looked heavy, like oil. It was spilling over, seething, as if something were pushing it up from underneath. There are limestone stacks under there, Ted had told me, and the tide rushes up and spills over them—it's like a fountain under the sea. Even on a calm day the water's rippling, pushing one way and then pushing against itself, as if it doesn't know which way to go. It's a huge mass of water, running in and running out. I noticed a man on a dark rock shelf right on the edge.

I went down toward Pearce Barracks. The building's derelict, it's out of bounds. I could see the roof of the old quarantine station. The buildings, the fortifications, most of them are ruins now. The concrete bunkers reminded me of burnt-out buildings I'd seen on TV.

Afghanistan. The Gaza Strip. Baghdad. You don't see ruins like that in Australia. They look wrong here. Like a monument to some war that we were never told about, that maybe never even happened. But here I was, standing among them. I could see the car ferry. It looked tiny. It started to rain again, through the sunshine, so I sat in one of the concrete shelters and watched the waves lift and curl and crash, their foam making lace patterns on the surface as they reached the shore.

Maybe I was imagining things. Overreacting. Maybe that Andrew guy had just been embarrassed to see me again. But then I'd brought it upon myself, their suspicion. If I hadn't spoken to Ted in the first place, it wouldn't have happened the way it did. What sort of loser was I to try to make friends with some creepy weirdo? Had I even tried to make friends with him? I wasn't sure.

That afternoon I felt so lonely, as if no one in the world would ever understand me, would ever believe me about anything, that I'd never even understand myself. I knew my parents were really worried and they were disappointed in me. It's the worst feeling to think that you've disappointed someone. That you're a disappointment.

Then I felt bad that there was a girl missing and I wasn't even trying to find her anymore. I was wallowing in my own pathetic problems. But it was hopeless trying to find that girl—as if I would be able to do that. This was just another one of my stupid ideas that I seemed to be having lately.

A kid came up to me. She gave me a fright. I recognized her from the paper. She was Grace's sister, Annie. She stood there, staring at me like I was an animal on display in my little broken-down fort.

Then she just came out and asked me. She asked me if I knew where her sister was.

At least this kid could say it straight, what I knew other people were thinking.

On the way back there were more signs. Whoever was in charge of them must really be over the top. Maybe I was tired because even the signs began to annoy me. In the toilets it said: DO NOT DRINK THE WATER. Steep hills had Beware signs at the top. Since when was a steep hill so terrifying? Live Firing in Progress. I doubt it.

There was a piece of modern equipment on the cliffs above the ancient buildings. It was radar, and it made an eerie ticking sound.

I walked around the old cemetery. There were crooked graves, from the different shipwrecks and from the first settlers. A neat white picket fence surrounded them, tidying up all the history inside.

I took the narrow track to the bay beach and came out near the old jetty that I'd jumped off that night. The tide was out so more of the jetty was exposed. The gray posts looked like stepping stones into the sea. And the sea itself looked pretty harmless—it was hard to imagine getting into trouble in that water.

I stood there for ages. I could see Melbourne—it looked like a floating city. We were due to go back there in two days. But all the days had lost their rhythm. They had begun to drift into each other and I felt tense, I felt worried all the time now. I'd be going back to school. I started to think about Abbie and the bra. But mostly about Abbie. When we had "family life" class at school, and in the books that parents buy for their kids, it says that people have sex when they love each other, two consenting adults and all that. Like it might be tender. But when you see it, like in a magazine, it doesn't look like that. I reckon it looks violent. It looks like animals. And it's not how I feel either—when I think about stuff like that, it isn't a tender feeling. That makes me more worried than anything. I mean, I dream about having a girl I could love, but that just seems like some stupid fantasy; nothing like that would ever happen with any girls I know.

The water looked clear and clean. I remembered the way it had risen and fallen that night, how it had tossed the Boogie board high into the air. I wondered about Ted. Had it been his Boogie board? The one at his house? It was so hard to get a straight answer out of him. He was so unlike anyone I'd ever met. He had a sort of sadness in him all the time—even when he seemed happy—and then without warning that sadness would turn in on him and became rage.

A policeman came up to me. "You shouldn't be here," he said.

"I'm helping, I'm a volunteer."

He paused, his expression changed.

"Tell me, Kip, is there anywhere you think we should look? Anywhere you'd like to look?"

Annie

I was up to Point Nepean on my list.

Dad let me come with him in the end because I'd hassled him all day. It was late in the afternoon. As we walked along the road he held my hand as if I were seven or something. I let him do it. Poor Dad. I'd heard him in the early morning, walking around. Sitting in the kitchen on his own. He looked so worn out and tired.

A policeman was standing outside the Visitors' Center. He was talking on his cell phone. Dad spoke with him—in whispers again. Then we walked to the cliff with the radar. A man was standing on his own. Dad stopped and stared at him. I could hear the ticking of the radar as it circled around. It sounded like a giant clock.

"Who's he?" I asked Dad. "Is that guy helping with the search?"

"What?" Dad looked past the guy and out to the ocean. Huge white waves rolled and crashed onto the rocks.

Dad is someone who knows the answers. He knows scientific answers. He knows what temperature water has to be to boil, and what temperature it has to be to freeze. He can explain why you see your reflection upside down in a spoon. He's told me how rocks are formed. But now I know it: Grace is gone, and my dad can't find the answer.

I pulled at Dad's hand. "I said is he helping, that man?"

"Yeah," said Dad, in a dream. "He's helping."

We saw Geoff, the policeman who had come to ask me questions. He was with a group of people. Dad went over to talk with him. They zipped up their jackets because it had started to rain again. They pointed in the direction of the guy standing by himself. He looked miserable. I heard them say something about "surveillance" and "observation." I heard Geoff say those words again—*young person*. I watched the man or boy or whoever he was. He looked up. He was crying. What did he have to cry about? If he was one of the helpers, then I could ask him if he'd found any clues. He looked alone. He was stabbing a stick into the ground.

Dad was still talking with Geoff, so I went toward the boy.

Neither of us spoke. Then I asked him something.

"Are you the young person?"

He looked at me.

Then I said something else. People are always telling me that I should think before I open my mouth. But I didn't think. I didn't even know what I was going to say.

"Did you take my sister away?"

He shook his head. He started to stand up. He started to say something. He said, "I. . . ." Then he stopped and sat down again.

"Annie!" Dad and Geoff both yelled at me at once. Dad ran closer. "Keep away from her." He said it the way you shout at a dog.

It made me frightened. I ran over to Dad. He grabbed me. "What did he say to you?"

"Nothing," I said. "He didn't say anything."

When we walked home, the sun was going down through dark pink clouds. We went in the back way and Dad helped me climb the fence so we wouldn't have to go past the TV people.

I was feeling a bit confused. I was feeling that Dad was cross with me. And it wasn't just because I had spoken to the young person.

Nobody said so, but I knew myself that I had lost Grace. It was because of me. Because I never think. It was because of me that Grace was gone.

Grace

I dreamt there was a man who came.

I dreamt of a book and a picture.

There is a painting—a man wears a bright coat. Children are gathered around him. One little girl has round, wide eyes. She looks up. I touch the picture, I touch the little girl's hair that looks so soft and I whisper to her, "Don't worry, little girl, I'll save you. You don't have to go into the side of that dark mountain with the others. Turn back. Please, I'll rescue you."

Kip

On the way back from Point Nepean I saw Ted. He was sitting in an old Toyota Landcruiser outside the shops. His headlights were on.

He beckoned me over. "G'day, mate." He was eating a hot dog, spilling over with sauce. I wondered how a vegan did that.

I pointed to his lights. "You might get a dead battery."

He switched them off. Darkness flickered outside. "Happy?"

I nodded, but I wasn't happy.

"The police were looking for you," I told him.

He rested his elbow on the open window. "You working for them now, soldier?" he asked.

In his car was a whole lot of electronic stuff and a tripod and camera. "Where have you been?" I asked him. "I thought you said you lost your license."

"Yeah, well I got it back, didn't I."

I put my hand up against the glass and peered in. There was something purple. A colored T-shirt draped over a bulky shape.

"Where have you been?" I asked again.

"I've been out. Enjoying the natural world. That all right with you?" he snapped, then leaned toward me. "Never trust anyone who doesn't appreciate nature. They can't see past themselves." He finished the hot dog and held out the empty paper bag, which was covered in grease and sauce and bits of onion. "Throw that in the trash for me will you, soldier."

What was I, his slave? I did what he said, and came back to the car.

He reached into the back and grabbed the T-shirt.

Black umbrellas tumbled from underneath it. They were wet. They looked like bats' wings. Ted used the shirt to wipe his hands.

"You know that Boogie board that I asked you about, the one that was in your house and then it wasn't there—"

"What are you, a forensic scientist?"

"Do you know where it is?"

He didn't answer.

"Did you put it somewhere?"

"Listen mate, I can't remember where I put my cup of tea in the mornings. I have whole days that I can't remember!" He opened his arms as wide as they'd go in the car. "Big chunks of time."

That's because you're always drunk, I thought. Then it made sense, why he'd looked so blank when I'd mentioned how he'd told me to piss off the evening I went around there. I bet he hadn't been able to remember me being there at all. And that worried me, because if he couldn't remember that, then what else had he done that he couldn't remember?

He took a swig of beer. "You know they're watching us, they're watching both of us, mate, thanks to you."

"I wasn't turning you in," I said. "I had to tell them what I'd been doing, that's all."

He snickered.

"You're drunk," I said. "You shouldn't drive when you're like that."

"I'm not driving, officer. I'm sitting in a bloody car."

He pointed to the western sky where the charcoal clouds hung like gauze above the setting sun. "That's where I've been."

"Where?"

"Chasing."

"Chasing what?"

He rolled his eyes as if I were the dumbest person in the world. "Chasing the storm, you idiot! Western Victoria. Big event. Could be here in a couple of hours." He swung an arm around wildly to the back of the four-wheel drive. "I got all the equipment here—I got satellite, my computer, I can pick it all up on radar. I got as far as Alexandra. Dark as midnight up in the Black Spur it was." He smiled, his green eyes alive. "You'd love it, soldier. When you're in a supercell, you're caught in time, man." He laughed. "The whole shebang could go one way or the other—bring on something bloody wonderful, or destroy everything in its path." He was slurring his words. "It was a ripper, it was a *tornado*, soldier."

He sounded like a bragging kid, as if he wanted me to say something like, "Wow, a tornado, unreal!" But I was sick of trying to say the right thing to him. I didn't even believe him. A tornado? Come on!

"I didn't hear about it on the news," I said.

"Australia's got the second highest number of tornados in the world. Most of them aren't reported. And half the time *I* have to tell the weather guys what's coming."

Yeah, I could really imagine the weather bureau waiting on a reliable report from Ted.

He downed his can and started to rave. "You've got to have moisture in the air, you've got to have instability, you've got to have lift and wind shear—"

I'd stopped listening. I could see a poster advertising the fundraiser in the window of the deli. Ted's name was on it.

"Hey," I interrupted, "did you go to the rehearsal? Is that gig on tomorrow?"

"Rehearsal? We're talking about a supercell, man, I didn't need to go to their bloody rehearsal. I could play any song they want standing on my bloody head." He drank from the can. "Anyway, I'm not playing in their stupid fundraiser."

"Why not?" I had wanted to go and see him play. "I thought you were going to help them, so they could raise money for the national park. You said it was important."

"First they tell me they're going to pay me. Five

hundred bloody dollars. I used to get ten grand to do a concert." He wiped a greasy hand on his jeans. "But I said okay, because I'm a reasonable guy." He glared at me as if I were going to dispute him. "Now they say they want me to donate my services. *Everyone else is donating their services,*" he said in a mimicky voice.

"Isn't that what people do if it's a benefit concert?"

He crushed his can with his foot then chucked it beside him on the seat. "Look, I don't care what they do. I said I'd help them out but I never said I'd do it for nothing. I bet they've paid other people for their services, what about me?"

"I thought you said people are doing it for nothing."

He ignored me. "Now they're going back on their word. Never trust a do-gooder, man. They've always got a bloody ulterior motive." He looked like a sulky child. He shook his head and opened another can. "I was really big, man," he said. "They don't realize how big I was. They're bloody ignorant."

He drank some of his beer. "Want some?" he asked me.

He was such an idiot! "No, thanks."

"That's right, you're a rum and Coke man."

A police car pulled up outside the shops. Who cares, I thought. It's a free country. I'm allowed to stand here. Why should I feel guilty all the time?

"What happened?" I asked Ted.

"What do you mean?"

"Well, you had the number one albums, then what happened?"

Ted screwed up his face. "Record company cheated me." He saw the policeman get out of his car.

"Oh, Christ," he muttered, "here we go again." Then he went on. "You should have heard me, man, I was so good. I could have been a virtuoso guitarist if I'd wanted—the best. Better than that Tommy Emmanuel guy. I mean, they compared me to Hendrix, to Clapton. And I could sing—you should have heard my voice then." He shook his head. "I had talent."

That's like me, I found myself thinking. Like me and the swimming.

The policeman went into the soda shop. We watched two girls come out with ice creams. They were good-looking girls. Long hair. Slim.

"You got a girlfriend?" he asked me suddenly.

"No," I said, and he snorted as if I were a loser. "I've only just turned fourteen, remember."

"Yeah, well when you get one, don't get a skinny one. Never trust a skinny woman. Bloody neurotic, every single one of them." He rolled his eyes. "I had a skinny girlfriend once. Father was a bloody lawyer. He and his mates let me down, too."

Honestly, was there anyone in the world who hadn't let Ted down? "How?" I asked. "How did he let you down?" I was almost smiling but at the same time I wanted an argument.

He shrugged. "Girl was a bit younger than me, that's all." He fiddled with the radio.

I wondered how young the girl had been if lawyers had got involved. It was hard to know what to say to that, but it didn't matter because Ted was on to a new topic. He was raving about some other girlfriend he'd had who was neurotic. I wasn't listening because I'd noticed the girl I'd seen at Point Nepean. Grace's sister. She was marching by herself, striding along like those mothers you see who power walk around the streets in the mornings. She was heading up the hill. I took a step away from Ted's window. She looked over at me, then away again. Her arms swung. She looked determined.

I interrupted Ted. "See that girl, that's her sister," I said.

He looked around quickly. "Who?" he snapped. "Where?"

I pointed. "Over there. I saw her at Point Nepean."

"What were you doing up there?"

"I was looking for Grace. I was helping the volunteers."

Ted laughed, shaking his head.

"Anyway," I said, trying to lighten things up a bit, "I've seen one of your girlfriends."

He looked up, wary. "What? Who?" he demanded.

"The one in the photo. At your house."

"Oh. That's not a girlfriend, that's my *wife*." He spat it out as if a wife were not a good thing to have at all.

I didn't realize that he was married. "Where's she?" I asked.

He glared at me. "Well, she's not here, is she!"

Everything I said seemed to make him hurt or angry. As if I were hitting him on a bruise. And he was so bruised. Everywhere, he was bruised.

He kept turning his head and glancing back toward Grace's sister. She was at the top of the hill and moving out of sight. He fiddled anxiously with the coins in the compartment between the seats.

I had to ask him.

"Ted, you don't know anything about that girl, do you?"

"Which one are you talking about now, mate? The missing girl? Course I don't."

"It's just that, that night, there was a Boogie board in the water."

I could see that he wasn't following. That I'd lost him already. I persevered.

"It was purple, like the one I saw at your house. Except now it's not there."

"What is it with you and that bloody Boogie board?"

"And the police keep asking me about you. Was that drink you gave me just Gulf War Coke? What was in the drink you gave me?"

"A bit of rum. You were freezing, man, soaking wet. Don't you know rum warms you up? It wasn't much, big guy like you, you could drink a bottle of the stuff before it'd kick in. Remind me never to do you another favor, pal."

"You shouldn't give kids drinks with rum in them."

"Well so-rry!" He rolled his eyes. "Crime of the century!" He held his arms out through the car window. "Handcuff me and put me away."

For some reason, I laughed.

Annie

The fifth night.

Dad couldn't sleep. A tennis match was on late. I got up and sat with him on the couch. It was dark in the living room, but I could see his face in the green light from Wimbledon. Lleyton Hewitt was playing but we didn't care if he won or not.

Dad hugged me and he said, "I'm sorry, Annie. I shouldn't have let you and Grace go off to hide that last time. It was too late. It was a king tide. It was getting dark. I'm so sorry."

Kip

The next day we were supposed to be going home. Dad was keen to get back, so he left early in his car. I felt restless all day. I packed my stuff and in the afternoon I walked down to check out the benefit gig. It was held near the Visitors' Center. There were food stalls and a stage where the bands were playing. One of the bands was packing up their gear when I got there. It was even a beautiful day, but it was as if no one wanted to be there. People were quiet. The mood was flat.

A policeman went up on the stage and thanked the volunteers who had helped the search-and-rescue people. He said that the search was being called off. He looked tired.

It was pathetic that I'd thought I could find her when no one else had managed to. The small crowd broke up and people moved off in a huddle, murmuring. I could hear bits of what they said. *Probably drowned and her body's been swept out through the Heads. Eventually what's left of it will be washed back in with the tide.* I heard other things, too. *Wedged under a rock. Knocked unconscious. Eaten by sharks. They think she's somewhere under the sand.*

And the worst one, *She was seen with a teenage boy before she disappeared. The police know who he is.*

I felt like screaming at them. "I'm the teenage boy, and I didn't even speak to her. I'm not even sure that I saw them. I didn't do anything!" I went down to the beach on the bay side, the sparkling bay. I shuddered. That bay was tricking me. Water could do that when it looked so calm and clear, but I would never forget the night when it had been so wild, so deep and strong.

Almost as soon as I got there, I didn't want to stay. I wasn't in the mood to wait and hear the next band. On my way back through the Visitors' Center I was surprised to see Ted. I wondered if he'd changed his mind again and was going to play. It didn't look like it because he was sitting on a pine bench, drinking. He was wearing a long black coat. He was actually really drunk, as drunk as I'd ever seen him.

He gave me a nasty look. "Someone's friendly to you on a beach, they let you play their guitar, they jam with you and you shaft them."

"What?"

"You let me down, you little shit." He spat out the words. "Why did you tell the police you were running away from me? *Oh, the bad man's got dirty magazines,*" he mimicked me. "Haven't you ever seen one before? Don't you go on the Internet?"

"Of course I have."

He scowled at me. He wanted to hit me, I could tell.

"We're heading back today. To Melbourne," I said. It was awful to say good-bye like this. I hadn't meant to shaft him. "Ted," I began.

"Yeah," he said, looking uninterested, "well see ya." He walked off.

It struck me that all Ted's relationships would end like this—so that he could feel sour and misunderstood. Let down. Lost.

I stood there, watching his black coat get farther away from me. He turned around. I was ready for one last insult.

"Good luck with finding your friend."

"She's not my friend," I said. I looked at the ground. "And anyway, I figure she'd be dead by now."

My voice shook when I said that word. But suddenly Ted seemed to brighten up. He took a step back toward me, leaned against a fence rail to steady himself. "Don't worry about it, soldier. She'll turn up."

What a stupid thing to say. What did he mean, she'll turn up? She was a girl, not a lost book or an odd sock. She'd been missing for five nights! "How is she going to turn up?" I asked him. Just for once, I wanted a logical, proper, adult answer from Ted.

He waved an arm nonchalantly. "I bet she's around. I bet she's found shelter somewhere," he said casually.

I looked at him. Why would he say something like that.

He walked off toward the ruins.

"Where?" I yelled. "Where would she be sheltering?"

He staggered off the path and into the scrub.

There was something about the way he'd said it. I ran up to him, grabbed him, spun him around. He fell against the bushes and they scratched him. "Tell me!" I screamed. "Tell me where she is."

He tried to stand up. "I don't know where she is, Kipling." I put out my hand to help him but he ignored me. "Now piss off and leave me alone."

But I couldn't. He got up and I followed him. He walked crookedly, recklessly, lurching through the thick scrub toward the ocean to the top of the tall limestone cliffs. He was peering around as if he'd lost something.

"What are you doing?"

He turned to me. "We both want to find her. We both want to clear our names, soldier." He took off again. I followed him. I was staggering, too, now, as I ran through the grasses and scrub. We reached the edge of the cliffs on the ocean side above Cheviot Beach and couldn't go any farther. Ted stumbled as he looked over the cliff to the ocean. "The Y-shaped pool," he said.

"Watch out, come back, you'll fall off," I said as if I were talking to an eight-year-old. These weren't small sandy cliffs like on the bay side, where it had all happened. These were tall, towering limestone cliffs, sheer in places, steep. These cliffs would never come down in a storm.

"The Y-shaped pool, that's where Harold Holt got swept out in the riptide."

He was so stupid; he made no sense. "Ted," I yelled, pleading with him, "come back from the edge. Please!"

"I'm looking," he shouted back, then stepped farther out, making my heart beat hard. "I'm looking for the Y-shaped pool." He leaned over—

I had to leave. I couldn't watch. He was going to fall. I turned around. The wind picked up, and I thought I heard something. A call, a shout, a child.

Then Ted spoke again.

"She's down there somewhere . . ."

It took me a second to register what he'd said.

"What was that?"

He didn't answer.

We both stopped.

"You have seen her, haven't you."

He staggered in the wind.

Without thinking I charged forward and grabbed both his arms, holding him up, shaking him, dragging him away from the cliff.

I let go of him and he fell sideways.

"What?" I yelled.

"A couple of days ago."

I took in his battered face, his helpless, lost expression.

"What have you done with her? Where is she?"

He was almost completely incoherent. "I couldn't lift her. In a cave, man . . . she's all cut up." He looked at me as if he were a child. For a second, something about him looked just like that little kid David when I'd seen him crossing the road—all screwed up and desperate for some sort of help. Then Ted started to cry. "I can't remember where she was, man." He kept calling me *man*. "I'm thinking it's a dream," he went on. "I'm waking up and I'm thinking maybe I've dreamed the whole thing. I can't remember."

We both stood staring, each unable to help the other. I heard music, the last band starting up at the Visitors' Center. "What are you saying?" I whispered. Then louder, "What are you saying? If she's in a cave, if you saw her, then why didn't you get her out?" I was yelling now. "What sort of adult are you? There's a girl stuck in a cave and you *leave* her there? You don't help her? What is *wrong* with you?"

"I was going to go back, but I fell asleep . . . I lost track of . . . then I got a call, for a chase." His eyes were pleading with me. "But I've been looking for her, soldier. Then because of you the bloody cops were following me everywhere."

Because of me! I was completely furious with him. All I'd done was tell the truth. But the truth had never been so confusing to me. And to think I was worried about him being blamed for something he had nothing to do with. "If you had nothing to hide," I shouted at him, "then why didn't you tell the cops that you saw her?"

"Neither did you. You had nothing to hide either." He started to stagger off again. Then he turned on me. "Why did you listen to me? Don't listen to me. You're so bloody naïve," he hissed. "A bloody child is what you are. I told you not to trust me. Didn't anyone ever tell you, never trust a . . . never trust . . ."

He couldn't finish what he was saying.

I stood there. My shoulders fell. I had no energy, no life left in me, helpless.

He looked at me, smirking now. "Go on, run off and tell the cops. Off you go."

The ocean roared. "You bastard!" I shouted. "If you hadn't been so pissed, you could have helped her. Now she's . . . she'll be dead because of you." I wiped my eyes, my face.

"What's your problem? Stop blubbering," he said. "Grow up, man."

"No," I told him, "you grow up."

Annie

That afternoon my uncle took Simon out. Dad was packing up our things. The vacation was almost over, and we were supposed to be going home.

But nobody said anything about leaving. I wanted to ask Dad, "Will we really go?"

Mum sat on the couch and stared. She didn't speak. She didn't even whisper. My auntie wiped the sink.

Dad drove down to the concert to thank the volunteers. I went with him. The reporters followed us in their vans. "Whatever they say, just ignore them," Dad told me.

When Dad was talking I couldn't watch, I couldn't listen. I looked at the people around me instead. I saw a boy who looked too young to be out on his own. He was crying. He ran up the hill after two men walking in the distance. He was probably crying because his father was walking too fast for him. Imagine crying about that. Something so small and simple.

When we got home, Mum stood up. Tears ran down her face, but there was no sound. She stood straight and still. She was holding the phone out to Dad, and as he took it I could hear Grace's voice. "Hi, you've called Grace. I can't get to the phone right now so leave a message and I'll call you back. Thanks."

It made me cry to hear it. It scared me.

"I'm her mother," Mum said to Dad, as if she had to make him believe her. "She needs me." Mum put a hand across her mouth. She looked at Dad, shaking her head. "She needs me to come and get her."

How could we drive back to Melbourne without Grace?

People will ask us all the time what happened.

I'm not the oldest child.

I want my sister back.

Kip

I left him staggering around like the pathetic drunk he was.

I ran all the way back to the Visitors' Center. I told the guy on duty. He said he'd call his superior and tell them. I had to wait a few minutes for the other policeman, Geoff, to come. There was a copy of the newspaper.

> Police hold grave fears for safety of Grace
> Search hampered by severe weather
> Twelve-year-old girl presumed drowned

Geoff came in and I told him that Ted said he'd seen the girl, that he'd mentioned something about a cave. I told him that Ted was drunk, he hadn't made much sense and might not even remember what he'd said to me.

"I think we'll go and have a chat with Ted then," Geoff said. "Although I wouldn't get too excited—he's not exactly reliable."

They got a map and asked me to show them where I'd left Ted. On the map, I could see what a big area it was.

"I hope you can find him," I said. "It would have been almost half an hour ago. He was up here, on the cliffs, in the out-of-bounds area." They gave me a pen and I put an X, like I was making a treasure map. A few of them set off to look. I waited at the Visitors' Center. One policeman stayed behind. He was on the phone.

I sat there for ages. I walked around and around, waiting. I went outside for a while and watched the people packing up the stalls. The bands had finished and everyone was leaving.

Should I go home? I wondered. I couldn't leave, but I couldn't stay there. So I started walking again, automatically putting one foot in front of the other, following the track, trying to walk it all away. It was cold. A gray sea. The dusky mist. I was worried that Ted had fallen off the cliff. I should have told the policemen how close he'd been to the edge. Now two people were lost. I couldn't see the police who were looking for him. I'd become like Ted, I thought, wandering around on my own like a complete loser. I went all the way past the ruins, past where I'd left him, toward the Heads. Maybe the police had already picked him up and I'd missed them. It was a big place and there was lots of bush. I looked over toward the ocean side. Maybe he'd made the whole thing up, maybe he'd dreamed it, who knows.

I felt so angry with Ted. I felt sorry and sad as well. He must really hate himself now. I was so uncertain about him. I mean I could see that he was someone that guys at school would laugh at, but were the guys at school really any better than Ted? They were the types who were always polite to your parents, they knew how to behave when they had to. Ted seemed to have no idea.

In the distance, through the spray, two people were walking down on the rock shelf. I had a feeling of déjà vu, like when I had seen the figures in the distance on that afternoon when everything had started.

I went right to the edge of the tall cliff. I squinted, trying to see—that long black coat . . . was it Ted?

I ran along the ridge, getting closer.

He had someone with him.

It must be her. He'd found her! "Ted," I called out,

cupping my hands. "Ted!" He'd remembered and he'd looked and he'd found her. He was okay! I suddenly thought. I was okay. That girl was okay—Ted had found her. He'd bring her back to the police and everything would be right again.

But wait, this figure was little. I kept running along the edge of the cliff. I got closer and when I called again, Ted didn't turn around, but the person beside him did. I saw his face.

It was the kid, the little kid David. He turned and looked up but he kept walking away from me. He was holding Ted's hand.

Ted was leading David away and into the cliff, toward the dark sky at the Heads.

"Stop!" I cried out to him. "Stop!"

They kept walking.

I was letting him go.

"Stop!" I yelled again.

But they didn't even hear me. They didn't look back.

I took off, running as fast as I could. I came to a point and I couldn't get any farther. So I climbed down to the rock shelf. I had reached the sea. But I couldn't see them anywhere. Where were they? It was as if they'd walked into the side of the limestone cliff.

"Ted!" I called out. "Ted! David!" I couldn't let Ted take him. I couldn't let that kid go again.

I looked around for the police, but there was no one. I stumbled, grazed my hands, and fell in a deep rock pool. There were blowholes, waves, arches. The waves were coming. "Ted, where are you?" I called.

I looked in the hollows along the inside of the cliff. Marbled waves flew at me.

Where were they? They hadn't gone over on the track, but they weren't around the rocks either. The cold water gripped my legs, making them hurt. I could see dark pools. Kelp swirled heavily in the water, like soup.

I scrambled up to a higher rock shelf. The ocean roared, it filled my ears like amplified music. It wasn't sandy here. The cliffs were tall and rocky. The cliff top was overhanging above me, like an arch. The sun came out; it cast a long shadow.

Was that what made me glance up? Or had I heard something?

Above me, high up, a color was hanging. It moved.

A patch of red.

An edge. A dirty yellow sleeve.

I climbed, slipping, my wet sneakers scrabbling as the sand and rock gave way.

Pulling, reaching.

Still.

She was still. She had no jeans on. Her leg was swollen and covered in blood.

Grace.

I dragged myself into the cave. The waves went quiet.

It was nearly dark. My shadow moved over her as I reached out and touched her arm. She turned. She made a sound.

"Grace," I said, starting to cry.

Her mouth was open, salt had dried on her face, her lips. Her head rolled to the side.

I put one arm under her legs and one around her back.

"I'm going to put your arm around my shoulders," I told her. "I'm going to lift you up and take you out of here."

She hardly moved. She was heavy. I lifted her arm and put it across my neck. Long hair lay on my shirt.

I fell down, holding her, to the water below.

I carried her out to the beach. I carried her all the way up to the Visitors' Center where I could get help.

Annie

It had started raining again. It was almost nighttime. I was watching TV. I heard heavy steps running to our back door. Someone banged on it. I went to open it.

It was Geoff the policeman. He wasn't wearing his

uniform. For a minute I didn't recognize him. Water tumbled off his woolen sweater.

"Where are Mum and Dad?" he asked me, huffing.

Mum was already coming. "Oh no, no," I heard her whisper. I turned around. Her hands were gripping the frame of the living-room door.

Geoff came toward her. His boots dripped on the floor tiles.

"No, it's good news," he said. "She's been found. She's alive." He took a breath. "She's going to be fine."

Dad ran up the hallway. Mum fell onto him, crying, crying even more than when Grace was gone.

Kip

I haven't seen Ted since then.

I went to his house the day after I found Grace but no one was there. I knocked and knocked. I held my hand to the glass doors. His stuff was lying everywhere.

I was about to leave when a woman arrived with a key.

"I'm looking for Ted," I told her.

"Ted's gone AWOL," she said. Her thin fingers fiddled with the lock. She leaned her weight against the sliding door and pushed it back.

"I saw him on the beach. Cheviot. He was with a little boy."

"David," she said, walking inside and not looking at me.

"Do you know David?"

She turned and smiled sadly. "He's my son."

Why would this woman trust Ted with her son? Maybe she didn't know Ted very well.

She stood in the doorway as if she didn't want me there; she just wanted me to go.

"I'm the person who saw him in the water," I said. "I'm Kip."

Tears came to her eyes. She had dark, sparkly eyes and long black hair. She gave a kind of sigh and moved toward me. She was wearing lots of silver jewelry and it jangled.

"Kip, thank you. Thank you." I just stood there. I thought I might cry. It was just those words, *thank you.* It was embarrassing.

"Did you get my note?" she asked.

"No."

"I sent a note to the hospital. I left my number asking you to call me. I wanted to thank you in person. They said at the hospital that they'd pass it on."

"They probably sent it to our address in Melbourne. We were supposed to leave yesterday but we got a bit . . . held up." I wasn't about to start telling her the whole story. "What was he doing in the water?" I asked.

"He was trying to find his father's boat. He was very

distressed. His father . . ."—she paused—". . . Ted, and I separated last year and he's taken it very badly. They both have."

"His father?" I gasped. "Ted is his father?"

She nodded. "David had run off and turned up here that night. He's done it a couple of times. House wide open, of course. Ted wasn't here, but David saw him down on the boat. He must have been checking the mooring or maybe even going out in it, who knows. Look, David was so upset he didn't know what he was doing. He got his Boogie board and was trying to get out to his dad's boat." She paused. "Ted goes out in the storms."

"Yeah, storm chasing, he's told me about it."

She stared straight ahead as if she wasn't talking to me at all. Under her breath, she said, "What a fool."

"But Ted didn't know, he didn't know that it was his son in the water. He never told me." I remembered telling him about the boy who was rescued.

"He didn't know because I didn't tell him. The police came to tell him that night but he wasn't here, or he didn't answer. Then when David was safe, I asked that they didn't let Ted know. Ted has had no contact with me or David for a few months," she said, turning to face me. "Believe me, it's easier that way."

Then it clicked. I knew her. I'd seen her before.

"You were the person driving the car. And the person in the photo."

"What car?"

"The other day, when David ran off. At the shops."

She nodded.

"I saw him," I said. "I wanted to stop him, but he ran off, down to the beach."

She sighed. Her jewelry rattled. "Look, you probably think I'm a terrible mother. A terrible person."

"No," I said. I had no idea what sort of mother or person she might be. But she kept talking.

"I thought he'd go to his dad. I'd had enough." She shook her head, looking around at the filthy house. "I'd just had enough."

We both stood there awkwardly amid the mess. She looked at me as if I were expecting some sort of explanation for it. "God," she sighed, "we just wore each other out."

I didn't know if she was talking about her and David or her and Ted.

"He told me he didn't have any kids," I said.

She looked distracted. "His child was lost to him. His child was already lost."

"Where have they gone?"

"I don't know. David ran off again yesterday. He'd seen all the posters, he knew his dad would be at the fundraiser. Now Ted's taken him and they've both run away."

"How do you know?"

"I phoned him. I know he's got David with him, but I don't know where they are. And now he's turned off his phone. Helpfully," she added. "That's why I'm here. To find his address list. It's in his computer." She pushed aside those magazines as if they were *Reader's Digest*s. They toppled onto the floor and lay open, exposing limbs and flesh and hands. I kicked one closed with my foot. David's mother switched on the computer.

"It was last night that I saw them," I said. "They were walking along the beach, toward the cliff." I paused. "I didn't know where they were going. It was like they just . . . disappeared."

She was scrolling down a list of names and numbers, distracted.

I was worried about David. "Ted," I said, "he seems like a pretty angry sort of guy."

"He'll be furious with me that I didn't let him know about David being rescued in that storm," she said, to herself rather than me. Then she looked at me, as if our whole conversation had just come into focus. "You poor kid," she said, "how did you get yourself mixed up in all this?"

"I don't know," I said. "But don't you know where he is? Where they've gone?"

"They'll be in Melbourne, they're probably staying with his sister."

She came to the door where I was standing.

"Maybe he's run away because he feels ashamed."

She looked at me through her bangs.

I went on. "Guilty." I didn't know how much she knew. "You know, about the girl? Who was missing?"

She nodded.

"He'd seen the missing girl, but he was so out of it that he couldn't remember where she was. The only reason I even saw her was because of his jacket. He'd left his jacket with her. She'd been able to push it to the edge of the cave with her foot, and it was hanging out."

She had a small frame, like a child. She leant against the sliding door again, slamming it shut. "Yep," she said quickly, as if she wasn't really interested in Ted's jacket or his feelings right then. She locked the door. "Now he's got my son so I need to find him."

Annie

In the end, it was the young person who found her. He brought my sister back.

She had been swept out of the bay, through the

Heads, all the way around to the ocean side. There'd been timber floating in the water. The police said it was probably a broken bit from a boat smashed in the storm. Grace held on to it and the waves had washed her onto the rocks and into a cave.

I don't understand how the volunteers didn't find her. She wasn't that far away. But Geoff said that they could only search that part of the beach at low tide, and it was hard to search there at all in the bad weather. They had looked above where Grace was, up on the top at Point Nepean, and they'd looked below, on the beach, but they hadn't looked in the middle, where the cave was. They said that it was only because of the king tide and the storm that she'd been swept up so high.

The police drove us straight to the hospital. Grace had already gone there in a helicopter, but she doesn't even remember it. Grace did have hypothermia, like I thought. The doctor said that having the dry jacket probably saved her life. She nearly died. Death from hypothermia, it was in the book I read. The jacket be-longed to that creepy guy. He had heard Grace and seen her one night. I don't know what he was doing on the rock shelf at night. Geoff said that he likes walking around in storms. But he was drunk. He was too drunk to remember where he'd seen Grace or what had happened. I don't understand that but Mum says it can happen. It's called alcoholic amnesia.

The police said to Mum and Dad, "Your daughter should be praised for her resourcefulness." Grace had tried to move to where the sun was, she drank rainwater when it came into the cave and made puddles. She had a broken leg and a bump on her head from when the waves swept her into the rocks. And even before it was broken, her leg was cut because her jeans had been caught on rocks and been torn. She couldn't move her leg. Even after she came out of the hospital, for a few weeks she couldn't walk at all.

I asked Mum if it had been the same as when Grace was a baby, the time that they thought she'd die. I wondered if they loved Grace more now that they'd got her back again.

Mum said that it's a complicated thing to love someone as much as parents love their children.

I didn't understand what she meant. Loving your *parents* isn't difficult—it's something you're born with.

"It's because you open yourself up for everything that might happen," she said.

"Like what?" I asked her.

"All the joys, all the happy times," said Mum, "but other things as well."

Her eyes were sparkling and I remembered Mum when Grace was gone. How she stared but didn't see.

"Do parents get afraid in the happy times?" I asked her. "That the other things might happen?"

Kip

We saw the family a few times. Once we went for dinner at their place. Grace was quiet, but her parents said she was getting much better. She was lucky she found a bit of timber. Heaps of stuff get washed around in storms as big as that one. She was lucky she didn't get knocked out by the rocks. She was lucky she didn't drown. The doctors said that she was lucky to survive.

It was embarrassing with Grace. The parents were nice to me. Andrew apologized because he said he hadn't been very friendly to me on the beach that night. I thought he probably wouldn't want me hanging around his daughter but he said, "Why not? Grace is old enough to choose her own friends."

At first, Grace and I didn't have much to talk about. After what had happened, it seemed strange to ask her questions like, "What CDs do you have?" or "Have you seen the new Harry Potter film?" What had happened made it different for me and Grace. As if we'd started a friendship from the inside out—and somehow we knew the private things but none of the everyday things. Like me, she looked older than she was. She was tall. People might have thought she was in ninth grade or something, but Grace was young—only twelve, only in seventh grade.

One thing I talked to Grace about was Ted and David. My parents hated me talking about Ted. I think they just wanted to believe that he didn't exist, that he'd never existed. Every time his name came up, Dad would say, "No need to keep going on about it." Sarah would roll her eyes and say, "Kip, just get over it."

Grace and Annie had a brother who was about David's age. Simon.

I told Grace that I felt sorry for David. I worried about him. I wondered if Ted still had him or whether he'd gone back to his mother.

"Imagine having a dad like Ted," I said to Grace.

Grace closed her eyes for a moment, as if she really were trying to imagine it. She had long dark eyelashes that rested against her skin. Grace's eyes were big, they were beautiful. I'd never seen eyes that color before. A dark, greenish gray. Like water, like the sea in winter.

"If Ted was your dad," she said, "you'd still want him there."

She was right. Even I had wanted him around for a little while.

"I can hardly remember him in the cave," she said.

"I bet he still feels really bad about that," I said. For some stupid reason I felt I had to stick up for him.

It was as if Grace understood what I meant. She spoke softly—she had this slow, thoughtful voice, a deep voice for a girl. "I don't think he's bad, Kip."

I shrugged and let out a laugh. "Yeah, but I wouldn't exactly call him a good guy."

Annie

Grace's leg is nearly better. We've made some new friends. The young person's name is Kip and his sister is Sarah. She's my friend.

Grace never said that I'd told her she had to climb up the cliff. She didn't talk about it much at all. Mum said not to push her into talking about it unless she wants to. We wondered if she'd want to go back to Portsea, to Point Nepean, but we've been back a few times and she doesn't mind. Last time we were down there and Mum and Dad went for a walk, Grace and I were looking after Simon. There was a thing on TV about people who have survived landslides and being lost in the bush and things. I asked Grace then, "Did you think you would die?"

"I thought of different things, but it was like dreaming," she said. "I thought of people coming to rescue me. I kept thinking about how to get water to drink. At first I could drag myself to the edge where the rain was. And other times the sun came in there."

"I never thought you would, Grace," I told her. "I never thought you'd die."

"I remember the cold," she said. "At first I was shouting out, but the sea was too loud. I lost all my energy. I was shaking. I thought that someone might find me, but I always imagined that it would be Dad," she said. "But it wasn't. It was Kip."

"And that other guy, the drunk guy who left you his jacket."

Grace nodded. She didn't say anything for a moment. Then she said, "Time went differently when I was there."

"Time went differently for me, for us, too," I told her.

Mum and Dad are watching her. I notice them doing it, maybe they always did it, but I don't feel as if I need to look after Grace anymore.

Kip

I went back to school. Even though most of the kids in my class had heard about it, I never talked about what happened. But I know I'll remember it for a long time.

I still look out for Ted. I think of him often. I watch the old music shows in case his song comes on, but I haven't seen it again.

I can picture him easily in my mind, holding a can in one shaking hand and smiling—that crooked, lousy, annoying smile.

Grace's mum told my mum that Ted's house was sold. So I've got no idea where he is. Sometimes I imagine him sitting alone in some dingy apartment with torn curtains and crap piled up everywhere. I'd like to do something to help him, but I don't know what. I wish I'd been able to tell him that he probably saved Grace's life by leaving his jacket with her. Not just because I noticed the sleeve, but because it had kept her warm. I think that's why I look out for him. I want to tell him that he actually helped, tell him something good about his life. I don't think he had many friends, maybe none.

I know that what happened will fade. Already it sometimes feels like a dream. When I'm playing my guitar, I write songs about it. I do a chord progression and write lyrics. I even wrote about Ted and the jacket in a song. I tell him what I would tell him if I ever see him again. Who knows, Ted might even hear it one day.

When we'd been back at school for a few weeks, I decided to phone Grace to see if they would be spending summer vacation at the beach. They would, she said. She asked if I was still playing my guitar. I told her yes. Now that I've stopped swimming I can really concentrate on it. I'm saving up for a Les Paul. Not one like Ted's. I'll get an Epiphone.

Sometimes we IM. Grace told me that she's going to learn the drums in eighth grade. I've always thought that girl drummers are cool. And she'd be good at it, I bet; a tall, strong girl like Grace.

It's good to think that I'll be seeing her again in the summer.

I like to imagine that when Grace and I are older, we might go out together. And when people ask us how we met, we'd tell them about being lost, about that winter day when I found her, that fantastic day at the end of June.